Dark Paradise

Dark Paradise

ANGIE SANDRO

FOREVER
YOURS

New York Boston

Copyright © 2014 by Angie Sandro
Excerpt of *Dark Sacrifice* copyright © 2014 by Angie Sandro
Cover design by FaceOut
Cover copyright © 2014 by Hachette Book Group, Inc.

Forever Yours
Hachette Book Group
237 Park Avenue
New York, NY 10017
hachettebookgroup.com
twitter.com/foreverromance

Forever Yours is an imprint of Grand Central Publishing.
The Forever Yours name and logo are trademarks of Hachette Book Group, Inc.

The Hachette Speakers Bureau provides a wide range of authors for speaking events. To find out more, go to www.hachettespeakersbureau.com or call (866) 376-6591.

The publisher is not responsible for websites (or their content) that are not owned by the publisher.

ISBN 978-1-4555-5482-9

For my family and friends. I love you.

Dark Paradise

Chapter 1

Mala

Floater

Black mud oozes between my toes as I shift my weight and jerk on the rope, sending up a cloud of midges and the rotten-egg stench of stagnant swamp water. The edge of the damn crawfish trap lifts out of the water—like it's sticking its mesh tongue out at me—and refuses to tear loose from the twisted roots of the cypress tree. It's the same fight each and every time, only now the frayed rope will snap if I pull on it any harder. I have to decide whether to abandon what amounts to two days' worth of suppers crawling along the bottom of that trap or wade deeper into the bayou and stick my hand in the dark, underwater crevice to pry it free.

Gators eat fingers. A cold chill runs down my spine at the thought, and I shiver, rubbing my arms. I search the algae-coated surface for ripples. The stagnant water appears calm. I didn't have a problem wading into the bayou to set the trap. I've trapped and hunted in this bayou my entire life. Sure it's smart to pay attention to my instincts, doing so has saved my life more times than I can count, but this soul-sucking fear is ridiculous.

I take a deep breath and pat the sheathed fillet knife attached to my belt. My motto is: Eat or do the eating. I personally like the last part. A growling belly tends to make me take all kinds of stupid risks, but this isn't one. If I'm careful, a gator will find my bite cuts deeper than teeth if it tries to make me into a four-course meal. Grandmère Cora tried to teach her daughter that the way to a man's heart was through his stomach. Since Mama would rather fuck 'em than feed 'em, I inherited all the LaCroix family recipes, including a killer gator gumbo.

Sick of second-guessing myself, I slog deeper into the waist-high water. Halfway to the trap, warm mud wraps around my right ankle. My foot sticks deep, devoured. I can't catch my balance. *Crud, I'm sinking.*

Ripples undulate across the surface of the water, spreading in my direction. My breath catches, and I fumble for the knife. Those aren't natural waves. Something's beneath the surface. *Something big.* I jerk on my leg, panting. With each heave, I sink deeper, unable to break the suction holding me prisoner. Gator equals death…But I'm still alive. *So what is it? Why hasn't it attacked?*

A flash of white hits the corner of my eye—

Shit! I twist, waving the knife in front of me. My heart thuds. Sparkly lights fill my vision. Blinking rapidly, I shake my head. My mind shuts down. At first I can't process what I'm seeing. It's too awful. Too sickening. Then reality hits—hard. The scream explodes from my chest, and I fling myself backward. The mud releases my leg with a *slurp*. Brackish water smacks my face, pouring into my open mouth as I go under. Mud and decayed plants reduce visibility below the surface.

Wrinkled, outstretched fingers wave at me in the current. The tip of a ragged fingernail brushes across my cheek. It snags in my hair. I bat at the hand, but I can't free my hair from the girl's grip. She's holding me under. Trying to drown me. I can't lift my head above the surface. *She won't let me go!*

My legs flail, kicking the girl in the chest. She floats. I sit up, choking. I can't breathe and scream at the same time. I'm panting, but I concentrate. *Breathe in. Out. In.* The girl drifts within touching distance. Floating. Not swimming. Why doesn't she move? Is it stupid to pray for some sign of life—the rise of her chest, a kick from her leg—when I already know the truth?

Water laps at my chin. I wrap my arms around my legs. Shivers shake my body despite the warmth of the bayou, and my vision's fuzzy around the edges. I'm hyperventilating. If I try to stand I'll pass out. Or throw up. Probably both 'cause I'm queasy. I close my eyes, unable to look at the body any more. Which is so wrong. I've studied what to do in this sort of situation. Didn't I spend a month memorizing the crime scene book I borrowed from Sheriff Keyes? *Come on, Mala. Pull it together.* A cop—even a future one—doesn't get squeamish over seeing a corpse. If I can't do something as simple as reporting the crime scene, well, then why not drop out of college, get hitched, and push out a dozen babies before I hit twenty-five, like everyone else in this damn town?

I lift my hands to scrub my face. Strands of algae lace my fingers. I pick them off. My legs tremble as I rise, which keeps me from running away. I have to describe the crime scene when I call the Sheriff's Office, and I imagine myself peering through the lens of a giant magnifying glass like Sherlock Holmes—searching her body for clues. Each detail becomes crystal clear.

Her lips are slightly parted, and a beetle crawls across her teeth, which are straight and pearly white, not a tooth missing. She's definitely a townie. A swamp girl her age would have a couple of missing teeth, given she appears to be a few years older than me. Her expensive-looking sundress has ridden up round her waist. Poor thing got all gussied up before she killed herself.

The deep vertical cuts still pinking the water on both of the girl's wrists makes my stomach flip inside out. I double over, trying not to vomit. It takes several deep breaths to settle my gut before I can force myself to continue studying the body.

Long hair fans out like black licorice around her head, and her glazed blue eyes stare sightlessly at the heavens. Faint sunlight glistens on the flecks of water dotting her porcelain skin. I've never seen such a serene expression on anyone's face, let alone someone dead, like she's seen the face of God and has found peace.

After seeing her up close and personal, I can't stomach leaving her floating in the foul water. Flies crawl in her wounds, and midges land on her eyes. Slimy strands of algae twine through her hair. Soon the fish will be nibbling at her. Unable to bring myself to touch her clammy-looking skin, I take a firm grip on her dress and drag her onto the bank—high enough above the waterline that she'll be safe from predators while I get help.

I'm halfway across the stretch of land between the bayou and my house when a shiver of foreboding races through my body, and I slow my pace. *Shit! I took the wrong path.* Usually I avoid traveling through the Black Hole. It's treacherous with pockets of quicksand. Cottonmouths like to hide in the thick grass, beneath lichen-smothered fallen trees. Those natural obstacles are pretty easy to navigate if you're alert. What makes the hairs on the back of my neck prickle is the miasma that permeates every rock and rotten tree in the clearing I cross to get home. A filmy layer of ick coats my skin and seeps in through my pores until it infects my whole body with each step. I feel…*unclean.* I'm not big on believing in the whole concept of evil, but if there's any place I'd consider to be tainted ground, I'm walking across it.

Instinct screams that I'm not alone. I'd be a fool to ignore the warning signs twice. If I listened to my instincts earlier, I never would've found the body. I stretch out my senses like tentacles waving in the wind. Nothing moves…chirps, or croaks. A strange, pungent odor floats on the light breeze, but I can't identify it. My darting gaze trips and reverses to focus on the *Bad Place.* I swallow hard and yank my gaze from the dark stain on the rock in the middle of the circle. Mama said our slave ancestors used this area for their hoodoo rituals because the veil between the living and dead is thinner here.

It's always sounded like a whole lot of bullshit to me until I stumbled across the blood-stained altar and shards of burnt bone scattered across earth devoid of grass or weeds—salted earth, where nothing grows. Mother Mary, it creeps me out.

'Cause what if I'm really not alone? What if something stands on the other side of the veil, close enough to touch, but invisible? Watching me.

Whatever's out here can go to the devil 'cause I'm not waiting to greet it.

By the time I burst out of the woods that border our yard, the sun has started its downward slope in the sky behind me. I double over, hands on my knees, to catch my breath after my half-mad run. Our squat wooden house perches on cinder-block stilts like an old buzzard on top of the hill. The peeling paint turns the rotting boards an icky gray in the waning light, but it's sure a welcome sight for sore eyes.

With a final glance over my shoulder to be sure I wasn't followed, I dash beneath the Spanish moss–draped branches of the large oak that shades our house, dodging the darn rooster running for me with tail feathers spread. I brush it aside with my foot, avoiding the beak pecking at my ankle.

"Mama!" My voice trembles. I really wish my mother had come home early. But the dark windows and empty driveway tell me otherwise. I track muddy footprints across the cracked linoleum in the kitchen to get to the phone.

Ms. Dixie Fontaine answers on the first ring. "Sheriff's Office, what's your emergency?" The 9-1-1 dispatcher's lazy drawl barely speeds up after I tell her about the dead girl. "All right, honey. I'll get George on over. You be waiting for him and don't go touching the body, you hear?" She pops her gum in my ear.

A flash of resentment fills me, but I'm careful to keep my tone even. "Don't worry, I know better, Ms. Dixie. I only touched her dress—to drag her from the water."

"That's fine, Malaise, quick thinking on your part. Bye now."

"Bye," I mutter, slamming the phone in the cradle. I breathe out a puff of air, trying to calm down. I'm antsy enough without having to deal with Ms. Dixie's inability to see me as anything but a naive kid. I'm not an idiot. How can she think I'd make a rookie mistake like contaminating the crime scene? I've been working with her now for what? Nine…no, ten months. Hell! What does it take to prove myself to her? To the rest of the veterans at the sheriff's office who remember every mistake I've ever made and throw them in my face every chance they get?

Disaster. That should've been my name. Instead, I've been saddled with Malaise. Well, whatever. I stomp into the bathroom, slip off my muddy T-shirt and cut-off jean shorts, and take a scalding shower. I scrub hard to get the scummy, dead-girl film off my skin. It takes almost a whole bottle of orchid body soap to cleanse my battered soul and wash the tainted, dirty feeling down the drain with the muck.

The whole time, three words echo in my head. *Deputy George Dubois.* My heart hasn't stopped thudding since Ms. Dixie mentioned his name. The towel I wrap around my heaving chest constricts my rapid breaths like a tightened corset. Hopefully, I won't do an old-fashioned swoon like those heroines from historical novels when I see him.

It's a silly reaction, but George comes in third on my list of People I Want to Impress the Most. It's not that his six feet of muscled, uniformed hotness tempts me to turn to a life of crime just so he'll frisk me and throw me in the back of his patrol car. Nope, that pathetic one-sided schoolgirl crush passed after we graduated and started working together. I'd be as cold as the dead girl if I couldn't appreciate his yummy goodness, but the last thing either of us need is for a romantic entanglement to screw up our professional relationship.

George epitomizes everything I want to become when I "grow up." He graduated from Paradise High School my freshman year and went to the police academy at the junior college. Once he turned twenty, he got a job at the Bertrand Parish Sheriff's Office.

When news of a part-time clerical position floated around town, guess who stood first in line for the job assisting Ms. Dixie with the data entry of the old, hardcopy crime reports into the new computer system. It's not always what you know at BPSO, but *whose* ass you kiss to get hired as a deputy. The recession left few open positions, forcing rookies to compete against seasoned officers who were laid off at other agencies. I don't have family to pull strings for me, but I've made job connections with people in positions of authority while obtaining practical experience working for the Sheriff's Office. I refuse to leave my future to the fickle whims of fate.

My last year at Bertrand Junior College begins in two months. I'll graduate with an Associate of Arts degree in Criminal Justice. I haven't decided whether to transfer to a larger university for a BA, but if not, I will definitely enroll in the police academy next summer. One year. I just have to survive one more boring year, and I'll finally get to start living out my dream of becoming a detective.

Calm down, Mala. I fuss with my thick, russet curls for a few minutes in the bathroom mirror then give up and pull it back in a high ponytail. My hair's a lost cause with the darn humidity frizzing it up. I finish dressing in my best jeans and a lavender T-shirt. Rocks pop beneath tires traveling down the gravel driveway. Instead of remaining barefoot, I slip on my rain boots, not wanting to look like a complete heathen or worse, reminding the higher-ups at the crime scene of my true identity—the prostitute's bastard.

Rumors about Mama's choice of occupation have been whispered about since before my birth. You'd think being the daughter of the town whore would be humiliating enough to hang my head in shame. Then add in the fact that most folk also think she's a broom-riding witch. The kids in school were brutal, repeating as gospel the stupid rumors they overheard from their parents, who should've known better. It boggles the mind that people in this day and age can believe ignorant stuff like Mama can hex a man's privates into shriveling if he crosses her. The only good thing about being the witch's daughter is it keeps most boys from straying too close. I don't have to deal with a bunch of assholes who think I'll blow them for a couple of twenties and an open bar tab like Mama.

With one last rueful glance at my face in the mirror, I shrug. This is as good as it's gonna get. I run onto the front porch and freeze halfway down the steps. The patrol car I expect to see in the drive turns instead into a good view of Mama on hands and knees beside her truck with a flowerpot stuck under her chin as she pukes in the geraniums. *Crud! Georgie will be here any minute.* I've got to hide her in the house. She can spend the night heaving up what's left of her guts in the toilet without me babysitting her.

Mama senses me hovering. She rolls onto her backside and holds out her hands.

"Don't just stand there gawkin' like an idiot, help your mama up," she says.

With a heavy sigh, I trudge to her side. I grit my teeth and lift her to her feet while she flops like roadkill. Upright, she lists sideways. A strong wind would blow her over. The vomit-and-stale-beer stench of her breath makes my nose crinkle when she throws her skinny arm around my shoulders.

"What you been up to today?" She tries to trail her fingers through my ponytail, but they snag on a knot I missed. She jerks her hand free, uncaring that it causes me pain since she's purposely deadened her own feelings with booze. Mama can't cope with her life without a bottle of liquor in one hand. It's like the chicken-and-the-egg question. Which came first? Was her life shitty before she became an alcoholic, or had booze made it worse? I can't see how it could be better, but maybe I'm naive, or as stupid as she always calls me.

I rub at the sting on my scalp. "Why are you home so early?"

She sways. "Can't I miss my baby girl?"

"Missing me never slowed you down before. What makes tonight any different?"

"Why you so squirrelly? You act like you don't want me here." She pulls back far enough to look me over. "Expectin' someone or you all dressed up with nowhere to go?" She cackles, slapping her leg like she's told the funniest joke ever.

"Georgie Dubois's coming out."

"Why? I know the deputy's not comin' to see you."

I grit my teeth on the snappy comment that hovers on the tip of my tongue. "Found a dead girl floating in the bayou."

Mama pulls her arm back and strikes cottonmouth quick.

I end up flat on my back with stars dancing before my eyes. My cheek burns. I blink several times, trying to clear my head, then focus in on the shadow hovering over me with clenched fists. "God damn it! Are you crazy?" I roll over and stagger to my feet. She steps forward again, fist raised.

"Don't you dare, Mama!"

"Don't take the Lord's name in vain. Or threaten me."

"I haven't threatened, *yet*. But I swear, you hit me again, I'm out of this rat hole you call a house. I've earned enough scholarship money to move into an apartment."

"Why you sayin' such things, Malaise?" Tears fill her eyes.

Money. The only thing that still touches Mama's fickle heart.

"You just backhanded me, Mama! What? Do you expect me to keep turning the other cheek until you break it? Or accidentally kill me like that girl I found..."

Mama's mocha skin drops a shade, and she sucks in a breath. I don't think it has to do with any feelings of regret. No, it has to do with the girl. She hit me after she heard about George coming out for the body.

"Why do you look so scared?" Suspicion makes my voice sharp. "What did you do?"

Mama staggers toward the house.

"Don't walk away from me," I yell. "What's going on? Georgie will be here any minute. If I've got to cover for you, then I need to know why or I might let something slip on accident."

Mama makes it to the stairs and collapses onto the bottom step. She buries her face in her palms. Shudders wrack her body. "I need a drink, Mala. There's a bottle in my bottom drawer. Bring it out to me."

"That's not a good idea..."

She lifts her head. Her dark brown eyes droop at the corners, and I see the faint trace of fine lines. Strangest of all, her eyes have lost the glazed, shiny appearance they held a few minutes earlier. *The news shocked her sober.*

"I'm not askin' again, Malaise. Get in there if you want to hear the story."

Chapter 2

Mala

Trigger Happy

I scramble up the stairs. It doesn't take but a minute to find the bottle hidden under her nightgowns in the dresser drawer. The seal on the bottle of Johnnie Walker Red remains intact. She must've been saving it for a special occasion. That doesn't bode well for the direction of the conversation we'll be having in a moment. I don't bother with a glass. Mama always says, "Don't need one for beer. Don't want one for liquor." I ease down the staircase. She doesn't even look up, just holds out a shaking hand.

"Want a swig?" she asks, opening the bottle with a deft twist. A slight smile dances on her lips. "No? My, my, such a good girl I got. Funny thing is, girl, I was just like you at your age. Thought I was better than my mama. Thought she was trash."

Silence fills the space between us, but I twitch first. "That's not how I feel—"

"Don't lie. I see it in your eyes. You'll learn different when your time comes." Her chapped lips purse. She takes a long drink and sighs. "Come on over here. Sit by me, *cher*."

I shuffle forward then stop.

She stretches out the arm not holding the bottle. "Come on, I won't bite."

When I sit down beside her, she pulls me close, and I lay my head on her shoulder. For a long minute, we sit in silence, staring out toward the woods. The sun has almost reached the tips of the moss-draped trees, and the clouds have turned crimson and gold. Day and night. Love and hate. One can't exist in the world without the other. They come together at twilight—the perfect symbol for my chaotic feelings for Mama because, as much as I hate how she treats me when she's drunk, I still love her.

"Mama, I'm sorry I cursed you," I whisper, head tilting to stare into her pensive face.

She squeezes my shoulders. "Don't worry, *cher*. I won't be around to hurt you much longer."

"What does that mean?"

"Means I had my death vision and I'm gonna die. Soon. I'd hoped to keep the news from you for a while yet, but I need to set my affairs in order before I pass."

I snort and pull free of her embrace. "That's silly, a death vision." The wellspring of anger reserved just for her crazy shit has been tapped, and it bubbles up again. "The drink has you hallucinating."

"Wish that was the case, Malaise. The day's comin'. I'm not sure exactly how or when, but it's tied to that girl you found. I dreamed about her." She takes another drink then burps. "S'cuse me."

I shake my head. Mama, the epitome of a southern lady.

"I don't believe in dreams that foretell the future." My arms fold across my chest with a chill that caresses my spine like an accordion being played by a zydeco master. "You're just *crazy*—"

She rolls her eyes at me then shakes her head. "Sure, I'm crazy. I know I am, but it's those dreams that done drove me nuttier than Ida Jean's fruitcake, not the other way around. After I die, the visions will pass on to you like mine came from my mama and hers from her mama, and so on, all the way back to mother Africa. Then you'll sit on my grave and beg my spirit to teach you how to control the horrors you see." She takes another drink. "Maybe I'll have forgiven you by then and will help you out."

"I'm not sitting on your tomb. That's creepy. And I'm the one who should be forgiving you," I say, voice rising. "Why you always got to turn things around and make yourself the victim?"

"Talk to my bones and find a bottle of whisky. Both'll be your best friends. Helps ease the pain of dreaming of deaths you can't change."

I roll my eyes, careful not to let her see. No use arguing when she refuses to listen. "Tell me about the girl."

"Long black hair? Blue eyes to match her fancy sundress?" Mama sits the bottle between her legs. "A spoiled, rich brat from town."

"Yeah, I guess. You met her before?"

Red and blue flashing lights and a siren drift from the end of the long driveway leading to the house. The patrol car's wheels had rolled over rain-filled puddles that splattered the sides with mud during its close to thirty-minute journey through unpaved woodland.

Mama reaches for the railing and uses it to pull herself to her feet. "I'm going to bed. You tell little Georgie Porgie to tell his daddy hello for me. We go way back, me and Dubois senior. He'll remember me."

Does that mean Georgie's dad and Mama did the nasty back in the good ol' days? *Eww.* "Yeah, sure," I drawl. *Thanks, Mama. Scarred for life with that image.*

I squeeze my eyes shut and shove the thought of Mama dying into the farthest recesses of my mind. As much as she drives me crazy, I love her. The idea that she won't be around forever terrifies me.

George parks his patrol car and steps out with a scowl. My gaze travels over his body. I compare the change in his appearance. It's been a month since he went to the graveyard shift, and the beginning of a Dunkin' Donuts belly stretches his starched, tan uniform shirt, but he still looks mighty tasty.

He catches me staring. A smile lights up his face. "Hey, Mala Jean." He waves me over. "Dixie said you found a body?"

"Uh yeah, down in the bayou." My feet tangle together. I must look as drunk as Mama when I stumble over to him on wobbly legs. *Stupid feet.* "Just you coming for her?" I ask, glad my voice doesn't shake too. I wipe sweaty palms on my jeans. *I am a professional.*

George blushes, a light dusting of freckles standing out against his pale skin. The setting sun brings out the fire in his reddish-gold hair. "Sheriff Keyes, Andy, and Bessie are out on Route Seven. A bunch of buffalo broke free of McCaffrey's pasture and ran out into the road. It caused a major pile-up."

"Merciful heavens, anyone dead?"

"Four buffalo got killed. No human fatalities, but some pretty serious injuries. A little boy needed to be flown over to Lafayette. The sheriff's ETA is in an hour with the coroner." He remembers to take a breath before continuing, "So, where is my crime scene?"

"About half a mile away. Got a flashlight? It'll be dark by the time we get there."

George climbs back into his car and comes out with a long-handled flashlight and his shotgun. He pulls a mini-flashlight from his duty belt and hands it over.

"Okay, let's go," I say, leading him into the woods.

He walks with the shotgun pointed skyward, alert for trouble. His eyes scan the dense foliage completely oblivious to my desperate attempts to keep the conversation going so I don't have to think about our destination. How can silence be so deafening? *Say something. Anything.*

George clears his throat. "How's your ma? She been staying out of trouble? I haven't seen her at the station for a few days."

Heat floods my cheeks, and my steps quicken. I swallow hard around the lump in my throat. "Mama's doing just fine, Georgie." Somehow I manage to answer without my voice betraying the immense humiliation I feel. Why did he have to go and irritate me by bringing up Mama? "I'm sure she'll be real grateful for your concern over not seeing her in the drunk tank."

God love him, but it takes a few seconds for the sarcasm to sink in.

"Oh, Mala, you know I didn't mean anything bad by that. I hadn't seen her is all, and I usually see her every weekend…uh, this isn't going too good for me, is it? Might be better if I shut up, huh?"

My eyes roll at George's horrified tone. He has a good soul, not a mean bone in his body, and the faux pas leaves him flustered. Wanting to put him out of his misery, I look over my shoulder with a forced grin that I hope doesn't scare him. "Don't worry. You mess with me, I mess with you."

"Still, I'm sorry. I wasn't thinking. Truth be told, I'm a little nervous." He gives me a sideways glance. "I wouldn't say this to anyone but you 'cause…"

"'Cause you know I'll have your back?" I arch an eyebrow and echo his relieved smile. "Stop avoiding the subject by buttering me up with compliments. What's wrong?"

His hand tightens around the shotgun. "Fine, but don't laugh. Swear."

I cross my heart.

"I've never seen a corpse before, and Sheriff Keyes expects me to work the crime scene alone until he arrives with the coroner." He pauses, and I give him a blank face—the expression I hide behind whenever someone says something hurtful. Or in this case, to keep from laughing my head off over seeing big, bad, ex–football player, super-cop Georgie shaken. It makes him a little less superhero-like and more human.

He gives me a relieved smile. "I don't want to make a fool out of myself."

"Don't worry, I won't let you do anything stupid, like vomit on the body," I tease. A slight chill in the air makes me shiver, and I wrap my arms around myself for comfort. I smell the sulfur stench of the water before I see the girl's body lying on the muddy bank. "There she is."

George plays the flashlight across the corpse. "Oh Jesus, damn it," he whispers, voice choked up. "It's Lainey—Elaine Prince."

"*Lainey*." I sigh the nickname. Knowing it makes her feel real. She didn't before, not totally. I turn to George, unable to face her glazed stare. "She's exactly how I left her."

"O-oh, well, that's good."

We stand side by side over her body, coming to grips with the harsh reality of her death in our own ways. Seeing her again stirs up volatile emotions I refuse to contemplate too closely. I can't afford to look weak, and breaking down in front of George is not an option. Finally, I can't take the silence and ask, "You gonna pass out?"

"Nah, I'll be fine. I knew Lainey." George clears his throat. "She's…she was a couple of years ahead of me in school. I had a huge crush on her in ninth grade."

He squats down beside Lainey and pulls her dress down over her legs. I almost remind him to put on gloves, but it doesn't matter. Any evidence probably washed away in the swamp.

"Lainey comes from a good family," he says. "Her father's a well-respected preacher. Her mama's always donating time. You know, doing good deeds like feeding and clothing the poor. They'll be crushed."

My rubber boots squelch in the muck as I hunker down next to him. "Prince, huh?"

The name sends tendrils of unease down my spine. The image of Landry Prince's gray eyes form in my mind. His heavy stare followed me whenever I walked past him at school. I memorized his schedule last semester to avoid going to the places where he hung out with his friends. I'd shaken him until a few weeks ago when he started coming into Munchies on the weekends when I work a second job—not sure why he finds my waiting tables so fascinating. The irritating thing is he never speaks to me. Hell, he doesn't even come in alone. He has a different bobble-headed girl clinging to his arm each time, but do his dates keep his attention from turning to me like a needle drawn to a lodestone? Nope!

George glances over at me. The shadows make it difficult to read his expression, which means he can't see how freaked out I am either. "Her younger brother, Landry, went to your school."

My chest tightens. I can't breathe. I close my eyes and focus on drawing in air.

Crap, she is *related to him. My juju's the worst today.*

"Mala, are you okay?"

I twitch, blinking in George's direction. I wipe my sweaty palms on my jeans. "Oh, yeah, Landry got accepted to play football at the JC. I've seen him on campus."

I try to picture Landry's face, but I've always avoided studying him too closely because he makes my stomach squiggly. The only image that forms clearly is of eyes like the sky before a hurricane. The rest of his features blur and morph into his sister's bloated face and dead-eyed stare. My stomach sours like I ate a tainted batch of crawfish, and I swallow hard. Desperate for a distraction from how queasy I feel, I walk over to a downed log and sit down. "He's never said two words to me, but he struts around campus like he's the king and we're subjects who must bow down before him. He's an arrogant jerk."

Landry watches me, Georgie, like I'm a deer he's tracking. I shiver, rubbing my arms. I've had boys interested in me before. Some hate me. Others are scared or curious because of the witchy rumors. But Landry...he creeps me out but also strangely fascinates me. I can't tell what he's thinking, and the touch of his eyes on my skin feels…electric, like when thunder rumbles overhead just before lightning strikes. I hate it.

George follows and sits beside me. His arm brushes mine. "Sounds about right from what I know of Landry, but Lainey was a good person." I can't see his eyes, but I feel his gaze fall on me. "You know, Mala, you've never gone out of your way to try to get to know folks. Not everyone has it out for you."

I tense up. Of all people, he knows better than anyone the sort of special hell my life has been. "Maybe if I hadn't been bullied all through high school, I'd be more social, Georgie. I can't help that I didn't always have clean clothes, let alone name brands…" I trail off, feeling hot and sticky. *Hellfire! Arguing over the body of a dead girl. How low could I get?* "Look, I have my reasons for not liking Landry, but this is his sister, and I don't mean to disrespect the dead."

George blows out a breath, running a shaky hand through his hair. "No, it's my fault. I shouldn't have said anything. It's not the time or place."

"But you *did* say it."

"Yeah, I did. 'Cause it's true. And life's kind of short to leave things unsaid, don't you think?"

No, I've never thought that. I draw in a deep breath. His fresh, clean scent washes away the scent of decay. George bumps his shoulder into mine, and I almost tumble off the log.

"Damn it, Georgie." I jab my elbow into his side. "How about if we agree to disagree on this issue and call it even?"

George's mouth opens. I can tell by the set look on his face that he has an argument prepared and ready to launch. Then his eyes follow mine. When his gaze lands on Lainey, he shudders. The radio connected to his belt crackles. He speaks quietly into the microphone attached to his lapel and then turns to me.

"We'll finish this discussion later. Sheriff Keyes, Detective Caine, and Coroner Rathbone are at your house with the crime scene techs. You okay to get them alone?"

"Sure, if you aren't too scared to stay here by yourself. I think you'll be fine. Just march around and make a lot of noise to scare off any critters. Don't get trigger happy when we return and shoot us on accident," I tease with a flashlight-enhanced grin, then shut off the light to fade ghostlike into the brush.

* * *

The moon lets in faint light through the treetops. I allow my eyes to adjust, then lead my group toward the crime scene. Sheriff Keyes, the parish coroner Dr. James Rathbone, Detective Bessie Caine, and two crime scene technicians with their large flashlights and bags of equipment follow like the pack of stampeding buffalo that caused the traffic accident.

Damn. I'm sick of this crawling, choking feeling of dread. It smothers me with each step. My breaths quicken. I desperately try to take my mind off of seeing Lainey again. I really, really don't want to go back. But I owe it to George to suck it up. Only a self-ish loser would abandon him when he's waiting for me. Plus it's part of the job description.

Sheriff Keyes pats my shoulder, and I flinch. "Are you doing okay?" he asks.

My voice cracks, but I manage a shaky smile as I say, "Well, sir, stumbling across that girl's body tonight certainly put some gray hairs on my head. I'll look as stately as you soon enough, if I'm not careful."

He runs his fingers through his silver hair. "I've seen a lot of untimely deaths in my life, and it's never easy or kind on the living."

My head drops as I sigh. "No, it's not."

"All things considered, you handled a difficult situation like a professional."

Joy rushes through me. I squeeze my hands together and hold in my squeal. It won't do to act like a dippy-brained teenager after getting such a high compliment from my hero. The sheriff doesn't know it, but he's the closest thing I have to a father figure. I've idolized him ever since I was a little tot, hanging onto Mama's skirt and trying not to cry as she was carted off to jail. He teases me to make me feel normal. And I tease him back to feel strong. He'll never admit it to me, but he likes my spunk. I overheard him tell Bessie so.

Keep it cool, Mala. "I hope you'll remember you said that when I apply for deputy next year and not all the silly things I've done since you've known me, Sheriff."

He gives me a weary smile. "I don't think that will be a problem. Ah, Bessie's coming. I'll let the two of you take point."

"Yes, sir."

When the chief detective reaches me, I wrap my arm around her waist. "Hey, Bessie, *konmen to yê?*"

"*Cé bon, mèsi,*" Detective Bessie Cainc says, squeezing me so tight that I almost trip. When she loosens her grip enough for me to step aside, I see her solemn expression, but I also detect a bit of a twinkle in her dark eyes. She's always been nice to me. Hell, to be honest, she raised me. At least once a week, when Mama got too drunk to drive home, Bessie dragged her out of the bar and dropped her off at the house. She even stayed a bit to make sure I had something to eat since Mama tended to forget that a growing girl needed food.

Bessie sighs. "So, tell me what happened."

I shrug and pull from the safety of her arms. "Pretty much what I told Ms. Dixie. I found the girl—Lainey Prince—floating in the bayou…"

Bessie places her hand on my shoulder and squeezes. "You didn't mention a name when you called, Malaise. How do you know her?"

"I don't. Georgie recognized her. Speaking of, maybe we can move a little faster 'cause he's all alone and kind of freaked about the gators."

Sheriff Keyes chuckles from behind. "Oh, is he?"

Instant regret stabs a hole in my chest. I didn't realize he'd be able to overhear our conversation. Why did I open my big mouth? Not wanting to make George look bad, I say, "George secured the crime scene, and he's protecting it from gators. I also saw tracks this morning for Mamalama. She's the biggest razorback we've got in these parts. It's lucky I found Lainey before that old boar came for water and smelled her, or the boar might've eaten her."

Sheriff Keyes points the flashlight directly at my face. "That's a gory thought."

Blinking, I shrug and pick up my pace. "I like to watch mob movies. Pigs eat anything. I've heard the best way to dispose of a body is to throw it in a pigpen. Not that I've been researching body disposal for a specific reason or anything." *Oh God, Mala shut up.*

Bessie's shoulders twitch, her version of a knee-slapping guffaw.

I blush and duck my head, wishing I could rewind the last few minutes. Great. I protected George's reputation by making myself look like a blithering idiot.

The report of a gunshot fills the air and, with it, a shout.

"Georgie!" I yell, and lurch forward. *I never should've left him alone.*

Chapter 3

Landry

Speak of the Devil

Drum beats and guitar riffs blast my eardrums as I shuffle through my iPod in search of the perfect song to pump me up. I settle on Nine Inch Nails—"Mr. Self Destruct." It weirdly fits my mood. Not that I'm about to explode. Yet.

Sweat glues hair to my forehead and stings my eyes. I squint against the light overhead, staring at the cardboard boxes stored in the beams of the rafters in my parents' garage. Each breath of muggy air I draw into my lungs holds the taint of gasoline. With a grunt, I press my sweaty back against the leather bench, plant each foot on the ground, and press the weight bar overhead.

Two hundred and forty pounds. No spotter. No problem.

Yeah, bullshit.

My eyes blur. I keep pressing. *One, two. Twenty-nine. One, two.*

Thirty... The burn turns to pain, but it's good. My muscles shred with each rep. Later they'll reknit, adding mass. I think of myself as an artist sculpting my body into a work of fine art. As conceited as that sounds, it's not. It's my reality. I'm not the sharpest tool in the shed. And I don't have a whole lot of goals. But the ones I've got involve transferring to a university. If I don't bulk up another twenty pounds before football season, I won't be playing this year. Then it's bye, bye, scholarship, and hello to slinging drinks at some dive bar downtown.

I set the bar in the rest, then readjust my grip. With a deep breath and lift on the exhale, the bar rises. I lift it over my chest, then slowly bring it down, up, down. The muscles in my chest and arms burn—twitching spastically—and the bar wavers.

If I keep pushing it, I'll regret it later. It'll be a day of whisky shots on top of ibuprofen to kill the pain so I don't walk like an arthritic old man. But I can't stop. If I do, the irritating itch in my brain will burrow through my mind like a worm bores through an apple. It started yesterday afternoon—a tickle of worry that kept me up all night, tossing and turning, unable to fall asleep. Each creak of the floorboards had me rolling out of bed as I listened for footsteps that never came. I gave up the fight around three a.m., took a five-mile run through the park, and now weight training, all to keep from freaking out about my big sister disappearing.

When did Lainey turn into a selfish bitch? Sneaking around and staying out all night. Not bothering to call or text that she's okay. She's driving me batshit, and I'm pissed that I even care. Not like Lainey gives a damn how anyone else in the family feels. It's all about what *she* wants. And I'm the idiot who suffers because, instead of being at my apartment sleeping in my own bed, I'm stuck at my parents' house waiting for her.

The temperature in the garage suddenly drops. One minute it's eighty plus degrees, and I'm soaked in sweat. And the next ice covers my skin, like I've stepped into a meat locker. I huff out a ragged, surprised breath. The air fogs over my head.

A shadow darts past the corner of my eye, and I flinch. The metal bar I've been holding in the air slips, and two hundred and forty fucking pounds slam onto my rib cage. Air jets out of my lungs, and my legs jerk in the air.

My vision blurs as the shadow blocks the overhead light. *Speak of the devil and she'll arrive.*

I squint until Lainey comes into focus, barely. She looks a little blurry around the edges. She crouches beside me, so close that I can see a white haze of vapor roll from her mouth. Her lips move. What is she trying to say? Probably an insult. Maybe it's a good thing I can't hear her over the music blaring through my earbuds. Why does she look sad instead of laughing her head off at my situation? Better yet, why doesn't she help get this thing off me?

"What the—" I choke on the words. "Help me."

My sister stares back with blue eyes tipped down at the corners, unmoving. I can't even detect the rise and fall of her chest. It's like she's holding her breath, waiting…for me to die? Is that it? Does she hate me so much she'll watch me suffocate?

I gasp like a fish flopping on pavement. I don't see her anymore. If I could move, I'd ring her scrawny neck. I'm gonna make her suffer. I don't know how to top this shit, but I can't let her get away with this. It's not like stealing the last doughnut. This is torture.

A face floats in the darkness. Eyes like bitter coffee, full lips, and a bold, no-nonsense nose dominated by skin as rich and creamy as melted caramel. Hair curls untamed around her beautiful face, catching fire in the sunlight, no matter how tight her ponytail. Regret, a bitter pain, stings deep. God, I'm such an idiot. I can get with girls I don't give a shit about, but the one person I really like I've never said a word to because I'm too afraid she'll tell me to piss off.

Well, screw that. Anger burns, and I dig deep for one last burst of strength, rolling sideways while using my upper chest and useless arms to fling the bar to the ground. I fall with it, hitting the grease-stained floor facedown. Air tastes better than water after ten laps around the football field, and I drink it in until I feel like I'll drown.

I hurt, but it's a good pain. It means I'm still alive.

Footsteps run into the garage, but I'm too spent to look up. My neighbor, Clarice Delahoussaye, kneels beside me. Her long, chestnut brown hair brushes my face as she lifts my head and rests it on her lap. I inhale her clean, strawberry scent.

"Are you okay, Landry?" she asks, brushing my hair out of my eyes with a shaking hand.

"I'm cool," I whisper. Jeez, it hurts to talk.

"Good, so I don't have to feel guilty about doing this." She smacks the top of my head, then shoves me off her lap. Dazed, I don't catch my head before it smacks against the cement. I let out another grunt, and Clarice snaps, "What the hell were you thinking to lift that much weight without a spotter? Do you have a death wish?"

I sit up, rubbing my head. "Actually, it's Lainey's fault for distracting me. Where did she go?"

Clarice shrugs. "I don't know."

I try to push myself up off the ground, but my arms stage a rebellion. I'm not sure how to get back on their good side. I'm gonna hurt for days. Should've drunk a couple of shots of Dad's Irish whisky before bed instead of staying up all night worrying about someone who doesn't give a damn about me.

"Get me a beer," I say, jerking my chin toward the refrigerator in the corner.

Clarice's mouth draws down at the corners. Not her best expression. It makes her look like a pug that pissed on the bed after being left home alone. "The sun's barely up," she scolds. "If your mom catches you drinking, you're so busted."

"Mommy Dearest had a migraine and took sleeping pills last night, which is why I'm here playing at being the man of the house while Dad's out of town. She won't roll out of bed until noon." I glare at Clarice until she stomps over to the refrigerator. "Are you sure you didn't see my sister? She was right beside me only a few seconds before you came in."

"No." Clarice slams the door closed. "I went out to get the paper and saw you from across the street. I ran right over. Nobody else was in the garage. I swear."

Did I hallucinate my sis from lack of oxygen? I glance at Clarice, who seems pretty straight up. Lainey on the brain...that's what caused me to be in this mess in the first place. I gotta get her out of my head. Distract myself before I go insane.

I'm a poet and didn't know it. The laughter doubles me over, gasping as pain rips through my chest. *Oh, jeez, it hurts.*

Cold aluminum presses against my chest, and I take the beer

from Clarice. "Can you open it for me?" I try to look as pitiful as I feel. "I overdid it."

She snatches it back and pops the top. "You think?"

"Sarcasm isn't your best quality."

Clarice flicks her hair over her shoulder. "I'm pretty. I don't need to be sarcastic or witty. I can get by on my looks, and you'll still love me in the morning."

"Oh, the vanity is blinding."

"It's called a good moisturizer with sunscreen." She flashes a dazzling white smile. Her mother paid the dentist a lot of money for that birthday gift. Spoiled brat.

My chest throbs when I lift the can to my lips. Even swallowing hurts. I chug the whole can 'cause I'll need something to take the edge off when I try to stand. I hold out a hand to Clarice. "Get me to the hot tub before I stiffen up."

"I was kind of hoping you'd stiffen…up." She pops the *p*. A wicked smile tips her lips, and I sigh. *Here we go again.*

"You're banned from entering the hot tub if you can't promise to behave like a lady." I wag a finger in her direction, but even that small action makes me wince. Without her, I won't be able to get to my feet. The brat knows it too. Threats don't work on her.

"What kind of lady? Naughty schoolgirl?" She claps her hands. "Oh, I know. Dutiful nurse." She wraps her arms around my waist and helps me stand, cooing and patting me. "You poor thing, want me to kiss your boo-boo?"

"Now you sound like a pedophile." I disentangle myself from her arms and limp through the side door leading into the back-yard. My nose wrinkles as I pass Mom's roses.

Clarice follows from behind. She runs a finger up my spine,

and I twist away. "Fine, I get it," she says, sulking as only she can. "You're not in the mood."

I raise an eyebrow. "When have I ever been?"

"Can't you try?"

Her voice is softened by an underlying pain that I wish I could ignore. All jokes aside, Clarice's one-sided crush is real. And the girl's no quitter. No matter how many times I tell her that I only see her as a slightly annoying best friend, she keeps trying new and more inventive ways to convince me to take the from-friends-to-lovers route in our relationship.

Maintaining a friendship when the other person keeps putting her own selfish emotions before yours is exhausting, but I'm no quitter either. And I'm not ready to cut her out of my life yet. I decide to throw her a bone. "How about if I buy you dinner at Munchies later?"

It's Sunday. Mala works tonight. It's been over a week since I last saw her. Maybe my near-death experience will make me grow a pair and I'll talk to her. I'll start with something easy like "What's up?" or "Hey, good-lookin.'" Nah, too cheesy. "Hi." Yeah, short and sweet. Not overwhelming at all.

A finger pokes my bruised ribs, and I wince.

"Were you even listening to me? I said I have a date. Rain check?"

"Whatever." The hot tub beckons like a lover. Only less clingy. I cast a sideways grimace in Clarice's direction.

Clarice gives me what she thinks is a sultry pout but actually makes her look like a suckerfish stuck to a glass aquarium. "You're seriously not jealous, are you? Don't you care that I'm seeing another guy?"

Loaded question. Time to change the subject, since I'm in no condition to fight her off if she tries to drown me. I drop my shorts. I'm wearing boxers, but they're tight enough for Clarice to stop and stare like I'm a slice of prime rib served up rare. I slide into the water with a sigh. Clarice smiles. She lifts the edge of her T-shirt and slowly raises it. A wink of gold in her navel narrows my gaze. That's new. When did she get pierced?

"Like it?" she asks a bit breathless.

"It's cool." I wave my hand. "If you're getting in, come on or you'll miss the bubbles."

She frowns but is not deterred. You'd think she'd finally get a clue that I don't find her remotely attractive. It's not that she isn't beautiful, she is. Stunning, if you like her type, but her pale skin and willowy—that's what they call model-skinny girls—willowy frame isn't what I crave. I want a girl with meat on her bones. Okay, I'm only obsessed over one girl's curves, and Mala's the exact opposite of Clarice. And Clarice stripping down to her panties and bra in slow motion is nothing but pure comedy.

Her brother said she's been going to girls' night at the Armadillo Strip Club. I guess she picked up some moves, but her jerky hip thrusts aren't exactly a come-on. I suck in my lips so I don't laugh when she wiggles her narrow hips as she sinks into the water beside me. She's got nothing I haven't seen before, and she's nothing compared to the girl I want to see do a striptease for me.

The cool morning breeze blows across my overheated skin. The contrast feels good.

"Oh, yuck. Smells like something died out here," Clarice says, pinching her nose. "Is Sasha still bringing her kills in for inspection?"

"Yeah, but it's not the cat." I tip my chin toward Mom's prized rose garden. "Fertilizer."

"Ah, gotta love the smell of shit in the morning."

I grunt.

"Man, you're red. It's going to turn into a nasty bruise," she says, staring at my chest. She glances up to catch me watching her watching me, and she blushes. "Why were you working out so early?"

"Lainey didn't come home last night."

"So? She's grown."

I shrug, but I don't feel it. "I don't know. I've got a strange feeling that she's in danger or something. It's like an itch in my brain that I can't scratch. The more I think about it, the more it bugs me."

"Is it like the time you warned me not to ride my bike?" Her bottom lip pokes out in a pout as she crosses her arms. "I still think if you'd said to watch out for stray dogs running in the road, I wouldn't have crashed into the tree and broken my collarbone."

"If you hadn't gotten on your bike in the first place—" I splash water in her face, and she squeals. "Fine, blame me if it makes you feel better. At least you believe me, right?"

"Yeah. I remember when you dreamed about your grandmother passing the night before her stroke."

My heart skips. *Don't even think it. Lainey's okay.* "Nah, ignore me. I'm being stupid. It's probably nothing. She's out with that guy she's been sneaking around with but is too scared to bring home."

"I don't blame her after what happened with her last boyfriend. Did you ever figure out who the new guy is?"

"Why should I care? She should just move in with him so I don't have to worry about her anymore."

"Living in sin…" Clarice fake gasps, covering her mouth "…making the beast with two backs without the sanctity of marriage. Your daddy would kill her."

Yeah, she's probably right. I tip my head against the side of the tub and stare at the shimmering golds and reds that fill the sky. The pain in my body starts to fade. The itch returns like a vengeance-packed wallop in the gut, and I sit up. "I should call the Sheriff's Office," I say.

"Stop stressing out. Gray hair looks distinguished on your dad, but you just turned twenty-one. I'm sure Lainey's fine."

I growl.

Clarice rolls her calf brown eyes. "Hey, do you want me to distract you?"

"Like you can."

"Wanna bet?" She scoots closer with a smile that tightens my ab muscles. I scowl at her in suspicion. The last time she gave me a look like this we got suspended for putting a frog in our teacher's desk. She reaches toward me.

I flinch, brushing her hand aside. "I don't trust you."

"Chicken," she taunts in the exact same tone she used back then. "It won't hurt. I swear. Cross my heart. Close your eyes."

You'd think I'd know better, but my early years of being her sidekick keep me docile. Just because she's turned majorly scary since hitting puberty shouldn't be a reason not to trust her. Right. I'm such a fool.

Clarice throws her leg over mine. Water laps between us. I hiss with the pain of her breasts rubbing against my bruised chest. I press back until I'm pinned against the wall of the tub. She can't weigh more than a buck twenty, but she's like a jellyfish. I'm wrapped in her slimy tentacles as if she injected a toxin into my bloodstream. The more she wiggles, the less I want to get away.

Not like I have a girlfriend. Yet.

What are friends with benefits for if not this sort of situation?

Her mouth slams onto mine.

I shove her back and touch a finger to my bleeding lip. "Damn it!"

Clarice gives a wicked laugh, but this isn't funny. "Sorry, I promised that it wouldn't hurt," she whispers. Her lips nibble the skin beneath my chin. My eyelids flicker. I'm super sensitive to a girl sucking on my neck. "I'm distracting you, right?"

Right. No. Wrong. Very wrong. I have to stop before this goes any further. I don't want to take advantage of her feelings for me. Rejecting her later will only hurt her worse. And damn, yes, her roving hands feel too good. *I'm only human.*

I spin, grabbing her by the waist and lifting her up onto the lip of the hot tub. Her hands lift to wrap around my neck as she struggles to hold on. "That's enough, Clarice."

Clarice gasps and scrambles backward, like a crab scuttling across the sand. A bit extreme for the situation, but I shouldn't look a gift horse in the mouth. She stares, slack-jawed enough to be impressive if I trusted her not to bite. It takes a couple of seconds before I realize I'm not the subject of her awe. She's looking over my shoulder. I follow her gaze and almost shit my pants.

My voice cracks. "W-what are you doing here?"

Chapter 4

Mala

Kill Spot

It totally sucks to be short.

Sheriff Keyes's long legs outstrip mine. He disappears down the path, and I try to keep up. Even Bessie passes me. Shouts come from up ahead. I burst into the clearing, gasping for air. Colorful spots dance in front of my eyes. God, I need to work out more. It takes a few seconds before I see George hanging from the branch of a tree with the thrashing body of an alligator directly below him. He drops to land a few inches from the gator's mouth. My heart lurches when the head jerks, its teeth snapping shut.

George shouts, kicking the gator in the snout, and lunges backward. The animal's dead, not stunned, but I can't fault George for being freaked since even in death those teeth almost took a huge chunk out of his calf. The still-twitching creature stretches a good twelve feet from snout to tail. He'll net about fifteen hundred dollars if we get him on ice before the meat goes bad. To hit the quarter-size kill spot at the back of the creature's skull in the dark—well, the word "miraculous" comes to mind.

Sheriff Keyes slaps George on the shoulder. "Damn! Nice shot."

George staggers. His legs fold, and he slumps to the ground to sit with his knees drawn up to his chest. "Thanks, Sheriff. It came up out of the water so fast…" He pauses and looks around. His eyebrows draw up as if surprised to find he has such a large audience. "One minute, I'm on the ground, and the next, up in the tree. I don't even remember aiming the gun before I pulled the trigger."

Sheriff Keyes shakes his head. His rotund belly stretches his duty shirt so much when he chuckles that I fear he'll pop a button. "Well, that's quick thinking. It probably saved your life. Training doesn't mean a damn thing in this line of work if you don't have the instinct and good sense to use it."

George ducks his head. "Sir, I didn't do anything special."

"You let me be the judge of that, Deputy Dubois." The sheriff walks toward the body, saying over his shoulder "See there, Mala Jean. You didn't have to worry about George *freaking out* after all."

I swallow hard, blushing. *God, I hope George didn't catch—*

"What did he mean by that?" George looks a little pasty in the faint light. Shock can do funny things to a person.

"It means I shouldn't have left you alone." I drop down next to him. "You're lucky you didn't get a chunk taken out of your ass. I told you not to stand too close to the water."

He holds his hands over his face, and his body trembles. He glances over his fingers to meet my eyes. "Shit, Mala, stop yelling. I'm fine."

Crap, I hadn't even realized I'd lost control. It's just…if anything had happened to him…

Dr. Rathbone crouches beside him. "Are you going to be okay, son? You're not gonna throw up, are you?"

"I've got Georgie, Doc." I pat George on the back. "Why don't you do what you came out here for and check out that girl's remains? She's not getting any fresher from lying in the mud."

Dr. Rathbone gives me a hard look but doesn't utter a peep. I've never cared for the man. Elections are held every four years for parish coroner, and he's won for the last twelve without anyone running against him. Rumors float around town about him taking bribes and being selective on whom he chooses to autopsy. Bessie nearly foams at the mouth whenever she has a case that gets kicked out of court for lack of evidence simply 'cause the doc can't be bothered to do his job, but the sheriff sticks by his friend. Good ol' boys.

Dr. Rathbone stalks over to stand next to Sheriff Keyes. They begin whispering and gesturing at the deceased. Then Keyes gives Bessie and the crime scene techs orders to start setting up. Soon the whole area fills with light from their big lanterns.

George swats my hand aside, like it's a pesky mosquito. "I'm fine, Malaise."

My hand clenches into a fist at my side. "Are you sure about that? You still look a little green."

"I said I'm fine. You don't need to coddle me."

Logic tells me that his anger and embarrassment over his loss of control in front of the other officials, especially the sheriff, is directed toward himself, like mine was earlier, but he proceeds to take it out on me the same way I turned my frustration on him.

I take a deep breath, trying to cool my temper. "Just trying to help. No big deal."

George shoots a glare over his shoulder. "No big deal? If I needed help looking even more incompetent than I already feel, I would've had my mother come out to hold my hand."

I throw my hands in the air. "Don't be stupid. I don't think you're incompetent."

"No? Well, everyone else does, thanks to you." He pushes to his feet and dusts off his pants. "Why don't you go home? Your mama's probably worried sick. If we need help, I'll send someone for you."

My face flushes. He knows darn well that Mama doesn't care where I've gotten off to. He just wants to share the humiliation. *Stupid, stupid me.* It takes all the strength I can dig up inside me to practically beg "Can't I stay and help work the crime scene?"

"You're not trained for this. Legally you're a liability, and in reality, you'll just get in the way."

* * *

Dawn finds me curled up in the rocking chair on my sagging front porch with a cup of coffee and sleep-deprived eyes. I'd been too wound up over finding Lainey and fuming over Georgie's jerk-move to get any sleep. True to his word, George sends Bessie to the house, rather than showing his face in front of me again. The coward. When she steps out of the trees and heads in my direction, I go inside to warn Mama so she can hide in her bedroom from her least favorite law woman. We don't think Mama has any outstanding warrants for her arrest, but it's better to be safe now than sorry in lockup for thirty days.

I meet Bessie on the porch steps with a steaming cup of coffee. Weariness sits heavy on the detective's broad shoulders. Skin like polished mahogany glistens with perspiration, and she wipes her forehead on a large handkerchief. "Gonna be another scorcher."

"Yeah."

"Sorry to do this, but I need you to come to the station so I can get your witness statement on tape. Just explain how you came across Lainey while the details are fresh in your mind."

I stifle a sigh, knowing my job. It's why I studied the body so thoroughly, even though the sight made me want to vomit. "I know. I've been expecting it. Every time I close my eyes, I see Lainey Prince's glazed eyes and smell the stink of her blood." I take a deep gulp of my coffee, hissing when it burns my tongue.

"Yeah, you look worn out. You did a good thing, dragging her out of the water and all. You could've left her there. Nobody would've been the wiser."

"I couldn't stomach living with myself if I'd left her there, Bessie," I say softly. "Her family deserves to have peace of mind. How much longer before you're done out there?"

Bessie takes a sip of her coffee. "We moved the body to the morgue. Andy brought out Rex. I tell you, that dog can sniff out blood from miles away. With the way the girl bled, it shouldn't take long to find where she cut herself before entering the water."

Saints, I hope she didn't kill herself on our land. We own five acres of prime swamp. The house stands on the highest hill, a fragile peninsula in the middle of all that water, on a cleared half acre. Only our gravel road provides entrance in or off our property, unless you count traveling by airboat through the bayou. Rex will find her car in no time.

Speaking of, only one patrol car remains parked on the side of the driveway bordering the woods. If Andy and his K-9 had driven out, then—"What happened to the other cars?"

"Sheriff Keyes and I rode in together. He and George went to give the death notification to the Prince family. George will come back to pick us up in a couple of hours. If you're feeling up to it after the interview, Maggie said she'll make you lunch."

Ha! Score. I'd throw myself in front of a bus for a batch of Maggie's blueberry muffins. I guess seeing my best friend makes up for having to ride to town with George, but unlike him, Bessie trusts my judgment. So does the sheriff. I won't disappoint them by acting like an idiot just because I have to breathe the same air as Deputy Dubois.

* * *

I take a long shower that steams up the bathroom. The hot spray beats into the kinked muscles in my back, working loose knots of tension I hadn't realized I had. I lean my head against the tiles and close my eyes. The image of Lainey Prince floating in the water invades my thoughts. Even though I never met her in life, the *whys* of her death haunt me. Why did she kill herself? Why did I find her? From what Georgie said, she had parents who loved her and provided everything she needed: food, clothes, shelter. Maybe she killed herself once she grew up and learned how rough life could be. Still, what could've been so bad?

I shake off my gloomy mood. As I step out of the tub, cold air slides around my body, and goose bumps rise on my arms. Shivering, I wrap the towel around my shoulders. Steam covers the mirror, and I swipe the edge of the towel across it. Eyes of cobalt blue, wide and staring, meet mine.

I scream, jumping back. My foot slips in a puddle, and I fall to my knees.

"Mala?" Mama must have jumped from the bed the second I screamed. She jiggles on the handle. "You okay?"

My heart races. Never in my life have I felt such deep, overwhelming fear. I can't think. The air feels thin. I can barely breathe, and what breath does come out crystallizes in the air. Panicked, I try to stand. My feet slip on *ice*. The top of my head slams into the underside of the sink, and I fall back again. Sparkles flash in front of my eyes as I cry out.

"Mala, answer me!"

Cold seeps down my palms and into my bones. "Mama, help!"

"Unlock the door."

The chill worms its way up my arms and legs and settles as a heavy weight on my chest. I start to hyperventilate, dragging air into my lungs in short gasps. Tears well up in my eyes, hard frozen shards that ice my eyelashes together.

"Please, please, Malaise."

"I can't—" I stare at the door, willing Mama to open it. Why doesn't the doorknob turn? The popped button proves it's unlocked.

"Open the door. *Please, baby,*" Mama yells, pounding on the door.

Why can't I move? I squeeze my eyes shut and suck in a deep breath. It catches in my chest. My vision blurs...

...then darkens.

Chapter 5

Landry

Hold Together

Deputy George Dubois, legendary prick of all pricks, stands by the back gate with his thumbs hooked in his duty belt. His expressionless face means he definitely saw Clarice with her hand down my boxers. I throw a grimace in Clarice's direction, but she's staring at the water. Damn right! She'd better be embarrassed trying to give me a hand job without asking permission first.

George nods to Clarice. "I need to speak with Landry in private."

She grabs her clothes off the ground. It takes less than ten seconds for her to abandon me to deal with the fallout alone. How is it I always end up taking the blame for her stupid ideas? You'd think after twenty years I'd know better.

"Landry..."

I meet his gaze. "What did you say?"

"I need to speak with your parents."

"Sorry, Dad's in Lafayette, and Mom's asleep. Why don't you come back tomorrow?" The hope in my voice makes me cringe. He stares at me with cold green eyes, and I shiver. "Come on, Deputy. Give me a break. This isn't what it looks like."

Why am I making excuses? I'm an adult. I signed up for the draft. I'm in college. I'm not the kid he used to babysit, but suddenly I'm twelve again when George says, "Stop dicking around, Landry. Sheriff Keyes is waiting for us out front."

Mom's gonna skin me alive. I rise and walk toward him. The closer I get to George, the less intimidated I feel. I've got three inches and about fifty pounds on him.

But he's got a gun.

I grab a towel off of the deck chair and wrap it around my waist. I'm about to go inside when I turn back around to beg George for a pass one last time. I catch the deputy at a vulnerable moment. Deep lines are etched around his eyes. It feels like he rams his fist in my gut. *Why would Sheriff Keyes be here? He'd only want to speak to Mom and Dad if something bad happened. It doesn't make any sense.* My palms begin to tingle. The sensation travels up my arms then spreads through the rest of my body. I'm about to jump out of my skin. *Lainey…oh, God.*

A gust of cold air chills my skin. I squeeze my eyes shut, shaking my head. "I know why you're here. It's Lainey. She's dead, isn't she?"

Silence falls over the yard, but I still have to strain to hear George's whispered "Yes."

The sound of glass shattering whips my head around. Mom

stands in front of the screen door. The drink-filled tray she'd been carrying dangles from her fingers. Broken shards of glass litter the concrete.

"Momma," I choke on the word, breathing hard.

Her mouth opens, and a keening wail cuts the air…like a knife…each scream jabs deeper and deeper into my chest.

My throat tightens around my own cries. They fight to get free. To release the pressure building inside my chest, but I hold them in. I have to be strong.

Mom takes a step forward and stumbles. I lunge for her, but I'm too far away. George catches her as she falls, scooping her up in his arms like she weighs no more than an infant.

My legs don't catch my forward motion. I drop to my knees. Pain stabs my hand, and I look at my palm, dazed. I yank out the sliver of glass. Blood oozes from the puncture wound and drips to the ground. The dime-size crimson splatter widens. Now it's the size of a quarter…a silver dollar.

"Landry, I need your help. Your mom's cut herself," George yells from inside the house.

I tear my eyes from the blood and push to my feet. My thoughts are fuzzy. I feel disconnected, as if I'm watching from outside of myself. I step carefully to avoid the rest of the glass and pause in the doorway, letting my eyes adjust. Sheriff Keyes sits on the sofa next to Mom. He has his arm around her shoulder and pats her back as she cries—and it's not her usual ladylike misting of the eyes that she dabs away with tissue during sad movies—I mean, she bawls, as in snot dripping and tears streaming over the sheriff's starched, khaki uniform shirt. It's a total loss of her vaunted self-control. I've never seen her break down before, and it makes the situation even more surreal. 'Cause Lainey being dead, it's bullshit!

The more I think on it, the more I know for sure. Lainey can't be dead. I saw her not more than half an hour ago in the garage. Sure she looked kind of filmy and way too quiet, but she didn't look dead. And that stupid itch…fleas. The cat brought the parasites into the house. Sasha's always hunting mice and dumping them on our beds. Bet one crawled up my nose while I was sleeping, and that's why my brain itches.

Lainey can't be dead.

A sound breaks into my thoughts. It takes a second for words to form from the meaningless mutters.

"Landry…" *That's my name.*

I blink then focus on George. "What?"

"Snap out of it."

"Out of what?" My gaze travels back to Mom. She's stopped wailing and now clings to the sheriff, shuddering and hiccupping. A shadow crosses my vision. *How long have I been standing in the doorway? In a towel. Surrounded by broken glass. Barefoot.*

I shake my head. "What the hell?"

George grabs my sandals from beside the doormat. He holds them out to me. I'm not sure exactly what I'm supposed to do with them. Does he want me to go with him somewhere? Didn't Sheriff Keyes tell Mom they found Lainey? Where is she?

My head's killing me. I squeeze my eyes shut, pressing my palm against the throbbing vein between my eyes. Hands lift my leg. George slips first one foot then the other into the sandals. "Why don't you go sit beside your mom?" he says.

He takes my arm, and I let him lead me to the sofa. I sit next to Mom with my hands folded between my legs so they don't shake. Sheriff Keyes continues to rock Mom like a colicky baby. His voice is too low for me to hear what he's saying to comfort her. I guess he and George decided to split us into easily handled chunks, but it wasn't necessary.

"I'm fine," I whisper.

"No. You're not. Where's your first aid kit, Landry?" George asks.

I glance down at my injured hand. The bleeding has stopped, but dirt crusts the puncture wound. I'd better wash it out with peroxide so it doesn't get infected. I'd hate to get my hand amputated for a stupid reason like gangrene.

Oh, yeah. Mom got hurt too.

Her foot's propped on the table with a bloody dishtowel wrapped around it. I stand up and walk toward the staircase. George puts out his hand, and I ram chest first into his palm. I hold my breath against the pain in my ribs.

"Damn it, that hurts." I smack his hand aside.

"Where are you going?"

"For the first aid kit. It's in the upstairs bathroom."

"I'll get it."

No, I need to be alone for a minute. "It'll be faster if I go."

George's doubtful expression makes it seem like he doesn't believe me. I bark out a choked laugh and wince as my ribs protest. I step around him and take the stairs two at a time. I'm breathing hard when I reach the top, and I lay my arms against the railing until I catch my breath.

Downstairs the murmur of voices captures my attention, and

I strain to hear the conversation. A thump from down the hall turns me in that direction. I pause for a minute. I listen but don't hear anything else. Probably my imagination on overtime. I start toward the bathroom. The thud from Lainey's room is louder this time. A rush of excitement floods through my body, clearing the fog from my mind.

I run to fling open her door. It bounces against the wall and rebounds closed. I stop it an inch from smacking my face. The image of her empty bedroom is branded in my mind. Without opening the door, I imagine her lavender and white bedspread and fluffy pillows on her made bed. The spotless floor and organized dresser. What the hell?

"Landry?"

I spin, falling back against the wall. My heart almost explodes out of my chest. "Don't sneak up on me."

George's voice is gentle, like he's trying to talk a guy off a high-rise ledge. "Does he think I'll jump?"

"I don't think you're gonna kill yourself," he says.

Oh, jeez, I asked the question out loud. "I'm not crazy."

"You're in shock. It's normal given the circumstances. Why don't you go downstairs and sit with your mom?"

"I heard someone walking around in Lainey's room. What if she came home while we were talking?"

George reaches around me and opens the door.

"See," I say, pointing at the bed. "Her room's usually a mess. It drives Mom crazy. They're always fighting about her making her bed and picking up her clothes."

His sharp gaze travels around the room, settling on each piece of furniture for a second before moving on as if cataloging the contents for future reference. Once done, he looks back at me. "Maybe she didn't want to leave behind a dirty room and cleaned up before going out."

I snort. Obviously he doesn't know Lainey as well as he thinks he does. "Why would she? She thinks making her bed's a waste of time since she'll have to get back in it again later. Plus her cleaning would make Mom happy. Lainey never does anything for anyone but herself."

George nods as if what I said makes perfect sense. He waves his hand. "Can I look around? Maybe she left a note."

"Sure, go ahead. Check the closet to make sure she's not hiding in there." I sit on her bed. I've been banned from coming into her bedroom for years. Lainey had been pissed at how girly Mom decorated it, but after she grew out of her tomboy stage, she came to love it. It'll serve my big sis right having her ex-boyfriend pawing through her private stuff after pulling a stunt like this. For a minute, I really thought she'd died.

George starts riffling through her desk drawers. He glances over his shoulder at me with a frown. "You doing okay now?"

I laugh. "Yeah, sorry. I guess I lost it for a minute. What made you think Lainey was dead anyway?"

"Are you saying you think she's alive?" He turns slowly. "I thought you understood what I was telling you earlier."

"You think she's dead, but she's not. I swear." I hold up my hand. "Scout's honor. Lainey ran off with her new beau. She's been sneaking out with him for about eight or nine months."

God, the look in George's eyes.

I lift my head to stare at the ceiling. The blood coursing through my body pulses in my ears. His voice comes as a muffled shushing. "Landry, I'm sorry. I thought you heard the sheriff tell your mom…"

I wish I couldn't hear at all.

"We found Lainey." George stands over the bed. He wants to be sure I hear him this time. That I don't mistake the words coming out of his mouth. He's gonna force me to face the truth whether I want to or not. No more living in denial. No more pretending. No more hope.

I breathe out the words, "Found her where?"

"Her body was found floating in Bayou St. Louis. She's dead, Landry. Dr. Rathbone plans to conduct an autopsy later today to determine the cause of death."

I'm not sure when the tears start to fall. My face feels numb. I watch them drop from my eyes to form a violet stain on my sister's lavender bedspread. A thump comes from inside the closet. George walks over to open the door. Sasha looks up at him and hisses, then runs to hide under Lainey's bed.

"I need to get dressed." I run for the bathroom.

Everything moves in slow motion.

My brain shuts off.

I'm cool with the emptiness.

I take a quick shower to get the chlorine off my skin and get dressed, but then I'm forced to crouch over the toilet, dry heaving. When I can stand, I splash my face with cool water. The Landry in the mirror looks like a zombie. Dark-rimmed, hollow gray eyes and wet black hair I don't even bother combing. I remember to grab the first aid kit and walk downstairs.

Sheriff Keyes stands by the front door with Mom. I thought he would've left by now. I'm glad he waited and didn't leave Mom alone. She's in bad shape. Now that my brain is partially functional again, I think I'd better take her to the ER so she can get stitches. I go to stand with them. Outside, George paces with jerky steps in front of the patrol car with one hand pressed against his shoulder mike.

Sheriff Keyes pats my shoulder. "I'm sorry, son. I wish I could stay until your dad arrives, but there's been another development in the case. I'm sorry for your loss."

I nod and wrap my arm around Mom's shoulder. "Thank you."

Sheriff Keyes walks down the sidewalk and meets up with George. They speak in low voices as they move with measured but urgent strides to climb into the car. The patrol car's engine revs then peels out with squealing tires and sirens blaring.

We stand in the doorway in silence for I don't know how long. Mom and I are lost in our own worlds until they collide. She twists out of my arms, and I let them fall to my sides. My shoulders slump, a heavy weight presses down on them. The sudden urge to punch a hole in the wall has me balling my hands into useless fists.

Mom's gaze flickers downward, and I shove my hands into my pockets. "Do you want breakfast?" she asks, heading toward the kitchen, not waiting for my answer.

I chase after her. She moves fast. It doesn't seem like her injury even hurts. Then I notice she walks with a slight limp, not putting all of her weight down on her foot. She bustles around the kitchen, leaving bloody footprints on the tile with each step. She pulls out packages of bacon and eggs from the refrigerator then slams the door. The expression on her face terrifies me. She's totally blank.

"Mom, why don't you take a sleeping pill and rest? I'll cook up something for you."

"Don't patronize me," she says serenely. Too calm to be real.

I swallow hard. Maybe *I* should take a sleeping pill instead. Wake up once this nightmare is over. Except it never will be. I'll replay this moment over and over for the rest of my life. The day my sister died.

"When is Dad coming home?"

"I don't know."

"Did Sheriff Keyes call him?"

She lays strips of bacon into the skillet. Her eyes meet mine. "Mind your own business, Landry. What were you and Clarice doing in the hot tub?"

Old eagle eyes. So scary. I hide my shiver by sitting on a stool. The counter hides my hands as I rub the goose bumps rising on my arms. "I bruised my ribs while weight training. Clarice saw what happened and came over to see if I was okay."

Mom nods. "She's a nice Christian girl."

Nice, right. I almost choke. Lainey would've busted up if she heard Mom say that. She hates...hated Clarice with a passion. She called Clarice a hypocrite. "Sweet on the outside, Satan's handmaiden on the inside." They had a lot in common.

No. I can't think of Lainey like that anymore. She's dead.

Mom's focus returns to cooking breakfast. I'm not sure what to say to her. Should I try to get her to talk about what happened? I need Dad. He'll know what to say...to do next. Do I need to call the funeral home? Schedule a service? How long do we have to get everything ready? I have to tell him what happened so he can come home. He's only an hour away, but it feels like he's clear across the country. I creep out of the kitchen. My cell phone sits on the table by the door, and I punch in Dad's number. It only rings once before he picks up.

"What's going on, Landry?"

He's psychic like that. He can always sense when something's wrong.

"Dad—" My voice cracks, and the line goes silent. How do I put what happened into words? I try again. "Dad, you've got to come home. It's Lainey—"

Mom's fingernail scratches my cheek when she snatches my cell out of my hand. I press my palm against my stinging face. She throws the phone at the wall, then spins.

"Don't tell him a bunch of lies over the phone!" she shrieks, shoving me into the wall when I try to pick up the cell phone.

"Stop!" I yell, pushing her off. I barely touch her, but even laying hands on her that much sends a wave of guilt rushing through me. I pick the phone up. It's dead. *Crap! Did Dad hear?*

Mom grabs my shirt in her balled-up fists. This time I don't fight her. She's so tiny; she's like a sparrow pecking at a raven. "Sheriff Keyes, he's an idiot. You know that. Right, son? He's never been the sharpest tool in the shed. Not even in high school." She laughs, wrapping her arms around my waist and pressing her face into my shirt.

I hug her back. Her body trembles. She looks up at me with tears darkening her blue eyes. They look so much like Lainey's that my stomach twists.

Mom gives me a watery smile. "Don't worry." She pats my cheek. "Sheriff Keyes made a mistake. I know you *feel* it too. It's not our Lainey's body. There's no way. It's someone else."

I want to believe Mom. Maybe they did misidentify her. Who knows Lainey well enough to be one hundred percent positive except family?

"George said it's Lainey," I say reluctantly. "He seemed pretty sure, and even if he made a mistake like that, the sheriff wouldn't back him on it. They said they took her to the coroner's office. Uncle Jay plans to do an autopsy."

Mom sucks in a breath. Her wild eyes send me stumbling back. "I don't believe it. They have the wrong body. I'll prove it. We'll go see for ourselves. I'll prove they're wrong. It's not Lainey."

Chapter 6

Mala

Soul Sucked

My eyes feel sticky and dry and my vision hazy when I force open my eyelids. A slick, burnished brown cockroach the size of a half dollar crawls out of a crack in the wall and skitters across the underside of rusted pipes leading into the sink. I hate roaches. I can handle near 'bout every other critter found in the swamp, but roaches in my house turn me homicidal.

I stare at the hole it exited, planning to get the insecticide as soon as I figure out why I'm lying on the floor in the first place. More antennae wave at me from the mouth of the crack. A slender roach crawls out. Another follows behind, and another. The bodies scramble free in a flood of wiggling legs, scurrying down the walls directly toward my open mouth.

With a squeak of panic, I roll backward and bump into the legs of an African American soldier in tight green Vietnam-era camouflage BDUs. The man crouches beside me, fiddling with the bathroom door. I rise up onto an elbow, trying to see. He keeps shifting his heavy body into my line of sight to block his actions from me. I swing a fist at his thigh. It passes right through and out the other side.

I exhale the prayer in one breath. "Holy Mary, Mother of God, pray for this sinner, now and at the hour of my death, amen."

The helmeted head turns at my words. Hooded eyes, pitiless orbs of darkness, connect with mine. The intensity reflected within the ebony gaze mesmerizes me like a snake charmer entrances a cobra. And I learn how helpless the snake must feel, dancing to someone else's tune. Helpless.

Then he blinks and sets me free. "Ready?" he asks.

I shake my head. "For what?"

He points to the door, and the C4 molded into the lock. "Fire in the hole," he yells, with a grin that stretches his face like rubber. He raises the detonator and presses the button.

The wave of flame engulfs his body, ripping him to pieces.

"No!" I scream. My arms wrap around my head to protect it from the chunks of meat and blood raining down on me. Cold rather than heat sucks the air from my lungs.

A deafening crash fills the room. My eyes pop open. The door vibrates and then swings wide with so much force the knob breaks a chunk of plaster out of the wall. I draw my knees up and fumble to pull the bath towel higher, but it's too late.

George strides into the bathroom with a look on his face that I've never seen before. Worry wars with fear. Then, when his eyes fall on me, they widen. "Oh, baby girl," he whispers so softly that I barely hear the endearment.

He bends down and scoops me up like I weigh no more than a child. The top of my head fits perfectly beneath his chin. I press my ear against his chest. His heart races. The arms wrapped around my body squeeze me so tight I can barely breathe.

I shiver, gripping the towel against my breasts.

Mama hovers at his side. Her face has drained of color. Black lines from her mascara run down her cheeks. "Is she okay?"

"Ms. Jasmine, I need you to move back a bit."

"What? Oh, sorry." Mama stumbles back into the bedroom, twisting her hands together. "Is that blood on her head?"

"Yes, ma'am." George lays me on the bed, pulls the blanket up to my chin, and tucks the edges under me so tight I can't move my arms. "Where's your medical supplies?"

Mama shakes her head.

George's mouth turns down at the corners. "She's freezing, probably in shock. Keep her covered while I get my first aid kit." He pats my leg. "Will you be okay while I'm gone?"

I lick my lips then whisper, "I'll be fine."

George hesitates. Indecision flickers across his face. I think he debates picking me up again and carrying me out to his car rather than leaving me alone in Mama's not-so-tender loving care. Finally, he mutters something about remembering to restock his medical supplies and leaves the room. My heart crawls after him.

"I need some water," I say.

"I'll be right back. Don't move." Mama runs from the room, and I gape after her in shock. She's never moved so fast to attend to me. Not even when I got pneumonia as a child and had been admitted to the hospital. She made me buzz a nurse whenever I needed a drink or help to the bathroom.

She returns in less than a minute holding out a glass of water. "Here, drink it fast."

I take a large gulp, swallow half, and spit the rest across the bed, choking. "It's vodka!"

"Shh, of course," Mama cries, glancing nervously toward the door. "That's why I said drink it fast. I don't want to get arrested for contributin' to the delinquency of a minor. Lord knows, I'm sick of goin' to jail for stupid shit."

Tears sting my eyes, and my throat burns from the alcohol. "That's nasty. How can you drink it?"

"Tastes better with cranberry juice, but we don't have none. Feel better now? Warmer?"

"Yeah," I drawl. "How'd you know it'd work?"

"Works for me in these situations." She sits on the edge of the bed. "Drink up. I hear Georgie's big ol' feet crunching in the gravel. He'll be back in a couple of minutes."

Frowning, I rub my eyes. My vision looks filmy, and my thoughts are sluggish. "Mama, what's he doing here?"

"What do you mean?"

"Why's he in the house?"

She takes the glass from my hand then sticks her face close to mine, staring into my eyes. "Are you serious?"

I lift the blanket up and glance under the covers. Yep, it's worse than I thought. The towel lies at the foot of the bed. "Oh, hell, he saw me stark naked," I choke. "How can I ever look him straight in the eyes again?"

"Did that knock to your head scramble your brain? Embarrassment is the least of your worries. Rather than bein' angry, you should be thankin' me for gettin' Georgie to break open that door."

"But why, Mama? Last thing I remember, I'm taking a shower, and the next, Georgie's bursting into the bathroom." I wrap the blanket around my nakedness and roll from the bed. "I don't want him seeing me like this again. Don't let him come in until I'm dressed." I stagger toward the bathroom.

"Mala, don't you dare go back—"

I slam the door and lean against it to catch my breath from the dizziness that makes the room swim.

Mama's voice moves into the hall, and I hear the rumbled bass of Georgie's answer. They argue, too low for me to make out distinct words. Finally, another knock sounds on the door, and I open it wide enough to take the first aid kit from Mama, ignoring her protests, and close the door again. I stare at my reflection in the mirror, horrified. A trickle of blood has dried on the side of my face, and I wash it off. The shallow cut on my temple's all bark and no bite. It'll swell up into a formidable knot, but I can hide it beneath my hair.

"Pathetic. I look like I got dragged through the mud behind a pickup." *And George saw me looking like this, ugh.*

Since I don't have time to blow dry my hair, I towel dry it and put in some anti-frizz goop to deal with the muggy air. I even put on makeup and have to admit that while I usually don't pay a whole lot of attention to my appearance, I clean up well. I look polished and mature—maybe even beautiful in a Jessica Szohr kind of way once I slip into the low-cut, vibrant purple dress I'd hung over the shower bar to steam out the wrinkles, and slingback heels.

Mama knocks on the door. "Bessie says it's time to go."

I run out of the bathroom.

"Hold on, let me look at you." Mama grabs my face and tilts my chin up. She stares into my eyes with a frown then roughly fingers the knot. "You sure you want to go? Be better if you stuck ice on that lump and rested."

I wince and push her hand aside. "I'm fine. What's the big deal?"

"The fact that you don't remember what happened scares me."

"Nothing happened."

"Mala, I had to beg Dixie to get her to send George. You were locked in the bathroom for thirty minutes with me not knowing if you were dead or alive. So don't tell me nothin' happened. That's thirty minutes you scared off my already short life."

Mama calls me hardheaded for good reason. A little bump won't keep me from making George squirm like a night crawler on a hook for treating me like an outcast at the crime scene.

"Well, I'm fine now. And Bessie's waiting." I hug her and give her a kiss. "Stop fussing, it'll give you wrinkles. I've gotten worse lumps from falling out of trees."

I try to pull back, but Mama's arms tighten. "Tell me what happened, Mala. Before you passed out—did you see anythin' *strange*?"

"No, I—"

"Try to remember. It's important or I wouldn't ask."

"All I remember is getting out of the shower. I must've slipped and hit my head." I stare at the velvet picture of Elvis Presley hanging over the fireplace mantel, trying to replay the last moments before everything went dark. My thoughts grow fuzzy, and my vision clouds. The vibrant baby blues of Elvis's eyes darken to cobalt, the shape elongating to tilt slightly at the corners.

The hairs on my arms rise, and I shiver. "It's cold, Mama, like ice running through my veins."

"What else? Do you smell anything?"

"The swamp…the smell of decay," I whisper, swaying in her embrace.

"Don't let go, baby."

"I'm dizzy. My head's pounding."

"I know. One last thing. What did you see?"

I'm whimpering. Tentatively, I probe the dark corner in my mind. The place that feels glossy, slick to the touch, like oil coating the top layer of water. I don't want to go deeper. I don't want to relive an experience that obviously scared the hell out of me the first time.

I raise a shaking hand to cover my eyes.

Mama shakes me so hard my neck snaps back. "Damn it, Mala. Why did you scream?"

Footsteps thump on the porch stairs.

"Stop, let me go!" I jerk her hands off of my shoulders. My head's pounding again, and I almost wish she snapped my neck.

"Wait, we need to talk about what's happening." Her expression breaks my heart, but I learned how to cut off the hurt as a child. I lock away the guilt and toss the imaginary key out the window.

"No, *we* don't. I've got to go." I throw open the front door, not wanting to make Bessie wait any longer. George stands on the porch instead, and my smile wilts as I snap, "Oh crap, it's you again."

George stands flatfooted in my path.

"Move," I say, edging around him and slamming the door closed behind me.

His eyes travel leisurely down the length of my body. "Mala, I—"

"Sorry about Mama dragging you from *your* crime scene. As you can see, I'm fine." I slide my hands down across the slick silk clinging to my hips.

George's green eyes darken as his gaze follows my hands, and he licks his lips. "Yeah, you look real pretty..." He frowns and shakes his head. "Shouldn't you be in bed? You took a nasty fall. What if you have a concussion?"

Now he's acting all nice. If I'd knocked myself unconscious last night, would he have felt sorry enough to let me work the crime scene? I jerk my head aside and force my voice to sound cold, even though I feel hot, hot, steaming up...*whew, breathe, girl. Calm down.* "Thanks, but I don't need your 'coddling' any more than you need mine."

He stumbles when I brush past. "What? That's not—"

"Look, you made your feelings clear last night." I exhale the heavy breath tightening my chest. I turn and start down the stairs.

George grabs my arm. "Hold on, Mala. You can't go flinging out accusations, then storm off without letting me defend myself. Hell, I'm not even altogether clear on what you're going on about."

"Then maybe you are *incompetent*. 'Cause it's pretty obvious." I snatch my arm away. My heels click loudly on the stairs as I stomp down them. *Idiot!*

"Mala," George yells back. "Tell me what I did."

I spin around. "Nothing. You didn't do anything. And I'm fine. See"—I wave a hand down my body—"no lasting injuries. Mama scared the living daylights out of you, and you rescued me. Just don't assume I fell on purpose to get your attention."

He digs his fingers into his hair. "I never—"

"Well then, good." My face burns hot enough to go off like a Fourth of July firecracker. Colored sparkles flash before my eyes as I hurry across the lawn to the patrol car. Each step spears a clod of earth, and I wobble rather than storm gracefully over to the car.

Chapter 7

Mala

Stuck on Stupid

Bessie leans against the passenger door of the car with her arms crossed. She raises an eyebrow, and I drop my gaze, unable to maintain eye contact. Part of me feels like a weight has been lifted off my shoulders at not being a dishrag and confronting George over how he humiliated me at the crime scene, but the other still fumes that he has no clue why I'm angry. He's like a kid who can't figure out why his mama's mad at him for eating all of the Halloween candy in one sitting. Serves him right if he gets sick with the guilt.

Let it go, Mala. He's not worth it.

"Mala," Bessie says, and I jerk to a halt. "I need to remind you to keep quiet about finding Lainey. With so many people involved in documenting the crime scene, I'm sure a bunch of rumors are already floating around town. People will be hungry for particulars about how Lainey died, but for the time being, the details of the case need to remain confidential."

My face grows hotter. "Who exactly do you think I'd tell, Detective Caine?"

"Don't get mad," George says, coming up beside me, and I spin. "I asked Bessie to talk to you. This is an active investigation, and the fewer people who know what's going on, the better."

What's this? Gang-up-on-Mala day? I share my glare with both deputies. "And you think I can't keep my mouth shut? I'm not an idiot."

Bessie returns my glare with an even stronger one. I wilt, feeling all of four years old. "Don't get smart. I mean for you to keep quiet around Maggie too."

I glare at the mixed pink, yellow, and purple pansies in the raised beds bordering my vegetable garden. Their little pansy heads bob in agreement with Bessie as the wind brushes their delicate faces. Little traitors. See if I water them anymore.

"This is a big trust being laid on you, Mala," Bessie says. "I know once you've given a promise you'll keep it."

Her faith in my judgment melts my anger. "Fine, I'll exercise my right to remain silent even if Maggie uses her blueberry muffins to torture me for information. Promise."

"Thank you," Bessie says with a smile.

I shrug. I've gotten off easy. At this point, I'd agree to cutting out my own tongue if it meant getting free from George.

Bessie's and George's radio mikes beep. Ms. Dixie's voice comes through as a scratchy, high-pitched, inaudible squeak. Not her normal even tone. Something's up. Wish they'd turn up the volume so I could hear what's being said because worried frowns settle on both of their faces.

Bessie lifts a finger. "Come on, Mala. You're riding with me."

George grabs my arm when I start toward the car. His eyes flick over to mine, and I read the worry darkening the jade depths. "Are you crazy, Bessie? Don't tell me you plan on taking Mala with you?"

Bessie stiffens from her slouch. "I think it'll be a good experience for her."

"She's still a kid. It's not a good idea…"

My chest puffs at the kid comment. Who does he think he is? He's only three years older than me.

Bessie swells up even bigger than I do. "I didn't ask for your opinion, Deputy Dubois."

I hide my smug grin as the color leaches from his already pale face. *Ah-ha, you're busted. Take that, Mr. Smarty Pants.*

Red-gold lashes brush his high cheekbones when he lowers his gaze to stare at my feet. I shift from one foot to the other. The stupid heels make my toes feel like I set hot coals beneath them. His eyes narrow, but he shakes his head. "Sorry, Bessie. Do what you think best. You're the boss."

"Yes, I am." Bessie waves me toward the car.

The vibe between them makes me cringe. The boy's lost his ever-lovin' mind. What was he thinking to challenge Bessie's authority? Especially in front of me. As his supervisor, she could write him up for insubordination. Their cryptic conversation convinces me of one thing though; I'm not blowing my chance of seeing whatever it is that George thinks I shouldn't.

Andy's caged K-9 car comes down the driveway. He rolls down

the window. "Mala, Bessie," he greets us with a wave then turns to George. "Let's get this show on the road, man."

The shadow of Andy's partner, Rex, a black Labrador, fills the tinted window. He barks his give-me-a-Milk-Bone greeting, not his I'm-gonna-bite-off-your-face greeting. Andy will kill me if he ever finds out I sometimes sneak in treats for his dog, but how can I say no to Rex's sweet puppy face?

As I slide into the passenger seat, I catch George watching me. He gives me one last indecipherable glance then heads for Andy's car. Was that a flicker of worry in George's eyes? Nah. Whatever happened has George spooked.

George gets into Andy's car, and they drive off in a peal of squealing tires and flashing lights. Bessie waves me over, and I slide in beside her.

We ride in uncomfortable silence for a while. I stare out the window, watching as woodland turns into fields of sugarcane and then, upon entering Paradise Pointe city limits, to the main street lined with beautiful, colonial houses beneath towering, moss-draped ancient oak trees. My favorite home belongs to my boss, Ms. Marcheline Dubois. It resembles Tara in *Gone With the Wind* and has an award-winning rose garden, which I help keep up in the summer. I do other sorts of yard and housework for her, in addition to working at Munchies.

The best part about working for Ms. March is sitting under the ceiling fan on the veranda and watching HBO on her giant television with a huge bowl of popcorn propped on the couch between us. The woman loves her some *True Blood*. She told me in confidence that she hopes a sexy, elderly vampire will move to town someday and make her *his* before she gets too shriveled up to appreciate him. I can't imagine actually living in a house so big and fancy—but old, yeah.

Gerard Savoie built my house in the 1840s for his slave concubine, my ancestor, after he freed her and their children and gifted them with twenty acres of swamp. I wish he passed along a little more money to his illegitimate descendants for upkeep on our drafty, rotting homestead. Still, we made out better than the ancestors of my friend and cousin Dena Ackers. Savoie's inheritance bypassed his legitimate female descendants. The Acker clan survives on less than I manage to scrounge from the bayou, and at least Mama's pastime brings in money for decent clothing.

It's not until we pull onto Court Street that it dawns on me that Bessie doesn't seem inclined to explain where we're going. Or share why George was so upset that he threw in his two cents. I turn in the seat so I can read her face. "Is something going on that I need to be worried about?"

Bessie's eyebrows shoot up, but she keeps her gaze on the road. "No, why would you think such a thing?"

I frown. "Seriously?"

"It's nothing to worry about. I have an emergency that takes priority over your interview. I thought you might like to do a ride-along. Was I mistaken?" She slants a look in my direction. "I can always drop you off at the station."

I frantically wave my hand. "Oh, no, that's okay. I'm fine." I avoid her eyes and stare out the window as we pull into the parking lot for a two-story, redbrick building with a sign—Coroner's Office—posted in the landscaped lawn.

My eyes widen. "Bessie, am I going to the autopsy?" A grin stretches my lips. I wiggle in the seat. I've researched what happens in an autopsy. I've memorized all the steps, from placing the cadaver on a body block to expose the chest, the Y-shape incision…I know it all, but I thought it'd be years before I'd ever see one.

Bessie laughs and pats my hand. "Girl, I must've been a good role model if you get all giddy over seeing a body get dissected." She shakes her head and unbuckles her seat belt. "I'm not staying for the full autopsy. I need to chat with Dr. Rathbone about the case. It's against department policy to leave the keys or the car running when I'm not in it. Go wait on that bench in the garden. I shouldn't be long."

My smile fades. "I guess that means it's also against departmental policy for me to watch the autopsy, isn't it?"

"Yep. Besides, George would kill me," Bessie says with a laugh. "The fact I respect his opinion is between us, though."

"You're such a tease, Detective Caine." I stifle a groan, fanning my face with my hand as I climb out of the car. Until she said I'd be sitting outside, I hadn't noticed the sticky, wet patches under my armpits. Bessie walks me as far as the bench then leaves me to go inside. I sit down. The metal seat burns right through the lightweight fabric of my dress, and I hop back up with a hiss.

Rubbing my bottom, I kick off my heels and move deeper into the garden. A magnolia tree offers a secluded spot. Shiny, dark green leaves of a camellia bush form a private nook around a grassy knoll. I curl up with my back against the tree, smoothing my dress over my legs and closing my eyes. Tension flows from my body as I breathe in the mingled sweet scents that drag me into a low doze.

Lainey stands barefoot on a carpet of red rose petals. Her glorious, shiny black hair, without a stitch of curl to mar its smooth perfection, hangs past her waist. Her robin's-egg blue dress blows in the wind. She stares at me with her black brows furrowed and her jaw tense. I can't make out the expression in her eyes, worry or anger, maybe both. She holds out her right hand, gesturing for me to follow, then points at the morgue with the other. When I don't move, her expression tightens. This time I know what she feels—rage. It rolls off her and settles on me, a heavy weight sitting on my chest, pressing me down so I can't breathe.

Choking, I wake up with a gasp. The sun shines through a break in the leaves overhead, and a beam stabs into my eyes. I roll onto my knees, sucking in great gulps of humid air. The dream lingers in my mind, but the details drift on the breeze until only the feelings the dream inspired remain. Anger, fear, and despair roll through me, and I huddle in a ball with my arms around my legs. Mama always threatens to "give me something to cry about" when I act like an idiot. Why am I so emotional over a stupid dream? Exhaustion and stress play a part, but I don't have any excuse to keep feeling sorry for myself.

I clench my teeth and sit up, brushing tears from my cheeks. I've been so wrapped up in my own pain that I've ignored the yelling coming from the cab of a black truck in the parking lot. It continues on for about a minute, but I can't hear individual words. The tinted side windows make it difficult to see inside the cab, but it looks like the passenger slaps the driver in the face—once, twice…I duck behind a bush when the passenger door flies open. A tiny, middle-age woman with a mussed, black bob haircut hops to the ground. She sprints for the entrance to the Coroner's Office before the driver gets his door open.

"Momma, wait for Dad!" Landry Prince yells, and I grab onto a branch so I don't fall when my legs wobble. I press my hand to my racing heart. His black hair blows in the breeze. His lips are pinched into a thin, stern line as he runs to grab his mother's arm. She throws her elbow back into his stomach. With a wheeze, he doubles over. His mother twists out of his hand, pulls open the front doors, and runs inside.

"Damn it," he curses, following ten strides behind her.

I rock from one foot to the other, but, really, there's no decision to be made. Curiosity propels me to follow them into the dark, gray-walled corridor, and then it's simply a matter of following the screams.

The doors to the morgue swing open with the slightest push, and I step inside. The floor feels like ice beneath my bare feet. The stench hits at once—a sickening sweet, rotting-gas smell like wet dog fur fills my nose. I spare a single glance for the hysterical woman and her son surrounded by Bessie, Dr. Rathbone, and a couple of lab technicians and deputies, arguing in the corner on the far side of the room. Then my gaze turns to the corpse on the metal slab.

Lainey's chest has been sliced open, and her heart rests on a scale beside the table. My stomach bucks and tries to crawl out of my throat. All the peace and grace Lainey radiated in the water has been ripped from her, leaving her exposed and vulnerable to the stares of those observing the official autopsy.

My eyelids flutter, and my knees buckle. A hard shoulder slams into mine, and I grab onto the door to catch my balance as someone shoves past me. I stare at the ground, unable to focus my blurry vision.

"Oh, Mother Mary," I whisper, backing out of the room. The images replay in my mind. Over and over. *The heart. The body.* The wail from the woman—Lainey's mother. *The poor woman. To see her daughter cut…*

My stomach turns over, and I run for the front door as wobbly and blind as a day-old kitten. I need fresh air. If I stay trapped within these walls, I'll lose it. My eyes burn. I can barely see where I'm going, but the scent of roses replaces the rot of decomposition. I drop to my knees in the grass and breathe in deeply, try to settle my stomach.

I'm not alone. The prickle of awareness spins me around.

Landry has collapsed beneath the magnolia tree not two feet from where I sit. The storm clouds in his eyes churn with the intense emotion flowing through him. My skin tingles as if zapped by electricity, and I shudder. I can't breathe.

"I'm sorry, I didn't see you…" I crawl backward. *How could I be so blind? He's huge.*

"Mala, wait…don't go." His raw voice echoes deep inside me. My body screams with the need to run, but my mind refuses to obey. I pause, trembling as I picture his expression when his mom elbowed him in the gut, the horror in his eyes when he saw his sister cut open on the autopsy table. He's devastated, and I can't leave him alone with his grief.

I stare at an ant crawling across my knee. If I meet Landry's eyes again, I'll break. They reflect so much pain that they threaten to overwhelm me. I speak to my folded hands. "Are you okay?"

"My sister's dead," he says, voice thick with horror. "I saw her…h-heart."

A quick glance upward shows him resting his head back

against the tree. His eyelids squeeze shut, giving me a split second to study his tearless face before his red-rimmed eyes open and almost catch mine.

"I know. I saw. I'm *so* sorry, Landry."

"You were inside?" He leans forward, reaching toward me with a bandaged hand.

I scoot back, and his hand drops onto his upraised knee. "Yeah, I—"

"I remember...standing by the door." Landry frowns at me, but his gaze focuses inward. "You work at the Sheriff's Office, don't you? Is that why you're here?"

It's kind of unnerving that he pays so much attention to my comings and goings. *Stalk much, Landry?*

Goose bumps prickle on my arms. "Yeah, I came with Bessie...I mean, Detective Caine. I wasn't supposed to go inside."

"I shouldn't have either." His eyes close again as if he's too exhausted to keep them open. "My mother thought the sheriff made some kind of horrible mistake. That's why she couldn't wait for my dad to come. She had to see Lainey with her own eyes."

I bite the inside of my cheek, brimming with guilt. I totally understand how Mrs. Prince feels. If Mama was in the morgue, I'd need to see her for myself too. I wouldn't believe her dead otherwise. The not knowing has to be the worst. I want to blurt out the truth about finding Lainey so bad that blood trickles into my mouth from clenching the information behind my teeth.

"I have to go," I say, as much to myself as to him.

"Can't you stay a little longer? I don't want to be alone."

"I'm sorry. Detective Caine will worry if she can't find me." I stagger to my feet, legs numb.

"Wait." Landry lunges toward me, and his face blanches. His feet tangle together, and he falls forward. I grab for him at the same time that he grabs for me. My arms wrap around his chest, and he moans. His legs go out on him, and we tumble backward. He twists his body, taking the impact of the fall. I don't think the bristly thicket of jasmine cushions his landing. Vines snap and tangle around our thrashing limbs. With a heaving grunt, Landry rolls us sideways back onto the safety of the lawn. When our wild roll comes to a stop, I realize I've been screaming the whole time. My throat burns like I've turned into one of those folks who make a living eating fire.

Landry's chest heaves. He sucks in air, trying to catch his breath. Which can't be easy since I'm draped across his chest like an itchy wool blanket. The muscles in his abdomen ripple, and even though shock still fills me, I flush.

Our gazes meet, and he frowns. "Are you okay, Mala?"

White sparkles explode in front of my eyes, and I squeeze them tight. "Oh, yeah," I say, breathless. "You?"

The arms encircling my waist flex, then release.

I desperately try to lasso my rampaging emotions. My body tingles like I've stuck my finger in a light socket. Energy pours off me and zaps into Landry. I've never felt so alive or so turned on by a guy in my entire life. *I hate it.*

Chapter 8

Landry

Curiosity Kills

Mala rolls off of my chest, but not fast enough.

My body reacts like it didn't with Clarice and doesn't listen when I tell myself to chill. I'm breathing harder than if I sprinted a half mile. All the blood rushes from my brain and heads down to my little brain, which seems to be running the idiot show. It's gonna get me kicked in the balls for being a perv.

"I totally groped you, didn't I?" I say with a moan.

Mala's huge, dark eyes widen, like a deer startled in the brush. Any minute she's going to run for her life. Not that I blame her. I try to head her off at the pass. "Sorry, I didn't mean to scare you."

"I wasn't scared." Her chin juts out, and her eyes narrow.

I raise an eyebrow at the obvious lie. She looks ten times worse than scared. More like horrified. Her breath comes in heaving gasps that do wonderful things to her breasts squished in the tight purple dress that's wearing her. It's hard, but I force my eyes up, up, and away from temptation, leaving me gazing into the inky pools of her eyes.

God, I hope I'm not drooling.

Mala surprises me when, instead of breaking for the parking lot, she runs trembling fingers through her curls, grimacing. "Seriously, I'm fine. Did I hurt you?"

"Huh? Oh, no." I pull my hand from beneath my shirt. I'd been subconsciously poking at my tender ribs. "It was stupid. I dropped the weight bar on my chest during my morning workout." I lift the edge of my T-shirt to show off my bruise, but let it drop when she averts her eyes. "I'm fine. Nothing's broken."

Her bottom lip pokes out, but she just nods.

God, she's beautiful. I pluck a jasmine blossom from her hair and tuck it behind her ear. My heart stops beating for a few seconds when my fingers brush her earlobe. It's soft, ah, silky. I stiffen my knees and focus on breathing in one slow breath at a time. If I dare touch her one more time, I'll die, and she'll have no idea she killed me.

Or maybe she *does* know how twisted up inside I've gotten.

Mala pulls the flower from behind her ear and folds it in her fist. "I should go. Bessie's waiting. You should go find your mama."

The crash hurts.

Mom…Lainey…her heart on the autopsy table. The memory hits harder than a three-hundred-pound offensive tackle. I forgot why I'm here for a few moments. Being with Mala, holding her in my arms…I've had plenty of fantasies about the day I figured out how to talk in her presence. None of them ended like this.

We walk side by side into the Coroner's Office. The air-conditioned air blows over my heated body, cooling me down. Raised voices have me grabbing Mala's arm. I wrap my arm around her waist and drag her back against my chest. She looks up, mouth opening. I press a finger against her soft lips, shushing her. She goes along with it.

She crouches down, and I lean over her. We peek around the corner. Mom stands near a potted rubber tree in the hallway with Uncle Jay. I never really thought much about his job before, but as parish coroner, he's in charge of autopsying Lainey. God, I couldn't do it. He's known us our whole lives. What a shit job.

Mala leans up until her breath brushes against my ear as she whispers, "Can you hear them?"

I shake my head, shushing her again. She flushes. I like how the blood rushes into her face. My smile drops when Mom grabs the lapels of Uncle Jay's lab coat. She speaks in a low voice, but a slight rise of hysteria infuses her tone. "You promised, James. Is this how you keep your word? Defiling my daughter's memory?"

"I'm doing my job, Theresa." He yanks his coat out of her balled fists and backs away, but she steps forward.

"You swore—"

"I didn't have a choice. It's protocol when there are suspicious circumstances." He glances over his shoulder and waves over Detective Caine, who stands near the operating room doors. "Theresa, I swear I'll take care of Lainey. I'm handling the autopsy myself."

Mom glares at him for a long moment before her shoulders crumple. She covers her face with her hands and nods, backing up. She starts sobbing again. I start forward with a muffled curse, but Mala shoves me back with a scowl. "Let Bessie calm her down."

"She's my responsibility."

Mala shakes her head and pokes a finger into my bruised ribs. A white-hot shaft of pain doubles me over, and she catches me. My face presses into her curls, and I inhale. She smells like flowers. Not sure what kind. She holds me, stronger than she looks, until the pain fades enough for me to straighten up. Course, Mother Dearest didn't raise a fool. And maybe I overexaggerate my weakness a bit to stay in Mala's arms.

Mala pushes me against the wall and wrinkles her nose. "I'm sorry. I wasn't spying on purpose, but I saw your mama elbow you. Maybe you're new to getting walloped on, so take my advice. The best way to avoid a beating is to figure out when one's coming and hide." Her eyes drop to the floor. She bites her lip and turns back around. I stare at the curve of her back, wondering who she has to hide from.

Detective Caine reaches Mom's side and places her hands on her shoulders, but Mom twists away. "Don't touch me! Where's my son?"

Detective Caine raises her hands in the air. "He's waiting for you outside. He's devastated and confused. He needs his mama to pull herself together. You need to be strong for him."

"How dare you! You know nothing about my son's needs." Mom draws her shoulders back and lifts her chin. "You…all of you, will be hearing from my lawyer. My husband never gave consent for an autopsy. It goes against our religious beliefs to desecrate the dead."

"Legally, we didn't need permission from the family. It's time for you to leave." Detective Caine takes a firm step forward.

Mala exhales. "Uh-oh. Hurry, go get her before she gets arrested."

Yeah, Detective Caine's badass. I recognize the set of her shoulders. If Mom attacks the detective the way she did me earlier, she'll get slapped in handcuffs and hauled off to jail in the blink of an eye. Mom figures out the same thing. She spins on her heel and briskly walks in my direction, brushing past me and Mala as if we're invisible, to stride out the door.

I debate whether I should follow, but something Uncle Jay said niggles at me: "suspicious circumstances." What about Lainey's death has everyone in an uproar? They wouldn't be so on edge if she died from an accident.

Mala eyes me with a frown.

"I'm hiding," I whisper.

She gives a tiny smile and a nod.

I smile back and acknowledge my biggest reason for not following. I'm not ready to leave Mala yet. What if this is the last time I feel somewhat normal? What will I do at home but mourn? Mom's crazy behavior scares me. I'm embarrassed, but, at the same time, I understand her. Well, not totally. I lost a sister, but I can't begin to understand how it feels to lose a child. It must be all kinds of devastating. Still doesn't make me want to go home with her.

I'll do anything to keep back the memory of Lainey on the autopsy table.

"You two can come out now," Detective Caine says.

Mala stumbles. "Crap, I swear the woman has eyes in the back of her head. Come on. There's a time to hide and a time to take your knocks."

I follow Mala, sliding around the corner. Guilt over spying on their conversation bothers me a little, but I'll get over it.

Uncle Jay follows Bessie's gaze with a start. "Mala, Landry, I didn't know you were here."

I clear my throat. "Yeah, you seemed a little busy."

His eyes narrow. He glances down at his bloodstained smock and shakes his head. "Never had such a thing happen in all my time as coroner," he says softly. "A parent should never see their child the way your mom saw Lainey."

Detective Caine wraps her arms around Mala's shoulders and tucks her head against her chest. "Landry shouldn't have been forced to see his sister like that either. Her behavior was purely selfish," she snaps.

I'm pissed at the woman's shit-talking. Who does she think she is? Then I see the tears swimming in Mala's eyes. Detective Caine pats her on the back, but she stares at me. The sympathy in her expression overwhelms my defenses. The detective is angry for me. I try to stay strong, but I start trembling again.

Mala's bloodshot eyes meet mine. "I'm sorry," she mouths.

"I'm going to take Mala home," Detective Caine says. "I thought she'd be sensible and stay outside like I asked. Seems I'm just as guilty as Mrs. Prince of exposing the innocent to horrors they're not old enough or equipped to deal with."

Rathbone shakes his head. "Nobody, no matter how old, is equipped to deal with the death of a child. And poor Lainey was still a child. She had her whole future ahead of her. I delivered her, you know. Back when I was in general practice. Mine was the first face Lainey looked on, and I watched her grow into a lovely young woman over the years." He rubs his eyes. His cheeks are wet when he turns to go back into the morgue to continue with the autopsy. "I'll phone you with the results, Bessie."

Mala shoots one last glance over her shoulder as they leave. I force myself not to follow.

When I look back, the hallway is empty. I stand outside the lab doors. My hand shakes when I reach for the handle. I don't have to do this. If I wait, I'll find out what he meant later. Mom or Dad will tell me. Or not. I may legally be an adult, but they still see me as a kid.

I push open the door and step inside. The smell almost drops me to my knees again, but I stiffen them and step forward. I avoid looking at the autopsy table. I don't have to see it. The image is branded into my mind.

"Uncle Jay," I call.

He turns, eyes widening. "What are you doing back in here?"

One of the officials observing the autopsy starts in my direction, but he waves them off. "I'll be but a minute," he promises, and rushes over. He takes my arm and steers me back out the door.

"I'm sorry, I can't leave. Not yet," I say. "Not until you tell me what's going on."

"What are you talking about?"

"I heard you talking to Mom. What did you mean about Lainey dying under suspicious circumstances?"

"Didn't Mala tell you?"

"Tell me what?"

He frowns. "I guess she would keep quiet, given her part in this."

"Will you stop being cryptic and spit it out."

"Look, the only reason I'm telling you this is because you're family. Don't share this information with anyone but your father. He'll know what to do." He glances over his shoulder at the sealed doors to the autopsy room. "Sheriff Keyes and Detective Caine will cover this up. They won't want a witch hunt on their hands. Nobody believes in a bunch of superstitious nonsense in this day and age, but I've seen things on my table that would make your hair fall out."

He pauses, eyes staring though me. I don't know what memory he's reliving. I don't want to know. "You know the LaCroix history? The rumors of witchcraft and devil worshiping."

"Yeah, so what? It's bullshit."

"They say Jasmine LaCroix is a witch. That the LaCroix women inherit their powers from their mothers. From blood sacrifice. That's what they say."

"You're a doctor. You can't believe a bunch of rumors."

"I'm a Christian first. I believe Satan comes in many disguises. Some are sweet and innocent. They tempt you to want to taste their ripe lusciousness. To bathe in their embrace even though you know it's a sin. The LaCroix women are temptresses. Don't ever forget that when dealing with one, Landry. Mala appears as innocent as new-fallen snow, but she comes from a long line of evil."

The memory of holding Mala in my arms returns with his words. I swallow hard. He's creeping me out. I never pegged him for a religious fanatic. "What does all this have do with my sister?"

Uncle Jay blinks. "Everything," he breathes. "Lainey was found on LaCroix property. She'd been dumped in the bayou like garbage. Judging from the ritualistic symbols carved into her abdomen and the cuts on her wrists, Lainey bled to death slowly, in terror and agony." Tears fill his eyes. "In my professional opinion, your sister was sacrificed in some sort of satanic ritual."

Chapter 9

Mala

Stalked

Bessie hustles me out to the car.

I check the parking lot for Landry's truck. It's gone. His mama left him. She shouldn't be driving in her condition. Then again, neither should he. I should've stayed to be sure he's okay. I feel even worse for him now after seeing his mama in action. I sigh, staring out the window. The town fades to be replaced by fields of sugarcane, then woodland. "Hey, Bessie. I thought we were going to the station."

Bessie grips the steering wheel. "I want you to go home and get some rest before you collapse. I'll get your statement tomorrow."

I sigh, leaning my head against the seat. I'm too exhausted to argue. The last thing I want to do is spend hours talking about how I found Lainey. "I'm working with Dixie tomorrow. I'll give you my official statement afterward." I chew on my lip, then blurt out, "So, what's really going on, Bessie? And don't tell me 'nothing.' Not after what just happened. This isn't a normal case, is it?"

"It's turning out to be more than I bargained for," Bessie says, turning on the air conditioner.

Lukewarm air hits me in the face, and I adjust the vents onto my sweaty body. "It's more than just Mrs. Prince?"

"I shouldn't be talking to you about this, but I think it may affect you in the long run." She sighs. "I'm afraid Reverend Prince will stir up trouble once the autopsy results are in. The man has some beliefs that I don't hold with."

"What kind of beliefs?"

"Nothing worth repeating, but we've gone rounds about it in the past."

"So you're not besties?"

"Not even close. He prefers that I don't have dealings with him or his family. And after what just happened with his wife, I don't expect things to get any better." She glances at me. "The sheriff put George nominally in charge of the investigation."

My mouth drops open, and I force it closed. "But he's a rookie."

"Yeah, but he's the face of the investigation. He still comes through me for everything important, but he'll pass along information to the family."

"So, is it the fact that you're black or a woman that the good reverend finds unforgivable?"

Bessie shrugs. "Who the hell knows? I bet both. Mala, you should've seen his wife before today. I met her a few times doing charity work. A more broken, spineless creature I've never seen. Poor thing never spoke above a whisper. I tell you, seeing her charge into the morgue so filled with grief and rage—and dragging her son in with her. It shocked me."

Mrs. Prince shocked me too. Should I tell Bessie how the woman beat on Landry? I've never told anyone about Mama slapping me upside the head. I've made excuses for her my whole life. What if I'm doing the same thing for Mrs. Prince, excusing her behavior due to grief, when maybe the public face of a cowed, submissive woman hides the true, hateful woman inside?

The scent of roses blows out of the air conditioner. I turn the vent toward Bessie, shivering.

"What's Landry like?" I ask.

Bessie cuts a sideways glance in my direction. "Oh, I don't know. I've never had contact with him before today. The whole situation must be pretty traumatic for him." Bessie casts a sideways glance in my direction. "The two of you seem pretty close."

"No, no, I felt sorry for him is all." I wave my hand. "I've never talked to him before today either, that's why I asked."

"Hmm, well. Best you stay away from him. I've kept your part in finding the body from the family. So don't go blurting out the truth. If Landry's inherited his pa's disagreeable streak, it could go bad for you."

I close my eyes and picture the face that resembles his sister's—masculine features instead of Lainey's soft beauty. The same black hair hiding tortured gray eyes, instead of blue, that couldn't tear his gaze away from his sister's body. Landry should've been angry. He should've been cursing God, fate, his mama for bringing him to the morgue, his sister for dying, and me for intruding on his grief, but he didn't. I felt gentleness in Landry…he made me want to protect him. I'm not sure how. Or why? But I don't think Landry would hurt me—even knowing the truth about me finding his sister.

If I hadn't promised Bessie, I would've spewed my guts to him. Maybe it's good she made me swear to keep my mouth shut. Landry's parents sound like they're judgmental and unpredictable people, the kind who give good Christians a bad name by manipulating scripture to justify their evil ways. As their son, he'd be obligated to tell them about me if he knew.

Mama's truck is gone when I arrive home, a relief and a worry at the same time. I can't help but think about her death vision. How much of the events playing out in the Prince household have to do with her? She seems to feel that the girl's death and hers are tied.

* * *

The fire burns high. I stare into the flames, mesmerized by the flickering colors. Orange, green, and yellow all blending together. Sparks dance in the air, swirling in the warm wind. Shadows gyrate at the edge of the light—amorphous shapes without form, but alive with an energy that makes my skin tingle. I sway from side to side, my feet lift, and my arms stretch up to the night sky. With fingers splayed wide, I shift my weight, first to one leg and then the other. The breeze blows across my palms, wetting my skin with dew. I dance.

My movements are slow at first, then pick up speed to the pulsing rhythm. Bullfrogs croak, crickets scratch their legs in a whistling tune. An owl hoots, signaling death. And I spin, circling the oak tree, my fingers caressing the knobby bark. The wind blows hair away from my face, and my heart pounds in tune with the natural world around me.

I whirl faster and faster until I can't breathe, but I don't care.

From the corner of my eye, I see a flicker of blue. Bare white legs dance. The girl's blue dress swirls around her ankles and floats into the air when she kicks her feet. Black, thick, straight hair blends with the darkness that shrouds the girl's features—all but her blue eyes, which reflect the light of the fire. She stretches out a hand and beckons with her long fingers. Laughing.

I laugh with her. Her joy is so infectious that she draws me to her. I skip toward the fire, heedless of the heat or the flames that set my nightgown ablaze. Her hand beckons again, and I reach for it. Then notice I'm burning.

I jerk upright, slapping at my nightgown. Panic fills me, and I breathe in tainted air that tastes of smoke. The smell saturates my hair. Sweat plasters my nightgown to my skin. I thrash beneath the blanket wrapped around my legs, trapping me.

The soldier sitting on the floor at the foot of my bed has a stripped machine gun between his outstretched legs. He keeps his helmeted head down, and his fingers swiftly clean and re-assemble the rifle.

I pull the blanket up to my neck. "I thought you blew yourself up."

He lifts the assembled rifle and sets the scope to his eye. "It's ready," he says. "Are you sure you know what you're doing?"

I shrug. "Can't be too hard."

"Got to know what you're aiming for." His head turns. The skin has burnt from his face, leaving a red ruin of muscle and bone. His lipless mouth stretches in a permanent smile. "If you miss, you're dead." He points the barrel right between my eyes. "Only got one shot. Aim to kill, and shoot." He pulls the trigger.

I wake with a scream and scramble from the bed. My foot slips in something slick, and I fall, which gives me a closer view of a pale, brown oil stain smeared on the hardwood floor. I touch it lightly, rubbing my fingers together.

Mama bursts into the room, wide-eyed with fear, with her nightgown flapping around her knees. When she sees me kneeling on the floor unhurt, her eyes narrow. "Girl, what're you about? Screamin' like that? You 'bout gave me a heart attack."

"I saw…" The finger I point trembles. The oil stain on the wood and the one on my finger have vanished.

Mama presses her hand to her heart and stares inquisitively at the floor. "Somethin' startle you? A spider?"

Laughter bursts out, and it has a slightly hysterical pitch to it. I hug my arms around my stomach, giggling so hard that it hurts. Tears roll down my aching cheeks. I try to rein it in, but I can't. Raw, wild emotion rips out of me. Poor Mama stares at me in confusion, but I can't control my reaction. She sounds so disgusted at the thought of me screaming over a spider…good heavens, a spider is the least of my worries.

Mama's lips purse. "I take it that's a no?"

"No," I wail then snort.

"So why'd you scream?"

"Oh, Mama, does it matter?" I stand up, still clutching my stomach as the muscles cramp. "I had a nightmare."

"Humph, been havin' more than your share of bad dreams since you found that girl's body. Don't think I haven't felt you tossin' and turnin' at night."

My mood shifts to anger lightning quick. Why does she have to ruin my morning by bringing up Lainey? I'm trying hard to forget. Her being nosy and acting like she cares only gives me a headache. "It's only been four days since I found Lainey. Not nearly long enough to get over the memory, especially with everyone weeping and wailing about the poor girl killing herself. Folks who probably never spoke to her while she lived are going on about how she was their best friend. It's total bull. If Lainey had all these friends that cared so much about her, why did she commit suicide?"

With each word I speak, my resentment grows. A bunch of hypocrites infest our town, and I despise them. "Do you think if I died they'd act like that? Or do you think it's because she's the daughter of the reverend and sister to their star quarterback?"

"Mala, it ain't like you to be so uncharitable."

"I know." I wipe perspiration from my face then stare at how my hand trembles. "I've just been so out of sorts—getting angry over little things." I sit on the edge of my bed and pull the blanket over my lap. Part of me wants to lie back down and go to sleep. But I'm afraid I'll dream again. "I just want this week to be over."

"I think what's goin' on with you is stronger than just feelin' sad. I know you don't believe in the Sight, but—"

"Leave it, Mama," I snap, shoving the blanket back. "I don't want to hear any more mumbo jumbo about spirits."

Mama crouches down in front of me and places her hands on the sides of my face. I try to pull back, but her hands grip my head. "Tell me about your dreams." She removes her hands and places them on my knees. "Remember any of the details?"

"No, and I'm glad! Once I wake up, the nightmares get hazy,

and the details fade. All I know is that I'm afraid. That I'm being warned something bad is coming, and I've got to be ready."

"Ready for what?"

"I don't know or care." I shiver. "I think all your death talk messed with my head."

"You're treadin' a slippery slope, Mala Jean. Haunts won't go away simply by pretendin' they don't exist, but the more credence you give to them, the more they take advantage and worm their way into your thoughts. Soon you can't get rid of them."

"My brain's not infected by parasitic ghosts. They're dreams. Bad dreams. But it's normal to have nightmares. That's human nature, not haunts." Tension tightens my shoulders. Mama's voice grates on my nerves. I'm sick of talking about death, of spirits or her stupid vision, of how helpless we are. I glance at the clock and gasp. "Shoot, I overslept. I've got to get ready for work."

Mama stretches her arms around my waist and holds on. "Munchies or BPSO?"

"Munchies."

"Then bring me home a Reuben dog and a pint of butter pecan."

"Hope you don't plan to eat that combo together." I hug her tight. "I'm sorry if I've been grouchy. *Mo laimm twa.*"

"I know," she whispers. "I love you too."

* * *

The outside matches my insides. Thick gray clouds cover the sun, and a cold rain bounces off my canary yellow rubber raincoat. The walk to the bus stop takes fifteen minutes. Even layered up, I'll get wet since my umbrella blows into a tree the minute I step off the porch. I run for the woods, pushing aside wet branches until the thick leaves overhead shelter me from the downpour.

If I hadn't been so annoyed with Mama, I would've put aside my pride and begged for a ride to the crossroads where the transit bus would pick me up. The steady drum of pelting rain muffles my footsteps. I miss the hush that usually comforts me. Today I'm on edge, nervous. Like some predatory critter hides in the bushes watching me, but I can't see it. The hairs rise on the back of my neck, and a nervous energy has me practically running despite the ankle-deep mud that tries to suck off my boots.

Halfway to the bus stop, the rain slows to a low drizzle. I pause.

Footsteps. Their pace matches mine. First one foot then another, two, not four paws. My heart stumbles in my chest, then races. I hold my breath, straining to hear what direction the steps come from, but the rain distorts sound. It comes from in front, the side. I spin to squint behind me. The empty path stretches back toward home. I'm tempted to go back. The woods look like an oversaturated watercolor painting. Colors blend together, faded and hazy. Bushes and trees in the distance blur to melt into a glob of varying shades of green and brown. I can't tell if what I sense is real or the remnants of my earlier nightmare bleeding over into reality.

I can't pretend everything is okay when I know it's not.

"Who's there?" I yell.

The crack of a snapping twig is followed by a muffled curse. I let out a high-pitched scream and spin in the direction of the noise. A flash of red in the distance darts behind a bush.

I grab a baseball bat–size branch from the ground. "This isn't funny. Come out!"

The toot of a horn signals the bus's arrival, and I sprint toward the road. I shove branches aside, ignoring the scratches to my face and hands. Running steps follow me, but I don't look back. I dig in deep and pull on my reserve of energy. I burst from the trees, slip on the embankment, and slide down the muddy hill on my butt. At the bottom, I roll to my knees and look over my shoulder. The same flash of red moves at the edge of the undergrowth, but the person doesn't show his, or her, face.

"Coward!" I throw the stick. It crashes into the trees where the silhouette of a figure had been standing, and the thrashing of the bushes makes me think I hit someone.

The bus driver honks the horn again. "Mala, I'm on a schedule. Playtime's over. Get on the bus!"

"I'm coming, Mr. Johns." I pick up my supersize black leather purse and wipe mud and crushed leaves from my jeans as I climb up the stairs onto the transit bus. My boots squeak all the way down the aisle. The seats are full, which isn't surprising. This is the only bus that runs through the swamp to town. If I needed any other affirmation from the heavens that luck abandoned me today, it appears in the identical forms of the fourteen-going-on-four Acker twins, Carl and Daryl, who keep up a running commentary of increasingly stupid insults about my appearance as I clump down the aisle.

"Mala went dirt surfing." Carl snorts.

"She doesn't look any different than normal," Daryl says. "Maybe cleaner."

The twins laugh.

"Best keep your opinions to yourselves or lumps are gonna sprout on other pieces of your anatomies, you little brats," I threaten, slapping the back of their knobby blond heads as I walk past their seats. They may not be afraid of my wrath, but if they keep messing with me, their big sister will make their lives miserable. It shames me to know the twins and I are blood relatives, thanks to sharing a great-great-something-grandfather who lusted after his slave. Not that the boys or their racist father will ever admit kinship. The only one in their family who gets a kick out of being my cousin is their sister, Dena, who currently frowns over her shoulder at me from the front of the bus.

I wave her off. I hold onto the top of the empty backseat when the bus lurches into motion, then take off my rain jacket, stuff it and my purse under the seat, and sit down. My wet jeans stick to the vinyl as I turn to stare out the back window. Headlights shine from the corner we just left, coming from the road leading to my house. I press my nose to the glass trying to see who's driving the black Ford that pulls in behind the bus, but the truck stays far enough back that I can't make out a face.

A tap on my shoulder startles a yelp out of me. I spin in my seat. "What?"

Dena settles into the seat beside me and raises her hands. "Sorry. Gosh, what's got you so jumpy?"

"Sorry, cuz." Wet hair sticks to my cheeks, and I push it out of my eyes with trembling fingers. "Somebody followed me through the woods. Scared the shit out of me."

"What?" she shrieks. "Did you see who?"

Her panic reignites mine. "No, but I think it's whoever's in the truck behind us."

Dena stares out the back window, and her freckled nose scrunches up. "I don't see anybody."

I look back. The truck is gone.

Chapter 10

Mala

Munchies Memorial

It takes an hour to wind through the woods to pick up the rest of us country folk. Those of us living out in the sticks have never fit in with the townies or with each other. By the time we park at the bus stop in front of town square, my head pounds and my nose feels stuffy. I rise slowly, dizzy. My temples throb when I lean forward to pull my stuff out from beneath the seat. It's going to be a long day.

Dena leans against the metal frame of the bus stop with her arms folded and her toe tapping while I take my time getting off the bus. Our gazes meet through the window, and she rolls her eyes, a silent signal for me to get my ass in gear before we're late for our shift at Munchies.

Daryl and Carl shove past me. One of them yells, "Move it, fat ass!"

I trip on the last step. "One day, I'm killing those brats."

Dena grabs my arm, steadying me. "Warn me ahead of time so I can set up alibis." She yells at her brothers' retreating backs, "Evil twins, meet me at Munchies in an hour for lunch."

Daryl raises a hand but doesn't turn around. They head toward Playtown, the place where kids their age hang out. The park has a swimming pool, skating rink, batting cages, and a mini golf course.

Dena and I walk down the narrow sidewalk in silence, which must be torture for my chatterbox cousin. The sun beats down onto my head, soaking up heat, until my hair burns to the touch. I swat at the mosquito on my neck and glare at the roses around the gazebo in the Vietnam Memorial garden housed in Paradise Park across the street.

"I hate roses," I mutter. *Roses smell like death.*

Dena shrugs. "That's because you don't have a romantic bone in your body."

"I don't like you either, Dee."

Cold air feels like a slap upside the head upon entering Munchies Diner & Ice Cream Parlor, and my headache eases. The large, saloon-style building, with its gaudy pink, balloon-decaled front window, is my home away from home. I've worked here every summer since starting high school, but this is the first time it's ever been full of customers on a Wednesday morning.

"Saints, is it somebody's birthday?" I say, checking out the packed booths.

Dena shrugs. "Not sure. Look, there's Maggie and Tommy."

Our friends sit cuddled up close in a corner booth. They look so happy to be with each other that I avoid their table and head toward the employee bathroom. I don't feel social, and I don't want to ruin their obvious good mood.

Maggie catches me sneaking past, and her face lights up. She slides out of the booth and charges down the aisle, like the hounds of Hades chase after her. But, instead of looking terrified, her face glows. She grabs Dena in a bear hug, lifts her in the air, and spins her around. She then turns and does the same to me.

"Put me down before you suffocate me," I say, trying to catch my breath.

Maggie takes after Bessie in looks and size—big-boned, flawless cocoa skin, stunningly beautiful. She gives me a hard kiss on the cheek, laughing when I rub it off, and releases me.

"How are you feeling today?"

"Not too good. I'm sick."

Maggie pulls out a tissue and hands it over. "You got a little drainage going," she says, motioning to my nose.

"Thanks, Ma."

"Sure. What happened to your clothes?"

I twist around to stare at my muddy butt. A snicker comes from beside me, and I glance down at a table full of prissy-looking sorority girls. One of them gives my pants a pointed stare and waves her hand beneath her nose with a snooty expression. The girls cover their mouths and laugh. One of the perks of having a junior college in our town means that, even if these girls were too dumb to get into a university, they have someplace to hang out while they search for a suitable husband. Idiots.

Assaulting customers isn't allowed, Mala. With the reminder ringing through my head, I give the girl a sunny grin, turn my offensive ass directly toward her seat, and continue with my rudely interrupted conversation. "Had a bit of an accident walking to the bus," I tell Maggie. "Don't worry. I have an extra pair of jeans in my locker."

Dena grabs Maggie's arm and whispers, "She has a stalker. He followed her to the bus stop."

Maggie's dark eyes widen. "Seriously? Should I call my mom?"

I glare at Dena. I should've warned her to keep her mouth shut. The last thing I need is for Maggie to wind Bessie up. She's already stressing about my part in the Prince case. She'll station an armed deputy at my house if she thinks I'm in danger. With my luck, it'll be George. I've avoided him all week. *The jerk didn't even call to apologize.*

I cast a sideways glance at my friends. "I need to change. Can you handle all these people alone, Dee?"

"Go on. Sam and Tabitha haven't gone off shift, and you stink."

I roll my eyes. "Gee, thanks."

I bypass the counter and go down the hall to the employee break room. A barrage of varying shades of pink blind me for a minute. I focus on the white lockers for Munchies employees gracing the wall beside the sink, ignoring the garish walls painted in clashing carmine and amaranth.

Maggie stays right on my heels as she follows me across the room. "Okay, what's up?" she demands, hands on her hips. "And don't say 'nothing.'"

I pull a clean pair of jeans from my locker and head into the small bathroom. Maggie doesn't completely violate my privacy by following me inside, but she stands in the doorway with one hand on the knob, in case we're interrupted, while I begin to change. Silence stretches between us for a long, tension-filled moment. Then Maggie, being Maggie, charges ahead. She's not even subtle.

"George and Mama were talking on the porch after work last night. The kitchen window was open, and I overheard them discussing the case they're working on."

"Oh?" I pull off my tennis shoes. "What did they say?"

"They were talking about you." Maggie stares expectantly. When I remain silent, she continues, "George said he couldn't stop thinking about you."

"About me? Georgie told your mom he was thinking about me?" My heart speeds up. "What else did he say? Did he sound guilty? Ashamed? Don't keep me hanging."

"He said he's worried about Landry Prince going after you."

"Ah." I shrug. *Total letdown.*

"Feels like you're hiding something," Maggie accuses, "a secret that Mama and George are in on. Why won't you talk to me?" Her voice rises. "What's going on between you and Landry Prince?"

While I hadn't really been aware of the girls' voices coming from behind Maggie while we were talking, the hush following my best friend's shout is noticeable.

"Shush," I hiss. "This is why nobody tells you anything. 'Cause you can't keep quiet."

Hurt fills her dark eyes. "So there is something going on? I knew it."

I slip on my shoes, preparing to do battle with whoever ignored the Employee Only sign on the break room, and brush past her. Three girls stand in front of the break room door, blocking our exit back to the safety of the packed dining area. When they see us come out of the bathroom, they give us, or rather me, hard stares.

"Hey, Malaise." It's the rude bitch who waved her hand in front of her nose. Tall and willowy, she looks like a model as she glides toward me. "Can I speak with you?"

I glance at Maggie, who shrugs. "Do I know you?"

"No, we've never been introduced. I'm Clarice Delahoussaye." She says her name like I should immediately fall down and kiss her feet. Not happening in this lifetime.

"Obviously, you know my name already," I say.

"Everyone knows you."

"Yeah, sure." If she thinks that will make me more receptive to her, she's mistaken. "Look, this break room is for employees only. If you want to talk, we can do it after I finish my shift."

Clarice raises an eyebrow and gives Maggie a knowing look. She smiles. "I didn't mean to run you off. I just want to chat for a moment."

"I've never run from anyone in my life." *Except for the stalker in the woods this morning.* "I have work." I calmly pull on my fuchsia apron and ball cap, with "Munchies" emblazoned across them in white. I'm afraid of turning my back on her to walk to the door. The glitter in Clarice's brown eyes reminds me of a rabid raccoon. Her girlfriends pick up on the psycho vibe. Their eyes shift between us, and they clump tighter around us.

Maggie tugs on my arm. "Seriously, we've got to go. Dena's waiting."

Clarice graces me with a hard smile, like Maggie hasn't just spoken. "I overheard you gossiping about my boyfriend."

Boyfriend? I share a confused glance with Maggie, who jerks on my arm again. I shift my stance, knowing I should leave, but I'm too curious. Which boy does she mean, Georgie or Landry? Not that it matters who she's dating. Neither of them have anything to do with me. I shove my wet clothing inside my locker and slam it closed.

"Overheard, huh? Okay. It's pretty obvious you and your friends followed me in here on purpose. So did you come to fight or what?" I crack my knuckles. "Am I kicking just your ass or all three?"

Maggie sighs. "I'll take the two little ones, but you're explaining this to Mom when she comes to arrest us. She said if we get in any fights after we turn eighteen that she's not bailing us out of jail."

"God, you two are so ghetto. I didn't come to fight," Clarice says quickly.

"Then stop with the insults 'cause every word out of your mouth so far only makes me want to punch you in the face."

Maggie nods. "Yep."

Clarice's nostrils flare.

I'm kind of worried she hasn't backed down. Most girls stopped messing with me after I got fed up with the bullies in junior high and made a few examples out of them. Maggie and I've avoided getting into full-on brawls for years with bluffing and smack talking.

Clarice flicks a strand of hair over her shoulder, saying "I came to have a civil conversation—"

"Fine, say what you need to say," I interrupt. Time for her to get to the point. Dena's going to kill me if this takes much longer.

"I want you to back off. Landry's understandably upset about his sister's passing. He's vulnerable. The last thing he needs right now is a bunch of ridiculous rumors floating around town about him being in some imaginary relationship with the witch's daughter."

My face heats with each word. "Relationship? With Landry. Look, I've never—"

"Just stay away from him."

Did he tell her about our meeting at the Coroner's Office? Is that why she's so angry?

"Are you listening to me, Malaise?"

I blink at her, finally understanding. She's totally jealous. Imaginary relationship my big toe.

"Yeah," I drawl. "Loud and clear."

A smile that isn't reflected in her eyes twists her lips. "Landry's grieving. Don't confuse his vulnerability for weakness or you'll regret it. People do all kinds of *crazy* things when they're grief stricken. And they're forgiven. I just don't want *you* to get hurt. Maybe you should take off today. We're holding a memorial service here this afternoon so Lainey's friends can say good-bye. A lot of people will be emotional." She reaches out and pats the top of my head, like I'm her obedient poodle.

I jerk my head away and ram my shoulder into hers as I shove past. She catches her balance on her friend's arm. My fingers twitch with the desire to yank out a huge clump of the hair she flippantly tosses over her shoulder.

Her laughter-choked words follow me out of the locker room. "Thanks for the chat, Malaise. I'm glad there won't be any misunderstandings between us in the future."

Misunderstandings? Oh, no, her threat was crystal clear, and I suspect that this is only the beginning.

* * *

Clarice and her friends cover the tables in the private room in the back with black cloths. Lainey's blown-up portrait sits propped up on the middle table surrounded by flowers, stuffed animals, and handmade cards. *Lainey, we love and miss you.*

For most of my shift, I avoid their part of the restaurant, but Dena's on break having lunch with her brothers. I have no choice. I hold the stacked tray of food and drinks over my head and wind through the tables of mourners. From the corner of my eye, I see one of them point at me. Whispers follow.

When I walk past Lainey's picture, her cobalt blue eyes follow me. She looks pissed, like she's mad at being the object of such intense scrutiny and gossip. Or maybe I'm projecting my own emotions onto her. My chest tightens. The air around me chills, icy cold, and each breath has to be sucked into my lungs.

"Mala," a voice yells.

Startled, I glance up to see Dena waving furiously from the booth she shares with the knobby-headed twins. She points at something behind me. I spin and almost face-plant into a wide chest. I stagger backward with a startled yelp. The tray of food I'm clutching falls to the ground with a loud clatter that draws everyone's attention. I squat and grab the cup rolling toward a boot-clad foot.

"Sorry," I whisper, then grit my teeth.

"Watch where you're walking."

"Me watch…" I sputter.

"Pretending like you don't see me again?" the guy asks, stepping on the plastic tray. It cracks in half. The cold that settled around my body earlier vanishes to be replaced with heat. This is the last straw. First Clarice, now this idiot's trying to start a fight. The image of me stabbing a fork into this guy's thigh flashes through my mind, but I stop myself from acting on the crazy impulse and rise to my feet.

"Look, jerk, you bumped into me first. Apologize!" I step forward and glare up into a face that is a masculine copy of the portrait of Lainey Prince. Black, tangled hair hangs over bloodshot gray eyes filled with so much anger that I wince.

"I'm not apologizing to you." Landry doesn't back up. If anything, his body hunches toward me. Way too close. I can't even breathe he's so in my space, but it's my own fault since I stepped up to him. I stumble back into an empty table and let out a trickle of air. His eyes go flatter, dull, as he says, "Tell me what happened to my sister."

"To y-your sister?" My mind scrambles. Why is he asking me about Lainey? She's dead. We saw her body. What's changed between now and the day in the garden other than his shitty attitude. Unless…My eyes widen. Did he hear I found his sister's body?

My mouth opens to ask, then closes. What if I'm wrong and he doesn't know? Or doesn't know all the gory details? I promised to keep my mouth shut. I can't break my word to Bessie and George, but Landry has me cornered. I don't know what to say…truth or lie. I suck at lying.

So I go with the truth. "What do you mean?"

"Stop pretending like you don't know what I'm talking about. Lainey was found on your land. She'd been murdered." Landry pushes forward. I edge around the table, backing up until my back presses against the wall. I can't escape. "But you knew all that, didn't you? That's why you were really at the autopsy. Tell me what happened to her."

"Murdered?" I almost choke on the word. "I don't understand."

"Why do you keep lying to me? Is it because you feel guilty? Did you cut her up and throw her into the swamp like trash?"

"No! No, why would I?" I glare at the crowd gathered around us. "Get him off me!"

"They're not gonna help you."

He's right. They're all his and Lainey's friends. I'm doomed. How did I get myself into this mess? Oh, right. Found a body, pulled her out of the swamp. I should've minded my own damn business. This so isn't fair.

"Damn it, Landry! Yes, I pulled her out of the water and called the police. I could've left her there, but I didn't. I did the right thing." Tears burn my eyes; I'm so freaking pissed. The jerk accused me of murdering his sister in front of a roomful of people, and these idiots believe his lies. I can tell by the disgust stamped on their faces. I've got to get him to listen to reason before he ruins my life.

"Nobody told me that she'd been killed. I thought she committed suicide." I push at his chest, trying to shove him back. It's like pushing a boulder.

"I can't believe I felt grateful to you for comforting me." He squeezes his eyes shut, breathing hard. "You were so sweet. God,

I'm such an *idiot*. I totally fell into your trap. You should've told me the truth."

"Landry, stop it." He's lost. He hasn't heard a word I've said. It's like I'm trying to tend to a tomcat with a thorn in its paw. No matter how I try to help, he claws at me. "Please. Get away. I don't want to call the cops."

His eyes pop open. "What? Not gonna use black magic on me? Or is it just your mom who's a witch?"

My mouth drops open. This is the second time today someone's come right out with the whole your-mama's-a-witch bullshit to my face. He quivers with anger, and his eyes, well, they don't look completely sane.

I grab the arm planted by my head and try to move it, but he resists. "Blaming me for your sister's death won't get you any closer to finding the truth."

His icy gray eyes drill into mine. They make me feel like I'm skinny dipping in my pond in the middle of winter. Chills ripple across my skin, and when I exhale the breath I've been holding, mist forms between our bodies. Landry stares in shock at the dissipating cloud. From the corner of my eye, I see a shimmer of cobalt blue, and a frigid touch crosses the hand holding Landry's arm. We both look down.

"Do you see that?" Landry whispers.

I move my hand, and he lowers his arm down between us. Condensation moistens the black hairs on his wrist in the image of a handprint.

"Lainey," I breathe, partly in denial, but the other part senses her presence. If asked, I can't explain how I know it's her spirit. I just do.

Landry knows her too. Horror fills his eyes.

He stumbles back. "No, no."

"Landry, wait," I yell. I don't want him to leave me alone with Lainey. She scares me spitless. Her rage settles on my skin like a cloud, dripping with venomous hate so cold I don't think I'll ever warm up. I can't even chalk this experience up to delusions. Not if Landry saw the handprint too.

Unless we've both gone round the bend.

"No!" He spins on his heel and pushes his way through the people who've surrounded us. They stare at him in surprise. I don't think they saw or felt what we felt. I hope they have no idea what just happened.

My stomach twists, and I fight down the vomit that creeps up my throat. Jelly-legged, I shove through the crowd and enter the bathroom. I stare at the person crossing the room in the mirror. She looks like my doppelganger, a creature who resembles me enough that strangers will accidentally call her by my name. I tear my gaze away, unable to stand seeing the fear twisting my face into a frozen mask. I cup my hands beneath the faucet and splash warm water across my icy cheeks, then look up.

Lainey stares back at me. She presses her hands flat against the mirror. Blood runs down her wrists and drips into the sink.

Chapter 11

Landry

Haunted

My wrist burns.

Not an I-spilled-hot-soup burn, but the kind you get after taking a dare to see how long you can hold a piece of ice against your bare skin. The ache goes all the way to the bone. The red handprint glows. I wrap my hand around my wrist, pressing it against my chest, hoping nobody will see it.

I've got to get out of here.

I stumble across the room. The door seems to get farther and farther away. That, or it's shrinking, like in a trippy *Alice in Wonderland* way. Floating circles swim across my field of vision. My lungs tighten. With the effort of each step, my breath becomes harder to draw in. I recognize the signs.

"Landry, wait!" Mala's voice vibrates with fear.

I don't stop. Not even when someone steps in my path. I barrel right over them and ignore their cry. I've got to get out of here. Away from Mala. Away from the ghost of my sister who's haunting her…or me? Lainey's voice…I can't escape it. She whispers, her cold breath against my ear, "*Go back.*"

I spin from her voice. "No!" It echoes in my head. The itch in my brain intensifies. Worse than after I fell into a patch of poison ivy. At least then I could scratch. I can't dig this feeling out of my head. I thrust my fingers into my hair, grabbing a handful and pulling hard. The pain clears my head.

I stumble against the door leading out of Munchies. A quick glance over my shoulder shows the wide eyes of all the customers focused on me. Then, almost as one, they turn to Mala, tracking her as she runs toward the back of the restaurant.

My legs barely keep me upright. I press a hand against the brick wall, using it for support. The sun blinds me. Breathing in the muggy air feels like I'm inhaling water vapor.

A hand touches my arm, and I jerk free. "Landry? Stop."

Clarice.

I suck in a wheezing breath, and her eyes widen. "Oh crap, you're having an asthma attack. Do you have your medicine?"

I shake my head. Squiggly, multicolored spots dance in front of her face.

"Is it in your truck?"

I can't remember. I haven't had an asthma attack in years.

"Maybe in the glove box," I manage to say. She stuffs her hand into my jeans pocket and pulls out my keys. She doesn't even try to cop a feel, which shows how worried she is. I lean against the wall, then slump into a crouch. I close my eyes and concentrate on each breath.

I can't calm down.

It burns.

I'm not aware of Clarice's return until she grabs my chin to open my mouth and thrusts the inhaler against my lips. I breathe in the shot, then grab the inhaler with a shaking hand and take two more hits. Each time, I'm able to draw in a little more air. Fingers brush sweaty hair off of my forehead, and I duck my head.

"Ungrateful ass," Clarice snaps, dropping her hand.

I stare at her splotchy face and feel like shit. I scared her.

"I'm okay."

"You don't look it. Come on. I'm taking you to your parents' house in case you have another relapse."

"I'll be fine."

"No way. Your mom would kill me if something bad happened to you. You'll stay there until you're able to drive home."

I push up off the ground. It takes two tries before I can stand without wobbling. Sweat soaks my shirt. I'm shaky, and my mouth feels like sandpaper. *I need a drink.*

Clarice takes my arm and wraps it around her shoulders. I want to pull away, but I'm too unstable. It's worth having her hands on me if it means I don't do a face-plant on the cement. For the first time, I regret the oversize tires on my truck. My legs tremble. I grab onto the bar to pull myself up. Clarice takes advantage of my instability by placing her hands on my ass and shoving me up onto the seat. When I look back at her, she wears a smug smile. I frown down at her, but she gives me a quick wink and slams the door in my face.

Damn. I'm not up for her flirting today.

I lean my head against the passenger seat and close my eyes.

She gets my not-so-subtle hint that I'm not in the mood to chat about what's wrong when I ignore her hesitant attempts at conversation. Takes her a while though. My thoughts jumble together. I try to tell myself I'm confused about what happened in Munchies. That Lainey's ghost didn't come to me. Didn't touch me. But the burning sensation on my wrist is an unwelcome reminder that I can't lie to myself. Not anymore. I keep my arm hidden against my side.

When Clarice parks in front of the house and turns off the ignition, her head dips. "So? What happened in there, Landry?"

I hold in my harsh laugh. It rings through my head, bordering on insanity. If I let it out, I'll frighten her. She cares about me. I wish she didn't, but I'm not a complete ass. I won't insult her by ignoring her feelings for me. If I could tell her what I saw…it would be so much easier to have someone to confide in. Someone who understands what I'm going through, but nobody will believe me if I say I'm being haunted by my dead sister. If I tell Clarice, she'll think I'm nuts. She'll tell my parents.

I haven't lost my mind. Yet. 'Cause seeing ghosts isn't crazy, but seeing ghosts will drive me crazy.

Stop thinking. I clear my throat and twist in my seat. I focus on her rich brown eyes, trying to keep this panic from showing in mine. "What do you mean?"

"Don't play stupid. What did Malaise do to make you freak out? Did she fix a curse on you?"

"A curse?" I run fingers through my damp hair, see the handprint on my wrist, and drop it. I glance at Clarice. She's staring at my arm with a frown. Did she see it? Her mouth opens, but I beat her to the punch. My words come out hard, mean, as I try to distract her. "Are you an idiot? Did you really ask if I've been cursed? Tell me you don't believe in that hoodoo shit."

Her face crumples. "Don't call me names. It's a legit question. God, Landry. Malaise LaCroix made you scream like a scared little girl and run out of the room. I'd laugh if I didn't see you afterward. You couldn't breathe…"

"I had an asthma attack."

"Not for years. She fixed a curse on you."

"That's ridiculous."

"No, you're being stupid for denying it. Everyone who saw what happened knows she cursed you. Maybe they'll be too embarrassed to admit it out loud, but they'll be thinking it. Just like I am."

I know. God, I know exactly how it looked. That's why I'm freaked.

I open the door, not wanting to have this conversation. It's ridiculous for me to even think this way. I don't want to lie. But I can't say the ghost of my sister burned her handprint on my arm. I'd sound nuts. "Thanks for driving."

Clarice grabs my arm. "Stay away from her, Landry. Please, for me."

I pluck her hand off my arm and jump out of the truck. Clarice follows. The whole time she stares at me. I won't meet her gaze. Finally, she gives up and walks slowly across the street. I watch her until she enters her house. It's the least I can do after her saving my ass with my inhaler. Plus I'm avoiding going into the house. I'm scared Lainey will be waiting. I don't know what she wants. Maybe she needs something from me or from Mala to put her spirit to rest.

When I finally work up the courage to go inside, I'm surprised. The house is quiet. Peaceful. I pause in the entryway and inhale. The thick aroma of onions, garlic, and spices mingling with rich beef comes from the kitchen. Mom cooked beef stew. It has a distinct odor. Lainey loved Mom's stew. It was her favorite dish. I follow my nose into the empty kitchen, then check the simmering pot. My mouth waters, and I give in to temptation. Heaven.

A figure passes the window as I'm rinsing out the bowl. Mom, wearing a straw hat, pushes a wheelbarrow with an unopened bag of fertilizer toward her rose garden. Her cheeks glow from the heat. Her serene expression lightens my heart and puts a tiny smile on my lips. I didn't realize how worried I've been about her. The way Dad talked, well, I'm glad she's okay. For right now, she seems normal.

I've put off what I need to do long enough.

The stairs creak. Sasha runs up with me, tangling around my feet. I scoop her up so I don't trip and rub her head. The poor cat must be lonely. She slept with Lainey every night. Mom won't let her in the master bedroom. And I'm not living here anymore.

I pause in front of my sister's bedroom and prepare myself for the emotions that will sweep over me once I open the door. The room has become oppressive. Each item contains a memory. An imprint of Lainey. It's intense. I haven't been able to go back inside since the day George told me she died.

Hell, I've avoided coming back home even though Dad begged me to visit Mom. I couldn't do it. My roommate went home for summer break, and I have our place to myself. So I hid out in my tiny-ass apartment for the last four days, drinking and playing video games. Alone. Maybe I should bring Sasha to my apartment. At least we'll have each other.

My hand shakes as I open the door. Sasha lets out a yowl and twists, clawing at my arm. I drop her with a muttered curse. She's a black, furry blur as she darts beneath the bed. Fickle cat. The room hasn't changed. The bed's still made. Her clothes hang in the closet. George searched the room when he was here last. Now I know why. He was looking for clues to her murder. Now it's my turn.

I search beneath her bed and inside her dresser drawers. The walk-in closet holds a trove of personal information. Lainey kept a diary ever since she learned how to write. The old ones are still stored in a trunk in her closet, but the newest diary is missing. A whole documented year of her life has disappeared. It has to be here. Where else would it be?

In one of her tennis shoes, I find a key with a tag: #101. It's too big to be for a locker…maybe it's an apartment or hotel room key. It must be important if she hid it in her shoe, right? I stuff it in my pocket and keep searching. In the farthest corner of her closet, beneath a pile of clothes, I find a bottle of whisky.

Oh yeah! I take a shot directly from the bottle—a silent toast. *To Lainey. Thanks for caring enough to beat my ass with a shoe after catching me drinking in high school. And for not telling Mom and Dad. Love ya, sis.*

After a few more shots, I'm ready to tackle the big job. The bookshelf's one of those floor-to-ceiling, custom-built jobs. My sister liked to brag about reading a book a day. A couple hundred books line the shelves. I start pulling them to see if one may be the diary in disguise.

Lainey liked to do that. Hide her diary in the dust jacket of another book. She was tricky, but I still knew all of her secrets. Mainly because when I was a kid, I didn't care that her diary was off limits. To counter that, she started writing in French. She knew I was too lazy to learn another language.

"Landry?" Mom stands in the doorway. Her eyes widen as she looks around the room. "What are you doing?"

I follow her gaze. I've trashed the place. Crap!

"Mom, I'm sorry. It looks bad, but I swear I'll clean up after I'm done."

"Do you know how long it took me to clean up your sister's mess? I wanted this room to be perfect." Her blue eyes bore into mine. They're filled with confusion. Her hands shake. "What are you doing in here?"

Her words filter in. It took a while. I guess I drank more of the whisky than I thought. My tongue feels thick in my mouth. "Lainey's diary. It's missing. Did you find it when you cleaned the room?" I drop the romance novel I'm holding onto the pile on the floor.

Mom lets out a tiny wail when it hits, and the pile slides to the floor. She staggers forward to collapse onto the bed. Her dirt-encrusted hands rub her face, leaving mud streaks on her perspiration-damp forehead. "Why are you doing this to me?" she mumbles.

I go to her side and sink down beside her. "It's important, I think. Finding it."

Her hand rises to cup my cheek. "Son, this is no longer your home. You can't barge in here doing as you please."

"I *said* I'll clean up. This is important."

"Your sister doesn't want you in here messing things up and neither do I. Get out of my house, Landry. And don't come back unless invited."

I rear back, shocked. "Wait...you're kicking me out?" My heart thunders. She doesn't mean it. I'm her son. She'd never kick me out. Not for real. She loves me. "Mom, don't be like this. Please."

"Go," she hisses. She shoves my chest, and I fall backward. She rises. Her eyes flick over me. "Stop by the barber shop. You need a haircut. You're getting shaggy."

What the hell?

Her lightning-swift mood change sends a chill down my spine. Her eyes are cold. They used to be so warm. Filled with love. Now it's gone. No wonder Dad wanted me to stop in to check on her. She's not handling Lainey's passing well after all.

Hell, neither am I. Most people would say seeing your sister's ghost means a psychotic break from reality. I'm going crazy. Mental illness clusters in families, so why couldn't I be nuts if Mom keeps flipping the switch on her sanity? My shoulders slump once Mom walks out of the room. The jittery prickles on my arms fade with each step she takes down the stairs.

I kick the pile of books, wishing I had the guts to go full-on temper tantrum and trash the bedroom. A random key, a missing diary, a bottle of whisky, and the privilege of getting booted out of my parents' house like a teen delinquent who smokes pot all day. Obviously, this search for clues is an epic fail.

Why did I think I'd find anything here anyway? It's obvious Lainey's trying to send me a message. What? I don't know. But Mala saw the imprint of Lainey's hand on my wrist too. She spoke

Lainey's name. She breathed in the cold spot and felt the icy energy coat her lungs. Does Mala know why I'm being haunted? Did she purposely sacrifice Lainey in some hoodoo ritual and trap her spirit on earth for nefarious purposes?

Nefarious, I like the word. It reminds me of a black widow spider that lures its prey and eats its mate.

I grab the bottle of whisky from the closet and down a huge gulp. The liquid burns down my throat, and I breathe out heavy fumes. Warmth burns in my belly and spreads out to relax my muscles. I have to learn the truth from the source. Rumor says the LaCroix witches speak to the dead. If that's true, Mala can ask Lainey why she keeps coming to me.

Chapter 12

Mala

Through the Looking Glass

Go away! You're not real." I squeeze my eyes shut, suck in a deep breath, and let it out in a heavy sigh before I crack open one eye. She's still there. Unlike a framed portrait, she seems solid enough that I can reach out and touch her. I bang my palm against my forehead and wince. "I'm hallucinating."

Lainey dips her finger into the cut on her wrist, then scribbles letters on the mirror in blood.

FIND. HIM.

My stomach heaves, and I back away from the sink. "What're you trying to tell me?"

Lainey slams her fist against the glass. Again. And again.

Cracks spiral across the glass from the impact. The fractures separate my face into red-tinged fragments—wild eyes, mouth open—a jigsaw puzzle. One last hit and the mirror shatters. Jagged shards of glass fly at me.

My hands rise to protect my face as I duck beneath the counter. I curl into a ball, pressing my back against the metal pipes. I can't stop shuddering. Cold settles so deep into my bones. They ache, and the more I shake, the harder I rock back and forth.

"I'm okay. I'm okay. She's not real," I chant.

I sniff, wiping my face on my upraised knees, leaving a red smear on the denim. My hand flies to my nose. A thick clot of bloody mucus plops from my nostril onto my palm. I must've jammed my nose when I dove for cover. I reach out from beneath the counter and grab a handful of paper towels from the dispenser above my head.

This totally sucks. I'll die of shame if anyone finds me like this—hiding under a sink like I've lost my ever-lovin' mind. I pinch my nostrils shut, roll onto my knees, and crawl out. My gaze skitters sideways, darting to the mirror. The glass is unbroken, but the words Lainey smeared in her rage have been rewritten. *I'm not crazy.* I bite my lip to keep from speaking the words. I don't want to believe I'm imagining the whole thing—but, on the flip side, it can't be real. *Mama's insane. Not me.*

Unless she's right? If Lainey's haunting me, it's for a reason. What does she want from me? I draw in a deep breath and hold it. *MIH. DNIF. Doesn't make sense. Stupid ass backward ghost.* I blow out the air in a giant gush. *Backward, duh.* Lainey had written FIND HIM. *Find who?*

* * *

The ride from town to the bus stop takes forever. I huddle in my seat with my eyes closed and my headphones blasting. Nobody talks to me, not even Dena. Although I know she doesn't try only because my body language screams FUCK OFF!

When the bus pulls up at my stop, I pick up my purse. Liquid drips on my foot, and I glance down to see a spreading yellow stain. I glare at Thing One and Thing Two, the only jerk-offs left in their seats.

"Which one of you pissed in my purse?" I yell.

Carl shrugs and holds up his hands. "Not us. We didn't do nothing. I swear, Mala," he says, but with a smirk on his lips that itches to be smacked.

God, I wish I really could lay a *gris gris* on them. Twist a curse that'll make the boys' lips swell up or give them the squirts. "I'm sick to death of getting messed with by you two. Keep it up and you're gonna be in a world of hurt. Don't forget, I know where you live. And I know how hard you sleep at night. You won't even hear me coming."

I stomp off the bus to the sound of their laughter.

"Hold up," Dena yells. "I'm walking with you." She jumps off the bus, bypassing the stairs. She lands in the mud and hops out with a laugh. "Guess I need to start looking before I leap."

The laugh sticks in my throat and turns into a snort. I choke it off with a scowl. "You didn't have to come, I'm fine. No lasting injuries from my run-in with Landry Prince."

Dena blows a ragged curl out of her eyes. "I'm not doing it just for you. I don't want to get grounded for beating up my baby brothers. Those boys have gotten on my last nerve. 'Sides, I've been thinking. What if the stalker's back?" My glazed look prompts further explanation. "The guy who followed you to the bus stop this morning."

"Oh hell, with all that's been going on, I'd put that out of my mind. Thanks a lot for reminding me, Dee."

I pause at the base of the trail through the woods. With the sun shining and birds singing, it looks normal. I can almost convince myself that my experience this morning is a figment of my imagination. Or if it did happen, that someone had just been wandering innocently across our property. Maybe I scared them more than they scared me. But, then again, if Landry had been telling the truth, his sister had been murdered.

I assumed the cuts on her arms were self-inflicted. But no, someone deliberately stole her life and dumped her body in my bayou. I've always felt safe roaming around, but now I get the shivers thinking that someone may be lurking behind a tree watching me. Thing is, I have to know for sure. I can't let fear hold me back from finding a clue if the killer has indeed been stalking me.

"I guess I'm glad you're with me," I tell my cousin.

Dena bounces up and down on her toes. The girl can't stay still to save her life. "Lead the way."

We climb the hill and enter the woods. Sodden leaves and thick mud cling to my boots once I move off the trail and into the deeper underbrush. The beaten-down area where the person hid so he could watch me climb onto the bus is easy to locate. "Check it out, Dena. I guess I wasn't seeing things." I pick up the stick I threw and point to scuffled boot prints in the drying mud. "From the raised sole, I think they're men's hiking boots. Shit!" *What if the murderer is still lurking about?*

Dena glances around. "You should report this to the sheriff."

Not a bad idea. "What about you? Want to come over and have your daddy pick you up?"

"Are you kidding? He'd rather shoot himself in the head then come onto your land. You know how he feels."

I roll my eyes. "I don't know why he hates me so much."

"It's not you. He still claims his great-something-great grandma should've inherited the LaCroix land. He'll be perfectly happy to know some crazy stalker is out to get you—" Dena's eyes widen. "I said that out loud, didn't I. Sorry. I swear I'm adopted."

"Don't say that. I like being related to you." I bump her hip with mine.

Her grin quickly fades. As much as she'd like to deny her Acker blood, her daddy's DNA doesn't need a test to be revealed. It's obvious in the red hair and freckles his daughter inherited from him. Course, my hair also has the Savoie red highlights.

"I'd better go," she says. "I'll call you once I get home. Be safe."

With a wave, Dena turns onto the path that winds around the pond and continues to the Acker homestead. Part of me wants to beg her to stay. I don't want to be alone. Not because I'm scared for her safety but because I fear for mine. Which is totally selfish and wrong. Tears burn in my eyes. I try to hold them in, but they disobey me. I let out a loud sob. *God, why didn't I leave Lainey in the water?* My head aches. My nose feels stuffy. Damn it. I feel terrible.

Shivering, I wrap my arms around my waist seeking comfort that I can't give myself. I sneeze four times in a row. Each one comes out louder and harder than the last. I blink quickly to clear my vision as a shadow moves across it, then yell, "Oh hell, no!"

Landry rises from the porch steps. How did I miss seeing him sitting there in his red T-shirt? It's not like he blends in against the dingy gray of the house. I turn to scamper back into the woods but stop. I'll be damned if I ever run from him. I stride forward, shoving past him to climb the stairs. "Go away, Landry."

"Wait, I need to talk," he says, slurring the words. The strong scent of alcohol fills the air.

Panic spurts. "You're drunk."

"I know." He vibrates with barely leashed anger, and like our old washer, he looks about one rinse cycle away from shaking apart at the seams. He stalks me up the stairs and blocks the front door. He's so big, so out of control. He scared me earlier, and he'd been sober at the time. I can't begin to predict what he'll do now that we are alone.

"Leave me be, Landry. I know you only did that because you're upset—"

"I *am* upset. Tell me that wasn't my sister's spirit we felt."

"I can't. I don't know what we felt."

"You said 'Lainey.' I heard you." He moves in front of me. His gray eyes squint with anguish. "She's haunting you. Why? What do you know?"

"I said I don't know anything!" *Why, oh, why did I think I wanted to talk to him about Lainey?* The saying "Be careful what you wish for" echoes in my head.

"Liar." He stalks forward. "I felt her hand on my arm. So did you."

I hold my hands up, warding him off as I back across the

porch. I don't dare turn my back on him; I'm afraid he'll grab me. "Please, leave me alone. You're not thinking clearly."

"I am." Landry matches my retreating steps. He shoves aside the rocking chair that I push in front of him with a swipe of his hand. I'm cornered quickly. I can only see one way to escape, but if I try to jump over the flimsy porch railing, I'll probably land headfirst.

Saints, Mala. What happened to not running from him? I straighten my shoulders and step forward. His chest brushes against mine when he draws in a ragged breath, but I don't back off. "What more do you want from me, Landry?"

His eyes lift to meet mine. I expect to see anger, but instead confusion swirls in the gray depths. "Ask my sister who killed her."

"What?"

"She'd know, right?" His hands land on my shoulders, squeezing. "So ask her."

The boy's lost his mind. "She's dead. How am I supposed to ask her anything?"

"You're a witch. Talk to her spirit."

"That's stupid talk. Let me be clear: I. Am. Not. A. Witch." And even if I were one, I'd never admit it to him. To anyone, not even to myself, without them thinking I've lost my mind. "Okay, I get it now. This is some kind of twisted joke." I shove him, and he stumbles a few steps back. I scan the empty yard. "Where are your friends hiding? Is that bitch Clarice out in the woods recording this to make me look like a fool?"

The door slams open, and Mama runs out of the house. I've been so focused on Landry that I didn't notice her truck parked in the driveway. I sag against the wall as she inserts her tiny body between us.

"What's goin' on? Why're you attackin' my daughter?" Mama stands with her shoulders back and her head held high. In my eyes, she towers over Landry's much larger form.

"Mala knows how to find out who killed my sister. But she won't help me," Landry tattles, and then, to my surprise, he buries his face in his hands and begins to cry. Not something a manly guy like Landry would do if his friends plan on posting the video online for the world to watch. This will be reputation destroying if it goes public.

Mama and I share the "look." We each take one of Landry's arms and maneuver him into one of the three rocking chairs sitting in the east corner of the porch. If Landry turns squirrely, I want to be able to move away quickly. But I doubt he'll be capable of doing anything soon. A dam burst inside of him. He bawls, body shaking, snot dripping, crying as if his world has shattered. And maybe it has. I've never felt as helpless in my entire life as I do watching him.

And Lainey, damn her restless soul, comes back to comfort him, which makes the situation worse.

The air temperature around his body drops, and when he breathes out, a cloud of mist hovers in the air, catching his attention. He looks up in surprise. The tears on his face crystallize. I can't help myself. I brush a finger across the frozen layer on his cheek, and the ice flakes away.

Mama gasps, falling heavily into the other rocking chair. "Is that Lainey?"

"Yes," Landry and I say together. Our eyes lock. Heat rises in my chest then spreads through my body, and my breath catches. I tear my gaze free.

"Well, I'll be…And she's been hauntin' you since you found her body?"

I squeeze into the rocker between Landry and Mama and trace my fingers over the smooth surface of the table, trying to decide how much I want to share with them. The words Lainey wrote on the mirror float in front of my eyes. *Find him.* Did she mean for me to find Landry? Should I tell them about Lainey trying to communicate with me in the bathroom?

No way. They already stare at me as if I've grown a second head. If I tell them about the ghostly visitation, their suspicions will be confirmed. *I'm not a freak.*

"I've had nightmares," I say. "I couldn't remember them after I woke up. Then today when Landry came to me at Munchies, it's like she wanted us to stop fighting and talk. We both felt her, like now."

Mama rubs her arms against the chill. "Her spirit's strong. Stronger than any ghost I've ever felt."

"She scares me, Mama. Landry asked me to talk to Lainey's spirit. See if she'd tell me how she died. Do you…" *Merciful heavens, I can't believe these words are about to come out of my mouth.* I draw in a deep breath and spit out the question in a rush. "Do you think you can do a séance or something?"

Mama pinches my cheek. "My little skeptic. What a question. You're serious, ain't you?"

My cheek stretches like Silly Putty as I pull it free of her talon-like fingers. "I'm not stupid. After what I've seen, denying the existence of ghosts is like saying chiggers don't bite. They're both crimes against nature and shouldn't exist. But I'm scratching the bumps on my legs and Lainey's still hovering over my shoulder."

"That's a mighty fine argument you've wasted on me, Mala," Mama says. "I've spent the last fifteen years drunk so I can't hear the spirits. I don't think they'll talk to me now even if I put them on speakerphone. Sorry, *cher*. You got a better connection to Lainey's spirit than I do."

"Is there any advice you can give me?"

"Nope."

"Thanks a lot, *Mama*. That's so helpful."

Landry tenses beside me when Mama rocks forward in the chair, hands fisting on her lap. I wonder if he thinks he should protect me. What would he do if she lashed out?

Mama catches his movement. Her eyes narrow, but she leans back. "Don't sass me, girl. You asked. I answered. Did you want me to lie? Say it'd all work out? Well, I can't do that. Your grandmère Cora tried to teach me how to control my abilities 'fore she died, but I was just as stubborn as you. I thought she was crazy and pushed her away so I could do my own thin'—hangin' out with older men, drinkin', and gettin' pregnant with you. After she died, I inherited her powers, and those she'd gotten from her mother, and so on. I couldn't control the spirits. They swept over me like a hurricane. Bashed me up somethin' terrible, and I never fully recovered. That's what I worry will happen to you, *cher*. I don't know what it takes to be able to control these gifts."

"Well, maybe there's someone out there who can help—a medium or medicine man."

"There's that psychic, Madame Rubine." Mama's lips pucker as if she sucks on something sour. "Course, she's paid by the hour.

Think you can afford her prices only to find out she's full of shit?"

"Depends on how desperate I am, I guess."

Landry rubs his face with his hands. "We're wasting time. None of this helps. There has to be a reason why Lainey's drawn to Mala. One of you knows something or she wouldn't be telling me to come to you."

I rub my hands on my jeans. "I'm sorry. I wish I did. I'd never seen her before I pulled her from the water, but it scares me to think someone killed her out here…" I trail off with a choked cry and take a deep breath, trying to calm down.

"I did," Mama says softly.

Landry rocks forward. "What did you say?"

I put a hand on Landry's shoulder and press him back in the rocker. The fact that he lets me raises my eyebrows a notch. "Mama, what do you mean? Did what?"

"You stayed over at Maggie's house some months ago. Lainey came to me that night. Poor girl was desperate. She begged for my help. Said she'd heard I knew spells."

I cross my arms and snort. "Bah…spells? That's *crazy*."

"Any crazier than ghosts, Mala?"

"Yeah, okay, maybe ghosts exist. They're made of energy, right…and Einstein said 'Energy never dies, it just transforms.' I remember that from my physics class. But magic spells, there's no proof. It's all smoke and mirrors." I lean toward her trying to get a whiff, but with Landry smelling like a bar, I can't tell if Mama's been spending time with her good friends, Jim Beam and Johnnie Walker.

"A spell is just an old-timey way of sayin' medicine." Mama rocks back in the chair. Her gaze settles briefly on Landry then skitters to the roof. "It's just a concoction based on herbal remedies and years of tamperin' by the women in our family. Lainey wanted somethin' to knock loose the baby growin' in her belly."

Landry groans like a cow being slaughtered. "A baby…oh God, Lainey." His head drops into his trembling hands. "I had no idea."

I want to hug the boy so bad my palms tingle. That's what you do when someone's in pain, but I'm not sure if he'd be open to being comforted by me. I pop my knuckles, processing what I've been told. "This doesn't make any sense. Why go to a 'witch doctor' for an unwanted pregnancy? This isn't the Middle Ages."

"Because our dad would've killed her if he ever found out," Landry says. "And if she went to a clinic, he would've heard about it. His congregation pays close attention to those places."

I chew on my lip, trying to figure out a delicate way of asking the question, before I finally just spit it out. "Did you do it, Mama? Give her something?"

"I did, but I don't know if she took it."

Chapter 13

Mala

Ghost Talker

Enough! I can't do this." Landry pushes out of the chair. He stumbles down the stairs, heading for his truck.

I run after him. "Wait, you're drunk. You'll kill yourself if you drive like this." He fumbles, dropping his keys, and I grab them from off the ground. He spins and snatches for them, but I dance back.

"Don't. I'll call George Dubois to pick you up. You've got two choices: Wait here for him to take you home or have him arrest you on the road and cart your ass to jail. What's it gonna be?"

His fists clench. I rise on the balls of my toes, ready to dodge again.

"Fine, I'll wait. But keep away from me. I can't take any more."

"You're the one who came for answers."

"How can someone so pretty be so heartless? Can't you see

this is killing me?" He turns and stalks off to the side of the house, leaving me staring after him as the word—*pretty*—flashes through my mind. I shake my head. *Landry thinks I'm pretty.*

And heartless. Ouch.

A few chickens dodge his heels. I start to call out a warning about the rooster, but I'm afraid it might startle him. If he accidentally falls and breaks his neck, I'll have to explain how another dead Prince ended up on our property.

Landry walks far enough into the trees bordering the edge of our yard that he is out of earshot, but I can still keep an eye on him from the porch.

Mama comes back outside. "I called Dixie. George isn't far. He'll be here in about ten minutes."

I cross my arms, feeling cold, and this has nothing to do with a spirit floating around me. This has to do with the lies my mother tells and me believing them. "I asked you the day I found Lainey's body if you'd ever seen her. You didn't answer."

"Weren't none of your business. What she came to me for was private."

I throw my hands in the air. "What if coming to you got her killed? Don't you get it? If anyone finds out what you did—"

"I didn't do anythin' wrong. Told the girl to go find the baby daddy and get money to take care of her problem. That's all."

"But you said..."

"Said what? I didn't say that I gave her a potion. Just that I knew how to make one. I'm not stupid. Those spells are from back when women didn't have a choice but to go to a witch doctor to take care of an unwanted pregnancy. Half the time, the girls died from infection or blood loss. You think I'd wish that on some innocent girl or have her death on my hands?"

Guilt burns in my belly. "Oh, Mama, I'm sorry. I assumed when you said you gave her something…I'm stupid. I didn't think it would be advice." We sit on the step, shoulder to shoulder. "Still, how would a preacher's kid know to ask you for help in the first place?"

"The girls told Lainey I can work mojo. They come begging for spells to help with protection, love, and luck." Mama laughs and rolls her dark eyes when speaking of the other prostitutes who work out of the same motel she does. "They're pretty gullible, and I can't say no to making a dollar off of their stupidity."

"How do you even know how to cast a spell?"

"Ever hear of Google? Lots of companies sellin' made-to-order hoodoo products, so I buy in bulk. Protection and luck oils and cleansin' crystals are my top sellers. I also make a mean mojo hand, but it ain't got no magic juice." She sniffs. "Don't act all holier than thou. My side business helps to pay your college tuition."

"So you're swindling a bunch of ignorant women with fake hoodoo products, and Lainey learned about you from the 'girls'?" I frown. "Oh hell, Lainey was a prostitute?"

Mama laughs. "No baby, the girl wasn't no angel, but she didn't go in for my line of business. At least, she kept her clientele to one. Her Richie Rich boyfriend kept her a room at the motel so they had a private hookup spot. She didn't want her daddy finding out she wasn't as pure as he thought she was. 'Sides, he wouldn't of approved of her affair."

I lean forward, trembling. "You know who the baby's daddy

is? Don't you?" I grab onto her elbow and squeeze. "What's his name?"

"Why should I tell you?"

"Come on, Mama. This guy might've killed Lainey. You've got to tell me, or would you rather George do the questioning?"

Mama jerks her arm free of my grasp. "Don't threaten to sic Georgie Porgie on me, girl. We're already neck deep in this shit, thanks to you dippin' your nose into somethin' that's none of your business. Lainey's man doesn't know I know who he is, and I plan on keepin' it that way. We don't need any more problems showin' up on our doorstep. You hear me?"

"But, Mama—"

"I ain't sayin' another word on the matter, and neither will you."

I glance at Landry. He still remains upright. I'm not sure how he hasn't passed out yet. I finally have a clue to help him figure out who killed Lainey, but it's not enough. Mama won't budge on telling me the name. Even if it comes to a choice between jail and snitching on someone, she'll choose jail. She has before.

The crunch of wheels on gravel fills the air, and I stand. Mama beats a hasty retreat into the house, not wanting to be around when George arrives. I wait in the driveway, shuffling from foot to foot. It's been three days since I've seen him. When he steps out of the car, my breath sucks in. He looks exhausted. The shirt that had been snug at the beginning of the week hangs loose. Dark circles surround his cheerful green eyes.

"Hiya, Malaise. Heard you have a visitor that's not fit to drive?"

"Yeah, Landry Prince. He's worked up about his sister's *murder*," I hiss the word, surprised at the anger churning inside me over not being informed of that bit of news.

George stabs his fingers through his hair, making the short ends stand up in copper spikes. "He knows about that?"

The guilt on his face fuels my exasperation. "Yeah, he accused me of killing Lainey and dumping her body in the swamp. Then fishing her out again, 'cause that's what murderers do, apparently. Why didn't you tell me that Lainey didn't kill herself or warn me that you told her family that I found her body?"

He lurches forward, so close I smell the fresh rain scent of fabric softener wafting from his shirt. His hands lift toward me, but he lets them drop to his sides. "Did Landry hurt you?"

"I'm fine. See, not a mark on me," I say, glossing over the incident. "But he freaked me out. Course he has a right to be upset. I don't get it. The cuts on her arms…"

"I'm not allowed to talk about the case, Mala."

"But *he* knows." I point at the still form across the yard.

George's eyes fall on Landry, and his fists clench. "Yeah, but I didn't tell the family. It must've been Sheriff Keyes. He's been working double time to head off trouble. Reverend Prince isn't happy with how our investigation is going. I'm afraid he might take justice into his own hands."

"Oh, like Landry tried to do? I should've gotten a heads-up or something."

"I'll collect Landry and warn him to keep away from you." George starts in Landry's direction, but I grab his arm.

"Don't be too hard on him. He's upset. Turns out his sister was pregnant. Have you checked out the baby's father?"

George spins and grabs my shoulders. "Pregnant? What do you mean?"

"Like Baby on Board. What? You didn't know?"

"No, the autopsy report hasn't come out yet, but preliminary findings didn't suggest…" His eyes light up. "God, this changes everything. A pregnancy could be a proper motive. What if the baby's father murdered Lainey to rid himself of her secret?"

"He makes a great suspect."

George laughs and pulls me into a bear hug. He squeezes all of the air out of my lungs. My heart pounds. It makes me uncomfortable. My gaze darts over to Landry and I flush, seeing him watching us with an empty expression.

"You're suffocating me," I whisper, wriggling to free myself from his constrictive embrace.

He relaxes his hold. "I'm sorry. I didn't mean to hurt you. Damn, it seems that's all I ever do when I'm around you anymore."

"No, I—" *I'm just embarrassed.*

"Look, I'm sorry for not warning you about the Princes. I'll keep Landry away. Just be careful. If anyone finds out that you know about the pregnancy—well, it could put you at risk. This guy killed once to cover up his secret. By finding her body, you brought her into the light, and now he'll be scrambling to cover his tracks."

I nod, not promising him anything. This situation with Lainey has more twists than a pretzel, and I'm smack dab in the middle of it.

He brushes the back of his hand across my cheek. "You did good, girl. Don't worry. I'll be watching out for you."

I hand over Landry's keys. As George walks over to Landry, a chill replaces the heat of his presence, and I rub away the goose bumps that rise on my arm. When he reaches the grieving boy's side, he lays a gentle hand on his back. They exchange a few words. Then Landry weaves his way toward the patrol car. George speeds up to reach his car first and opens the door. Landry bends to crawl inside then groans. He falls to his knees, grabs a flower-pot sitting beside the tire, and throws up.

"Oh, Landry, not in my geraniums." I rush to his side. The poor plant already droops from the last time Mama vomited in it. I've got to remember to move the pot out of the danger zone.

George stands on the far side of his car. "Sorry, Mala. If I get too close, I'll start puking myself."

"Thanks a lot. What am I supposed to do?"

George shrugs.

Deserted. Crap! I kneel beside Landry and hesitantly lay a hand on his shoulder. When he doesn't pull away, I rub his back in a slow circle. He shakes with each heave. And the smell, boy oh boy, does it smell rank. I shuffle a little closer until he can lean on me for support and brush the dangling tendrils of his hair behind his ears so they don't get coated in vomit. Finally, when every-thing in his stomach fills the flowerpot, he turns toward me. His head lowers onto my lap and his arms circle my waist.

I throw my hands up in the air, not sure where to place them. "Uh, Georgie, a little help, please."

George comes over and wraps his hands around Landry's waist and tries to lift him—not sure why he thinks that will work without cooperation, given Landry's size. And Landry isn't cooperating. He seems content to nest in my lap. When George pulls on him, his arms tighten around my waist.

"Landry, let her go," George yells right into the softly snoring boy's ear.

I sit there, afraid to move.

"Mala, give him a push."

"But he might fall over."

"Do you want to babysit him all night?" George snaps.

Landry grunts. His head turns, and an eyelid slides open to reveal a bloodshot eye. "I don't need a babysitter," he mumbles. "Just a little dizzy."

"See, he's dizzy, Georgie. Be nice. He's under a lot of stress." I gently pat Landry on the head, and he rubs his bristly chin against my leg with a deep sigh.

George's face flames scarlet, and a vein pulses in his forehead. "We're all under a lot of stress. I'm supposed to be on patrol. How do you think the sheriff would take it if he found out about this?"

"Georgie, you're doing a good thing. Calm down."

"I *am* calm," he yells, running his hand through his hair. "Look at him. How am I supposed to explain to his grieving parents how he got in this condition? They've enough to deal with preparing for the funeral on Saturday. They don't need this worry."

Landry shudders at his words. He rolls onto his backside and sits up. "Cut the yelling. I'm fine, *Deputy* George. My head's cleared up. I can drive."

"Hell, no, you can't drive." George grabs his arm. This time, Landry doesn't fight as George lifts him to his feet and half drags, half carries him to the car. He isn't gentle getting him inside either.

I follow behind, feeling guilty and not knowing why.

George turns and gives me a hard, lingering stare.

"What?"

He shakes his head. "I don't know how you manage to get me worked up."

"But I didn't do anything." I step closer, staring into his eyes. The moss green darkens with an undefined emotion. I clasp my hands together and take a deep breath to calm the surge of panic building inside me.

"Mala...I—" he begins, only to be cut off by the sound of Landry gagging. He rolls his eyes and offers me a tight grin. "I'd better go before I have to spend the rest of the night hosing out my car. You take care, all right?"

"Sure." What I really want to ask is what he planned to say before he got interrupted. For some reason, I think it might...no, better let it go. "Be careful."

Feeling confused, I watch the patrol car drive off. I hate that George is upset, and I think his frustration has more to do with me than with having to take care of Landry. I totally understand because I'm feeling the same way. The whole day has been a nightmare. Part of me wonders if I really woke up this morning.

After dragging out the hose and spraying out my flowerpot, part of the driveway, and my piss-soaked purse, I go inside. It's time for Mama and me to have a little chat. I have a bunch of unanswered questions about Lainey that only she can shed light on.

A battered suitcase waits in the entryway.

"Mama," I call, shoving it aside so I can get through the door.

She comes out of her bedroom with a tote bag. "The boy's gone?"

"Yeah, but what's all this?"

"I called my great-auntie in New Orleans. I need to head down there tonight. I'll be back sometime tomorrow. You gonna be all right by your lonesome?"

"You're kidding, right?" My hands start shaking. I cross my arms and lean against the door to block her exit. "What's going on? Why the sudden trip, Mama? After all that's happened, I need to talk to you."

Mama fiddles with the strap on her tote bag. "That's why I'm goin', Mala. I don't know nothin' that would help, but my grand-tante does. She's your great-grandmère Dahlia's twin, and she's the only livin' female left in our family who knows how to control our gifts. She may be able to help us."

"Why haven't I ever heard about this aunt?"

Mama picks up her suitcase in silence.

"Wait, Mama, don't go," I beg, trying to snatch the bag from her hands. She jerks it free and steps around me. The fire brightening her eyes has me cringing, expecting a slap. When it doesn't come, I straighten in surprise.

"I have to go, Mala." Mama's breaths come hard. It isn't anger reflected in her dark gaze, but deep, soul-draining fear. And despair. "Lord knows I want nothin' to do with that wicked woman, but I'd eat my own liver if it meant figurin' out a way to keep you safe."

I shudder. "Wicked?"

Mama picks up her suitcase again and starts for the door. I try to block her, but she shoves past and heads outside. I run after her. My mind whirls. "What aren't you telling me?"

Mama meets my gaze, her own terrified. "Grand-tante Magnolia's a conjure woman. She practices hoodoo—root magic. Great-grandmère Dahlia and her sister had a fallin' out when they were young 'cause Magnolia apprenticed herself to a priestess who taught her how to raise the dead and twist dark curses. They never spoke after that, and your grandmère Cora refused to practice root magic." She drops the bag and comes over to wrap her arms around me.

I hug her tight. "I'm scared. Please, please don't leave me alone."

"I'm scared too. The spirits started whisperin' to me when I was about your age, but it wasn't until my mama died that I ever saw one. And I've never felt a spirit as powerful as Lainey. She almost killed you that time in the bathroom, and I think the reason you forgot when she touched you was that your mind ain't strong enough to control her. Magnolia's the only one who can teach you how to use your gifts, and she might turn me away out of pure spite. I have to do somethin'. You need to understand that, *cher*. I can't let you suffer the way I did."

With a fake smile plastered on my face, I release her. Now that she's made her decision, I just want her to go. I'll deal with this mess on my own. Like always. "Okay, if you think this is the way, I guess I'll be fine until you get back."

"That's my girl." She throws her bag into the back of her pickup, then points to Landry's truck. "When that boy comes back, don't go near him, you hear? Don't listen if he tries to talk you into contactin' his sister. Her spirit's too strong. You need the help of a professional."

I bite my lip.

"Grief's got that boy torn up in the head, baby. Swear you'll be careful. Don't trust him."

"I swear I'll be careful. You too." I wave her off, glad she didn't force me to swear to something that I can't keep.

Chapter 14

Landry

Stalker

George doesn't take it easy on the winding road.

Each curve we whip around makes me gag. He'll kill me if I lose it in his car. I press my fist against my stomach, trying to dull the ache from puking up the bowl of beef stew I ate earlier. Food and whisky don't mix.

Okay, it's official. Phase I of my plan to find out if the girl I like, who I finally talked to, the one who made me forget for a little while that I'd never see my sister again, may be the one who murdered her, is a total bust. It's my own fault. If I hadn't gone to her house drunk maybe I would've handled the situation better. Like not bawling like an infant for once.

God, I'm so embarrassed. I press my forehead against the window pane. My chest feels like I've taken a garden claw to my insides and raked my guts into a lump in my stomach. I never knew I could hurt so much.

It's killing me.

The trees in the distance blur into broccoli-stalk smudges. My stomach churns, and I close my eyes and Lainey's face floats in the darkness. Her sadness haunts me. I see her whenever I close my eyes. I haven't slept more than a couple hours at a stretch in days. When I lie down, Lainey's voice whispers in my ears. It's only one name spoken over and over: *Mala. Mala. Mala.*

Lainey drove me crazy.

By the time I confronted Mala at Munchies, I'd convinced myself of her guilt. I obsessed over each word and action she'd taken while at the coroner's, sure she hid something from me. Her glittering eyes and smile concealed the evil inside, but it all changed once I was with her. I fell under her spell.

Tears press against my sealed lids. I squeeze them away. I won't cry again. Bad enough I broke down in front of Mala and her mom when Lainey appeared. I've got to stay strong until I figure out who hurt her. Heaven help the person who killed her.

George parks in front of my parents' house. I bang on the glass partition separating the front of the car. "I'm not going in there. Take me to my apartment."

My face flushes. I don't want to confess that Mom kicked me out.

George climbs out of the patrol car, and I glare at him while he comes around to open the door. "You're not in any condition to care for yourself." When I don't move, he grabs my arm and drags me out. A heavy scowl pulls down his eyebrows. He shoves me toward the house, and I stumble. "Don't tell me I have to carry you."

He tries to take my arm again, but I jerk away. "I don't need your help, Deputy George."

"You need someone's help. What the hell were you thinking? Accosting Mala, driving drunk…" He shakes his head "That's not like you, Landry."

"I'm thinking my sister was murdered, and you're not doing shit to find the person who did it. That rather than following the evidence, you're gonna sweep it under the rug because of your personal relationship with the main suspect."

George stiffens. "Main suspect?"

I laugh. It's so funny it makes me sick. "Go to hell, George. I saw you hug Mala. Don't even try to deny you have feelings for her. If you can't do your job, I'll do it for you."

I'm shaking so hard I'm about to fly apart. He had his hands all over her. I wanted to rip his arms off and shove them down his throat. The only reason why I didn't…Mala hugged him back. It hurt, watching them. I couldn't move. But I'm not frozen anymore. I'm so hot that if I don't get away from him, I might do something I'd regret later. I turn toward the house.

George grabs my shoulder and spins me around. "If you're implying Mala's a suspect—"

I jerk my arm free. "Did I say her name?"

"You don't have to." He steps forward until we're almost nose to nose. I straighten up to my full height, ignoring the clench in my strained gut. His emotionless, bottle-glass green eyes send a chill through me. He could hurt me. He'd do it without any remorse. He sees me lower than dirt, and he'd feel nothing but justified because he thinks he's protecting an innocent person.

This basically sums up my whole problem. Mala has him snowed. Uncle Jay warned me. He said she looks innocent on the outside. It's the inside I'm not sure about. When I'm with her, I can't believe she'd be capable of hurting Lainey. Her warmth surrounds me like a warm blanket, and I want to wrap myself in her arms and never let her go. It's when I'm alone that the doubts chew me up. Like right now.

I meet George's eyes. "Someone killed Lainey."

"It wasn't Mala so back the fuck off and leave her alone. If I even hear about you harassing her again, I'll lock your ass up." He leans forward, and I take a step back. "Do you understand? This is your only warning."

"Crystal," I say, giving a sloppy salute and spinning on my heel. I'm not running from him exactly, more like making a controlled retreat. What he's saying isn't wrong. Confrontation won't help me find the truth. It'll only cause problems with the law, and I'll scare Mala into hiding. I need to gain her trust to dig up her secrets.

The front door slams open when I reach the porch. I back up, but a meaty hand grabs my collar and drags me inside. Dad thrusts me against the wall. His arched nostrils flare. I must be rank from the alcohol and puke. My face flushes hotter than if I sat too long in the hot tub. When I step forward, he shoves me back against the wall.

Rage replaces my earlier embarrassment. I thrust my arms up, breaking his hold on my shirt, popping a button. "Back off!"

Dad doesn't smack me. He's never laid a hand on me in anger in his entire life. He left disciplining his children to his wife. He says because as a man he's stronger than Mom. He didn't believe in sparing the rod, but he didn't want us to come to lasting harm. For him to shove me means I've pushed him past his limit.

He backs away and runs his fingers through salt-and-pepper hair. His thick beard bristles like a porcupine when he juts out his chin. "You've shamed me," he says softly.

That's it.

He walks toward his study with measured strides. He doesn't look back. Heat rushes through my chest, up to my head. I'll explode if I don't let out the rage eating me up. I've stuffed my feelings inside, but there's no room for a slice more. Shame...he dares to talk of shame. I'm full up with it. Time to share the blame with the one who deserves it the most.

"Damn right you should be ashamed." I step forward. "If not for you, Lainey would still be alive."

Dad lurches to a halt. His shoulders heave. "What did you say, son?"

I can't believe the words coming out of my mouth, but I can't stop them even if I want to. "I said it's your fault, *Father*. Lainey dying. It's all because of you and your rigid beliefs. She needed her family's support, and instead she went to Jasmine LaCroix for a hoodoo potion to abort her baby. How tragic is that?"

"Baby..." Dad slowly turns. "Did you say..."

"Lainey was pregnant. Imagine how terrified she must've been. How alone. She didn't have anyone to talk to. Nobody to confide in who wouldn't judge her. You've always preached about the sanctity of life, but Lainey's life is over. She died."

"Jasmine LaCroix..."

"Lainey went to her for help because she couldn't come to us."

The study door opens, and Uncle Jay steps out. He stands in the doorway, clutching the frame with both hands. Dad and I turn to him. He raises his hands. "No, I didn't keep a pregnancy from you, I swear."

"Then why didn't I know about it?" Dad's voice booms through the corridor.

The bedroom door upstairs squeaks, and Mom races down the stairs. Her white cotton nightgown flaps around her bare knees. "What are you saying? What's going on?"

Silence fills the room.

I swallow hard and say, "Lainey was pregnant."

Mom cries out. She falls forward. Dad catches her before she hits the ground and hoists her into his arms like she weighs less than nothing. She's lost too much weight over the last few days. Her eyes are ringed with dark circles. He carries her upstairs in silence while she sobs into his shoulder.

I turn to Uncle Jay who stares after them. Emotions flicker through his heavy eyes too quickly for me to read. "How could you not know?" I demand. "You did the autopsy."

Uncle Jay shakes his head. "There were no signs of her giving birth recently nor was her uterus enlarged at the time of death. I didn't think to look further."

"Then the whole pregnancy thing could be a lie?"

"I don't know, but I intend to find out if Lainey had a pregnancy terminated." A hard glitter turns his eyes to slate. "But more important, I intend to discover how it was accomplished."

* * *

I thought maybe I'd get some rest by sleeping in my old bedroom, but the implications of Uncle Jay's statement stick with me through the long night. Lainey went to Jasmine LaCroix for a magic fix. I heard it from the woman's mouth. She admitted to giving Lainey what she wanted. Women died from abortions before they became legal. What if Lainey's went horribly wrong and she died as a result? Would Mala even know about it? She seemed surprised when her mom mentioned Lainey went to her. Could she really be innocent?

If so, why does Lainey keep shoving me in her direction? Why can't I yank the guilt and suspicion out of my mind? I'd rather feel the agony of an unrequited crush than this churning pain. The last of Lainey's whisky calls to me around four a.m., but I pour it down the toilet and flush it. I scared Mala yesterday. If I don't go to her sober, she'll never let her guard down enough to trust me. And I have an idea I want to try out. It might not be the brightest plan—okay, it's more like shooting daisies—but I'm desperate.

I catch the bus at an ungodly hour. The ride up to Mala's place gives me time to work out what I'll say. I want to believe in her innocence. Until I have proof otherwise, I can't lie to her. Even if lying might get me farther to my goal. I wait by my truck until she comes out of the house. Mala stops short when she sees me and takes a step backward.

Crap! She's gonna run.

I raise my hand—Vulcan style. "I come in peace."

Mala bites down on her bottom lip.

Okay, good. The joke disarms her enough that she doesn't scream and run back into the house, but she flicks a nervous glance over her shoulder.

Mala hugs herself after a tiny shiver, but her expression remains calm. "I think you mean 'Live long and prosper.'"

Point one: Mala's a Trekkie. Who knew?

I can play it cool too. I shrug, sticking my hands in my pockets so I look nonthreatening. "That too."

"What're you doing here?"

"I came to collect my truck."

She raises an eyebrow. "Yeah, so why are you still here?"

"Figured you could use a lift to town. Don't you work today?"

She walks down the stairs and edges around me. She's careful not to come within grabbing distance. The lack of trust hurts, but it's not unexpected. "My shift doesn't start until twelve. I'm going early to buy groceries, but I can catch the bus."

"It'll be faster if I drive you." I fall in beside her.

She stretches her legs and walks faster.

Finally I can't take the silence. "Malaise, this is the best I can do for an apology."

"The best you can do?" She spins around, and I fall back. Damn she's scary when pissed. Her nostrils flare as she stalks toward me. "What about saying 'Hey, Mala, sorry I scared the snot out of you when I accused you of murder. Sorry I came to your house drunk and killed your favorite plant.' How about that, Landry Prince?"

I stand my ground. "I am sorry, Mala. For all that—and more."

"More? There's more?"

Time to fall on my sword. I glance toward the trees, then force my gaze to meet hers. I dredge up all the sincerity I can into my eyes and hope it'll be enough for a last-minute save. I can't believe I'm telling her this. I heave a heavy sigh and spill my dirty secret.

"Yeah, yesterday…in the woods, I'm the person who followed you to the bus stop." Her face reddens with each word, but I force myself to continue. "I'm sorry. I wanted to talk to you about Lainey, b-but I didn't have the courage. Then you heard me and got scared."

A choked gasp comes from her. Her trembling hands ball into fists. I take a quick step back 'cause she's gonna punch me. I know it. I deserve to get hit, so I won't defend myself. But damn, it'll hurt. She's not like Clarice. Mala's got muscles. With each second that passes, the tightness in my chest grows. She won't forgive me. I've blown it.

"Please, forgive me." I lift my hand, and she jerks.

"Why? Why should I?" Mala presses her palms against her eyes, then lets her hands drop. Her eyes shine like ebony piano keys. I hurt her. I'm such an ass.

I stare at a fire ant hill. I should throw myself on her mercy and let her drizzle chocolate over my body for the ants. I bite my tongue, seconds away from suggesting the idea when I catch the kinky implications. Besides, if chocolate's involved in any form of makeup negotiations, it'd be more fun if I poured it all over her.

I tear my gaze from her heaving breasts. It's like my eyes have a mind of their own. Thank God she's avoiding looking at me and didn't see. Was I this goddamn stupid before Lainey died, or have my brain cells deteriorated from alcohol poisoning and lack of sleep? How am I supposed to come up with a decent plan to find my sister's killer when I can't focus long enough to manage an apology?

I should fall to my knees and beg. "I really am sorry, Mala." Pain flares in my right knee when I hit the ground. Crap, I fell on a rock. "I haven't been thinking straight since Lainey was killed. Something kept whispering your name in my ear. All I could think about was getting to you."

Mala stares down into my eyes. "Do you think Lainey's spirit has been telling you to find me? That somehow you sensed her desire and acted on it but didn't understand what she wants?" She sighs, breaking the connection between us by looking away. "Hell, why am I even surprised, Landry? I don't know what she wants from me either, and it's driving me crazy too."

"Maybe if we talk, we can figure it out." I stand, holding out my hand. She gives my outstretched fingers a suspicious grimace like I've been playing in the dirt making mud pies but turns to head toward my truck. My shoulders lighten as if a huge weight has been lifted.

Mala stands in place when I open the door, then glances up at me with a tiny sigh. "Uh…I ran from a crazy stalker and rolled down a hill yesterday. I'm a little sore. Can I get a lift?"

My cheeks heat. *I get to touch her! Play it cool.* "Yeah, okay." My palms tingle when my hands wrap around her narrow waist. When I lift her up, she lets out a small squeal, and I chuckle. "You weigh nothing but a minute."

"Maybe compared to you," Mala huffs, sliding across the seat.

I walk around to the other side and get in. We ride in silence for a couple of miles. I don't think either of us knows how to begin. Finally she asks, "What do you know about how Lainey died?"

"Dr. Rathbone's like family. He and my father grew up together, and they're still pretty tight. Anyway, Uncle Jay told us that Lainey had been murdered. He also said that her body had been found out here."

Mala snorts. It's not at all ladylike, but it works for her. She catches my sideways glance and scowls. "Your uncle's not my favorite person. I'm sorry if that offends you, but he has the ethics of a night crawler. Figures he'd be the one to blab. Sheriff Keyes ordered his deputies to keep quiet about the case. So what else did he say? Did he have any ideas about how someone co-erced a grown woman into the woods and cut her wrists without her putting up a fight? The wounds were perfect. No hesitation marks like she changed her mind like in a real suicide. I should've caught that myself when I found her." She sounds grumpy about that. Like missing a clue is a major offense.

Okay, go careful. Don't give out too much. "He said she'd been drugged."

She gives a sharp nod. "That makes sense. What kind?"

"What do you mean?"

"What kind of drug did the person use? If it was some kind of prescription medication or an exotic poison, the police might be able to trace who purchased it through the phar-macy or shipping company. Narrow down the suspects a bit. How long had the drug been in her system? Long enough to knock her unconscious at another location so the person had to physically carry her to the spot where he threw her in the water? Or did the drugging take place later, once they'd al-ready reached…"

God, she's intense. I'm not handling her questions well. I keep picturing my big sis on the autopsy table. My stomach twists, and I pinch my lips tight. *Please don't vomit again.*

Mala catches my puckered, prune-faced expression. "Oh, I'm sorry." Her hand lightly touches my tense arm. The heat from her palm warms my skin for a few seconds. Then she must remember I'm the crazed stalker and snatches it back. "This is your sister I'm talking about. I'm an idiot."

I swallow hard. "No, don't say that. I asked for your help."

"But my speculations aren't helping. They're just wild guesses with no evidence to justify them."

I glance at her. Her voice trembles. Sincerity shines on her face. I tear my gaze away and turn onto the main road leading to town. "There's one thing," I begin then finish in a rush, "I've been wondering how you found her. What did she look like? Did she look scared?"

Mala sighs, twisting her fingers together. "No, she appeared peaceful."

My hands tighten on the steering wheel. "But we both know that's a lie. If she was peaceful, we wouldn't still be seeing her."

"No, I guess not."

"I had an idea. Your mom mentioned that psychic, Madame Rubine, channels the dead. I thought maybe we'd go see her."

"Oh, I don't know. Did you also hear she's pretty pricey? I can't really afford to do something like that. Plus I don't really believe in all that mumbo jumbo."

"You've seen Lainey, Mala. How can you not believe?"

"Easy. How often do I see her? Not very. So how can this Madame Rubine call up the spirits of every grieving person who throws their hard-earned cash at her? That'd be a lot of undead running around."

"Come on, what would it hurt to try? I called her this morning. She has an opening at nine. Will you come with me? I guarantee it'll be more fun than grocery shopping."

I pull out my sad-puppy look.

Mala studies my face for a long moment and sighs. "Okay."

Chapter 15

Mala

Fake Madame

The mobile home looks like all the others in the Golden Garden Mobile Home Park, except for the fact that it's painted blue and white and boasts a large sign on the roof with a hand holding an eyeball in the middle of its palm. A robed woman stands in the front yard surrounded by a lush garden. She's youngish and wears her dirty blond hair pulled up in a scarf. Loose tendrils straggle around her chubby cheeks. Her large eyes have been lined with thick mascara and liner, but the rest of her face is free of makeup. A tow-headed toddler, wearing only his diaper, runs around her legs, avoiding her frantic attempts to corral him.

She waves to us when we pull in her driveway. "Hi there, ya'll are fifteen minutes early. I still need to get my boy next door to the sitter, but ya'll come on in." She lunges for the baby, grabbing him about the waist. He squeals with glee as he's hoisted into her arms. She gives us a harried grin and heads toward the neighboring home.

I don't move from the seat when Landry comes around to open my door. Instead, I lean my head close to his and whisper, "This is stupid."

"You've made your feelings clear on the matter," Landry drawls, his raven-wing brows drawing inward.

I ignore the hand that settles around my waist. "Did you tell her why we need her advice?"

"Nope." He gives a little tug, and I fall out of the truck into his arms. I inhale the spicy scent of his aftershave and catch my breath. Our eyes meet, and I try to read the emotions swirling in the smoky depths.

"Don't worry, I've got you," he says with a small smile.

My hands flex on his broad shoulders. For the life of me, I can't think of anything to say in response. His silky hair brushes the side of my cheek as he slowly lowers my feet to the ground. I lean against the side of the truck, expecting to be released, but rather than moving back, he keeps his arms wrapped around me for a long beat.

Flustered, I take a small step to the side, breaking the connection. "Good. Okay, then. Let's go see what the spirits tell her about us," I say, tone heavy with sarcasm, but my heart races like it has a mind of its own.

Landry gives me a breath-stealing smile. I let him walk in front of me and do a quick underarm sniff to make sure I put on deodorant this morning—yep, fresh as an orchid, but not for long. We await Madame Rubine's return in her front yard. Sunlight reflects off the white house paint. After five minutes, perspiration dots my forehead and soaks into my shirt. I fan myself with one hand, wishing for some shade and trying to sort through the confusing mix of emotions filling my mind about Landry. It doesn't help that my eyes keep returning to his firm backside, and my thoughts get wonky again. *Stupid brain.*

Madame Rubine returns like a mini-hurricane. Frenetic energy crackles off her body as she dashes over to us. The riotous colors of the plants jumbled together in tiny garden beds mimic the patterns in her paisley satin robe. She looks like she imitated the wardrobe of a clichéd gypsy queen from an old movie. Everything about her screams fake, money-grubbing con artist. She'll play on our emotions and tell us exactly what she thinks we want to hear. I have to catch her in her web of lies so Landry, in his desperation, doesn't get hooked.

Ruby, for that's what she asks us to call her, leads us into her lair. The room doesn't give off the exotic psychic mojo I imagined. I guess the poor woman can't afford the heavy velvet drapes, brass chandelier, and ornate crystal ball to really impress. Instead, she has a trunk full of toys stuffed in a corner and lots of plants. The warm air holds the scent of fresh earth and thick moisture like a hothouse. Sconces holding a multitude of burning candles hang from the walls throughout the room. Their scents mix together to form their own special, stinky blend. Tears fill my burning eyes, and I scrunch up my nose to hold back the threatening sneeze.

"I'm so sorry, I must look a sight." Ruby graces us with a sheepish smile that reveals deep dimples. She pulls the scarf off her head and fluffs up her blond curls. She reminds me of that little girl from those black-and-white movies. They even named a drink after her—Shirley Temple. Man, she's a cutie pie. Five minutes and she's already charming me into letting down my guard.

"Charlie, that's my little heathen, his daddy fed him doughnuts for breakfast. The sugar went to his head. He wouldn't settle down in front the TV long enough for me to get dressed this morning," she says, and I catch Landry averting his eyes to the ceiling. Wonder what just passed through his head to make him blush like that?

Time to leave. I step closer to Landry, ready to make up some excuse.

Ruby flutters her hands in the air. "I could go throw on some sweats…but ya'll didn't come for my looks, did ya? Sit down." She waves toward the table against the far wall, separated from the rest of the living room by a baby gate. She picks up a kettle. "Would ya'll like some tea?"

I hide my shudder, afraid to ask what sort of weird, psychedelic tea a medium might give her clients. I can totally see her tricking us into thinking our drug-induced hallucinations of dancing teddy bears are visions of the spiritual realm. I give Landry a warning shake of my head. "No, thank you, Ruby. Uh, I'm embarrassed to ask, but would you mind putting out the candles? I'm allergic to sage, and I think I smell that mixed in with the others."

Ruby's cheeks turn bright red. "Oh, Goddess, I'm so sorry."

Landry frowns and gives me a hard stare.

I shrug back, grab a tissue from the box on the table, and blow my nose loudly. "No, I'm sorry to be such a pest. I appreciate it though."

I stand by an open window, dabbing sweat from my forehead

with a clean tissue. No way can I survive without a breeze until this aroma factory of a deathtrap clears out a bit. Ruby snuffs the candles, then turns with a wide smile. "Better?"

"Yes, thank you."

"Good. Please, have a seat so we can get started."

Landry and I sit down at a round table covered with a thick red tablecloth.

"Give me your hands," Ruby says, reaching out to us.

I lay my palm on top of hers, and Landry does the same.

"Now take each other's hands."

Landry and I share another glance. He presses his thigh against mine, and I derive a bit of comfort from having his strong presence beside me. I draw in a deep breath, startled by my reaction to him, and take his hand.

Ruby smiles. Her hazel eyes close. Silence, but for our harsh breathing, fills the room for what feels like forever. I study Ruby's blank face. A minute crease forms on her brow then settles into deep grooves on her forehead. Her hand tightens around mine. "I see darkness," she says, and sighs. Her head tips forward, and she groans. "Ya'll have questions, fears for your future together."

I twitch, wishing I could take my hands back. My palms have gotten sweaty, but not nearly as moist as Landry's. Both of their grips keep me from pulling away.

"There's opposition to ya'll being together. Family? Mother? Father?" Her voice rises higher as if in a question then settles into authority. "They're not supportive."

My hand tightens around hers then releases as I think about how disappointed Mama will feel once she finds out I've disobeyed her wishes. And Landry's parents? Well, I can only imagine the righteous reverend's displeasure if he learns his son has gone to a practitioner of the dark arts with the witch's daughter. *Muwahahaa.* I stifle a giggle at that random thought.

Ruby rocks back and forth, moaning as if in pain. "Ya'll have to fight to be together. It'll come down to a choice. Love for one another or love of family."

I roll my eyes at Landry, about ready to burst out laughing. *Love for each other, ha!* But he's too busy nodding to notice. Ruby has sucked him in like a trapdoor spider and stuck him good. And poor Landry can't keep his big mouth shut.

"What about my sister?" He leans over the table, almost jerking me out of my seat.

Ruby's head tilts to the side, as if she listens to a voice we can't hear. "Your sister accepts and encourages the relationship."

I shoot Landry my shut-up frown and ask, "Madame Ruby, will she be my maid of honor?"

Ruby frowns in thought then nods. "Yes, she will. All ya have to do is ask. She'll do anything for her brother. They're very close."

Landry wilts in his seat.

I yank my hand from hers. "Wrong. Firstly, Landry and I aren't in a relationship for our parents to disapprove of. Secondly, his sister's deceased. That's why we came—to see if we could contact her spirit. Come on, Landry," I say, tugging on his hand. "She's a fraud. She can't help."

Ruby stands quickly. "I see the future. Not always is it clear, but what's coming in about the two of you is very strong. Your families disapprove, and ya'll have to choose whether to cave to their displeasure or stand up for one another. If ya don't fight, they'll destroy you."

"Just give it up, Yoda. You've been caught," I say.

"No, the only part I lied about was whether or not his sister would be your maid of honor."

"Mala, wait. What if she's telling the truth?" Landry says, breathing hard.

"Don't be naive. If she lied about one thing then she could be lying about all of it, Landry."

"Maybe if she knew more about what's going on, she'd be able to help."

"Help her get one over on us better, you mean?"

Landry pulls out four twenties and lays them on the table. "I want you to contact my sister's spirit."

Ruby shakes her head. "I can't do that. I'm sorry. All my information comes from my guardian angel, not the spirits of the dead."

Landry pushes the money across the table, desperation written clearly across his face. "Please. Ask your guardian angel what it knows about Lainey. She's been haunting Mala. Tell me who killed her." His voice rises with each word, and simultaneously the temperature in the room drops. His hand tightens around mine again, and his eyes glitter. "It's her, Mala. She's here."

"Oh, crap," I say, chilled. Mama's warning about contacting Lainey flashes through my head. Why hadn't I listened?

Ruby's eyes widen. "What's going on?" She loses her fake country twang for a northern accent similar to the one I've heard spoken on TV shows—*Jersey Shore* or *The Sopranos*. Ruby isn't even from the South, but Landry doesn't notice that either.

"It's my sister," he says, breathless. "It's Lainey."

"No, Landry," I say, heart pounding. "We should go. This is dangerous."

"It's why we came." He squeezes my hand so hard it hurts. I don't think he realizes. His eyes never leave Ruby's bloodless face.

"I came because I hoped Ruby was a real medium," I tell him, trying to pull my hand free. "She's not! Look at her, she's terrified. Lainey's dangerous—unpredictable. I don't want her inside me again."

"She can use me," Ruby offers in a rush, and her eyes take on a frantic glitter. "My chakras are open. My mind and spirit are in tune." Before I can pull away, she grabs my other hand and closes her eyes.

"Don't, Ruby. You don't understand—"

"Lainey, if you're here, give us a sign," Ruby says.

The cold spot settles over the table, and the overhead light rocks back and forth. We look up to see the rope cord sway then dip as the light flicks on. And off.

"Oh my Goddess," Ruby whispers. "Lainey, your brother wants to ask you some questions. Turn on the light once for *no* and twice for *yes*. Do you understand?"

Click, click. "Yes," Ruby translates. Her eyes roll back in her head, leaving only the whites of her eyes showing.

Landry stares at the light. "It's me, sis. Are you okay?"

Click—"No."

"Are you in pain?"

Click—"No."

"Do you need help?"

Click, click—"*Yes*," Ruby hisses, and a shiver runs down my spine at the alien sound. This isn't Ruby anymore.

A trickle of blood drips from Ruby's nose. The color drains from her face, leaving it a blank, ghastly mask. The blood thickens as it runs across her mouth. Her tongue darts out. The tip licks the blood from her lips, and a mirthless smile stretches her mouth wide.

"Landry," I whisper. "This isn't right. Please stop."

His hard gaze falls upon me. "Lainey, did Mala kill you?"

I gasp, frozen.

Ruby's sightless eyes focus on me, and I shiver. I can't meet her gaze. It takes all my strength not to run screaming from the room. Whimpering, I yank my hands from Ruby's and Landry's and back away from the table.

Landry's hard gaze follows. "Did she do it, sis?"

"No!" I yell.

Click. "No!" Ruby convulses so hard her forehead smacks the table. She tumbles sideways out of the chair. When she hits the ground, her eyes open, and she gazes at us, unblinking. I stare at her in horror, too terrified to care if she needs help.

Ruby coughs, spitting blood from her open mouth. "The baby's crying," she mumbles, sitting up with effort. "What happened? Where's my son?"

"Ask him. I'm done." I shove through the beads blocking the front door and exit the trailer into the light. Warm air wraps around my body and soaks in deep. My stomach clenches with nausea, and I bend double, sucking in air to keep from being sick.

"Mala," Landry calls.

I shoot upright then shuffle down the driveway on legs too shaky to run.

"Mala, wait!" He runs out of the trailer and catches my arm just as I reach the sidewalk in front of Ruby's trailer.

I twist my arm, but he refuses to let go. "Get away from me!"

He pulls me against him. "Damn you! Why did you leave?"

"Damn me? Right back at you, Landry!"

"What's the matter?"

I shove at his chest. "You're psycho! Like multiple-personality, stark-raving nuts if you can't figure out why I'm pissed."

"Is this about me asking if you killed Lainey? I had to be sure you weren't involved."

"You're a liar. This whole time we've been together you thought I was guilty. What would you have done if Lainey said yes?"

Landry doesn't answer.

"Oh my God, yesterday in the woods... What did you plan to do if you'd caught me?"

He juts out his jaw. "I didn't."

"Say I'd tripped and fallen. What would you have done to avenge your sister? Hurt me?"

"I don't know!" He turns in a half circle, then swings back to face me. "It didn't happen. I wasn't thinking straight. I'd barely slept in four days. When I did, I dreamed of Lainey and you. I got all twisted in my head."

"You're still twisted. Let me go."

"No! I need to figure out what my sister wants. She left when you walked out. She left with you."

"I don't care. You and Lainey can go to hell!"

He drops my arm and steps back. I take in a deep breath, looking around at the dilapidated trailers. Crap, not the best neighborhood to storm off in. I gritted my teeth. "I need to get to work."

When Landry doesn't answer, I snap, "I'm not rich like you. I don't own a cell phone. Give me yours so I can call someone to pick me up."

Landry crosses his arms, eyes hardening to ice chips. "Who'll come to get you?"

"I have friends, Landry. People who care."

"Not enough. Does anyone know where you are? Or who you're with? If you disappeared, nobody would suspect me."

I back up. "You're scaring me."

"I mean to. Lainey was murdered by your house. We don't know who did it, or why. Mala, it's not safe. You're in danger."

"From you?"

"No. Not now." He has the good grace to hang his head.

"Not good enough." *Not nearly good enough.* "For some stupid reason, I trusted you. I wanted to help you...and Lainey."

"You can trust me. I swear. I won't hurt you." Landry trembles with the strength of his emotions. The problem is that I can't read him.

But really, what choice do I have for the time being? He's right. I don't have anyone I can call to pick me up. No Mama. Bessie or George...I meet Landry's eyes. No, I don't even want to try to explain to either of them why I went to see a psychic with Landry.

"Mala—" a faint voice calls, and I jump.

Ruby stands in her doorway. She'd wiped the blood from her face, but a faint hint of crimson stains her too-pale skin. She squints, as if the light burns her eyes, but when she sees me watching, she walks toward us.

I take an unconscious step back, forgetting that Landry stands behind me, and I bump into him. His hands rest on my shoulders, not roughly, but firm and warm. I want to soak up his heat because I can't stop shivering but pull away instead. His touch makes me sick to my stomach.

"Are you okay?" Ruby holds out a shaking hand.

I take it. "I'm fine. What about you?"

Ruby laughs. "I've never had an experience like that before—an opening. That perfect feeling of connection to a departed soul. I've been blessed."

"More like cursed," I mutter.

"Don't worry. I'll be right as rain in a couple of hours. My next appointment isn't until twelve. I plan to soak in the tub and regain my equilibrium." She blinks, and I notice how watery and red her eyes have gotten. No matter how she tries to spin it now, she hasn't recovered from being possessed. She's even forgotten to start speaking in her fake country twang again. "I heard you and Landry," she says. "I know his betrayal has affected you, but I wanted to remind you of my earlier prediction."

With a scowl, I cross my arms. "You've already been paid. You can cut the bull."

"No bull, only truth. You need Landry, and he needs you. You've got to trust each other, or I'm afraid you won't be ready for what's about to happen."

My heart starts hammering…*Ready*. The word echoes in my mind. *I won't be ready*.

"Ready for what?" Landry demands.

Ruby's eyes turn from Landry to me. They've rolled up beneath her eyelids again. Merciful heavens, but that gives me the willies. Her hand tightens around mine. I try to pull free, but she holds tight. Her fingers dig into my skin. "I see fire. I hear screams...blood."

I quiver beneath her hand. Energy crackles between us. The heat of flames burns my legs. Thick smoke chokes off my breath and stings my eyes. Tears stream down my cheeks, but I can't free my gaze from Ruby's face as it blisters then blackens. Skin sloughs from the bone. Yet her lipless, grinning mouth still speaks. "Run," she whispers. "You're not ready. Run!"

Chapter 16

Mala

Cursed

By the time Landry parks across the street from Munchies and comes around to help me out of the truck, anger has replaced fear. I push his hand aside and jump down on my own. I forget to check for traffic until I'm halfway across the street and Landry yells, "Mala, wait."

The squeal of tires and a thump slows me down. A quick glance over my shoulder shows Landry limping around an idling car. The driver climbs out looking pissed.

"Sorry, I'm okay," Landry says to the driver, then yells, "Mala!"

I press my hand to my traitorous heart, which flipped when I heard him shout. "Don't say anything else," I cry, spinning around and running for the building. "I don't want to speak to you again. *Ever.*"

If I'm alone with him, I'll do something I'll regret, like smack him upside the head, or worse, forgive him 'cause I'm a pushover. "Can't hold a grudge longer than a minute," Mama always teases. And she's right. I'm already softening toward him, which kicks my fury up another notch. Now I'm also pissed with myself for believing his stupid I'm so sorrys.

The lunch crowd fills Munchies. Customers of all ages wait in line at the counter to order their meals, cluster together at tables or booths, and hang out in back playing video games. When I shove open the door, they stop and stare, eager to watch the drama unfold. We must look a sight—Landry chasing after me while I try my best to escape.

Landry blocks my path. I try to edge around him, but he mimics my steps. "I'm not leaving until we have this out. I need you. Please?" he says with a low groan that touches my insides and makes them clench.

Those three words conjure up a variety of dirty thoughts that have nothing to do with the actual conversation. Landry doesn't want me. He wants the power he thinks I have—the power to connect with Lainey. My mouth opens, but before I can say a word, a voice that makes the hairs on the back of my neck curl interrupts.

"Landry, I've been looking for you, *cher*," Clarice says, walking up behind him with her poseur posse of friends. A frown creases her perfect brow. Did she hear his last statement? I can't tell by the way she ignores me. She threads her arm through Landry's and caresses his forearm. "I've been so worried. You haven't returned my calls. Your mom said you'd left early this morning."

Landry pulls his arm from hers. Not in a mean way, more just irritated. "My mom has barely said two words since the police told us about Lainey, so I doubt that."

Clarice blinks, her only show of surprise at the rebuff. "So, where were you?"

"That's none of your business, Clarice. You're not my girl-friend, so stop acting like you are." Landry's eyes bore into mine as if by maintaining eye contact he can keep me from leaving.

A muscle flexes in Clarice's jaw, and she shoots a glare in my direction. Time to beat a hasty retreat. I turn to head for the employee break room. Landry sprints after me and grabs me by the waist, spinning me around like a top.

I press my hands against his chest to catch my balance. "Stop treating me like I'm your personal Barbie doll. I'm not yours to pose."

"Please, I'm sorry." He runs his hands down my back as if soothing an unruly kitten. "Let's talk."

"No."

Clarice stands with her hands on her hips. "Seriously, Landry," she yells. "You're gonna ditch me for that slut?"

I whirl in Landry's arms, fed up. "I'm not the one begging like a bitch for a bone," I say to her, shaking my head in disgust. "Show some pride. He's obviously not into you."

Clarice's hand lashes out, connecting with the side of my face. My cheek puffs out a bit of air and begins to burn. The skinny thing slapped me. Slapped, like a girl, and compared to getting walloped by Mama's closed fist, it barely hurts. She must've expected a reaction: crying, screaming, even getting a retaliatory backhand, but instead I stare the girl down. Her eyes widen, and fear fills them. Her friends start whispering.

One of them shouts in warning, "Clarice, she's putting a curse on you."

"She can't do that," Clarice says, but she backs up.

Landry keeps a firm grip on my waist as if afraid I'll go after her, but he still puts in his two cents just to mess with the girl I thought was his girlfriend. "You're the one who said she's a witch."

I roll my eyes, too honest to play along, regardless of the satisfaction I'd gain by freaking her out. "I'm not a witch, Clarice. If I were, I'd wish that all your hair would fall out and that you'd break out in itchy hives."

Clarice gasps. "Stay away from me."

"I'm not doing anything. You hit me first."

"This isn't Mala's fault, Clarice." Landry moves in front of me. Defending me against Clarice is one more clue added to my long list that he's just plain crazy. Hellfire, they're both twisted. And I'm stuck smack in the middle of their insanity. It's his fault I got slapped in the first place, since Clarice got pushed over the limit at seeing me in his arms. I don't blame her for being mad. Hitting me is another matter entirely. I won't forgive her for this. She's going down.

I step around him. "I fight my own battles, Landry."

He stares hard into my eyes.

"He's mine," Clarice whispers.

I don't break eye contact with Landry as I tell her, "I don't want him."

Landry winces. The hurt darkening his eyes almost makes me call him back when he turns and walks out the door, but I bite down on the impulse. Once he's gone, I glance back at Clarice and say, "Like I said, I don't want him. But if I change my mind, there's *nothing* you can say or do to stop me from getting him."

"This isn't over." She runs her hand through her hair. Her eyes widen when she sees the strands sticking to her fingers.

"No, it isn't." I pluck a hair from her palm. She watches the strand float to the ground with wide eyes. "It's just begun, Clarice. You should've kept your hand to yourself."

Part of me feels sorry for the girl who continues to run her fingers through her hair and whimpers slightly under her breath every time a strand clings to her fingers. That's the problem with believing in superstitious nonsense. Once an idea gets stuck in your head, you make it come true through your belief. You start seeing shadows that aren't there or, in Clarice's case, a normal shedding of hair as a curse. I wonder how long it will take before she breaks out in nervous hives.

Clarice gathers her friends and leaves. She's probably chasing after Landry. The fool. She can have the lying ass. I catch Tabitha staring at me from behind the counter. She'll report this to the manager. I'm so busted. I want to hide in the bathroom. Instead, I slink through the crowd to find Maggie, Tommy, and Dena seated in our usual booth. Maggie jumps up and makes me squeeze in between them. Surrounded by my friends, the knots in my neck loosen as I drop my guard. I slump sideways and lay my head on Maggie's shoulder. "I only have ten minutes before my shift starts," I say with a sigh. "I suppose you saw what happened."

Dena wriggles in her seat, shooting looks at Maggie. "Everyone saw you fix that curse on Clarice."

Maggie snaps, "How many times do I have to say that curses are a bunch of superstitious nonsense?"

Dena remains focused on me. "You told her that her hair would fall out."

"I said I *wish* it would fall out." I shrug defensively. "I was angry. She slapped me."

"After you cursed her," Tommy says around a bite of his foot-long hot dog.

My stomach growls. I haven't eaten all day. Maybe that's why it takes a while for his statement to sink in. "Geesh, Tommy. She slapped me before I said it. And it's not a curse."

Tommy finishes chewing. "'Cause I also heard you put Landry Prince under a love spell."

"Who've you been listening to?" I turn to Maggie. "Seriously, you need to limit who Tommy's allowed to talk to. His friends are corrupting his mind."

"It's not just his loser friends, Mala," Maggie says softly. "Everyone's been talking about it since yesterday. This blow-up only made the rumors worse. Tim just texted me that Clarice's friends plan on jumping you after work." She pats my thigh. "Don't worry, I'll call Mom. She'll pick you up after your shift."

I nod, feeling icky inside. *My life sucks.*

* * *

After my shift ends, I run for my locker. Bessie will arrive soon, and I'm ready to get the hell out of Munchies. A strange smell comes through the vent, like I've forgotten to take my lunch out and it's gone rotten, but when I open the door, I learn it is so much worse than a moldy sandwich.

The stench hits me first. I gag then scream at the sight

of the bloated possum carcass hanging from the hook by a shoelace wrapped around its flattened neck. Entrails dangle, and maggots crawl through the holes where the possum's eyes used to be.

The night shift manager, Annabel Jenkins, runs into the break room. When she reaches my locker, she backs up, covering her nose. Her pale face turns blotchy. "Merciful Jesus, why would you do such a thing?"

W-what? I stare at her, breathing hard.

Annabel slams the locker closed. "Go get something to clean up this mess. I'm telling Ms. March."

My stomach curdles. "Are you crazy? I didn't do this!" I swallow the mouthful of saliva filling my mouth and grimace at the taste. This smells worse than the autopsy. Probably because this is up close and oh so personal. And the way Annabel stares at me…"How could you accuse me of defiling my own locker, Anna? I thought we were friends."

Her face twists with a savage glee. "All of the employees put up with you working here because you're Ms. March's favorite, but we know what kind of person you are and where you come from. Trash! Just like your mama."

Bitch lost her mind. My hand lashes out.

"Mala, no!" a voice yells.

I pull the punch inches from connecting with her cheek, spinning around. Our boss, Ms. Marcheline Dubois, walks toward us. Her wide eyes focus first on my hands and then circle from Annabel to the locker, then back to me. I shove my hands into my pockets and step away from Annabel, breathing hard. *Shit! I'm getting fired for this.*

"Did you see?" Annabel cries. "Did you see her almost hit me?"

Ms. March's pale face has turned blotchy. "I saw and heard everything." She faces me. "Are you okay?"

Surprised, I nod.

"Annabel, go call the Sheriff's Office to come take a report. Let them know they'll need to contact animal control."

"But, Ms. March, she—"

"I said call them. Then meet me in my office."

Annabel's lips tighten. She gives a jerky nod and stalks out of the room. She's going to make my life hell if one of us doesn't get fired or quit. I'm rooting for her to get the boot. It's been a long time since I've struck someone in anger. Not even being slapped by Clarice pushed me over the edge. I think it's because Annabel and I have worked together for three years. We never hung out or anything, but I never saw any indication from her that her smile hid such a spiteful hatred. It hurts.

Ms. March fluffs her silver curls, a nervous habit she falls into whenever stressed. "Mala Jean Marie, what exactly is going on? Do you know how many calls I received this afternoon about you? I had to come in early, now this…Honey, this is my business…" She blows out a puff of air. "Take this weekend off, okay?"

I shiver and hug myself. *Does she hate me too?* "Why? Am I being punished? I didn't do anything wrong."

Her dark eyes study my face, and her shoulders slump. "I know, but people do insane things when they're afraid, and half the town seems to be terrified of you right now." She gives me a quick hug, and I inhale her baby powder scent. "You're not safe here. Go on home, sweetheart."

I'm shaky, almost sick, and every time my hair swings across my face, I inhale the stench of decomposition. I walk to the front doors and press my forehead against the cool glass for a minute to catch my breath. The heat radiating off my skin fogs up the glass. I can barely see the patrol car parked out front when I run outside, so it takes a second to register it's not Bessie climbing out of the car but George. I slow my pace to a quick walk while taking a couple of deep breaths. *I can handle this. I'm not freaked out.*

"Mala, you okay?"

I give a jerky nod. My voice only shakes a little when I say, "I'm fine. Are you here to take the police report?"

"No, Bessie put me on protection duty. Between the threats to jump you and the roadkill in your locker, you'll be safer with a police escort."

I frown up at him. "Then who's taking the case? Andy? Don't I need to stick around to give him my statement?"

"Aunt March said she'll take care of it."

I nod again. My legs feel wobbly. If I had to go back inside and smell…Ugh, thinking about it makes me want to vomit.

George studies my face for a moment. "Damn it. You're not all right, are you? Why do you always play the tough girl?" Before I have a chance to protest, he pulls me into a hug. He pats my back, trying to comfort me. Which scares me more than a dead possum ever could.

My arms hang stiffly at my sides. What should I do with them? Hug him back? Pull away? Friends comfort one another when upset, but this is so…public. It's not professional behavior. At all.

George squeezes tighter. "You'll be okay, Mala Jean. Andy will find out who vandalized your locker, and I won't let anyone hurt you. I swear."

"I believe you," I mumble into his shirt, but I'm lying as much to myself as I am to him. No matter how hard I try, nothing changes. Not in Paradise Pointe. The faster I accept the fact that I'll always be known as the witch's daughter, the better off I'll be.

George stares into my eyes for a long minute. I can't read the emotions flickering in the emerald depths, but whatever he feels grows more intense until he radiates an icy calm that makes him seem unpredictable.

I keep glancing at the people walking past, staring. If we stay like this much longer, people will get all kinds of crazy ideas about us. Should I break free of his hug? I wiggle a bit, but his muscles flex until I'm locked in a steel cage of his embrace. I glance back to his immobile face. With each minute that passes, my nerves shoot up a notch until I quiver with tension.

"Is something else bothering you, Georgie?" I ask hesitantly.

"Why did you get in a truck with that guy after what happened yesterday?" he asks, not breaking eye contact.

"Oh, uh…" He means Landry. Hell, Maggie and her big mouth. She told Bessie about him too. No wonder George is upset.

His arms drop, and I step back, twisting my fingers together. "It's no big deal. He offered me a ride, and I felt sorry for him. He seemed *so* sad. I know it was stupid."

The ice drains, replaced by heat as he glares at me. "It really was."

"Fine, I agree with you."

"We still don't know who killed Lainey. We haven't ruled out the family as suspects, and Landry doesn't have an alibi."

My eyebrows shoot upward. "Are you saying that you think he killed his sister? No way! He wouldn't do that."

"There's no proof he didn't do it, Mala," George says in a solemn tone that raises the hairs on the back of my neck. He believes what he's telling me. Could I be wrong? My gut tells me Landry's grief is too raw to be faked, but he's fooled me before. I'd hate to think he's that good of an actor or that I'm gullible enough to fall for his lies twice.

I lean against the hot hood of the car. "What about the guy that Lainey was seeing? Have you figured out who he is yet?"

George's mouth tightens. "You haven't said anything to anyone about that, have you?"

"No, I promised, didn't I? I keep my promises." And I protect my friends. I think on Landry's confession about stalking me. If I tell George, he'll arrest Landry for sure. I can't do that to him, no matter how scared and angry he makes me. I know, deep down, Landry is a good person, just confused.

"Lainey's friends all agreed that the guy had money. He bought her expensive gifts—a diamond heart necklace, clothes—took her out in Lafayette. They even rented a seedy room at the Super Delight Motel, but it had been cleared out before we got the search warrant. Their whole relationship was secretive."

"Sounds like Lainey had a sugar daddy. Some guy she used for his money. He's probably married with kids." I bite my lip. Mama told Lainey to go to the baby's father for money…did she listen?

Did taking Mama's advice get her killed? "If Lainey threatened to tell his wife about the baby, it would be the perfect motive for murder."

"I thought so too." We share a look. A meeting of the minds.

Heat floods through me. I've impressed him, for sure. "Oh, I almost forgot. Landry said that Dr. Rathbone's real close to Reverend Prince. He slipped them the autopsy results about Lainey. Did you track down where the drug came from?"

"She had trazodone in her system. Not enough to kill, but it probably knocked her out. It's an antidepressant, but some people use it as a sleep aid."

"Oh?" I say, softly. "So she might have been taking the drug to deal with depression and finding it in her system might not have anything to do with the killer."

George sits on the hood next to me. "Exactly! I'm at a dead end until we get a court order for Lainey's medical records. I do have some good news..." His voice trails off, and he looks at me expectantly.

"Spill it, Georgie."

"Well, this should set your mind at ease. Andy and his dog found the spot where Lainey was thrown in the bayou. It's about a half mile from where you found her. Forest Service land. Unfortunately, there are dozens of side roads into the park. That's another dead end."

"At least she didn't die on our property." *Thank God.*

George's grin makes his eyes sparkle with golden flecks amid the green. "You know, it's funny. Before I took this job, I never realized that most folks don't want to hear the gory details of my cases. I enjoy talking to you. It helps to work things out with someone else. You've got me thinking of taking the investigation in a different direction."

I'm so stuffed full of pride that I bet I'm glowing. "I'm glad I could help."

George stiffens, rising to his feet. "What does *he* want?"

I look over my shoulder and groan. Landry stands five feet from the car with his hands shoved in his pockets. Wind blows his hair back and a strange, unreadable expression fills his handsome face. *Oh God, did he overhear our conversation about Lainey?*

Chapter 17

Landry

Unmitigated Stupidity

Stay calm. Don't do or say anything you'll regret.

My gaze meets Mala's. She hates me. It flares in her eyes. I royally fucked up at Ruby's. Then made things worse in Munchies with Clarice, but she didn't have to go all dark side on me. Her words still echo in my head: "I don't want him..." Did she say it knowing how much it would hurt? Was it her way of getting even with me for accusing her of murder? Is she deliberately throwing her relationship with George in my face to make a point...to see me squirm like a worm on a hook?

No, she's not like Clarice. She doesn't toy with guys for shits and giggles. *Focus. Don't lose control.*

I have to keep reminding myself of this. I watched them from across the street. How George held her in his arms. The jealousy almost made me lose my mind. I wanted to ram my truck into the patrol car, damn the consequences.

I take a deep breath and step toward them. "Mala, I—"

George pulls Mala behind him, blocking her from view. "What the devil's going on, Prince?"

My jaw clenches when he lays hands on her. I pause a second, then say, "I came to see if Mala's okay."

"What's it to you?"

"She's my friend, George."

Mala sticks her head around George's back. Her eyes spark, like an obsidian arrowhead, sharp and cutting. "We're not friends, Landry. Friends don't accuse friends of…" She trails off with a hiss. I fill in the blank: *Murder.*

George picks up on her distress. "What did he accuse you of?"

"It doesn't matter," she says. "I told him earlier to leave me alone."

"I can't do that, Mala," I say. "I can't let you think…I'd never hurt you."

"But you already did. And Clarice, you hurt her too."

God, that girl! "What does Clarice have to do with us? She doesn't decide who I choose to spend time with."

"Tell her that."

George's head swivels back and forth between us. His face grows redder and redder with each word we speak. "Enough! I don't have time for your lovers' quarrel."

"We are *so* not lovers, Georgie. You of all people should know that," Mala snaps. The disgust in her voice punches a hole in my gut. Not lovers. Why should George know? Is he her lover? Oh, hell! Mom's friends gossip about George. How he's on track to becoming the youngest detective at BPSO. How he's handsome and well mannered. And his dad's rich and influential. Perfect. I don't stand a chance against him.

"Get in the car, Mala," George says firmly. "Landry, get out of here."

I frown. "Is that an order, Deputy Dawg?"

"Yeah."

I'm done taking orders. I pull my hands from my pockets and ball them into fists. My body visibly vibrates with tension. "You think because you have a badge and gun you can tell me what to do?"

George steps forward, his hand resting on the butt of his Taser. "If you're harassing her, then you're damn right I'm ordering you. I told you yesterday to keep your distance. You should've listened." George's voice has gone gunslinger low, and his normally cheerful green eyes are flat, hard as bottle glass. This is the face he wears when doing a traffic stop on a criminal or breaking up a domestic abuse disturbance. It chills me to the bone.

Reminds me not to be a fool.

"Fine, you win." I bend down and reach behind the wheel of the patrol car where I'd set Mala's purse. The Taser clears George's holster so fast that I barely see him draw. "Hands where I can see them, Prince!"

"Oh shit," I whisper, shaking. My hands rise into the air, and the purse dangles over the street. "Whoa, don't shoot, buddy."

"Georgie, it's okay," Mala says, laying her hand on his tense arm. He's already replaced the Taser, but he still holds himself as if prepared for a fight.

"Mala left her purse in my truck this morning," I say, voice hoarse.

"Hand it to me," George orders, holding out his hand.

"No." I clear my throat and move the purse out of reach. "It's hers. I'll give it to her, not you."

She steps around George and strides over. "I'll take it."

I meet Mala's worried gaze, and she grimaces. I know exactly how she feels. "When are you gonna forgive me?" I ask.

"Not now," she says, echoing my earlier words to me.

"Fair enough. I'll see you tomorrow."

"Arrogant *ass*!"

George frowns. "Mala, get in the car."

She turns on her heel, walks over to the patrol car, and slides into the front seat without a backward glance. George stands in front of her door with his arms crossed. He doesn't seem inclined to leave until he sees my back walking away. I don't go to the truck. I can't drive. I'm too pissed. I stalk past Munchies and ignore the people in the window who had a front-row seat for the whole confrontation and turn into the alley next to Revo's Boot World. The overpowering odor of rotten food and piss hit my nose. I draw in a deep breath.

I'm bricked in by buildings on either side. Nothing but trash around me. How fitting.

Fuck! My fist slams into Munchies' brick wall. I curse again at the unmitigated stupidity of my punching a wall. Unmitigated, yeah, the perfect four-dollar word to emphasize how idiotic I feel at getting my ass handed to me by that prick George. Maybe I wouldn't be so pissed if he hadn't tried to Tase me in front of Mala or if he hadn't had his hands all over her. And did she stop him? No!

"Oh, Georgie, you're so *awesome*," I parrot in my high-pitched Mala voice, which sounds exactly like her. The worst part is that I drove her into his arms. I betrayed her, but I *had* to ask Lainey if Mala killed her. Not knowing would've driven me insane.

I hadn't expected for George to treat me like I'm shit stuck to the bottom of his boot. Did Mala tattle to him about my stalking her? Or did Clarice say something after I left? That bitch can be vicious to her enemies, and Mala has moved into her number-one slot because of me. I hadn't realized how possessive Clarice had become until she put her claim on me in front of everyone.

I kick the metal Dumpster. A bag of trash slides from the top of a pile, spilling out rotting food, and I gag. The steel in my boots protects my toes from serious injury, and the resulting pain releases the anger churning inside of me. I slowly back away from the Dumpster, breathing hard. Rage still boils beneath the surface. I need to release it before I explode.

The perfect opportunity saunters down the alley in the pockmarked form of Redford Delahoussaye and his two hillbilly cousins—uncle, cousins, who the hell knows with that inbred family? One of them, Billy, I think, carries a baseball bat over his shoulder. All three guys outweigh me by a lot, but not one has the muscle. They're more into fried chicken and pigs' feet than salads. They can't take me in a fair fight, but I don't plan on giving them one even if they could.

Red sends a nasty grin in my direction. Too many bar fights and bad dental hygiene have made Red a very snaggle-tooth boy.

"You got a problem?" I stare at Red, licking the blood off my grazed knuckles. He's Clarice's older brother. We've tangled since we were kids. Maybe that's why he brought family to back him up. I didn't expect him to show up since he works on an oil rig out in the gulf, but I guess I should've expected someone from Clarice's large clan after what happened in Munchies.

The question is whether he came for me or Mala.

"Where's your girlfriend?"

Wrong answer.

I lean down and pick up a length of steel rebar lodged against the wall. I bounce it on my palm, then adjust my grip, feeling the ridged lines. Excitement makes my hands tingle, and my heart races as adrenaline courses through my body. A grin stretches my mouth. Billy and the other cousin share a glance. I'm guessing the smile doesn't look too happy.

God, this feels good—not having to back off. I can't afford to go to jail for hitting a cop, but these guys...whole other story.

Red raises his hands, palms upward. "I didn't come for you, Prince."

"Too bad. 'Cause you got me instead of a helpless girl."

"The witch didn't sound so helpless when she was cursing my sister." Red steps forward, holding his hand out. Billy glances at him, then hands him the bat. His cockiness fades once he loses his weapon. "Gotta say, I'm looking forward to kicking your ass. I never liked you, but Clary thinks the sun rises and sets on you."

"Then she's an idiot. Guess it runs in the family."

Red slams the bat against the wall. The sound of metal on brick echoes through the alley. It sets my teeth on edge and jolts my anticipation a notch higher. I'm trembling, I'm so juiced.

"Are you seriously trying to start shit?" Red yells.

"Who followed who into the alley?" I squint at him a second then shrug. "You know what? Who gives a fuck...less talking..."

Red doesn't stand a chance. No way am I gonna let him walk knowing he's after Mala. I aim my first swing of the bar at the arm holding the bat. He blocks the swing, but the recoil makes his fingers spasm. The bat drops from his hand. When he lunges for it, I kick his leg out from under him, and he goes to the ground with a howl.

Billy and the other guy stare at Red. The shock on their faces almost doubles me over it's so funny. Their faces pale, and their mouths hang open. I throw open my arms. "Come on!" I shout, chest rising. "You want me? Let's go."

Bravery comes in pairs. It builds when you're not alone. Strength in numbers and all that. I could've told them it's a load of bull. It's not about bravery but about how much damage you can withstand without folding. About how motivated the opponent is. I'm exceptionally motivated, and I don't have anything to lose.

Except Mala, and I won't give her up without a fight.

They run at me with shouts. I toss the steel bar to the side. I won't fight unarmed guys with a weapon. I duck Billy's swing, coming upward to nail him in the gut. The air whooshes out of him. The other guy hits my blind side. I don't know if it's a punch or a kick, but I take it in my still-bruised ribs. I stumble back, raising my arms. The uppercut slams into my chin. Where the head goes, the body follows. It's the law.

I slam into the Dumpster, stunned. Flickering lights spark in front of my eyes. I don't wait for my vision to clear. It's what this guy's waiting for—to take advantage of my confusion. I push off against the Dumpster, aiming my body in the direction I last saw him. He must've had the same thought. Our chests collide in midair. The impact knocks us to the ground. I recover faster, pulling myself on top of him and punching him in the face…once, twice. My arm goes back for another, but a hand grabs on. Billy shoves me off his bloody friend and tries to drag him away.

"What?" I scramble to my feet. My chest heaves as I try to catch my breath. "This isn't over. I'm still standing. Come on!"

"Let it go, man," Billy whimpers. "This ain't about you. Tell him, Red."

"It's about my girl." I kick at Red, who's lying with his back against the wall. He sees my steel-toed boot aimed for his face and ducks. "You think I'll let you go?"

Wild laughter barks out of me. It sounds manic, like I've gone batshit crazy. Maybe I have. Time to stick me in a padded room. "God, Lainey. What have you done to me?"

Billy glances at Red with wide eyes. *Shit.* I said the words out loud.

"I'm sorry," Red says, climbing the wall with his hands. "About Lainey, I'm sorry."

"This doesn't have anything to do with my sister." I brush my hand across burning eyes. "Leave Malaise LaCroix alone. I won't come at you straight if you go after her." I shove through them. "And you won't be crawling away the next time. I'll break every bone in your fucking body. Believe that if nothing else."

Chapter 18

Mala

Magnolia

George focuses on navigating the road leading to my house. When we round the corner and start up the hill, I see a familiar truck parked in the driveway.

"Oh, thank God! Mama's home." I open the door and jump out before the car comes to a complete stop. I stick my head back in through the open door and grab my purse. "Thanks for the ride, Georgie."

I slam the door on his response and run for the house.

"Mama," I yell, bursting through the front door. "You're not gonna believe how crazy my day's been."

"Hold on to your britches, *cher*. It's about to get crazier," Mama says, coming out of the kitchen followed by an old woman who sends chills racing down my spine.

I freeze, afraid to move farther into my own house. The air vibrates with a malignancy that sets off warning sirens in my brain. It takes all my strength not to run. I can't leave Mama alone, though even that isn't the truth. My legs won't listen. I've shut down—trapped in the hypnotic gaze of a predator.

The woman stares at me with pale brown eyes that have a golden cast. Her yellowed, parchment-thin skin stretches over high cheekbones dotted with liver spots that would've been considered freckles in her long-ago youth. Gray hair, long and wavy, has been pulled back into a braid that brushes the backs of her knees. She slams her silver-handled cane down on the hardwood floor with a loud *thud*, and I twitch.

"*Vin bay matant ou yon bo,*" the woman says, and smiles, showing a toothless mouth with blackened gums. She spoke in Creole, and my limited knowledge of French lets me interpret her words—"Come give your auntie a kiss"—but still, I hesitate.

Mama scowls. "Don't be rude. I taught you better." She grabs my hand and drags me over to the woman. The closer I walk, the more my skin itches. The hairs rise on my arms, and my body hums, like that tickle you get from walking under power lines.

Magnolia's eyes narrow. "You feel that, don't you?"

"*Oui*, Grand-tante Magnolia," I say, struggling to draw breath without hyperventilating.

She smiles. "I speak English." She holds her hand out to me. When I touch her, the hair all over my body stands on end. My scalp prickles. I grit my teeth because it hurts. Not the kind of hurt that comes from stubbing a toe or getting slapped silly, but a bone-deep ache that feels unnatural.

"She's a strong girl, Jasmine," Magnolia says, looking at Mama.

"Strong in the power. More powerful than you, and you got your full gift. When you die, this girl's gonna be fearsome."

I jerk my hand from hers and take a step back. "Mama's not dying anytime soon."

"Sooner than you both think." Magnolia lets out a low cackle. "Visions only come when the death is so violent that the passing shreds apart time."

Shreds time? Is she talking about time travel? "I don't understand. Are you saying Mama's dreaming of her future death—now—in the past?"

Magnolia's lips lift in a knowing smile. "*Oui, cher.*"

I shake my head in denial. "I'm not a genius so I'm not real familiar with the science behind time travel, but if what you're saying is true"—I look at Mama and frown—"then the…the what would you call it, psychic energy? Spirit?" I search Magnolia's face for some clue that I'm on the right track, 'cause the direction my thoughts are heading in chills me to the bone.

Magnolia cocks her head to the side. Her amber eyes brighten, but her face stays blank. Why? She knows the answer. Why doesn't she just tell me? Or is this a test? Doesn't exactly seem fair, using me as a chew bone, but I have to play along. For now.

I suck in a deep breath then spit out my answer so fast the words trip over my tongue. "So, this *death energy* is rippling into her past. Like a movie on a loop, replaying over and over, allowing her to see a vision of her future." I feel my way along this line of thought to its horrifying conclusion. "She's already dead. Nothing I do now can change what will happen to her."

"Not a damn thing," Magnolia agrees.

Bullshit! I refuse to believe that. I watched *Sliders* and *Fringe*;

even *Stargate* had episodes about parallel universes. So what if the time stream gets messed up if I save Mama's life now? Future Mala's life probably sucks. She'd want me to figure out a way to save Mama. And I will.

I glare at Magnolia, disliking the smug tilt on her liver-lips. The woman ignores me. She clumps across the room and sits on the sofa. "My, Jasmine," she says to Mama, "she's smart too. Not like you. I tried to explain this as we drove up here, but your brain's too full of holes from that moonshine you've been drinkin'."

"Why else would I be drinkin'?" Mama laughs. "Might as well enjoy what little time I got left."

"Stupid woman," Magnolia says with a shake of her head.

The way she talks to Mama makes me angry. Then I smell the liquor wafting off Mama's breath.

"*Oui*, Jasmine's been drinking since we got here. She forgets she's got to drive me home. I got a date with a corpse at midnight." Magnolia cackles, slapping her knobby knee.

I shudder, imagining her in the graveyard performing some sort of ritual. I hope a zombie eats her brain. The nasty old bat. No wonder she and her twin, Grandmère Dahlia, fell out. How could two women be such complete opposites in temperament yet come from the same womb?

"I thought I had more time to relax." Mama shoots me a disgusted look and falls hard into the armchair. A bottle sits on the end table next to her. "You're home early."

"I didn't ride the bus home today." I wish I could tell her why, but when she's in this condition, she doesn't care about anything but the drink. I give her up as a lost cause and address Auntie

Magnolia. "Why are you here? Not that I'm not happy to meet you, but it's a long drive from New Orleans."

"Despite what my sister thought about me, I value kin. Didn't have no kids of my own. It's why you're so powerful. You the last LaCroix girl, child. The power's split through our family lines, doled out from the mother upon her death throughout the generations. But it's all tied to you now. It's gonna blow your mind to bits."

"Yay for me," I drawl, but shiver.

Magnolia smiles. "Good, you got some spunk. Gonna help keep you strong, maybe even keep you sane. Jasmine said you've got a spirit haunting you?"

"Yes." I glance at Mama, but she's slumped in the chair. Her eyes are closed, and the soft buzz of a snore comes from her. "I went to a medium today, Madame Rubine, to see if she could figure out what the ghost wanted."

Mama snorts, eyes cracking open, and I cringe. "That fraud? Thought I told you to leave it be while I was gone."

"I know. I'm sorry. I thought it would help, but Lainey got inside Ruby. She spoke through her, and I swear, Ruby's nose started bleeding. She looked bad, real bad."

Magnolia nods. "Her mind wasn't strong enough. That spirit destroyed her."

"What do you mean, destroyed?" I ask.

"Scoured her mind. Never mind her. She's dead by now."

Shocked, I stumble back. "Dead? What?"

"Would've happened within a few hours of possession. Nothing to be done about it. Even if she went to the hospital, the bleeding in her brain would've still killed her."

Oh my God, it can't be true! She looked like she'd been wrung out and put away wet when we left, but she said she'd be okay. And I believed her because I was too angry with Landry to care. I should've stayed…done something. Her poor little boy. "It's my fault. I killed her," I mutter, barely able to speak over the lump in my throat. The awful revelations keep dropping faster than I can process them. First Mama, now Ruby. Is everyone I come into contact with cursed?

Magnolia's head tilts, and her beady eyes focus on me, like a crow eyeing roadkill. "You paid her, didn't you? She offered to open up her mind to the spirit. That's the only way it works. You got to be willing. It was her choice to make, *cher*. Not your fault she was stupid."

"At least it wasn't you, Mala," Mama says.

"No, I refused. The last time Lainey came for me, I didn't have any memory of her taking over. It scared me."

"Scared me too," Magnolia says with a gap-toothed smile. "That's why I cleared my afternoon appointments to come help you. You ain't supposed to be feeling the spirits so strongly, but you're getting a taste of the power you'll inherit after your mother dies. It's seeping into the past just like Jasmine's death vision. Tell me true, have you been feeling poorly lately?"

I rub my aching head. "I've had a bit of a cold."

Magnolia shakes her head. "*Non, ma petite*. That's the spirit eating up your life force in order to manifest. It'll suck you dry—driving you crazy. Unless you learn to control it, you'll wither away in a mental hospital unable to tell real from vision. Or die."

I pace in front of her, too jittery to be still. Power from three generations of LaCroix witches hums like a live wire stretched between us. I can't deny the connection because it zings through me, filling me up until I feel like I'll explode if I don't use it. My teeth chatter as I ask, "Are you saying this to frighten me?"

"Is it working, *cher*? Don't want you blaming me later, saying I never told you what you were up against. We got to put a wall up to keep this spirit bound."

"Will it get rid of Lainey?"

"No, she'll be hovering on the other side, waiting for an opening. Long as you keep the wall up, she won't be able to get to you. Mind you, this is temporary. Jasmine agreed you need to come to New Orleans for a few weeks. You'll be my apprentice. Learn how to build shields against this kind of psychic invasion. Don't want you ending up roaming around crazy like your mother or locked up in a funny farm. That's what happens to those with the Sight that don't get any training."

"But I don't want—" *to learn hoodoo.*

"Malaise Jean LaCroix, don't disrespect your auntie," Mama snaps. "She's gracious enough to help. This is all she asks in return."

I backtrack fast. "I was going to say, I don't want to be a burden." Which is a piece of the truth, just not all, and I hold onto the rest of my protest since it won't do any good. I have to learn how to control this magic even if it means being apprenticed to a conjure woman. I don't want to die or go crazy. 'Sides, I don't have to be wicked and learn how to raise the dead and twist dark curses. I can choose to be a good witch like Great-grandmère Dahlia.

Magnolia watches me with narrowed eyes and a smirk that

makes me think she listened in and believes my justifications are naive. When I meet her gaze, she says, "Good, let's finish this up. I want to get on the road 'fore it gets too late. Rush-hour traffic's gonna be fearsome if we hit Baton Rouge at the wrong time." She reaches into the pocket of her lacy black jacket, pulls out a tin of chewing tobacco, and stuffs a glob into her mouth. She gums the mix, and a bit of brown drool slides down her pointed chin. She catches my stare and the shudder I can't hold back and points toward the door. "Close your mouth 'fore you catch flies and grab my bag."

I follow her finger to a black leather satchel almost hidden between the umbrella stand and the front door. "Saints, it's heavy. How do you carry this?"

"That's what your mama's for."

I frown in surprise when I glance at Mama's toothpick arms. Though from experience, I know she packs a wallop and is stronger than she looks. "What's in here?" I carry it over and drop it at Magnolia's feet, careful to miss her toes. She leans over and paws through it, too busy working her chaw to speak.

The hand that carried the bag feels dirty, like I ran it through a layer of rotting scum. I wipe my palm on my jeans, wishing for some hand sanitizer.

Magnolia glances at me knowingly. "Get me a spit can unless you want to be scrubbing these floors tonight, though, by the looks of them, they could stand a good cleansing."

I tense up at the insult. The floor sparkles, clean enough to eat off of. I know that for a fact since I mopped the night before. *The old bat!* I tremble with suppressed anger and stalk toward the kitchen. At the doorway, I pause to look at Mama. She normally doesn't take criticism well, and I'm surprised she didn't chime in. But she's curled up in the chair and passed out, clutching her bottle of moonshine to her breast. A small smile lifts the corners of her lips—at least one of us is happy. She did her job by getting Magnolia here without getting her liver eaten. The duty of being a good hostess falls on me.

"Would you like me to pour you a glass of tea while I'm in the kitchen?" I ask Magnolia, in a voice as sweet as the mint tea I'll serve. "I can also microwave up a bowl of turtle soup?"

"No, that's fine, *cher*. Had Jasmine run through the drive-through at Popeyes—got some leftover red beans and rice and a bucketful of chicken sitting in the truck going bad in this heat. Best get a move on so I can be on my way."

"Okay." I run into the kitchen and bring her a metal coffee can.

"Sit it here by my feet," Magnolia orders and, without looking up, hawks a wad of tobacco juice into the can with spooky accuracy. I jerk my hand back with a squeal of disgust, but the juice doesn't even come close to splattering me. Practice makes perfect, I guess.

Magnolia thrusts a piece of paper into my hand. "Here, follow these directions."

I hold the paper up close to my face then invert the page that I'm trying to read upside down. The tiny, spidery handwriting makes my eyes cross. "It's written in French," I complain.

Magnolia spits again, and a metallic *ding* fills the air. "Never learned to write spells in English." She levels an evil eye on Mama's sleeping form. "Jasmine said you read French."

"Barely. I had two years in school. I might still have one of my old textbooks. Can't you just show me what to do?"

"It'll take too much time. Hold out your hands." She starts pulling leather bags tied with drawstrings out of her satchel. "This here's salt. Sprinkle it around doors and windows. It'll keep the spirits out of the house as long as you don't scrub your foot through the line and break the seal."

I pry open the bag and give it a test sniff. 'Cause really? I've got Morton Salt in my cupboard. How is this stuff any different?

Magnolia stands so swiftly that I blink in surprise; sure I'm mistaken when she leans heavily on her cane. "This here's a juju bag. Keep it on your body at all times, and it'll protect you from the spirits." The spidery fingers clutching the small cloth bag slide down the front of my T-shirt and into my bra.

I dance backward with a yelp. "Personal space, Auntie."

"No such thing, Apprentice. Best learn that quick."

My nose twitches at the smell wafting from my bosom. Snot forms in my nasal passages, and I sneeze. I raise a hand to cover my mouth, and the supplies I'm holding fall to the ground. "What's in this? Are you trying to kill me?" I dig into my shirt to pull the bag free, but every time my fingers brush against it, it shifts from my grip like it's skittering about on furry legs.

I sneeze again and groan. "I think I'm allergic." I sneeze three times in a row and stagger, which, ironically, saves me when the tip of the silver cane swipes at my head.

I drop down into a backward roll and come up in a crouch, balanced on the balls of my feet like I've been possessed by the spirit of a ninja. Or a cat hopped up on catnip. Neither option reflects my normal skill level, which freaks me out even more.

"Quick too," Magnolia mumbles, setting the end of the cane back on the floor.

"You tried to hit me." I stand, struggling to control the fury building inside of me.

Magnolia returns my glare with a menacing light that brightens her eyes to a golden glow. "But I missed. I misjudged. Next time, I won't."

"There won't be a next time, Auntie!" My voice resonates as a low growl. I don't sound anything like myself. My body trembles, and I rush the old bat.

I'm gonna launch her headfirst through a wall.

Chapter 19

Mala

Biggest and Baddest

Rage surrounds my body—a tainted black aura hovering above my skin that crackles with raw energy. Hate throbs. Burning and consuming like fire until only the ashes float through my mind. Of my conscious thoughts, there's nothing but the desire to destroy.

Magnolia doesn't move when I reach for her. My hands land an inch above her shoulders. I try to scream at the burning agony racing up my arms, but no sound passes my tightening throat. I can't even draw air into my lungs. I drop to my knees and cower before Magnolia with my hands cradled to my chest. Smoke mixed with the odor of burnt flesh sears my nostrils.

"You dare attack me, *cher*," she whispers.

Her arthritic hand reaches for my face, and I rear back. The hand fists and then rotates counterclockwise. My intestines form into a knot, imitating the twisting of her hand, as if she's reached inside my stomach and wrings out my guts like they're wet clothes going on the line.

Sweat runs down my face. I stare up at Magnolia, panting. "You're not strong enough to best me," she taunts with a toothless smile, and I know she's right. I glance at Mama for help, but she's passed out. Why can't she ever be there for me when I need her? Even when she's in the room, I'm alone. Helpless.

Maybe Magnolia reads the defeat in my eyes because she releases her fist. The pain in my stomach eases. When she reaches for my hands, I'm too afraid to pull away. She peels open my clenched fingers, and I whimper at the sight of black, flaking skin. "Magic for us is like breathing. It comes naturally from deep inside," she says. "It forms by our will. You only have to think of what you want and that desire becomes reality if you got the know-how." Breath ranker than a septic tank blows across my palms. My eyes close against the pain in my tingling hands. It hurts worse than when blood returns to a limb that has fallen asleep. "This is Lesson One, Apprentice."

God, please save me from Lesson Two.

The springs in the couch creak. Magnolia sits before me with her cane resting across her bony knees. "Now, where were we?"

I struggle to stand up, finally placing a hand to the ground. There's no pain. I lift my palms close to my eyes, studying the unmarked surface. "You healed me."

"Would you prefer I leave you broken?"

I grit my teeth, rising, but I don't get too close. Magnolia is crazy, which means unpredictable. I'd be a fool to challenge her again, but I'd be even crazier to let her stay. The rage still simmers inside me. I wasn't in control the first time I went after her. The rage took over. I'm more scared of what I'll do if she lays hands on me again than of what she'd do to me in retaliation. "I'd *prefer* if you left. Get out!"

"What did you say?" Her eyes still have that insane glitter, but I don't care.

"I said get out of my house." I kick Mama's chair, and she wakes with a snort.

The bottle falls to the ground, and moonshine pours onto the floor. "Oh, no," Mama wails, sliding from the chair. She lifts the bottle then bends over to place her lips to the spreading puddle and laps the liquid off the floor like a dog.

"Mama!"

She looks up with disgust. "Look what you made me do, Mala. What's the matter with you?" She glances from me to Magnolia. "What's going on?"

"Time for Auntie to get the hell out."

"But did you get what you needed to help with the spirits?"

"I'll take spirits over a crazy woman swinging a cane at my head and burning me."

Mama's eyes narrow in on Magnolia. "You hurt my baby?"

"Just a test."

Mama's lips purse but she remains thoughtful. What's with the women in this family thinking it's all right to resort to violence? I'm no angel, but at least I don't deliberately put out the welcome mat for the devil to take over my soul.

"Oh, no, Mama. That excuse won't cut it. I've been whaled on enough today. I'm not tolerating my own family taking shots at me."

The bubbling fury I've been struggling to control boils over, dark and pulsing. Red tinges my vision, and pressure builds inside my head. The air inside the house dips, like I turned on the swamp cooler. Goose bumps rise on my arms. The room pulses—a restless heartbeat within the walls. The floor buckles upward, tossing Mama's collection of knickknacks and curios off the shelves, and poor Velvet Elvis falls off the wall, the frame splintering when it smashes against the floor.

Fear tightens the corners of Magnolia's golden eyes, and I realize the rage isn't solely mine.

"Uh-oh," I whisper. "It's Lainey."

Magnolia shakes her head. "This ain't no everyday spirit." She sticks out her snakelike tongue and tastes the air with a dry hiss. Her eyes widen. "Oh, girl, what you conjure up?"

"I don't know," I cry, moving closer to her. She took me down with the twist of a hand. Surely she can banish whatever hormonal poltergeist threatens to demolish my house into splinters.

Magnolia backs up, hands raised in warning. "Don't come close to me. You fine. This an ancestor spirit sent to protect you."

"Protect me from what?"

"Oh, he's angry. Oh my, yes." She caresses the air with her hands. "He seeks to protect you from harm, never knowing he's the true danger to your soul. He fights to keep the girl's spirit from you, but it's a battle that spills over like a cup overflowing with tea. The cup—that's your mind, I'm speaking metaphorically."

"I figured as much."

"Like I said, you a smart-ass girl."

The floor shakes again, and I grab onto the back of the sofa for support. Magnolia picks up her bag and gestures to Mama who's curled up in a trembling ball underneath her chair. "Let's go, Jasmine."

"No wait, Mama." I turn to Magnolia, ignoring the fact I just tried to kick her out. I'd rather spend the night dodging her cane than trying to ride out the bucking bronco that has become my home. "Please, don't leave me alone with *him*."

"Girl, you can't escape an ancestor spirit. He's always gonna be with you, protecting you in his own way. He's angry at me. Not you. He'll settle after I leave." She lifts her cane to prod Mama in the back with the tip, and I flinch. The floor shakes again, and Magnolia's arms flail as she tries to keep her balance. Her face drains of color, leaving her freckles standing out against the bland backdrop. Whatever illusion she used to hide her wrinkles vanishes.

"Let's go, Jasmine. You sobered up enough to drive, or do I need to go into my bag of tricks for some special medicine?" She winks at me, obviously over her previous scare, and I shiver at the callousness of the woman. "Tastes real bad," she finishes with a laugh.

* * *

From the porch, I watch them drive off. New Orleans is two and a half hours, maybe three from here, depending on traffic. It'll be dark by the time Mama reaches Magnolia's house, and she'll spend the night again before returning home. Even as the dust of their passing fades, I remain sitting in the rocking chair, afraid to go inside. It was bad enough knowing the spirit of Lainey haunted the house. Learning that she isn't the biggest and baddest thing on the block terrifies me.

So I rock, staring out across the lawn as the sun lowers and shadows obscure the distant tree line. A cool breeze picks up, blowing across my skin. Crickets wake and start their nightly chirping. So do the mosquitoes. I dig out the juju bag wedged between my breasts and lay it out on the side table next to my chair.

Carefully, I dissect the ingredients, laying them in coordinating piles: animal bones, a large root that smells like cherry and cinnamon and a mix of other unidentifiable spices that makes it unique, a stone with a natural hole in the middle, other stuff I can only shrug over, and dried sage. The sage turns out to be the principal source of my misery. I toss the dried leaves over the porch railing and watch them scatter in the wind.

"I don't want any part of this hoodoo shit," I say aloud, sweeping the remaining ingredients back into the bag. I close my eyes and quickly throw the bag into the yard. When I open them to stare into the tall grass, there is nothing to show where it landed. "I should throw out the rest of that mumbo jumbo stuff too."

The rocking chair beside mine tilts forward, but unlike when the wind blows, it doesn't rock back, just remains tilted like whoever sits next to me leaned forward to better hear me.

I swallow hard. "Lainey?"

The chair doesn't move.

"Who are you?" I whisper.

The chair snaps back violently, tilting over backward to fall to the ground with a loud crash. My heart almost leaps out of my throat. I jump to my feet. "Keep away!" I scramble for the door, open it a crack wide enough to slide through, and slam it behind me. "Stupid! So stupid, Mala. It's a ghost. It can cross through walls."

Why did I throw away the juju bag? Why? Sure, I hate Magnolia with the passion of the damned. If I use her magic, I'm beholden to her. I'll end up as her slave, digging up corpses in a cemetery for all eternity. Unless the stupid ghost puts me in a grave first. I'm thinking this is a survive-to-fight-another-day scenario.

I run to the bedroom. My skin prickles. Someone or something watches as I grab my French textbook off the bookshelf. My brain races unable to focus as the words jumble. Letters like daddy longlegs skitter across the page. I chase their meaning, but I'm so freaked out it takes ten minutes to translate the directions Magnolia left for me. Part of me scoffs at my actions. A little niggle of doubt that this stuff really works keeps popping into my mind. Then I glance out the window to the newly upright chair rocking on the porch. Maybe the wind blows it—maybe not. If sprinkling salt in the corners of each room, across the windows and outer thresholds, and circling the house with brick dust keeps unwanted spirits out, then isn't it worth it?

By the time the sun sets, I'm ready to cast the final protection spell. "This better work—it'll suck if I burn the house down by accident," I mutter, before lighting the candles while reciting the Lord's Prayer. Whether it's hoodoo or the grace of God, I don't know, but peace fills the house now. I didn't even notice how uncomfortable being inside made me feel until the sensation faded with each waft of smoke from the herbal candles.

I fall into bed around midnight, glad I don't have to fight Mama for the blankets because I'm exhausted. The next morning,

I roll out of bed with a peaceful smile on my lips because, for the first time in four days, I don't wake screaming.

Landry's truck sits in the driveway when I stroll out of the house at a quarter to eight. I'm in such a glorious mood that I don't bother trying to sneak off without him catching sight of me. It would've been easy, I learn upon climbing on the bumper and sticking my head through the truck's open window. He has the seat pushed back and his legs stretched out kitty-corner across the passenger seat. Snores, loud enough to scare a bear, echo through the cab.

I reach in and poke his shoulder a few times. "Wake up, Sleeping Beauty."

Landry's thick lashes flutter then open to meet mine. "I'm supposed to be woken with a kiss, not a jab."

I snort. "I don't kiss slimy critters. You're playing double duty as a frog, and I throw *them* in a frying pan with a little butter and garlic."

"Oh, so *now* you're trying to butter me up?"

The heat of a blush rises. "Saints, boy. You're fraying my last nerve." I plant my hands on my hips, toe tapping. "What are you doing here? In case you forgot, I'm mad at you."

"No you're not." He grins and runs his fingers through his thick hair. My breath catches as my brain stutters. I shake my head to dispel the wave of pheromone-induced stupidity that washes over me. My nose twitches. Why does he have to smell so good? Like cinnamon and brown sugar. "Did you forget yester—"

An oily paper bag flies in my direction. I grab it out of the air before it drops to the ground. It's warm in my hands, and the smell makes my mouth water. "Ooh, cinnamon rolls," I mumble around the melting mouthful of cinnamony goodness. "I love these."

"I know," Landry says, throwing open the truck door.

I hop off the bumper with a scowl. The arrogant jerk thinks he has me eating out of his hands; all he has to do is flutter those insanely long eyelashes, smile to show off his pearly whites, and tempt me with fresh, warm buns.

"These *are* mine?" I clutch the bag to my chest as I eye him in suspicion.

"Yeah, they're your favorite, right?"

"Mmm-hmm."

Landry props his elbow on the open window and ducks his head. Black hair tangles across his face, hiding his eyes. "I hoped you'd be more accepting of my apology if I bribed you with sweets. Forgive me for being an ass yesterday?"

Lucky guy. He figured out the fastest way to soften my heartstrings—sugar. *Wait. How does he know they're my favorite?* Stupid question. It's like him knowing my nickname and my job. He pays way too much attention to me, and I'm kinda scared to ask why. I stare at my sticky fingers, then lick the icing off one by one. Landry's gaze draws my attention. He's staring at my mouth. My gut tightens in response, and I slowly lick my lips. *Get a grip. Don't trust him just because he says he's sorry.*

I concentrate on the mouthful of cinnamon roll. Each chew echoes the rapid patter of my heart. God, why does my body react like this when I'm around him? Why? He's still staring at me. Can't he tell I'm uncomfortable? Oh, I get it. He's irritating me on purpose so I can't totally ignore him.

I pass the empty bag to him. "You're not going away, are you?"

"Nope." He smiles.

Stupid question. I'm his only link to figuring out how Lainey died. The only way I'll get rid of the pesky Prince siblings for good will be to learn as much as I can about his sister's life before she passed. I just have to convince Landry of the danger of allowing his sister to possess me. The saying "Keep your enemies closer" bounces around in my head. It doesn't hurt that my enemy looks hella sexy with his sleep-rumpled hair, lazy grin…and whoa, holy bloodshot eyes.

"You drank again last night." I squint at him.

"Among other things." He rubs his face.

With a gasp, I pull down the hand trying to cover the violet bruise on his chin. "I know you're grieving, but turning to alcohol and drugs is about the most asinine thing you could do. Fighting is even stupider."

He blinks his tired eyes and sighs. "Look, I came to make up for yesterday."

Crap, I fell into his cinnamon bun trap and forgot that I'm angry with him. *Silly girl, stay firm. No sympathy.* "Well, thanks for the breakfast. Now go away!" I head toward the back of the house. The truck door slams shut, and I glance over my shoulder to see him following.

"Seriously, we need to talk without constantly being interrupted by your *boyfriend.*" Landry drawls the word, making it sound dirty.

"I don't have a boyfriend." I round the corner of the house, angling beneath the clothesline and grabbing my pink, flowered panties off the rope before Landry catches sight of them and has another reason to tease me.

Landry strolls along with his hands shoved in his pockets and a Cheshire cat grin stretching his cheeks. "Looked to me like old Georgie Porgie's got a thing for you, and the way you snuggled up in his arms said you have feelings for him too."

"Well, you're dead wrong." Red spots are flashing before my eyes. I exhale a deep breath. "Cut it out. I'm not letting you ruin my day, Frog Prince." I stomp up the stairs onto the back porch, grab two fishing rods and a can of worms, then storm down the stairs and shove them into Landry's arms. "You want to talk? Fine. We'll talk—on my terms. That means on the water. The sun's shining, and the fish will be biting if we get moving."

"Fishing?" Landry frowns at me. "Is that why you're dressed like Huck Finn's twin sister?"

"Call the fashion police," I drawl. "Oh, that's right. You and Clarice broke up."

"We weren't together."

"Like Georgie and I aren't together?" I choke on the words when Landry's face lights up. Warmth stirs in my chest and spreads upward. Merciful heavens, if I could stick my head in a hole, I'd be perfectly content.

"Well, good. Nice to know you've got better taste than to like that idiot," Landry says, eyes full of sparks. His gaze starts at my bare feet, works its way up the denim overalls, lingers for a spell on my chest that stretches the white, wife-beater tank top, then moves up to meet my glare. Yeah, that puts a damper on his lusty examination. The perv.

I huff a breath of muggy air and head for the woods, fully expecting Landry to follow. If the boy got up at the crack of dawn to bring me breakfast, a little fishing expedition won't put him off. Besides, we do need to settle some things. I push aside the thick branches hanging over the trail to the pond. Unlike the river where I found Lainey, the pond comes from an underground spring and runs clear of algae. Most days, it's safe enough to swim in. Every so often, I catch sight of a gator in there, but it moves along soon enough. The fish aren't big enough and the range is too small to support a healthy-size gator.

The path runs narrow, and branches hang down low. Landry has a time of it for a bit because the fishing poles keep getting caught up in the leaves. I finally take pity on him and take one pole. "The trail opens up in about half a mile."

Landry brushes aside the branch poking him in the head. "Good, I feared I'd lose an eye if this got worse."

"Poor baby," I say. "Look, I know the only reason you're here is to talk me into helping you with Lainey, but I'm done with all that. My auntie came and taught me how to cleanse the house. No more ghosts, so you might as well head on back home."

Landry stops dead.

I slowly turn to stare up at him. Crap, why did I drop that bomb on him? Especially when we're out in the middle of the woods. *Alone.*

Chapter 20

Mala

Gone Fishin'

I back up the way I'd retreat from an angry skunk.

Slow, careful. No sudden moves to set Landry off. I keep my voice calm as I say, "Ruby's dead. Having Lainey possess her burnt out her brain. If I'd let her enter me, I would've either died or gone crazy."

He blinks then lowers his face to study the ground. "How do you know she's dead?"

"My auntie's a two-headed conjurer—a hoodoo practitioner. Now, I don't completely believe in all that magical mumbo jumbo, but I think she told the truth about what happened to Ruby." Tears trickle down my cheeks. "Blood came out of Ruby's nose, Landry. I don't want a ghost-fried brain."

"So, that's it, then?"

I edge closer and lay a hand on his arm. His muscles tremble.

"I'm really sorry. If I could've helped, I would've, you know that. Don't you?"

"Yeah, well, I don't think Ruby's dead. I think your aunt just wanted to scare you so you wouldn't get hurt." He breathes out hard and gifts me with a smile that brings tingles racing through my palms. I move my hand from the warmth of his arm and wipe my sweaty palm on my leg. "Maybe I agree with her."

"You do?"

"I saw Ruby...Lainey fucked her up. I'm not a complete ass. If getting to the truth means you get hurt, then I'll find some other way. I'll respect your decision. Nothing I say will change your mind, right?"

I shake my head. "Not a damn thing."

"Fine. So how far is it to this fishing spot of yours?"

"Huh?" I blink up at him. *Why is everything so bright and shiny all of a sudden?*

He takes off my straw hat and sets it on his head at a jaunty angle. "Bet I can catch a bigger fish."

The boy's seriously bipolar. So am I.

Laughter bubbles up, mainly from relief at disaster being averted. But it also breaks the spell Landry put on me with his smile. The boy's more dangerous than a snake charmer. "It's not the size that counts, Landry. You're a guy, you should know that."

"Size isn't something any of the girls I've dated have complained about." He wiggles his eyebrows suggestively. I blush, wishing I kept my mouth shut.

I had no idea that he could be so funny. Maybe he's putting on an act to disguise his true feelings. He has to be upset, but it doesn't show. The trail opens to a small meadow. Wildflowers dot the waist-high grass, and the sun beats down on the dirt border-ing the pond so we don't have to worry about mud clumping to the bottom of our feet.

"There's my Daisy," I say with a proud grin, pointing to the ancient rowboat I found half sunk in the bayou after the flood last year. Nobody ever claimed my beautiful girl. I hauled her out, patched her up, and painted her green with tiny white daisies. Maggie and Tommy helped me move her here.

Landry stares at her skeptically. "Not sure Daisy will hold the both of us."

"Chicken, don't you insult my girl. She's perfectly sound." I take the rods and bait from Landry and put them in the boat with my tackle box, then get in myself. "Don't just stand there. Shove her in."

"Shove, huh?" He raises an eyebrow. I blink, not sure what he's insinuating, and he shakes his head, saying "Seriously, this is the only reason you dragged me out here? So you don't have to get your feet wet?"

"You're a big strong guy," I say with a flirtatious grin that I don't think will actually work on Landry, but he sighs. He sits down on a rock, pulls off his black boots, and rolls up his jeans. I give a wolf whistle. "Nice legs."

"If I actually thought you meant it, I'd blush." He places his hands on the wooden bow and pushes. The muscles in his arms and back bulge underneath his gray T-shirt, and my mouth goes dry. "Sure this isn't going to sink?" he grunts.

I clear my throat. "S-sure, yeah. I mean no, it won't…"

He catches me staring, and it's my turn to blush. "Ooh, so you don't like me, but the muscles turn you on."

"I'm not dead. I like muscles," I say, then grimace. *Stupid, dead reference.* I peek at him from beneath my lashes, hoping he hasn't noticed my slip of the tongue. He has his own tongue pressed to his top lip as he struggles to move the boat stuck in the dried mud. "Do you need help?"

"How much do you weigh? You look like such a tiny thing, but dang you're made of white dwarf metal."

"Holy Moses." I jump into the water. "Move back. I've got this."

Landry backs up and crosses his muscular arms. "This I gotta see."

"Watch and learn, city boy." I rock Daisy from side to side then give a good shove. The bow shoots out of my hands and into the water. I tumble forward, doing a face-plant into the mud, and roll onto my butt with a shout. "You did this!"

Landry raises an eyebrow. "Oh, really?"

"You faker." I rise to wade into the water, rinsing mud out of my eyes. Why did I fool myself into believing all those bulging muscles couldn't dislodge my tiny boat from the mud? Because the boy has me wrapped around his little finger. My gullibility has reached legendary status.

With a heave, I pull myself up onto Daisy's side, teetering on the edge of falling back into the water. Hands wrap around my waist, then I'm airborne. I land flat on my stomach across the wooden bench. All the air whooshes out of me.

Daisy tips when Landry climbs inside. A wicked light fills his eyes. "Are you okay?"

"C-c-can't b-breathe," I wheeze, tears filling my eyes.

"Sorry about that."

I sit up rubbing my chest. "You're still trying to kill me."

"No," Landry says with a firm shake of his head. "I was just playing. I didn't mean for you to get hurt. I've been so serious and uptight for the last week. I just wanted to have some fun. Guess I don't know my own strength." He strikes a pose, flexing a bicep, and I choke on my giggle. "Feeling better?" He squats and flexes first his right then his left butt cheek, and I just about die when he finishes with a tushy wiggle. "What about now?"

"Stop, please. I can't breathe," I wheeze.

Landry straddles the bench behind me. His hands settle on the curves of my hips, and he slides me backward until I'm snuggled between his legs. His thumbs massage the tight muscles at the base of my spine before traveling upward. He rubs my shoulders in slow, concentrated circles. The heat of his chest warms my back. "You're a tough audience to please. Do you like this better?"

Can't. Speak. Brain. Shutting down. My eyeballs roll up in pleasure. Tense muscles begin to relax, and my breathing eases. I try to shift away, but his hands tighten so I can't move. His fingers dance like he's playing the piano, kneading the tight cords in my neck. It feels like a little piece of heaven. No one has ever caressed me with such gentleness. He sweeps my braid over a shoulder. Warmth takes its place as feather-soft lips brush my skin. I clench my hands together—unsure if I'm afraid I'll touch him back or try to make him stop. 'Cause I don't want his kisses to stop.

My heart's racing. I can't catch my breath as I fight the overwhelming desire flooding through my body. I want to wrap my arms around him. I need to trace my lips across the prickles of hair growing on his cheeks. To slide my hands beneath his T-shirt and run my hands over his bare chest and feel the ripples of hard muscles beneath his smooth skin.

But, if I do, I'll lose control. I'm barely holding on.

Landry shifts my legs sideways and lifts me onto his lap. Cradled in his arms, I sink into the hollow between his legs. His hardness presses up against me. A blush burns through my cheeks, and I wiggle, sure my weight must be uncomfortable. His arm tightens around my shoulder, and his hand splays across my hip. His hand's so large that his fingertip brushes my navel.

"Don't move," he orders, pressing his forehead against mine. His breath comes in ragged gasps.

I freeze, afraid I'll push him over the edge.

His husky chuckle sends tremors through my body. "Breathe, Mala."

I draw in a hitched breath. Emotions tumble through my fogged mind, but I can't think rationally enough to work through them. So, I give in, allowing myself to enjoy the sensation of each caress searing its path across my increasingly sensitive skin.

Landry tilts my head and nibbles along the side of my throat.

"Oh, *God*…" I whimper, trembling. His teeth graze my earlobe, the tip of his tongue circling the gold ball of my stud earring. My thighs clench against the moist heat building down low with each warm breath. I had no idea my ears could be so sensitive. He slides a hand through the gaping side of the overalls. He trails his fingertips across my stomach, and the resulting explosion arches my back. Landry takes advantage of my position to cup my breast in his palm and roll my erect nipples between his fingertips.

I'm dying…

"Wait, Landry. Stop." *It's too much! Too fast.*

Breathing hard, I grab his wandering hand and pull it free of my clothing. I wrap my arms around myself, shivering against the mini-orgasms brought on by the wind blowing across my over-sensitized body like a warm caress, and climb off of his lap to kneel across from him.

Landry remains silent. He sits with his hands on his upraised knees, and when I glance down, I see the bulge of what I'd only felt pressed against me. He's gotten as turned on as I have.

Tiny sparkles dance in front of my eyes. My hand shakes as I wipe my forehead.

"Maybe we should head back to shore," I say with effort. The boat has floated to the middle of the pond. I can't escape unless I take a swim.

"I still haven't shown you how *big* a fish I can catch," Landry drawls.

I almost choke on my words, but I force them out in the same wry tone he used. "Oh, I see what you have is plenty big, but I told you before. Big isn't everything."

"Suppose you've got to be in love with the fish."

Landry picks up a fishing pole and searches the bucket for a worm. He baits the hook—merciful heavens, even that turns me on—and holds the pole out to me, then does the same for his own. We sit at opposite ends of the dingy, separated by only a few feet, and I'm intensely aware of him. The way his ebony hair tumbles across his face in the breeze. The faint scent of his spicy aftershave filling my nose every time I draw in a deep breath.

"Are you still mad at me?" Landry finally asks after a couple of hours with no bites or conversation.

"You didn't do anything that I didn't let you do," I say, giving a tiny jerk on the line.

He rests his pole on his lap and turns to face me. "Then why?"

The truth flashes through my troubled brain: *Because I liked having you touch me.* How could someone like him understand? Addictions run in families. It's why I rarely drink alcohol and why, at twenty, I'm still a virgin. I'm terrified of becoming so addicted to sex that I end up whoring myself out—like Mama.

"You're right, I want to love the fish or, rather, the guy. I don't want to be like those other girls you've made out with"—I frown over at him—"girls whose names I don't know, but who let you smile and charm them into having sex with you without love. If I let you, you'd break my heart, Landry Prince."

"Would it be that bad? To give in for a time and let your cares drift." Landry sighs and stares out over the water. "Can't it be enough that I want you? That I need the warmth of your arms to hold back the memories? I could get lost inside you, Malaise Jean Marie LaCroix."

His gaze captures mine when he says my name, and I whisper, "How do you know my full name? I never use it."

"I know a lot about you. I've been watching you for a long time." His voice is husky, and my body tightens in response. "You've just been too busy watching someone else to notice."

Georgie. Who else could Landry be talking about? Damn it! How many times do I have to say that George and I are coworkers—friends? No romantic feelings involved. Landry should know that much if he's being truthful about being interested in me. I still find it hard to believe. Maybe he's only saying this to get in my pants? *Boys.* They make my brain ache.

Landry jerks upright. The boat rocks, and I let out a little squeal. "Sure you won't change your mind?" he asks, setting my straw hat on my lap, then lifting the bottom of his T-shirt. My eyes widen as he slowly lifts it over his head, revealing chiseled six-pack abs leading to a toned chest. *Whew, boy.* I try to look away, but I can't pull my gaze from the hand that unzips his jeans and slides them down his narrow hips, taking his underwear with them.

"Lord, preserve me." All I have to do is say *yes* and this beautiful body will be mine. At least for today. Oh, the temptation. I cover my eyes with a groan. My body throbs. "Don't look, Mala, don't look," I whisper.

A splash drenches my head with water and I sit up sputtering. Ripples spread out from where Landry had gone in, but I can't see him.

"Landry," I yell, standing up.

Slowly the ripples fade. He still doesn't surface. "Landry!"

I unhook the straps on my overalls and kick them off. My dive into the water breaks the surface cleanly. I swim to the bottom of the pond, searching. The water looks like glass. Crisp and clear. Very little debris covers the muddy bottom. I stay under as long as I can, afraid if I surface, I'll end up going over the same area I've already searched and lose precious time. But finally I come up for air, choking from the water that burns my nose. I bend forward, trying to clear it out, but I dip under by mistake, breathing in more water. A cramp hits my calf, twisting it up.

"Shit! Landry…" I scream.

"Mala?"

I see movement on the shoreline. "Help me!"

Unable to tread water with one leg, I arch back, and the top of my head slams into hard wood. Everything dims, and I choke on the water filling my open mouth.

Daisy's trying to kill me.

Chapter 21

Landry

Spoiled Brat

Mala's been under too long.

Gotta calm down. If I panic, I won't be able to hold my breath as long. I focus on slowing the rapid beats of my heart, take a deep breath, then dive. The crystalline water makes it easy to see the fear on Mala's face as, with each frantic thrash of her arms, she sinks.

I kick toward her. Her face lifts. Bubbles leak out of her nose. I grab her outstretched hand and draw her to me. Once I have her, I seal my lips against hers and blow in a bubble of air. My arms circle her waist and with a strong kick we shoot upward.

As soon as Mala's head breaches the surface, she sucks in a large breath and hacks up a lungful of nasty water. She convulses in my arms, bent double with each barking cough. I fight my own fatigue and Mala's thrashing to hold her face above the waterline.

By the time I reach the boat and grab onto the side, I'm about done.

Mala wraps her arms around my neck. She's coughing and shivering at the same time. I pound on her back. "You okay?"

"Can't—breathe," she gasps. Her arms tighten around my neck.

"If you're talking, you're breathing."

I hear her whisper, "Liar," and hold in my laugh.

Hell, yeah. She's fine. She may feel like crap on toast, but it's not life threatening. She coughs again.

The adrenaline rush that flooded my body when I heard her scream starts to wear off, and exhaustion weighs me down. If I don't hang onto the boat, we'll sink like we have concrete blocks attached to our ankles. Mala doesn't seem to be in any better condition. She's falling asleep in my arms. I have to keep her alert.

Water laps at our chins. "What happened?"

"Idiot," she whispers into the cradle of my neck. Her soft lips brush against my skin, and I shiver. "I thought you were drowning."

"So this is my fault?" I hold her tightly with one arm, turning our bodies toward the boat.

"It's not mine."

I laugh, squeezing her, and she coughs. "So let me get this straight. You tried to save me but ended up needing to be rescued yourself."

"Stupid me."

"Yeah, but I wasn't gonna say it. Lucky for you, I've worked as a lifeguard over at the community pool since high school."

"Wish I knew that before."

"I also give swim lessons."

"Stop trying to be cute." She wheezes and coughs up some more water. "Ouch. My head's pounding." She touches the top of her skull. When she pulls her hand back, her fingers run red, and she chokes again. "Oh, I'm bleeding."

"Poor baby, you really had a time of it." I keep my voice calm so she doesn't freak out again, but I'm worried. I need to get her out of the water ASAP. "Do you think you can hold onto the edge of the boat while I climb back inside?"

Mala's actions speak for her. She removes her arm from around my neck and grabs the side. When I'm sure her grip's secure, I quickly climb inside, then grab her arm. With an easy pull, I lift her into the boat. She huddles on the bench, trying not to watch as I get dressed, but I see her peeking. Every place her eyes caress feels like the worst sunburn under creation. Only the touch of her lips will cool my skin. It takes every ounce of self-control to keep my hands off her.

Mala shivers, unable to warm up. The soaked tank top hangs to mid-thigh, showing her muscular legs. It's one of those men's wife-beater tanks—thin cotton, see-through. She wears a bra, but it's also white and wet, contrasting against the darkness of her skin. She catches me staring at her breasts and wraps her arms around herself to huddle in a sodden, pathetic little ball.

"Get over here," I say gruffly. I don't take no for an answer either. Just pull her across my lap and use my T-shirt to rub her shaking arms and legs with hard strokes to warm her up. She lets me. I think she's too cold and miserable to complain. Not at all Mala-like. "Are you sure you're okay?"

Mala shivers. "When I was underwater, I saw something," she says slowly, laying her head on my shoulder.

"Oh, what? A giant catfish?" I laugh, but it's not funny. Did she feel my heart stop at her words? In the water, I thought oxygen deprivation caused me to imagine the hands holding onto her ankles, dragging her deeper.

Mala shakes her head. Her pigtails thump against my chest, and she winces. "No, it…" She sighs, pressing her fingers to her scalp. "Never mind. It's stupid. I must've been hallucinating after I hit my head." *Yeah, me too. Gotta be.*

"Let me see." I pluck apart the hair on the back of her head and gently touch the swelling lump. "I've seen worse. There's a small cut. Do you have a medical kit on board so I can wash it out? I'm first aid certified too, in case you're worried."

She shrugs, snuggling deeper into my arms, like a cuddly bear on the verge of hibernating for the winter. She has no idea how sexy she looks with those heavy-lashed eyelids, or she wouldn't stare at me like this. My heart races, and my hands tingle like I've lain on them too long. A stirring in my pants has me sliding Mala off my lap. God, I hope she's too out of it to notice.

Pull it together. What if she has a brain injury? Trying to get laid right now would be wrong on so many levels. The guilt alone would eat me up inside.

Course, I might get lucky. No. Wrong. So very wrong.

Wrong enough I won't take myself seriously. I'm trying to distract myself, not only because of my arousal, but because her lethargy worries me. Her vulnerability only makes her sexier. She's so strong; it feels kind of good having her need me. I want to protect and cherish her even more. I want her bad. But not like this. When the time comes, I want to make it memorable for the right reasons. Not because I took advantage of her.

I pull on my T-shirt, then start searching the boat. "Okay, the first aid kit's in the tackle box, right?" I ask, trying to get her to focus.

Instead Mala lies on the bench and closes her eyes. The wet tank top strains against her breasts. She folds one leg beneath the other, and I get a peek at her white cotton panties, which for some reason turn me on more than if she wore a black silk thong.

Oh, God. She's killing me.

I'm trying hard to be noble. To respect her wishes. I drink in a warm gulp of air. The sun beats down on my head, soaking into my skin. I stare at the pale blue water lapping against the side of the shoreline. The lust fades to a hum rather than a throb.

Once I can think, I lift Mala upright with a little shake. "Oh, no you don't. Wake up."

She bats at my hands. I kneel in front of her and lift her chin until I can check her eyes. What are the signs of concussion again? It's been almost a year since I renewed my first aid/CPR certification. Her pupils aren't dilated, but… "You might have a slight concussion. Let's get you to the hospital."

"Nope, I don't have insurance." She squints as if the sunlight reflecting off the water hurts her eyes. "I didn't pass out. Just let me take a nap, and I'll be fine."

I sit on the opposite bench and row toward shore. Already-sore muscles cuss me out for using them so soon, but I ignore them. The old boat shoots across the water like it's jet powered. When it gets shallow, I hop into the water and pull the boat onto the embankment.

My girl watches me with a stubborn set to her chin. I already know how hardheaded she can be. She proves it by slapping at my hands when I try to lift her from the seat. "I said I'm not going to the hospital, Landry."

If I can get my hands on her, I'll carry her off whether she wants to go or not.

She shoves me away again and scrambles to the back of the boat. "Are you listening to me? I'm not going!"

"Head injuries aren't something to play around with. Now either stand up on your own or I'll carry you."

"You're not my father. You can't boss me around."

"If I was your daddy, would you listen and get out of the damn boat?"

Mala gasps. The corners of her eyes narrow. Did that daddy comment hurt her feelings? Her lethargy drains away to be replaced with indignant fury. "Do you know how much a trip to the emergency room costs, you spoiled brat? I can't afford the bill. I won't be in debt for years over an injury that's barely a scratch." Mala crosses her arms. "I've been to the hospital once, and that was when I was four and had pneumonia, and only because I almost died. We had to sell off five acres that my family's owned for over a hundred and fifty years just to pay those bills."

"Don't you think your ancestors would rather you survived than died to preserve their legacy?" My stomach twists at the guilt reflected in her dark eyes. "Don't you think you're worth it?"

She bites her lip then answers honestly. "No."

"Well," I sigh, "I do."

"Don't make me go." Mala wraps her arms around herself,

shivering. I don't think it's from being cold this time. "Please. Hospitals scare me."

"Fine. It's not like I can force you to go. Just promise to tell me if you feel worse, okay? Don't hide it. I feel shitty enough. I don't need any more guilt over someone I care about dying."

Mala's eyes turn to melted chocolate. "Oh," she chokes. Her arms open, and I fall into them. I lift her into a tight hug. Her heart pounds so hard that I can feel it. A drop of water falls like a tiny diamond to catch on her eyelashes. At first, I think it's water from my hair, then I realize I'm crying. What a mess.

Mala brushes it off and pushes free of my arms. "Enough of this moping around, Landry Prince, the day is young. We're not gonna spend it boo-hooing about how miserable we are, right?"

"What do you propose we do?" I wiggle my eyebrows with a little leer that turns her cheeks that cute shade of candy apple. "More fishing?"

"I'm not up for a fishing expedition. My head's a little swimmy—" She raises a hand, and I snap my mouth shut. "Not bad enough for a doctor so don't start in on that again. I'm hungry. How about if we go back to my house and make up some sandwiches?"

My stomach growls at her words. "You know what they say: The way to a man's heart is through his stomach."

Mala laughs. I hold out my hand. Mala grabs her overalls and climbs out, steadying herself on my arm. My gaze drifts downward, and I whistle. "Nice legs."

"I'm blushing 'cause I think you actually mean that." She lets out an un-Mala-like giggle and quickly pulls on the overalls. Very disappointing. She squeezes the excess water out of her braids with hard twists and wraps them in balls on the side of her head.

"Come on, Princess Leia," I say.

"You're such a geek."

"I'm picturing you in a gold bikini." Saliva pools in my mouth at the thought. I take a deep breath and chuckle on the exhale. "Yeah, for Halloween, I'll order one off the Internet for you to wear when we go trick or treating."

She pauses for a long second, then smiles. "As long as you go as Han Solo."

"What about Indiana Jones? I'll have a whip."

Mala blushes—and the image in my mind skews a bit to the raunchy side.

I let the 3-D fantasy of me swinging across a ravine while holding a gold bikini–clad Mala in my arms play out.

Mala pokes me in the stomach. "Earth to Landry."

"Hmm?"

"I asked if you can carry the gear by yourself. I'm a little unsteady."

Mala's skin has lightened to pale honey. She's about to pass out. I point to the oak perched on a wildflower-covered hill on the other side of the pond. "How about if we sit over there for a while?" Our fingers tangle together. It seems natural—holding her hand. Nope, I don't feel awkward at all.

We walk to the tree. I sit down with my back to the rough trunk and pull her across my lap. She wiggles into a comfortable position, and I hold my breath, trying not to think about her plump ass rubbing against me. It's not working. I bite the inside of my cheek. The trickle of warm, coppery blood on my tongue helps to clear the lust from my brain.

Once Mala settles, I tuck her head beneath my chin. "Rest for a while. I'll wake you in an hour to make sure you haven't slipped into a coma."

"That's reassuring," she mutters. Her body relaxes, conforming to mine as if against a memory foam mattress. We fit. She's soft and cuddly. No hard angles poke me. I begin to massage her neck, and she sighs.

The thick leaves overhead drop the temperature to bearable levels. Warm wind scented with wildflowers and rich earth blows over us. There's a faint lemony trace of magnolia blossoms coming from somewhere close by. A ribbon snake slithers from the thick grass and glides past my foot. I freeze until it's gone. I hate snakes.

I adjust my position against the tree. The rough bark catches in the threads of my T-shirt. I pull out the rock digging into my thigh and toss it into the grass, careful not to jostle Mala. She sighs, snuggling closer. Her heat and the scent of her hair relax the tension I've been holding. I'm afraid to fall asleep in case she does have a concussion. I have to wake her in an hour, but my body has other ideas. Insomnia brought on by grief, swimming across the length of the pond twice, and the warmth of the day make me sluggish.

Every time my heavy eyelids drift closed, I snap them open again.

Clear, blue water closes over my head. I float, cocooned in warmth. Long black hair waves in the current, and a pale hand reaches out, beckoning me to follow deeper. Part of me resists, but the other part can't stop from taking my big sis's hand. My chest tightens, and panic follows. I try to pull free, but Lainey's nails dig into my palm. She won't release me, just pulls me deeper until I can't see the light of the sky above the waterline.

I choke, unable to catch my breath.

I jerk awake with a short yelp. Damn my sister's unresting soul. She's dead but keeps trying to get back at me for all the grief I gave her when we were kids. I'm so sick of her haunting my dreams.

The unnatural stillness of Mala's body intrudes on my rant.

I press my hand against her chest, then lean close to her mouth.

She's stopped breathing. "Oh God, no."

I give her a little shake. Her head, cradled in the crook of my elbow, falls back. Her eyelids and lips have a slight blue tint. I shake her again, harder, and her head lolls on her neck.

"No!" I shout, "Mala, Mala, wake up!"

I look around for help, but there's no one. The stillness deepens until we're in a bubble, cut off from the rest of the world. Nothing else matters. A chill rushes through my body, but it can't compare to the icy coldness of her skin. A vein ticks in my throat in time with the frantic thumps of my heart. When I press my fingers to her carotid artery, it takes a few seconds before I separate her heartbeat from my own. My brain desperately files through the list of steps I learned in my CPR course: Check, Call, Care…no, wait: Look, Listen, and Feel.

Which comes first? In class, I got cocky because it seemed so simple. Now that I have to use it, I'm terrified I'll screw up. What if I'm forgetting steps? I should've taken her to the hospital right away. If she dies it's my fault. *Oh, God. What do I do?*

Two rescue breaths, chest compressions. Was it fifteen compressions to two breaths? I shake my head. "Thirty and two. It's thirty and two."

I roll her onto the ground and tilt her head back, making an airway, then use two fingers to open her mouth. I draw in a breath then press my lips against hers. I slowly breathe in the air, watching her lungs expand. The whole time, I pray for her not to die.

Chapter 22

Mala

Breathe

Lips press against my open mouth, and air fills my lungs, expanding them. I shove hard, breaking free. Landry leans back. His face has drained of color, and he pants, obviously freaked out. He gathers me off the ground. "You stopped breathing!"

I know. I felt myself drowning. My arms wrap around his neck, and I lean against him. I'm shaking so hard I think I'll break apart.

Landry's arms tighten, holding me together. "One minute you're fine, and the next, I couldn't feel you breathing," he chokes out. "I tried to wake you. You turned blue. I've never been so scared in my entire life."

"It was Lainey! She wouldn't let me go. She kept pulling me under the water. I couldn't break free. Why did she do it, Landry? Do you think she's trying to kill me?"

"I don't know." He rocks me in his arms, trembling himself. "She's trying to tell us something, but I can't figure out what. Or even why I keep dreaming about her. I'm not a witch. I don't have special powers like you."

"I'm not a witch," I mutter.

"Still, for you it makes sense."

"Nothing makes sense," I wail, choking on the sob fighting to get out. The fear and anger I've been trying to hide bursts free. I cry so hard I lose track of time. When I finally climb out of the pit of despair I've fallen into, I find I'm clinging to Landry like he's my security blanket.

"I'm sorry," I whisper, sitting back. "She's your sister. I shouldn't—"

"Don't apologize. If it's anyone's fault, it's mine. We used to be best friends—me and Lainey, fighting to hold onto our sanity in our parents' crazy, Bible-thumping world. You may not have noticed, but I'm not as religious as my parents. Lainey, though, she had the disposition of a saint when she was a kid. She was all fire and fun, but she never got mad. I tagged after her, and she never pushed me away even though we're five years apart in age."

"You're lucky to have had her. I wish I had a brother or sister. It sucks being alone." *I'm so tired of being alone.*

"Yeah, I know." He wraps his arm around my shoulders and hugs me. "Lainey went to Loyola University. Something bad must've happened to her last year because she came back home changed. She turned angry and cold. She'd stay out all night with her boyfriends but never brought one home to meet the family. Whenever I tried to talk to her, she blew me off. Finally I stopped asking. Now I'll never have the chance."

He looks down, and our eyes meet.

"Kiss me," I blurt out.

"What?" His breathing quickens. "What did you say?

Oh, shit! I just propositioned him. Me, squeaky clean, cowardly Mala. Lack of oxygen must've given me brain damage. I take a shaky breath and straighten in his arms. "I said kiss me." My voice cracks. "It's okay. I won't punch you or anything. You have my permission."

"Your head's not on straight." Landry gazes off across the water…distant, cold. Oh, so sad, and it breaks my heart. All I want at this moment is to drink the pain in his eyes. Guzzle it down so it never fills him again. I know nothing's forever. A momentary patch is about all the comfort I can give him, but maybe for now, it's enough. For both of us.

"I know. I'm scared." I take Landry's face between my hands, holding tight when he tries to pull away. "Stop. Listen. Why do I have to keep dealing with the craziness of my life alone? I'm so tired…Why is it wrong to want to escape?"

My trembling fingers lightly trace the curve of his jaw. I never in a million years thought I could be so bold. I've always protected my heart because I feared it would get squished. Being afraid hasn't gotten me anywhere but alone. "I *like* you, Landry. And…and I think you like me. At least a little bit, right? You make me feel safe…alive. Maybe…maybe I can make you feel the same way."

His eyes, thick black lashes outlining luminous silver, close as I trace my fingers across his eyelids. I press my lips to the angled plane of his cheekbone in a gentle kiss. His skin tastes salty from sweat and smells of grass. Rich and pungent. Intoxicating. His stomach muscles tighten against mine, but he doesn't move. I kiss the other cheek, then tilt his head toward mine and brush my lips across his, so lightly that it's more a mingling of breath.

My tongue caresses his lips. I taste him in small nibbles, and then, feeling bold, I pull his plump bottom lip between my teeth, gently teasing him until he finally responds.

Impatient, he threads his fingers into my hair so I can't pull away. His tongue flicks against mine as I open my mouth to his, deepening the connection between us. I've heard about French kisses—in high school, the girls giggled about them and rated the boys according to skill—but until now, I've never liked a guy enough to want his tongue in my mouth. Landry rated pretty high on the Awesome Kisser scale. Now I understand why.

The rush of excitement chases away any lingering fear. At some point, he stretches out on the ground, and I lay on top of him. My hands caress his wide shoulders and rise to tangle in his silky hair. I rub against his chest, wishing our clothing didn't separate us. I want to feel the softness of his skin against mine. I want to trace the tempting dimple in the small of his back and lick the faded scar to the left of his belly button.

Yeah, I totally peeked when he did his striptease in the boat. I may be the queen of denial, but I couldn't deny myself the sculpted beauty of Landry Prince in all his glory. I pull my mouth free of his lips and slide down the hard length of his body. He sucks in a breath, stomach tightening when I run trembling hands up his chest, lifting his T-shirt to give me access to that scar. I trace my tongue around it in a swirl of motion, like licking an ice cream cone. He tastes ten times better than chocolate—maybe like chocolate and caramel with marshmallow chunks—all gooey and melty in my mouth. So tasty that I want to lap him up. But I bite him instead.

Satisfaction throbs at his growl. The soft bit of flesh between my teeth almost sends me over the edge. I'm so hot…burning up inside.

I release him, licking the soft indentations in his skin.

"Mala," he moans, quivering when I pin his reaching hands to the ground. I give him a wicked grin, then lower my head. I steadily work my way up his chest, biting and licking until I reach his pecs. I run my tongue around his left nipple, then blow across the hard nub. His hips shift, a slight jerk upward. His erection presses against the fabric of his jeans. Is it uncomfortable?

I bite my lip, scared at the bold nature of my thoughts. It's like years of repressed sexuality screams to be set free. Too many romance novels have given me a working knowledge of what goes on. I can fake it until I make it, but I've got to decide right now how far I want to go. Soon I'll be too far gone. My body decides for me.

My hand slides between our chests and slips between the waistband of his jeans. Landry grabs my hand, breathing hard. I try to tug it free. I want to feel him. Is it soft or hard? Why is he stopping? He wanted me in the boat. Now I'm ready to take the next step. Lainey's trying her best to kill me, and I don't want to die a virgin. How sadly pathetic would that be?

Landry stares into my face, questioning. My pulse beats frantically. I lick my lips, not tearing my gaze from his, meeting it boldly. "What?"

His eyes squeeze shut, and he trembles. It's like he's fighting a battle for control, which totally sucks. He inhales, then lets the air trickle over his lips. His tense muscles relax. The enticing bulge in his pants shrinks. My self-control returns with his. I scowl, refusing to feel shame or regret. Confusion, though. My mind's cluttered with it. I never wanted to be labeled or judged. Mama, the woman everyone whispered about and ridiculed, left a stain on my soul. I've done my best through the years to prove I was not my mother—the whore. Yet here I am acting like a hoochie mama by trying to seduce Landry, and I can't seem to care.

"I'm sorry," Landry says, rolling me off of him.

Why the hell is he apologizing? I started this. I stare up at him, framed against the backdrop of leaves and sky. Emotions flit across his face: regret, shame…longing, all the feelings I refuse to acknowledge, hidden quickly behind a bland facade. *Well, now I feel like shit.* I sit up to rest on bent elbows.

He stretches out a hand, beckoning. "I'll walk you home."

I remain silent, staring at his hand while biting my quivering lip, trying not to cry. He wouldn't have seen anyway because he refuses to look at me. I sit all the way up and tuck my shirt into the overalls, buckling the straps with angry movements. Humiliation churns beneath the surface, building into a sticky web inside me as I consider my circumstances: I'm being rejected. Landry freaking Prince who slept with half the bobble-head girls in town, including that bitch Clarice, doesn't want me.

Ooh, I'm so pissed. I want to knock some sense into his fat head with a rock. Too bad the closest one is on the damn beach. I ignore his hand and rise on my own, not wanting anything more from Landry. Not help. Not condemnation or pity. I'm sick of his games. Sick of him!

"Mala, don't be like this."

Silently, I pick leaves from my braids and brush off my clothes.

"I'm sorry if I've hurt—"

Liar! "Could you get the fishing rods from the boat?"

"When I get back, will you let me explain?"

I can't meet his eyes. All I want is to escape. I wait until he's gathering our supplies, then break into a shambling run toward the tree line. A quick glance over my shoulder shows Landry's still facing in the opposite direction. If he doesn't notice me enter the woods, he won't be able to follow.

"Mala, stop!"

Panic spurts, and I put out a burst of speed fueled by adrenaline. Branches smack my face and scratch my arms as I shove deeper into the shady depths of the woods. I stumble over a rock and drop to my knees, sucking in great gasps of air. My head pounds so hard that my teeth ache. *What the hell am I doing?* I squeeze my eyes shut. *I'm so stupid.* I didn't do anything wrong—other than humiliate myself on an epic level. My aborted attempt at seduction and Landry's rejection isn't worth charging about like a rampaging bull. Why can't I think before I act?

A branch cracks to my left. The thundering roar of a gunshot drops me flat on my stomach. I wrap my hands above my head, cowering in the dirt, about as low as I can get without burying myself in a hole. A peek between my arms shows a shadow moving from behind a small elm tree, and booted feet plant themselves in front of my face. My focus rises to the barrel of the rifle pointed at the center of my forehead. It looms, shiny and big enough to blow a hole the size of Texas through my head.

I throw my hands back over my face with a piercing shriek.

"Mala?" the shout echoes from behind, but I'm afraid to answer Landry. I don't want him in the middle. This is between me and my surly neighbor, doing what he always does when we meet—trying to intimidate me. Dena inherited her dad's unruly red hair, and the twins got his awful disposition. Looking into his eyes is like staring into a dirty toilet. He doesn't even try to hide the hatefulness deep inside him.

Mr. Acker lowers the rifle and steps back. "Why you trespassing on my property?"

I push to my feet, glancing around me. I had stumbled into the old Savoie plantation graveyard—the section where they buried the slaves, not the family. That's up the hill closer to the main house. Still, it's Acker's land, private.

"Shit, you scared me half to death."

"Almost shot you. Pulled the barrel once I figured out you too stringy for a deer. Ain't enough meat on you to feed my kids." He leans his rifle against his shoulder. "It's dangerous for a girl like you to be roaming about in the woods alone. 'Specially after the rev's daughter got kilt. Know anything about that?"

A chill races across my skin. "Yes."

He squints at me and hawks a wad of tobacco in my direction. "Thought so."

"Didn't Dena tell you? I found Lainey's body."

"Said something about it." His head tilts as he studies me. "Also heard Lainey came to your mama for some kind of hoodoo shit. That true too?"

The spit dries in my mouth. How did Acker hear about Lainey coming to Mama? The only people who knew were me and…fucking Landry and his big mouth. He might as well kill me himself if he's going to go around spreading rumors. Doesn't he know how people round these parts feel? The old-timers still believe in hoodoo.

Mr. Acker's eyes narrow, and his fingers trace across the rifle. I work my throat trying to get out the words, but nothing comes. It's too late anyway. I've taken too long to deny it. He's considering whether to kill me. I'm so screwed. Even if I run a zigzag pattern like I'm trying to outrun a gator, I'm not faster than a bullet. My shoulder blades tingle, and I hunch my shoulders.

A crash of breaking branches comes from the side, and Landry bursts out of the brush. My legs wobble, and I stumble against the tree in relief. He freezes when he sees me, then his gaze moves to Mr. Acker. "Mala, you okay?" he asks, not looking away from the older man.

"I'm fine." *Now.* Acker would be crazy to try anything with a witness around. I hope.

I take the hand Landry holds out to me. With a quick tug, he pulls me toward him while simultaneously stepping forward to block my body from Acker's line of sight.

"Mr. Acker," Landry says with a nod.

"Landry, does the rev know you're associating with this girl?"

"Who I spend time with is nobody's business but my own," Landry says in a tone so chilly that I shiver.

Mr. Acker's gaze hardens, and he spits. Tobacco lands an inch from Landry's boot. "Best get this girl home before she gets hurt." He turns and walks off. I keep my eyes on him until he's no longer visible. Afraid he might return.

Landry pushes my head against his chest. "What was that all about?" His heart races beneath my ear. "Are you sure you're okay?"

"Yeah, I'm fine. He doesn't like me much. But you can't choose family, right?" I pull free of his arms, avoiding meeting his gaze. "Course, if you'd kept your big mouth shut about Lainey coming to Mama for a hoodoo spell, he wouldn't have been trying to scare me."

His face blanches. "What?"

"Acker thinks Mama and I had something to do with Lainey getting murdered." I squint up at him and snort. "Ridiculous, huh? About as crazy as George thinking you're guilty."

"George thinks *I* murdered Lainey? Why?"

"Why not? Obviously, you're insane!" I yell at him. "You stalk me. Threaten and reject me. Blab to everyone and their mother that I'm a witch. Yet I still trust you. Even when George said you did it, I defended you. I must be as insane as you are. Not only are you totally ruining my life, you're gonna get me killed."

Landry stiffens and steps back. "So that's how you want to play this?"

"This isn't a game. I'm telling the truth. One of us is going to go down for murder if we don't figure out who really killed Lainey."

"Fine, we'll solve her murder. Happy?" He stabs a finger in my direction. "Now, are you ready to talk about what's really bothering you?"

The apology he must think I owe him for sulking off looms between us, much like Mr. Acker's rifle. Pride keeps my lips sealed. "George said yesterday that Lainey kept a room at the Super Delight Motel where she met her boyfriend. He got a search warrant but they didn't find anything. Maybe *we* will."

Chapter 23

Mala

Super Delight

Landry left after dropping me off at home. I really didn't expect him to return tonight, but he's keeping his promise to help me search Lainey's motel room, despite still being pissed off. So here we are, pulling into the parking lot of the Super Delight Motel. I've never seen a more rundown hole. I've driven past the motel many times, but it's been years since I've visited the place where Mama whores herself four out of seven nights. I find it embarrassing, but Mama enjoys her job and takes pride in the fact she's never been on welfare. Independence comes at a high price in my opinion.

Daylight keeps the criminal element inside; maybe sunlight turns them to dust. Tonight feels different. Red doors stand out from graffiti-covered, canary yellow walls. Broken bottles, needles, and used condoms are scattered through the parking lot, adding to the seedy ambiance not even bright paint can dispel. One of these doors opens into Lainey's room. Her boyfriend was smart enough to clear it out before the deputies searched the room. He's staying one step ahead and doing everything in his power to hide his identity. His actions don't make him guilty of murder, but he definitely has something to hide.

Landry parks in front of the motel office by the pool. The silence in the truck has weight and texture. It vibrates with tension. I've let my anger cool with the setting of the sun. I welcome the night, knowing it's easier to let down my defenses in the darkness. Even if my emotions are painted across my face, Landry won't be able to see them. He'll only know what I want him to know. Maybe I'm naive to want to protect myself while being so willing to forgive him at the same time. I wish I could hold a grudge for longer than a minute, except this time, I think I'm the one at fault.

I turn until I can study Landry's shadowed face. My heart hammers in my chest. I'm scared to ask this question, but I should've before I made out with him.

I clear my throat. "Uh, can I ask something?"

"Oh wow, I exist in Mala's world again?" Landry drawls, not bothering to glance in my direction as he turns off the truck, and once again he sets my blood boiling.

Fine, let him play the martyr if it makes him feel better. "I'm serious. It's important to me. Please."

If possible, the tension thickens. He glances at me. I can't see because it's too dark outside, but I imagine the hurricane swirling in his storm-cloud eyes. "You're the one who thinks we'll find some clue in Lainey's room as to why our lives are falling apart. Let's go."

I grab his arm before he can open the door. "First, tell me why you're really here."

He frowns.

"I don't mean here"—I wave my hand—"I mean why you came this morning and why you stayed after you found out I couldn't talk to Lainey. When you stormed off this afternoon, I didn't expect to see you again. But you came back for me. I don't get it. Why are you even with me, Landry?"

He's quiet for so long that I don't think he'll answer. Then he sighs and shrugs, saying "What else was I supposed to do? Torture myself like I did last night?"

"What do you mean?"

Landry turns to face me. "I was lying in bed listening to my mother crying through the walls, and my dad working on his eulogy, and I couldn't stop thinking about you."

I scowl in disbelief.

He gives me a shadowed smile. "That wasn't too surprising since I think about you all the time. So I did what I usually do—tried to focus on something else. Football, supersexy Victoria's Secret models—that worked for about five minutes since you're way hotter."

"Oh sure, *way* hotter." I unbuckle my seat belt and slide across the seat. "Is that why you practically ran from me?"

"I wasn't the one who ran off." His voice softens. "I was worried about you. Hearing that gunshot…I don't know…"

He really does care about me, doesn't he?

My mouth on his stops the rest of his words. His tongue flicks against the roof of my mouth, and I melt. I press against him until there's not even an inch of space between our upper bodies. My legs shake. I want to lie back on the seat and pull him on top of me. But I hold back. Tingles race across my skin where he traces my arms with the tips of his fingers. Light caresses that drive me crazy with the desire to feel those fluttery shivers in areas protected by clothing. Why do I lose control only with him? How can a single, innocent kiss get me so hot?

Crap, I'm molesting him again.

I break the kiss with a sigh before he can. He presses his forehead against mine, breathing hard. I lay a hand on his chest and feel the rapid patter of his heart against my palm. My lips feel swollen, and my cheeks sting from his stubble. The scent of his skin mingles with mine. He's marked me. The whole time he massages my neck with his fingers, and the faint headache I really hadn't noticed starts to fade.

"Landry, I'm sorry. For some reason I can't keep my hands off of you." I rub my cheek against his shoulder.

"You're not the only one with control issues," he says softly, and I nod, acknowledging the truth. The attraction goes both ways.

"Yeah, but I handled it all wrong at the pond. I-I'm sorry I ran off. Being rejected hurt. I don't know why 'cause I should be used to it by now. Maybe because I actually care what you think of me." I shudder, knowing I should move from his arms but am unable to. "I don't know. It's silly, but I thought a clean exit would be better. Now you're confusing me again. I can't handle this back-and-forth drama."

"That's why I pulled away. The reason you kissed me was because Lainey almost killed you, and you needed comfort. If I'd let it go further, you'd end up hating me. I respect you too much to let that happen."

Respect, huh? "So we're back to being friends."

"With PG-13 benefits? Because now that I've gotten a taste of your minty-sweet kisses, I don't think I can go cold turkey." He wiggles his eyebrows, and I laugh. I can't go without kissing him either. It feels too good, but now I know he won't take advantage of my willingness to go all buck wild on him. He likes to flirt. So do I. And I won't feel guilty anymore about showing my affection to someone I care about.

On the other hand. Time and place. I would've regretted having my first sexual experience come from terror over my shaken sense of mortality rather than love—in the dirt instead of a cushy bed with unscented candles and chocolate. At the time, I thought it was okay to give in 'cause I didn't want to die without ever feeling loved, but Landry has reminded me that important things shouldn't be compromised.

I throw Landry a quick grin. "Now that we've hashed out our relationship issues, I guess we'd better come up with a plan to get into Lainey's room." I wiggle my fingers. "My lock-picking skills are nonexistent. But I'm pretty good at fast talking."

Landry leans back, crossing his arms. "Don't tell me you're quoting skills based on your online gaming profile?"

"Hey, I'm a seventh-level thief. Don't knock my imaginary skills. It's not my fault that up until this week I've never needed to resort to breaking and entering in real life. And I'm not too thrilled about it now. Maybe you can dig into your wallet instead, rich boy? We can probably bribe the owner into letting us into Lainey's room."

"Or we can use the key." Landry dangles what appears to be a motel room key in front of my eyes, then makes it vanish back into his fist when I try to grab it.

"No fair. Where did you find that?"

"This key is the reason why I went home after our fight, not because I was running away. A couple of days ago, I tossed Lainey's bedroom at home for clues. This key was stuffed inside her shoe, but I didn't know what it opened until you mentioned the motel. Her diary is missing, which sucks because the name of her murderer is probably written in it. Maybe she hid it in her motel room, and the cops missed it when they searched." He shrugs. "But my bet's on this being another dead end. Come on, let's finish this so we can go eat."

Landry presses a quick kiss to my forehead, then jumps from the truck. A warm glow starts to burn in my belly and spreads throughout my body. Happiness. It's such a rare feeling that I sink back into the seat and squeeze my hands together. I peek at him through the front windshield. He faces away from the truck. The lines of his body have gone from relaxed to tense in the space of a few seconds. His head cocks to the side as if he's listening to something in the distance. He throws a quick, wide-eyed glance at me, then runs.

A surge of panic races through me. I throw open my door and jump to the ground. "Landry, wait!"

He's moving fast, faster than I can catch. Nothing more than a dark blur speeding down the sidewalk between the motel and manager's office/recreation room. He turns left, disappearing around the corner heading toward the pool. Raised voices come from that area.

Landry yells, "Call 9-1-1." Then I hear a splash.

My mouth opens to call for him when a shadow tears around the corner. He wears all black, like a crook or a wannabe ninja assassin, and carries an object tucked in his arms like a football. I'm trapped in the narrow space between the two buildings about the width of my open arms. The guy doesn't slow when he sees me but charges forward, ready to bowl me over. I only have a split second to decide: black clothes, running away from the screaming.

Yeah, he totally looks suspicious. A real cop wouldn't have time to second-guess herself. If this guy has done something wrong, I'm taking him down. If he's innocent, well, I guess saying sorry is easier than asking for permission.

I squeeze back against the wall, but when he charges past, I lunge. A handful of his black shirt ends up in my fist. Not my brightest idea. His forward motion practically yanks my arms out of their sockets. I trip, and he ends up dragging me for a few steps before he twists, elbowing my shoulder and breaking my hold on his shirt. I don't fall flat on my face, but my elbows get skinned catching my fall. The guy makes a break for it while I stagger to my feet, weaving a little from the throbbing radiating up my shoulder and into my jaw.

Now he's gone and made it personal.

With each step, my anger grows. The pain fades beneath a black tidal wave of fury. Either he's slowing down or my rage increases my speed. We hit the parking lot in a flat-out run. He heads toward the main road. If he crosses it and gets into the woods on the other side, I'll lose him. The trees border a large residential area where he'll have plenty of places to hide.

My anger pulses, hotter, darker, more thinly focused than

when Magnolia attacked me. I thought I could launch her through a wall. She taught me a more subtle form of expressing my disdain. I stab outstretched fingers toward his retreating back. I picture the tips of my fingers slicing through flesh, fat, and muscles, splaying the layers open the way Lainey had been dissected on the autopsy table. With his innards exposed to my mind's eye, I clench my fist like Magnolia did. I imagine squeezing this jerk's guts into a ball like chitlins stuffed in a bucket.

The guy cries out. He stumbles but doesn't fall. The bundle he's carrying drops to the ground and slides under a parked car. He staggers forward, not bothering to pick it up.

"Stop," I yell, diving forward into a tackle that would've given Landry shivers of pride. I grab my suspect around the back of his knees. He hits the ground, but I don't give him the chance to catch his breath. Or me either, for that matter. I climb up his back, straddling him like he's a rodeo pony. He bucks, and I'm thrown backward. My upper back hits the fender of the car parked next to us. What little breath I'd managed to hold onto bursts from my lungs.

I struggle to sit up, but I can't do much of anything except struggle not to pass out. I stare at the swirling stars in the velvet black sky and listen to his footsteps fade in the distance. I'm still sprawled out when the ambulance passes by with blaring sirens. I must've blacked out because the ambulance is heading toward the main road, not coming in. I turn my head. I'm hidden, wedged between two parked cars. If I want anyone to notice me, I have to crawl into the parking lot and pass out in the middle of the driveway. Sure, I might get run over, but at least someone will find my body.

A face, like an overinflated balloon, floats over my head. I blink a few times to bring him into focus. "Landry." I gasp, tilting my head. "'S'up?"

"Shit, Mala." He squats beside me. "I've been looking everywhere for you. Why are you lying on the ground? Are you okay?"

The loopy, swimmy mess in my head begins to fade. I look around, finally aware of my surroundings. The motel is lit up like a Christmas tree with red and blue lights. Then I take in Landry's appearance and gasp. "What the hell happened to you?" I touch his wet T-shirt. "You're soaked."

He glances down at himself with a scattered frown. "Huh? Yeah, I've used my lifeguarding skills more today than I have in the last two years."

"Did someone fall in the pool? Is that why you ran off?" I straighten myself by degrees. A groan rips through me without permission. It doesn't feel like I've broken any bones, but I'm going to be black, blue, and sore all over come morning. "If the police came then it wasn't an accident, I assume. That guy..."

"Yeah...yeah, there was this guy. He tried to drown a...a woman in the pool." He runs his fingers through his hair. His gaze darts toward the flashing lights. "Shit! George is here. He'll want to talk to you."

Landry tugs on my arm, trying to encourage me to rise, but I can't. My eyes close against the throbbing in my head. "Stop yanking on me, Landry. Can't you see I'm injured?"

The shocked light in his eyes narrows and focuses on me like a laser pointer. I've finally gotten his full attention, and I kind of regret it. "How? I left you in the truck."

"I followed, of course. I saw this guy running toward me. He was dressed all in black and wore a mask, which seemed suspicious so I, uh, chased after him." I finish the justification for my stupidity in a rush. "An innocent guy wouldn't try to elbow someone in the face, right?"

"Let me get this straight. You chased after a masked man who's running away from the scene." Landry threads his arm around my back. The pain of his touch makes me wince as he helps me stand. His voice grows louder with each word. "He's the reason why you got hurt? Seriously?"

I nod, unable to speak. I wrap my arms around him and press my face to his soggy T-shirt.

His body vibrates, which makes mine crackle in response. He runs his hands up and down my arms and back, searching for injuries, then hugs me against his muscular chest. Air bursts from my lungs, and I gasp, trying to break his hold so I can breathe. "My God, Mala, he could've killed you…" Each word comes with a slight hitch in his breathing. Choked and raw. His fingers fist in my hair, yanking my head back. "I could've lost you."

"No, I—" His mouth slams onto mine in a rough, deep, tongue-thrusting kiss that makes my body sag, boneless. All of his fear and anxiety flows out of him and into me until we're connected. I wrap my arms around his neck and kiss him back hard enough to remind him I'm alive.

When he finally pulls back, I say, "I'm sorry."

He's right. I could've been hurt worse than I am. Chasing after that guy really was all kinds of stupid. I just wanted to capture the bad guy. Play the hero in my own little drama. I don't deserve to be a cop.

Landry blows out a breath. "Okay, okay, I…"

"No, you're right. I didn't think. I'm sorry I scared you." I lean heavily on his arm as we walk toward the patrol cars parked in front of the pool. The parking lot is full of gawkers milling around: druggies, prostitutes, even a couple of truckers who thought the Super Delight would be a nice pit stop in their travels. It's loud. The excitement has people talking over each other as they speculate about what's happening.

George stands beside his patrol car with a clipboard. He's talking to the motel owner, Mr. Khan, who looks shaken up. Andy notices us before George does and nudges him in the shoulder. When George sees me, his eyes widen. I must look a mess. Then I see the shadowed flicker of his lashes, the solemn lines in his face, and a chill of premonition fills me.

I glance up to meet Landry's worried gaze. "Something's wrong, isn't it?"

The trembling in his arm intensifies.

Landry leads me through the crowd. Each step toward George feels like walking through molasses. Dread presses heavier and heavier upon my chest. By the time we reach his side, my legs quiver with the weight of remaining upright. "You said a woman got attacked. It's Mama, isn't it?"

George glances at Landry. "You didn't tell her?"

"I couldn't," Landry says, voice breaking. He kisses the tip of my nose. "I'm sorry. I'll talk to you later."

I nod, tears burning my eyes when he walks off, leaving me alone with George and the news I don't want to hear but have to know. Time freezes. A million scenarios of what could've happened to her and the possible outcomes race through my mind, but I'm afraid to ask the next question. *Is she dead?*

George takes my hand and gives it a gentle squeeze. "She's alive, Mala. We need to head to the hospital."

"Why? What happened?"

"I'm not sure of the details, but she's hurt pretty bad. If Mr. Khan hadn't heard her scream and run out, and if Landry hadn't shown up when he did, it might've been a different story."

"What about Landry?" Andy has him and Mr. Khan corralled by his K-9 car. If either of them try to get away, he'll probably sic Rex on them.

George tugs on my hand, leading me toward the door. "He can go after Andy gets his statement. Come on. You're wasting time."

"Wait, I need to—"

"Bessie and Maggie will meet us at the hospital," George says.

Each word takes me a little closer to the edge. By the time George helps me into his patrol car, I've fallen into an abyss. I have no idea how badly Mama has been hurt, but I can tell that it's bad by how little of the details George shares. I want Landry. I'm so scared. I need his strength to preserve my sanity, because despite George's promise that Mama still lives, I still pray that whole drive to the hospital that her death vision won't come true tonight.

Chapter 24

Mala

Spirit Attack

I walk through the sliding doors into the hospital emergency room, instantly feeling claustrophobic when I see the sterile white walls, green-tiled floor, and fake plants. The pungent odor of antiseptic barely masks the scent of blood. Whispers, barely audible, tickle my ears, making me strain to hear them. Shadows flicker in the corners—*oh, merciful heavens. People are dying—I have to get out of here!*

"I can't stay!" I spin on my heel.

Maggie blocks my path with outstretched arms. I'm seriously gonna punch her if she doesn't move. I don't care that she's my friend or that she tore herself from a date night with Tommy to meet me here. It would be better for both of us if she leaves me alone.

I try to dodge around her. She grabs onto my arm, spinning

me around. It's the same arm the attacker almost pulled out of its socket, and I crumple with the pain.

George's grip on my other arm tightens painfully as he yanks me from the doorway. "What are you doing?"

"I've got to get out of here." I twist on my arms, trying to break their grips. "You don't understand. This is a bad place."

My hands tingle, and my chest tightens. The room spins and grows fuzzy. "I-I can't breathe."

"Nurse, a little help!" George yells. He wraps my arm around his shoulder and grabs onto my waist, half carrying me over to a plastic chair. "Lean forward and put your head between your knees." He brushes sweaty hair from my eyes. "Focus on breathing. It'll be okay. You're having a panic attack."

I shake my head. "I'm dying."

"No, you're not. Everything's going to be fine." He turns to Maggie. "Bessie said she'd meet us here. Have you seen her?"

"No, we came separately."

"Do you know what's wrong with Mala? She lost her everlovin' mind the minute we walked through the door."

Maggie pats me on the back. "She hates hospitals. She had a bad experience when she was little. Said people kept sneaking into her room, and it scared her something fierce."

Concentrate. Air in. Air out. Don't think. Everything will be okay. I'll be fine. They won't get me. Not this time. But it's a lie. The hairs on the back of my neck rise as the spirits run fingers across my skin. A shiver shakes me so hard that I grip the armrests so I won't fall off the chair. A hand touches my shoulder. I shriek, flailing out with my arms.

"Stop her," Maggie yells, grabbing my waist.

George wraps his arms around mine.

I kick my legs, trying to break free. "Let go!"

"Cut it out, Mala."

A nurse in navy hospital scrubs stoops down beside me. She pulls an oxygen mask over my mouth, and I take a deep breath. I can't hear what she is saying over the pulse beating in my head. Black spots dance in front of my eyes. Maggie has a death grip on my hand, and I squeeze back, trying to let her know I'll be all right. My breathing slows.

Then Bessie enters the waiting room. A frown mars the smooth plane of her forehead. When she sees George, she waves him over. Once he reaches her side and hears what she has to say, he starts scowling too. Oh Jesus, it can't be good. I start to panic again. This time, the fear focuses specifically on my mama.

George threads his way back through the patients. A few people seem put out at the attention we're receiving. A harried-looking mother shoots me a dirty look and lifts a crying baby over her shoulder.

"How are you feeling, Mala?" George asks.

I pull the oxygen mask down. "I'll be fine once I know what's going on."

"Ms. Jasmine should be fine. Her ribs are cracked, and she's bruised up. Her doctor will be running some tests." He glances over at Bessie, who stands by the door leading into the emergency room, wearing an impatient scowl. "We'll be going in to get her statement."

"What about me? Can I see her?"

"They said you can visit after she's settled in a room. She'll need to stay in the hospital overnight for observation. You gonna be okay waiting?"

Maggie squeezes my hand. "I'll stay with her."

"Yeah, I'll be fine. I don't know why I lost it so bad. I feel silly." I run my fingers through my hair and wince.

"What's wrong?" George places his hand over mine. "Is this a knot?"

I pull my head back. "It's fine. I bumped it while swimming." And hit it again while fighting the attacker. I still haven't told George. I'm not sure why. Maybe because I didn't see anything that would help to identify him but, mostly, I don't feel up to another lecture. The one Landry gave pretty much convinced me of my stupidity. I don't need a second vote from George to verify it.

"You need to get that checked out," George says.

"It's bad enough that Mama's in here sucking off all our savings. I'm not gonna contribute to our losing our house over a stupid bump on the head."

"George," Bessie calls, waving for him. "Let's go."

He pauses, then stands up. His mouth opens as if he plans to protest, but he takes a hard look at my face. He must realize I won't change my mind because he leaves without saying another word on the subject.

Maggie, on the other hand, can't let it go. "What happened?"

"I was swimming in the pond and hit my head on the side of the boat."

Maggie gasps. "You could've been killed."

"No, Landry hauled me out before I drank too much water. I'm fine."

"Landry?" Maggie's eyes widen. "Did you say *Landry*? What's going on with the two of you? Every time I turn around, he's showing up. He doesn't seem like your type."

"What do you mean?"

"You've only dated two boys up until last week: Jamal and Nadaedrick." Maggie wiggles two fingers in front of my nose then lifts a third. "Oh, and Adrian from kindergarten, but I didn't think you wanted to count him, since he came out last year. I think he's dating Osby Bryant who works at the Piggly Wiggly."

I fan myself with a hand. "Yeah, they're gorgeous together. You can totally tell how much they love each other." I feel jealous every time I see them. I hope I'll find someone who will accept me so unconditionally, especially with me toting around all Mama's witchy baggage.

Maggie giggles at my expression. "Anyway, about Landry, he's everything you've always despised: popular, entitled, arrogant, and, worst of all, a player. He's been with most of the girls in town our age, and I've heard rumors about some who are older. I bet he's just trying to add another virgin to the notch on his belt."

"If that's all he wanted from me, he could've had it today," I mutter into the oxygen mask.

"What are you saying?"

I pull the mask down. "I'm saying that I tried to seduce him. I probably didn't do it right because he turned me down flat."

Maggie's eyes flash. "How dare he say no to you? There's nothing wrong with you. You're beautiful. Any guy would be lucky to get you."

"Maggie, that's not the point." I stare at her for a long, hard second then laugh, unable to deny that Landry appears to be all those things. But he's also protective, honest, for the most part, and even when he tries to lie, he busts himself out. "Thanks for having my back, but really, it's not necessary. Contrary to rumor, Landry's a decent person."

Plus even a shirtless Taylor Lautner comes in second to Landry.

I press my hand against the flutters in my tummy as I picture Landry sliding off his jeans in the boat. The way his eyes darken when he looks at me, like I'm a stack of hotcakes he wants to gobble up. He makes me feel—desired. I like that feeling.

I gasp. "Crap on toast, I've fallen for Landry."

Maggie blinks again. "You say that like it's a surprise."

I stand so fast I knock back the chair. "I can't fall in love with Landry. He's only interested in me as a make-out buddy. I'm gonna get my heart broken. Oh, Maggie, what do I do?"

"Keep away from him," she says flatly.

"I can't."

"The hole you're digging for yourself is only gonna get deeper. Like Mama says, 'The more you stir in shit, the more it stinks.' Landry's getting riper the more you're together. I watched you with him at Munchies. Don't tell me you're just friends. The way he looked at you had nothing friendly about it. He's got strong feelings for you, and even if he can't admit it, it shows."

"I told you, he turned me down. I offered, and he said no."

Maggie snorts, shaking her head. "You're so naive. I can't believe you finally put aside your crush on the amazing George and start liking on the first guy who shows an interest in you."

"What!" My throat tightens as I spit out the denial, "Why does everyone think I'm crushing on George? We're just friends. I do *not* like him like him."

"Humph. Go ahead, keep believing your own lies if it makes you feel better, but everyone who sees you together knows different. There's no shame in liking him. Everyone loves George. He's like Clark Kent and Superman rolled up into one person."

"Clark Kent and Superman *are* the same person, Maggie."

She blinks twice and barks out a laugh that trails off uncomfortably. She glances up and gasps. I follow her gaze. George stands next to us. Double crap! I'm not sure how long he's been listening to our conversation, but he heard enough. Heat spreads up my chest and into my cheeks. I cross my arms to keep from fanning my burning face, playing it off. "Can I see Mama now?"

"She's upstairs. I'll take you to her room."

The shaking starts again. The deeper into the depths of the hospital I walk, the more it feels like the ceiling and walls press down upon me. I'm being caged into a shrinking box with no way to escape. I can't stop thinking about her death vision. If what Magnolia said was true, then the future has already come to pass and it echoes through time with no way to stop it.

"Are you sure she'll be all right, Georgie?" I ask.

"Her doctor said the injuries aren't life threatening."

"Did the guy just beat her up or did he do...more?"

George won't meet my eyes. "Bessie talked to her about that so I wouldn't know. They did a rape kit, but that's standard in these situations. Especially at the Super Delight."

I sigh. "The motel's where she usually sees her *clients*." A foul taste coats my tongue while uttering the word, and my lips twist bitterly. "Do they have security cameras posted?"

"No security videos, you pay by the hour, and it's situated close enough to the highway for a quick getaway. A lot of drug transactions are handled at the motel for that reason."

"Mama worked out a deal with Mr. Khan and rents her room by the month."

My chest tightens as I flash back to the dream of Lainey dragging me underwater, of straining to hold my breath. Had the dream been a warning of Mama's attack? If I'd listened, could I have prevented her from getting hurt? "She got lucky, didn't she?"

"The guy tried to kill her, Malaise. He would've succeeded if Landry hadn't heard the splash."

I nod stiffly, following George into the elevator.

"I heard your conversation with Maggie," he says once the doors close.

"Huh?" It takes me a second to shift gears from Mama's attack.

"I wasn't deliberately spying or anything. But I heard you say you're falling for Landry." George glares at the buttons lighting up as the elevator rises. With a jerky movement, he slams his fist on the emergency stop. The elevator freezes. "Seriously, Mala? Landry? Of all the guys—"

Oh God, why couldn't he act like a gentleman and pretend like he hadn't overheard my confession? This means he also heard Maggie's ridiculous theory about me crushing on him too? *Kill me now.*

"You…you can't stop the elevator!" I sputter. "This is a hospital."

"Are you insane? How can you associate with that asshole after everything he's done?" He steps too close, filling my vision.

I press back against the metal wall, wishing I could disappear through it. "I don't know what you're talking about."

"He attacked you at Lainey's memorial. He's playing you against his girlfriend, Clarice—"

"Hold on there, buddy. He didn't attack me. And Clarice is not his girlfriend."

"Tell *her* that. They go to church together every Sunday. Clarice was with Landry in the hot tub the day I went to his house with the death notification for Lainey. They were very obviously together. Do you really think he's interested in being with you?"

Very obviously together? What the hell does that mean? My face flushes with heat. *Duh, sex.* Now I'm pissed. I step forward, and it's his turn to retreat. "Why can't he be interested? Am I that hard on the eyes?"

"He's not your type. He's gonna play you for a fool and dump you."

"Good to know what you really think about me, George. With all I have to worry about, at least I've got you to remind me of how worthless, stupid, and ugly I am." This about sums up my frustration with George. He sees me as a naive little girl who needs protection from the big, bad Landry. It's not like I'm silly enough to think that Landry wants to be in a long-term relationship. So what if he's only turning to me for comfort? It's my choice how much of myself I choose to give him. Or anyone else.

I hit the button, and the door pops open. "What's the room number? I'll find it on my own. Spare you my company since I'm so unbearable to be seen with."

"That's not what I said."

"Yeah, it is."

Bessie waits outside of a room at the end of the hall, and I walk in her direction.

George follows, still yammering. "What if he killed his sister and he's trying to find out what you know?"

"I'm not listening to you," I say, covering my ears.

"He's dangerous. And every time you see him, you're putting yourself at risk."

No matter how hard I press on my ears, I can still hear his words. My hands drop and fist at my sides to keep from doing something I'll regret. "How many times do I have to say that he did not kill Lainey?"

"You don't know that for sure. You're talking with your heart, not your head. I'm following the clues, and they all lead home—Lainey's home."

I whirl around to face him. "What does that mean?"

Bessie had been slouched against the wall, but she stands upright and her eyes narrow on George. "Yes, George, what *does* that mean?"

George looks at Bessie with a pleading expression. "Will you talk some sense into her? Tell her to stay away from Landry Prince."

"Leave it alone, Deputy Dubois," Bessie warns.

George turns back to me, eyes wide. "Don't you see? I'm concerned. I'm not always going to be around to save you."

I squint up at him. The overhead lights turn his copper hair into a halo. I study his earnest expression. The poor guy. His protective nature has been sent into overdrive. No matter how I wish otherwise, he still thinks of me as that helpless little kid he protected from bullies in high school. Fighting with him feels wrong. "But you promised you would be, Superman."

George's eyes go flat and hard. "Stop thinking of me like I'm some kind of superhero."

Bessie raises her hand impatiently. "Enough, guys. This is neither the time nor the place for this discussion." Heat enters her voice. "I'm ashamed of both of you—acting like a pair of fools in front of a sickroom—but, George, you're a representative of the department. This behavior in front of our victim's family is unacceptable."

I duck my head, embarrassed, and sneak a peek at George's face. He doesn't seem at all remorseful. If anything, I think he wants to argue with Bessie, but the look on her face shuts him up faster than supergluing his lips together.

Bessie folds her arms. "Mala, get in the room and talk some sense into Jasmine. She's holding on to her story and claims she doesn't remember what happened to her."

"Is she telling the truth? If she has a head injury—"

"Hardheaded is what she's being. Says her work is confidential, and if word gets out that she snitched to the police about things getting 'a little out of hand,' that she'd lose customers."

I nod. "Can't fault her logic on that, Bessie. Those perverts she sees would scatter like cockroaches under a flashlight if they thought the police might get wind of their nighttime activities."

Bessie sighs. "Talk to her, Mala. Help me bag this guy before he kills the next hooker he 'dates.'"

"I'll try, but I won't make any promises."

I freeze in the doorway, unable to force myself to enter the room. I'm damn sure the woman lying in the hospital bed is not my mama. Mama isn't some frail, birdlike thing. She looms, larger than life, shooting sparks of energy from every fiber of her being, while this woman resembles a shriveled-up old lady, lingering on the brink of death.

"Go on in, Mala." George prods me forward.

"This is the wrong room." I turn to head back the way we came, brushing off his hand when he tries to stop me. "I don't know this person."

"Mala, stop this," Bessie orders.

"I *said* I don't know that woman. She's not my mother. You've identified the wrong person. How could you've made such a stupid mistake?"

"Mala," the woman in the room calls with Mama's voice, and I shudder. "Get your butt in here 'fore I got to pull my tired bones out of this bed and grab you."

I glance at George and wince. "Hellfire and damnation! It really is her, isn't it?"

Pity fills Bessie's eyes. She pats my arm. "I know this is hard for you to accept. Nobody likes to see a loved one in pain. Jasmine's tough, but you need to take it easy on her. She's not as strong as she sounds."

"She looks like she's been wrung out and put away wet. I seriously didn't recognize her."

Didn't *want* to recognize her with her eyes swollen and black, a cast on her arm, and white linen draped over her. Then she gestures imperiously. "Everyone get out except my daughter. Go on, I said my piece and ain't nothin' changin' my mind, so you might as well go."

"Ms. Jasmine, if you could—" George protests.

"I said get out!"

Chapter 25

Mala

Hoe

I close the door slowly, not wanting to slam it in their faces, then turn to Mama with a shake of my head. "Now that wasn't nice. They wanted to help."

"They wanted to get all up in my business." Mama taps a button on the medication dispenser. "Ah, that's better. I'm achin'."

"I get that you don't want to talk to the police, but tell me what happened. Who did this to you?"

"Never mind that, I'll survive. Guess that death vision wasn't such to cry about after all." She grins. "Came close to meetin' my maker, but I'm stronger than I look. And I float real good."

Anger twists my gut for whoever did this to her, but I force a laugh, as she intended. I rush to the bed and throw my arms around her narrow shoulders, careful not to hug her too tight. "I was so scared. I didn't even know you'd gotten back from New

Orleans, then to hear you'd gotten assaulted—" I pull away from her arms, clenching my fists. I want to hit someone so bad. My whole body vibrates. "Don't you *ever* frighten me like that again!"

Mama eyes me warily. Then understanding lights her heavy-lidded gaze. "Guess you do love your mama."

"Of course, don't be silly. I don't know what I'd do without you driving me crazy." I perch on the edge of the bed and lay my hand on the cast. "How long do you expect to be in here?"

"The doc said I can go home tomorrow night." Her eyes drift closed, and I think for a moment she's fallen asleep, but she opens them again to scowl at me. "'Fore I forget, what's this I overhear about you seein' that Prince boy?"

"You left me. I didn't have anyone else to turn to for help dealing with Lainey. Landry's been a friend to me the last week."

"That boy's no friend to you," Mama says, and her eyes close again. "Them Princes are a shady bunch. Keep clear of him. Do you hear?" One eye opens to glare at me until I nod. "Good. Now go on home. I don't need you no more."

Mama falls asleep. If she'd been in her right mind, I might've argued. But I'm grown. I don't need her permission. I tiptoe from the room to find Bessie in the hallway, and she insists I spend the night at her house.

Maggie and I lie in her bed, gossiping for hours. I fight falling asleep, not because I enjoy having my messed up love life dissected, but because after the emotionally exhausting day I've had, I'm terrified of the coming nightmares. When I do drift off, I dream I'm on fire. My clothes and hair burn first. Then my flesh blackens and peels. Blood sizzles on the ground. Worse, even though I choke on the smoke, I don't pass out. I wake up coughing so hard that I'm afraid I'll hack up a lung. I give up on sleep and watch infomercials on the TV in the living room for the rest of the night.

The next morning, I pull on my big-girl panties and return to the hospital to visit Mama. I get lucky. The spiritual attacks aren't as bothersome during the day. Or maybe I'm getting used to their goose bump–raising touch on my skin. A nurse finally kicks me out after lunchtime, saying Mama needs her rest, not that she knows I'm there. She's using a heavy hand on the morphine drip. I'm kind of envious. My bumps and bruises still ache, but the pain becomes manageable once I take the pain meds I bought at the gift shop.

A cab drops me off at the Super Delight Motel. I took Mama's keys before leaving the hospital so I can pick up her truck before someone jacks it. It's parked in front of room 105. I stare at the red door with the yellow police tape criss-crossing it while considering my options. We didn't get to search Lainey's room last night because of the attack, but the plan's still good. Nothing has changed except that I've added another psychopath to my list. Now, not only do I need to find Lainey's murderer, I also have to figure out which of Mama's clients attacked her.

Key in hand, I go inside. It looks like a normal bedroom. Mama rents by the month, and she's had this room for as long as I've been alive. It's totally trashed, and I don't think by the Sheriff's Office either. The mattress has been shoved off the frame. Clothes and shoes cover the floor. Boxes of oils, candles, and cleansing crystals are stacked in her closet. She even has a crystal skull, and I roll my eyes—the hoodoo supplies Mom buys off the

Internet to sell to the girls. I dab a dollop of Fast Luck oil on my wrists and sniff. *Mmm, cinnamony.* Hopefully it'll work. I could use some good luck.

Seeing the room so disorganized makes me jittery. What in the world was this guy searching for that would make him resort to attempted murder?

I spend half an hour straightening up. When I'm finished, her bed is made and candles rest on the bedside table. I hang Mama's work clothes in the closet—I don't find anything made with leather or holes that would scar my psyche, which makes me immensely grateful. I have a hard enough time accepting this part of Mama's life. I didn't need or want firsthand knowledge, but now, whenever I think of her at work, I'll picture her lying on this bed with the fuchsia and yellow tropical flowers reading *The Color Purple*.

I don't find any clues as to what happened last night. Maybe the police had better luck. I pocket the wad of money I find hidden in her shoe. I also decide at the last minute to take the book. Mama might like something to read while she's recuperating. After locking up the room, I walk over to the fence surrounding the algae-coated swimming pool. A dark blotch stains the concrete by the ladder. I assume the blood belongs to Mama, but it certainly could've come from some other poor soul. The gate looks rickety, but when I give it a jerk, it won't open. I contemplate how much pain and effort it will take to climb the fence. I want to get a closer look at the crime scene.

I've just thrown my leg over the metal railing when Mr. Khan opens the door to the recreation room and steps out. He wears a black turban, a blue silk shirt, and slacks. Coppery brown skin, slightly wrinkled with age, highlights dark eyes. Wire-rimmed glasses attached to a gold chain hang around his neck.

"Who are you?" he asks, squinting in my direction. "What do you do here? The pool is closed."

"Mr. Khan?" I jerk on my foot, which has gotten stuck in the fencing. "Don't you recognize me? I'm Jasmine's daughter. I heard that you helped pull Mama from the pool. You saved her life. Thank you."

Mr. Khan slips his glasses on his nose and shakes his head. "That was a very bad thing that happened to my good friend Jasmine. Very bad. I am only happy that I came in time."

He turns to go back inside.

I pull my foot out of my tennis shoe. The wire mesh shakes, and I half fall, half jump off the fence, landing a few feet from the man. "Mr. Khan, please. Wait."

"The pool is a dangerous place to play games. Go now."

"This isn't a game. Not to me." I limp toward him, talking fast. "I've got to ask. Did you see anything last night? The guy who attacked her…did you recognize him? Maybe something you didn't tell the police. If you did, you can tell me. I'll keep it quiet, I promise, but I've got to know if my mama's still in danger. Who do I protect her from?"

"Did she not tell you?" Khan's head tilts to the side. A furtive expression creases the corners of his eyes as he glances around to see if we are alone. "She would be quite upset if she found out that I spoke of her big meeting. We have an understanding. She pays me to keep quiet, so I keep quiet. But she did not pay me for last night."

"So you don't have to keep her secret?"

Khan sighs. "You will pay for this information? A hundred dollars."

"Hundred—" I choke on the word. "I'll give you twenty."

He shakes his head. "Now you insult me."

"Damn it, fifty. I can't go any higher."

"Seventy-five or no deal. What price do you put on your mother's life?"

I dig into the pocket of my jeans and pull out three of the eight twenty-dollar bills I found in Mama's room and hold it out to him. "Sixty. Take it or leave it. This is all I've got to spare, you cold-hearted old pimp."

He snatches the twenties from my hand and waves them under his nose. His eyes close as he smells the money, and I get an icky feeling inside. Finally satisfied, he smiles. "You drive a hard bargain. Jasmine would be proud."

"Save the compliments. Tell me what I just paid for."

"Jasmine told me she was meeting with a very important man last night—a very rich and powerful man—who has much influence in the community. She said she knows something about him that he would pay a lot of money to keep quiet."

"Blackmail?" Shocked, my hands ball into fists. "You'd better not be lying to me."

Khan raises a silver eyebrow, eyeing me wearily. "Oh, no. Jasmine was quite proud of her news. She said she has proof, written in blood. She asked me to pay close attention when he came. She didn't trust him. That he'd kill to keep his secret quiet. She feared for her life. I think this was very wise and unwise."

"I'd say unwise since the guy almost murdered her."

Khan shrugs. "Some risks are worth taking. Ten thousand dollars is what she asked for. Maybe the amount was too insulting. That's when he tried to kill her." He laughs, and I want to sock him right in his jelly-filled gut.

I take a deep breath instead, trying to calm down. "Did you get a look at him?"

"He wore a black mask. I could not see his face."

"That's it? You're the lookout and you couldn't even get a decent description of this guy?"

"He owns a large truck."

"Great, that's just fan-fuckin'-tastic. A truck. In Paradise Pointe, Louisiana. Wow, I'll get right on that clue. Hell, you've broken the case wide open. You're a hero, Mr. Khan. A regular Sherlock Holmes."

"What did you expect for sixty bucks? You get what you pay for." Khan waves the money in the air, kisses it, and turns to walk back inside to do whatever a lowlife scum bucket does when not bilking schmucks. *What the hell am I...* I pause, one foot raised to climb the fence, then let it drop. *A large truck...* Khan said he owns a truck, but the guy didn't drive away. He ran off on foot. So how does Khan know he owns a truck?

"Mr. Khan, wait." I hold the rest of the money I found in Mama's "office" in the air. "One more question."

The man turns with a sly grin and rubs his lips with two fingers. "Ah, it appears this question is worth more than your mother's life?"

"I think the answer may save her life...and mine." *Calm down. Don't spook Khan.* He's the sort who uses your weaknesses to his advantage. I breathe out a slow breath. "The man you saw. Ever seen him before without the mask?"

"I don't know who he is or his name, but yes, he frequently visits."

My heart skips a beat. "Which is why you don't know his identity, right? Because he pays you not to know?"

Mr. Khan shrugs.

"But the woman he visited is dead. So you no longer have to keep quiet about her."

His smile grows wider. "What do you want to know?"

Bingo! I hold the money out. He reaches to take it, but I snatch my hand back. "I want everything you found in Lainey Prince's room when you cleaned it out, Mr. Khan. No tricks. You give me Lainey's belongings, and you get the money. If you hold out on me, I'll know. My mama's not the only witch in town. I'll do worse than twist a curse. I'll go to the police and tell them you held back information about her murderer."

"How do you know I didn't give her belongings to the man who tried to kill your mother?"

Lucky guess. I mimic his conniving grin. "You're a businessman, Mr. Khan. And you're more cunning than my mama. You probably came up with the plan to blackmail him together. Now that your brilliant plan has failed, I think you should be more concerned about getting rid of this property before he comes back and tries to kill you for knowing too much."

The man gives me an elegant bow. "Jasmine pawned the jewelry, but she kept the rest of the girl's belongings. She planned to trade the box to the man last night. He must have taken it with him after he attacked her because it was missing when I found her in the pool."

I flash back to the night before when I chased after the guy. He had been holding something in his arms while he ran. It dropped and slid beneath a car after I tackled him. Could it still be in there? I don't bother to say good-bye to Mr. Khan, just sprint into the parking lot.

I find the small cardboard box holding what is left of Lainey's possessions beneath a purple Cadillac. It contains a bunch of toiletry items and clothes. Nothing worth murdering someone over. *Another fucking dead end.*

"Damn it, Mama!" I kick the box halfway across the parking lot.

Mama tried to blackmail her attacker, knowing he likely killed Lainey. No wonder she won't talk to the police. Either she fears she'll get arrested along with the guy she threatened or she figures, once she gets out of the hospital, she'll give another go at getting the money. But what does she have that he wants? He had the box, but he still trashed Mama's room. He was looking for something specific, and I don't think he found it. What does Mama have over him?

I gather Lainey's belongings. The whole drive home the puzzle of *why*s form and re-form in random, shifting patterns in my mind. I'm close to figuring out the mystery. I know it. I try to stop obsessing over what I've learned by applying myself to my chores. I feed the chickens, clean house, and, afterward, reapply my protective salt and brick dust. Then I start working on the vegetable garden. Hoeing works muscles in places I've forgotten exist.

The ground has dried out from the rain. I dig with a vengeance, chopping up roots and pulling out a gazillion rocks that seem to multiply like gremlins every spring. The monotonous work keeps me from worrying about Mama. Every time I picture her bruised face, I swing the hoe with all my strength, imagining the faceless man who hurt her and feeling angry at her for deliberately creating the situation that caused the attack.

The sun beats down. Sweat pours down my face. It's stupid. I'll get sick if I don't stay hydrated, but I'm driven. I clear most of the row I want to plant my tomatoes in, but one stinking root refuses to budge. It taunts me. A large white lump nestled in the red-brown earth, like a baby in its mother's arms. I can almost hear it wail each time the hoe cuts into the bulbous bark that runs with a thick, red liquid—like blood.

It can't be. My vision blurs. I blink salty sweat from my eyes, ignoring the burn. The root shimmers, twisting, and a tiny hand lifts, waving in the air. Eyes as blue as morning glory petals stare directly into mine.

The air grows cold, freezing the sweat to my skin. Mist forms before my eyes when I breathe. As the temperature drops, my body grows sluggish. I fall to my knees, unable to stand. My hands lift to cover my nose, trying to blot out the thick stench of roses and decomposition. Red rose petals float from the sky, landing in my hair and drifting down to cover the naked baby.

A dead baby. A boy, with Lainey's eyes.

"Lainey, stop," I whimper, grabbing a handful of grass, dragging myself forward because I can't crawl. Icy fingers dig into my legs and hold on. The hand caresses my skin, and her heavy weight presses full-bodied on top of me. I shiver, and my nose runs. I wipe my upper lip, but instead of seeing mucus on my fingers, I see blood.

"Please, stop. Lainey, you're killing me. Let go!"

My outstretched hand closes around a small leather bag, and I bring it to my chest. Warmth floods outward. The hands holding my legs vanish. I collapse, shaking so hard I can barely catch my breath.

When I return to myself, I realize I fainted. I stand up, swaying a little from dizziness, and trudge into the house, only stopping off at the fridge to grab the pitcher of mint tea before I collapse at the kitchen table. The juju bag has been clutched inside my fist the whole time, and finally after quenching my thirst, I take a hard look at the thing that banished Lainey. Opening it up, I see the sage that I tossed disdainfully into the grass has been returned to mingle with all the strange ingredients inside the bag—a bag that magically found its way into my hand when I needed its protection the most.

"You did this, didn't you?" I feel a little silly to be addressing the protector spirit of some unknown ancestor, but somehow, I know it listens. "You saved me from her. Thank you."

Warm wind blows back my hair.

I stuff the juju bag inside my pocket and head to the bathroom. I hope the protective charms around the house keep Lainey out, but even while showering, I hold the bag above the water so it won't get wet. The phone rings while I'm towel drying my hair, and I hear Landry's voice on the answering machine. I run into the living room, but he'd already hung up, and after listening to his message, I feel guilty.

I'd been so worried about my own problems that I forgot that today is Lainey's funeral. Not that this matters to her. She's too busy haunting me. Why would she show me a vision of a baby? She'd been pregnant, but I didn't think she'd been that far along. And Dr. Rathbone completed the autopsy; he'd know if Lainey delivered the baby. George never mentioned a baby was missing. Maybe it was one of the clues he'd been ordered to keep quiet. But if he didn't know…why did Rathbone cover up the birth? For my own peace of mind, I need to know the truth.

My mind tickles. Deep inside where my thoughts race and ideas form, a little tickle grows more annoying the more I mentally poke at it. The germ of an idea that sits just out of reach. Like most irritations, the prickle spreads, crawling down my tingling neck. When my hands start to burn, I scream in frustration. My hands tighten into fists, nails digging so deeply into the skin that blood wells up in the crescent marks on my palms.

I circle the room, moving from the living room to the kitchen, around the table, and back into the living room. My gaze darts to the television, to the King, across the porcelain curios Mama collected, unable to settle on any one object for too long.

The newspaper I bought at the hospital lies beside the door where I dropped it after I returned home this morning. It had fallen open, its pages scattered across the floor. I must've stepped on it several times while pacing and never noticed. A breeze lifts the straggles of damp hair falling loose around my shoulders, blowing into my eyes. The edge of one of the pages flutters like the wing of a baby bird. It spins in a slow circle, picking up speed like a dust devil. Then, with a *whoosh*, the paper flies into the air, brushes the ceiling, and drifts down into my outstretched hand.

I stare down at the obituary, into the dimpled face of the woman smiling at me from the black-and-white photo. Her hair curls around her face, beneath the edges of a scarf. Large hoop earrings brush her shoulders. She stands in front of her trailer, right in front of her sign, with her son perched on her hip. I can't tear my eyes from the hand holding an eyeball in the middle of its palm because, otherwise, I'd see Ruby.

"Oh, no. It's true…she's dead." My heart pounds like it will explode out of my chest and spray the room with my blood. "Why are you showing me this?" I yell to the silent room, shaking the crumpled paper at the ceiling. The walls expand then contract, like the house sighs. "What do you want from me?"

Chapter 26

Mala

Funeral

I was driven out of the house by an energy that set my hairs on end. But it fades the minute I step foot on hallowed ground, and I can think clearly again. In the distance, a large crowd of black-clothed mourners has gathered for Lainey's funeral. I feel too uncomfortable about intruding on their grief to join them, especially since my presence would be a reminder of how I found the body.

Sheriff Keyes, Dr. Rathbone, and Mr. Acker stand in the second row with their families. Landry is in front of the tomb with his folks. He has his arm wrapped around his dry-eyed mother. After her crazed behavior at the autopsy, I expected her to be broken up, but a more stoic and reserved facade I've never seen on a person. Clarice, wearing a wide-brimmed black hat, stands a little behind and to the right of Landry—the leech. She keeps touching him—patting him on the shoulder, rubbing his arm—I want to scratch her eyes out!

I'm carrying the small box containing Lainey's belongings under one arm as I climb up the stairs and sit down cross-legged on the concrete block holding Eulie LaCroix's remains above the waterline. The height of the tomb gives me a clear view of the service. The sun-bleached plaster feels cold through my light, black linen dress, and I shiver despite the heat of the day. I hadn't thought that Eulie would mind my company, but perhaps the chill settling into my bones is her way of expressing her disapproval over my not coming to visit more often.

Eulie is the first of my ancestors to be buried in the town cemetery. Her mother, Zouzoute, and her grandmère, Calixte, are buried in the Savoie cemetery. Calixte was Gerard Savoie's mistress, born somewhere on the Ivory Coast in Africa. I could've walked across her grave yesterday, and I never would've known since there aren't any tombstones. I'm a seventh-generation LaCroix—the seventh daughter.

Eulie was my grandmère Cora's grandmère. In fact, the tombs of my ancestors surround me: Great-grandmère Dahlia rests sandwiched between her children: Grandmère Cora and her twin brother, Gaston. Uncle Gaston died during the Vietnam War. He'd gotten blown up after stepping on a land mine. Dahlia's twin sister, Auntie Magnolia, will probably be buried with her mother, Eulie. Mama and I will be buried together someday 'cause, judging by the way the plots are laid out, the women in our family don't have a great track record of keeping a man longer than for procreation.

"Is dying alone the price the women in our family pay for

our gifts?" I whisper, letting the wind blowing around my body take the words to whoever might be listening. "Are we cursed?"

No answer seems forthcoming. Either Grandmère Eulie doesn't know or she isn't willing to share the secret with me.

Across the field of stone crypts stand two men who hold pieces of my heart—Landry and George. Yet I can't touch either one. It's like I sit in a bubble, separated from the rest of humanity by a thin membrane that I can't pierce. I see the world through a filmy haze. But none of the emotions spilling over from the mourners touches me. Not directly, not here in my isolation. No grief, no joy, and especially, not love.

I lightly trace my fingertips over the stylized cross carved into the plaster of the tomb. It seems kind of prophetic that, after slavery, my ancestors who practiced hoodoo had named themselves after one of the loa, Baron LaCroix, the spirit of death, and carved his symbol into their resting places. This crumbling cross beneath my fingers symbolizes the LaCroix family line—death and resurrection. Did the women in my family always have an affinity for the dead, or did some unknown ancestor ask this god for the power? And if the power was given, could it be taken away? If I pray real hard, could I be freed to live out my life with the man I love and be buried with him and my children around me? Could I break this curse?

Someday I'll know the answer.

Surrounded by a long line of strong LaCroix grandmothers, I can't sit around and cry about my fate, or I'll insult the women who lived and died with the same questions. And these ancestors are strong. Their power fills me. I inhale their strength with each breath. Eulie, Dahlia, Cora, and Gaston LaCroix are powerful enough to keep Lainey's spirit from bugging me. For that gift alone, I sit upright in pride and relief and feel sorry for Landry as, every so often, he rubs his arms like he feels a chill.

"Hello," a voice calls. "What are you doing up here?"

I turn around so fast I almost topple off the side of the tomb. "Oh, Georgie," I say, hand to my heart. For the split second it took before I recognized his voice, I thought Eulie had finally decided to answer my questions. "You scared the spit out of me."

George raises a copper eyebrow, and I flush.

"Sorry, you frightened me."

He threads his way through the graves and settles on the step below me. He waves toward the dispersing crowd of mourners. "You shouldn't be here."

"I know, but I had to come." *Or go crazy.*

"Everyone's heading over to the Princes' house after the service. Landry will be too busy with his family to talk to you."

"Maybe I can catch him before he leaves."

"Or you can stay with me," he says with a smile.

I take a deep breath to clear the sudden fog from my brain. *Whoa, Georgie.* I squint, studying his face. *Why is he being so nice all of a sudden?*

"Don't burn a hole in my forehead," he says, tipping his chin upward. "We've got company. Try not to embarrass me."

"As if…" I mutter beneath his laughter. We turn toward the footsteps heading in our direction. Ms. March and her brother, Georgie's father, George Sr., stroll toward us arm and arm. So sweet. Every time I see Mr. Dubois, I'm struck by how different he and his son are in appearance. Georgie takes after Ms. March.

They're both all sunshine and light, while Mr. Dubois is a handsome older man who embodies darkness. Brown hair glitters with silver at the temples, and he stares at me without cracking a smile, like always.

George rises. "Service over so soon?"

Impatience settles across Mr. Dubois's familiar features. "Your absence at the end of the service was noticed."

"I doubt it," George says as if his mouth is full of rocks. His jaw flexes, and I stand so it doesn't feel as if Mr. Dubois looms over my head like a stone gargoyle.

Ms. March shoots me a sidelong glance with a slight roll of her eyes toward her brother and nephew, and I stifle a giggle. Silver curls bounce on her shoulders. She pats her brother's arm. "Leave the boy alone, G.D. I'm sure you've met Mala LaCroix. She helps me out around the house. I wouldn't know how to get along without her."

Mr. Dubois nods but doesn't stick out his hand for me to shake. "Everyone's heading back to the church. I'll drive." He half turns as if expecting George to follow.

"I have to go," I say, resisting the urge to stick my tongue out at the man's back. "Ms. March, I'll be seeing you later this week. It was a pleasure seeing you again, Mr. Dubois." I grab the box and start down the tomb stairs, hoping to catch Landry before he leaves so I can tell him about Lainey's baby.

"I'll walk with you," Georgie offers, holding out his arm for me to take. I almost pass out in surprise.

Senior's brows draw downward. "Your mother's expecting you."

"No, she isn't, Dad. I told her that I have to head back to work after the funeral. Come on, Mala." Georgie takes my free hand and places it on his arm. Tension bunches the muscles beneath his suit jacket. Whew, his daddy has pissed him off good.

We walk away, leaving the Dubois siblings arguing. From their raised voices, Ms. March seems to be giving him hell for being such a rude prick.

George slants a glance down at me. "I can tell when you're upset. You get quiet and start chewing on your bottom lip."

"Yeah, I'm predictable." I wish I had the ability to hide my emotions. I want to tell him about the vision I had of the baby, but I can't think of a way to say "I see dead people" without sounding like a loon. Rational folk don't believe in ghosts.

I decide to take the cowardly route and leave my confession for a later time. Besides, I need to warn Landry first. I don't want him blindsided by the police about his nephew being murdered. He needs the truth from a friend. At least I finally figured out who the *him* was in FIND HIM. Lainey had been asking me to find her son. He should be buried with his mother here on hallowed ground, not in some unmarked grave somewhere. *Under red roses...*

"I'm surprised you came today," George says, interrupting my train of thought. "I thought you'd be at the hospital."

I give his arm a little squeeze. "They kicked me out. 'Sides, Mama's drugged up on painkillers. She's not much company, and I felt like I needed to be here."

"For Landry?" George raises an eyebrow. "Clarice seems to be quite capable of supporting him. She's been glued to his side all afternoon."

"Are you trying to be nasty?"

"Trying to get you to recognize the obvious—Prince is using you."

I pull my hand from his arm and take a giant step back before I smack him upside his fat head. My high heel digs into the soft ground, and my ankle twists to the right. My body falls to the left. George's arm wraps around my waist, and I end up with the box sandwiched between our chests.

"Whew, Georgie. Once again you've kept me from falling flat on my face."

"When are you gonna give up on heels? You're dangerous on them."

"I'm no quitter. Plus, heels are sexy. Don't you think?"

"I guess." The doubt in his voice makes me cringe. I free myself from his arms with a wince. He bends over and runs his hand down my left leg. I try to hide the quiver that spreads up my leg and through my back. My knees wobble.

George picks me up and sits me on a tomb. "Does this hurt?" he asks, feeling my ankle.

"What do you think?"

"Gosh, you're testy when you're injured."

"It hurts!"

"Look, you can't walk on this. Sit here while I go get my car and park it closer. I'll be back for you."

"Promise?"

He taps the end of my nose with his finger. "Cross my heart."

The last of the mourners file out of the cemetery in groups as the sun dips in the sky, creating deep shadows beneath the trees. The air cools and I shiver, rubbing my arms. Where in the world did George park, Outer Mongolia? Either he's stuck in traffic or he forgot and left me here—alone, in the dark, with the dead.

I sense Lainey's presence before I see who she shadows.

"Landry?"

"I saw you." He stalks more than walks toward me. A wild energy fills him, and it kind of makes me nervous, especially since I can't run.

"Okay." I force myself upright, placing my weight on my uninjured leg.

"It's good you stayed back. My parents would've freaked if you joined the service."

"They're not a fan of my charm and good looks?"

Landry's eyes glitter. "They're not fond of you. Or your mother."

Ouch, it's brutal honesty day. "Is it the fact that she's supposed to be a witch?"

"No, because she's a prostitute."

My throat tightens around the words I force out. "I can see how they'd disapprove of my mama given they're Christians, but I've never done anything wrong."

"Lainey died on your land." He wraps his hand around my neck, threading his fingers into my upswept curls. His grip tightens, and a couple of bobby pins slip. "They're angry about that."

"But she didn't. She was on Forest Service land. She just happened to float downstream." I jerk my head free, wincing with pain as a couple of hairs remain in his grip. "What's the matter with you today? Why are you being so mean? I swear I'm sick of you and Lainey haunting me. I never should've dragged her from the water 'cause now I can't get rid of her."

"She's here with us now." He turns in a full circle. "I can feel her."

"Landry, you're in full-crazy mode today." I step away from him, but I forgot about my ankle. I let out a yelp of pain, arms spinning as I try to catch my balance. *Why do I always have to be the sane one?* "Damn it, Landry—"

He wraps his arms around my waist and pulls me tight. His heart pounds as fast as if he sprints toward the finish line in a marathon. He presses his nose into my hair. "God, you smell so good. I want to—"

"Don't say it! We're not doing anything in a cemetery." I stare up into eyes so dilated they resemble a lunar eclipse—only a thin sliver of gray remains. I thump my fist into his chest. "What did you take? How much and how long ago did you take it?"

"It's all legal, Mala," Landry says with a little laugh. "Doc Rathbone prescribed it for Mama's nerves, and she shared some. I'll be fine once I get through the rest of this night. I swear. I needed something to keep me from losing it on all those people going to my house giving out false sympathy. Nobody knew my sister. Least of all me."

I press my palm against his chest. "Lainey did something scary today."

He steps closer. "I'm going to pick you up now."

"Say what?"

"I'm picking you up and carrying you to my truck."

"Wait. You don't have to." I scan the cemetery for George, not wanting him to catch me with Landry, but we're the only ones left in this section. It isn't like him not to keep his promise.

"It's getting dark, and you're alone. Do you really want to be in the cemetery when the sun sets, especially with your connection to the dead?"

"Not the dead. One dead person—Lainey."

"She's trying to tell me something." Landry slides his arms beneath my knees and behind my back. He lifts me like I weigh nothing. Shit. Why does crazy Landry seem hotter than normal? And why can't I stop noticing? He tosses his head, trying to move a lock of black hair away from his face.

"Can you get that, Mala? My hands are full."

"Oh sure, since they're full of me." I brush the silky strands out of his eyes and trail my fingers across his stubbly cheek. "You look exhausted. Did you sleep last night?"

Landry presses a kiss to the top of my head. "No, I've been having nightmares. Last night I dreamed of fire. Plus I kept hoping you'd call."

"Really? Me too. I mean, I dreamed of a fire. I couldn't sleep and ended up watching TV all night. I didn't expect you to call. I didn't even know you had my phone number until I got your message this afternoon. Thanks for asking about my mom…" I blink at him, realizing I've been rambling. "Do you think the dreams are what Lainey uses to warn us about the future?"

"I hope not. That's some messed-up shit."

The box rests against my chest like a lead weight. I have to tell Landry that the guy who shacked up with Lainey tried to kill Mama, likely murdered his sister, and buried their baby beneath a rose bush, but he seems fragile today. How do I tell him the truth when it will devastate him? Maybe I shouldn't tell him.

Give me a sign, God, please. I don't know what to do.

Landry adjusts my body higher in his arms. Hot breath sighs across my cheek, and I shiver.

"Stop squirming before I drop you."

"Sorry, I got excited."

"About what? Dreams of a future that may or may not happen? Or about me kissing your neck?"

My head tilts, and I close my eyes as he nibbles on the soft flesh beneath my jaw. "Mmm…" *Focus, Mala.*

"You taste like roses," Landry whispers, his breath tickling my ear.

I shudder, pulling my head back. "What did you say?"

He frowns. "I said—"

"Roses. You said roses, but it's not me." Now I smell the cloying scent. I begged for a sign, and I'm receiving it loud and clear. She's after me again. "It's Lainey. She's why I came." We've almost reached the road bordering the cemetery. I have to tell him…now. "The reason why we smell roses…Lainey showed me a vision of a baby—her dead baby, buried beneath roses."

Landry drops my legs, pulls my arm from around his neck, and steps back. Surprised, I barely catch my balance. "Damn it, Landry. Did you hear what I said?"

"No…stop," he begs, backing away. "Don't say any more. Not today, please."

I'm too scared to hold onto this secret alone. "Lainey delivered a baby boy. Landry, he was murdered—buried beneath roses—probably by the same man who tried to kill my mama last night. Afterward, he trashed her room looking for something." I hold the box out to him. "I found these. They're Lainey's belongings—"

Landry slaps the box out of my hand. It hits the ground, spilling its contents. "I said leave it alone!"

"Don't you get it? This is another clue. This guy's desperate to keep his identity secret, but we're closing in on him." I take a deep breath, studying his face. "I thought you'd be happy—"

He laughs harshly and waves toward the open grave behind us. "You thought I'd be happy about hearing my sister's baby was murdered?"

"No, I-I...that came out wrong." I limp toward him. "I'm sorry. I didn't think..."

He brushes my outstretched hand aside. "Because I'm the Frog Prince in Mala's fantasy world, a cartoon character whose feelings you don't have to think about. Right?"

"That's not true! I totally didn't mean it that way. I almost didn't say anything, but Lainey—"

"Why couldn't you just let it go for one day?" He spins around, hands covering his face. "Clarice, my father, everyone is right about you being a witch. You put a spell on me..."

"God, Landry, you're not bespelled. Those meds you took have you spun out." He has me seconds away from yanking all my hair out by the roots. Why won't he let me explain? Karma again. Hell, this must be how he feels when I flip out on him. "You know what Lainey can do. You've seen her ghost about as much as I have, and if that makes me a witch, what does it make you? A warlock?"

His mouth opens, then closes. Tension stretches between us like a rubber band about to snap. "Seriously, a warlock?" he finally says. "Worst comeback ever."

Yeah, it was pretty lame, but it distracted him. Maybe he'll actually hear me this time through his drug-induced fog. "I'm sorry I laid this on you today, but Lainey took me down hard when she gave me that vision. I had a bloody nose, and I passed out after she attacked me. Then I saw Ruby's obituary. The woman really died from being possessed. So I convinced myself that it would be okay to tell you. I thought you'd want to know. You came to me, remember? You asked me to figure out why Lainey's haunting us, and I did."

He rubs his eyes. "You're right. I asked and you got hurt again. We'll talk about everything...Lainey, the murderer, the"—he chokes on the word—"*baby*. Just not right now. I can't deal with this shit, or you, right now."

Landry's leaving me. I want to call him back, but again...stupid pride. It's getting me in all kinds of trouble. I cross my fingers, hoping he'll turn and run to me with outstretched arms. He'll sweep me up in a hug or nibble on my neck. We'll forgive each other's sins and solve the mystery of Lainey's murder and Mama's assault together, because I'm too exhausted to do this alone.

Landry passes beneath the cemetery gate and crosses the street to a limousine parked beneath a moss-draped oak. When the doors open, Reverend Prince and Doc Rathbone climb out. It's obvious they had a clear view of our argument. The rev—as Mr. Acker calls him—sends a look full of hatred in my direction.

George appears out of the shadows. A scowl creases his brow, but his anger doesn't show in his voice. "Still need a ride?"

I rub the goose bumps on my arms. "What took you so long?"

"Landry seemed to have the situation under control. Did he carry you the whole time?"

"If you saw him carrying me, then you also saw he got pissed."

He smiles a little and tips his chin in Landry's direction. "If it's any consolation, I don't think he meant whatever he said. More than likely, he was spouting off to placate his father. Mr. Prince doesn't look too thrilled to see his son associating with you."

Reverend Prince has his hands on his son's shoulders. He squeezes them so hard that I wince in sympathetic pain. Man, I wish I could hear their conversation because Landry's about to burst out of his skin. No, the rev's not at all pleased.

"Of course he's disappointed." I wince at the bitterness in my voice. "My reputation was established before Mama gave birth to me. Doesn't matter what sort of person I am, I'll always be judged by her actions."

George frowns. "Do you care so much about what Landry's father thinks of you?"

I shrug; it's not like Landry and I are getting married or anything. Poor Ruby failed utterly with that prediction. "No, I guess not."

George holds out his arms. "So, about that lift?"

"I can walk. My mom's truck is only parked half a mile away on Old Lick Road on the opposite side of the cemetery from where we are now."

George chuckles. "My, my, getting dumped makes you cranky."

I stuff Lainey's belongings back into the box, only pausing before throwing the book inside. *The Color Purple.* I stashed it in there after I dug the box out of the trash. I totally forgot to give it to Mama. The dustcover slips off, revealing a leather-bound diary hidden within. And I read the flowery handwriting—*Mon nom est Elaine Prince et ceci est mon histoire.*

Chapter 27

Landry

Misunderstandings

My shoulders burn as I walk toward the limousine. Each step feels like I'm dragging the weight of my guilt behind me. I pass beneath the arched metal gate and cross the street. Dad and Uncle Jay climb out of the limo and stand so they flank either side.

"Did you hear what you needed to convince you of her guilt?" Dad asks, bristled jaw flexing.

"No." I glance over my shoulder. George walks over to Mala, and she frowns at him. A happy scowl, I can tell the difference between them now. Dad's hands land on my shoulders, locking me in place when I turn to go back to her. I watch while George takes my place. He lifts Mala into his arms, and she lets him. Damn her!

"Let me go," I growl, straining against the hands.

"Why? So you can make an even bigger fool of yourself cavorting with the witch's daughter on holy ground?"

"She's not a witch."

"We both know that's not true, son."

What's true? I can't tell truth from fiction. I'm worn out. Mom said the medicine she gave me would help keep my emotions in check. It worked for her. She stayed dry-eyed and calm through the funeral. The whole time I fought not to cuss out the other mourners, my parents, even the preacher. I wouldn't have spared anyone if I lost control. The emotions of the mourners thrummed, like we're connected by an invisible current amplifying each other's grief, until I vibrated with it. Mala dropping a murdered nephew into the mix didn't help.

I don't know how much more I can deal with.

I meet Dad's eyes, then let my gaze drop. Guilt punches a hole in my chest. He's barely said two words to me this week. He sees my being with Mala as a betrayal to Lainey. I don't think he believed my lies about only hanging with her to get to the truth of Lainey's death. He doesn't need proof. He judged the LaCroix women off of what Rathbone found in the autopsy. I can't blame him. The evidence is pretty damning by itself. This morning I saw the cuts in Lainey's stomach at the funeral home. We all did. The inverted cross carved into her stomach right below her belly button.

Some sick bastard toyed with her. Rathbone said she was still alive while she was tortured. I know Mala isn't involved, but Ms. Jasmine knows more about what happened than she's saying. I should've gone to the hospital to check on Mala; instead I stayed at the hotel and paid Khan to let me search her mother's room.

I found herbs and hoodoo potions in her closet. Then I used Lainey's key to search her motel room. I found another bundle of herbs beneath Lainey's mattress.

The stupid part is where I got upset and told Dad about what I found. Mala's right. I've got a big mouth.

Dad drops his hands to his sides. "It's time to choose, son. Your family or that girl?"

"Why?" My voice cracks. "It's not about choice. It's about right and wrong. You're wrong about Mala. She wants to find out who killed Lainey, maybe even more than we do. She knows we're judging her. How do you think that makes her feel? How do you think it makes me feel knowing my family believes the girl I'm in love with murdered my sister?"

Uncle Jay shoves between Dad and me. "Love? Are you out of your mind?"

I shove him back. "Don't! This has nothing to do with you. This is between family."

"I told you to guard yourself. The LaCroix witches can twist your mind. Make you lust after them until you damn your soul to be with one of them. That's how Savoie became trapped by his slave and this town became saddled with those whores."

God, let me punch him, please. "You're a narrow-minded ass, Uncle Jay."

Uncle Jay glances down at my clenched fists and steps back. "I'm only trying to help."

"How? By poisoning my dad's mind against her? Spreading rumors that aren't true? You're more to blame than anyone, Uncle Jay." I look to my father. How can he tolerate this bullshit? He's a progressive guy. Sure he's a preacher, but he doesn't believe in this hoodoo voodoo stuff, at least he didn't before Lainey passed. Even with all I've seen, I don't believe in magic. What did Mala say about Einstein and energy again? Ghosts…make sense. Witchcraft, not so much. There's no supernatural bullshit behind my sister's death. It's some sick bastard who murdered her for some crazy reason. Why did it take me so long to figure this out?

I look to my father. "You say I've got to make a choice, then I choose Mala. She's innocent. I'll find the real killer, and when I do, I want your blessing. I want to be with her."

The backseat driver's side door opens, and I freeze. Mom leans out of the limo and stares up at me with an expression so coldly disapproving that I shiver. I can't tear my gaze from her icy blue eyes. She wilts me.

"Mom…" I beg.

She lifts up the hem of her black dress and holds out her hand. Uncle Jay helps her step to the ground. I stand before her, shaking. How can she scare the shit out of me with silence, while Dad only makes me sad? Maybe because I know Dad wouldn't hurt a fly unless it kept buzzing around his food, while Mom wields her flyswatter on flies and my ass without batting an eyelash.

Mom's head turns in Mala's direction. I watch as Mala and George pass beneath the cemetery arch. George puts her down once they reach his Land Rover parked by the curb. I guess she doesn't need me after all. The great prick will get her home. It should be me, but I don't trust myself. I'm too unstable. Plus I've got to make my parents understand how I feel. Things are spiraling out of my control. Tensions and hatred flare hot enough to burn. If I don't squash them, Mala will become an even bigger target.

"Theresa!" Dad yells.

I whip around. Mom is already halfway across the street and zeroing in fast on Mala and George. My chest throbs, an echo of pain from where she elbowed my bruised ribs when I tried to stop her from crashing the autopsy.

"Mala!"

Mala turns at the sound of my voice. She lifts her hand in a faltering wave when she notices Mom heading in her direction. I wait for a passing car, then sprint across the road. It's like I'm running through mud. Everything slows to a crawl. I don't know what Mom plans. She's been unpredictable since Lainey died. Grief took a bite out of her sanity. Maybe if Mom talked about her pain, she'd be able to work through it. But she keeps her emotions dimmed under a self-medicated haze, locked up and ignored. Inside the pressure builds and builds until she explodes, like now.

Mala's eyes widen when Mom walks up to her. I can't hear what Mala says, but I read her lips: "I'm sorry for your loss."

I've almost reached them when Mom's arm swings back. I try to catch her hand, but I'm not fast enough. Mala sees it coming, but she doesn't try to avoid the slap. The crack echoes off the brick wall surrounding the cemetery. Mala stumbles, falling back, and George catches her arm before she topples over.

Mom stands in front of them. She's not even breathing hard, like the slap came as an afterthought. I have no idea what she's thinking or feeling.

George and I share a look. "Get your mom out of here," he says.

My tongue's like a frozen *boudin*. I want to apologize, but I'm scared if I do, it will set Mom off even more. I lay my hands on her shoulders, ready to flinch back if she strikes out. She only turns in my arms.

"Family first, Landry," Mom says, patting my chest. "Now say good-bye to your little whore. It's time to get home. Lainey's waiting."

I glance over her shoulder. George holds Mala in his arms. Her face is pressed into his chest, and her shoulders shake. She's crying.

This is the second time Mala's gotten slapped because of me.

Dad reaches us, and I push Mom into his arms. "I'll be there in a minute," I say, unable to meet Dad's eyes. All of my bravado got whipped out of me. Mom figured out the best way to punish me was to hurt Mala. Now Dad knows how to keep me in check.

Dad nods to George. "Thank you for attending the service." His eyes flick to Mala as he says, "Both of you." He doesn't wait for a reply. He bundles Mom back across the street, helps her into the limo, and climbs in. He watches us through the window with fingers tapping on the steering wheel.

Mala's face is buried in George's suit jacket. The only features visible are a puffy eye and a tearstained cheek. She won't look in my direction. I reach toward her, but George bats my hand away.

"I need to know if she's okay," I say.

George growls a muttered curse. "No thanks to your mother."

"I'm sorry. I didn't know she'd…"

Mala lifts her face to me. "You don't need to apologize for her."

The bright red handprint on her cheek sends a burst of self-hatred through me. I should've been faster. *It's my fault she got hurt.*

"Damn right it's your fault," George yells, and I realize I said the words out loud. "Think I don't know that your family has been spreading rumors around town about Mala practicing hoodoo rituals?"

Mala gasps. "What?"

"Landry's parents think you and your mother sacrificed Lainey in a satanic ritual because she had weird symbols carved into her stomach. God only knows what they plan once they get proof, but it's why he's been hanging out with you. To get the evidence you murdered his sister."

"Weird symbols? Are you kidding?"

I shake my head. "I saw them myself."

Mala's face reddens. Shit. She's about to blow, and I can't duck for cover. Gotta take it like a man, 'cause I deserve whatever pain she dishes out for keeping this secret.

"Saints! Why didn't either of you tell me this before? I thought we were working this case together." A tiny furrow creases her forehead. "Unless *you* also believe I'm involved."

George lifts his hands, palms up. His tattle-telling totally backfired. "Whoa-there, I don't think—"

I interrupt, 'cause who the fuck cares what he thinks. "Come on, Mala. You know I believe you're innocent."

"I did before this startling revelation. Now all I know for sure is you've got more faces than a Rubik's Cube, Landry." She crosses her arms. "I thought you didn't want to 'deal with this shit' or me. So why are you still here?"

All the hot air rushes out of me. "I…yeah, I'm over it."

"Oh, hell no! It's not that easy."

Anger pinches the corners of my eyes and mouth. What does

she expect? For me to blab about my *feelings* in front of George? Not happening. My confession will wait until we're alone, but I'm telling her everything.

Lies. I'm sick of suffocating in a sticky web of lies.

"Fine, I'll be honest," I say with a hard grin. "If it's a choice between my family's bullshit and your drama, I'll pick you any day."

"Wow, I feel all weak and fluttery inside."

"You should."

George unlocks the door to his SUV. "Look, whatever childish rebellion you're engaging in had better not stir up trouble for Mala, or I won't look the other way."

"I'll protect Mala with my life before I ever let anyone harm her, George." It's the truth too. Whatever I've got to do to keep her safe, I'll do. Even if it means going against my parents, I'll be there for her. Decision made.

I hold my hand out to Mala. "Do you believe me?"

Mala's mouth opens, but George slaps my hand aside.

"She'd be a fool to believe you," he says, nudging her toward the open door. "Mala, let's go. I'll drop you off at your truck so you can pick up your mama."

"Hold on, Georgie," Mala says. "I can speak for myself."

I'm sick and tired of George's holier-than-thou act. Frustration erupts in a spew of acid-dripping words I've been holding in for days. "Why don't you get your own girlfriend instead of worrying about *mine*? Oh, right, 'cause Lainey dumped you on your ass. So what? Now that my sister's dead and there's no chance you'll get back together, you're trying to get Mala to take her place?"

Mala stiffens. "Now what are you talking about?"

"Didn't your best friend George mention he and Lainey dated last year?"

A hushed stillness comes over George. His voice vibrates with warning. "Not that it's any of your business, but Lainey and I agreed to be friends."

I roll my eyes. "Yeah, right. Maybe if you'd satisfied her she wouldn't have gone after some older guy who ended up getting her pregnant and murdering her and the baby."

Mala glances between us. "Landry—"

Oh shit, I've said too much. George's eyes sharpen to pinpricks. Dissecting my words. He noticed I mentioned the baby being murdered. Mala squeezes her eyes shut. We both wait for the explosion. I hold in my shiver when he says, "You want to blame someone, fine. Blame me, but we both know this little outburst has nothing to do with who I did or did not go out with. Let's go, Mala."

"Uh, you dated Lainey?" The shock in Mala's voice makes it warble. "Seriously? How did I not know? When you saw her at the crime scene, you said you had a crush on her in high school, but you never mentioned you dated."

"My personal relationships are none of your business," George says.

"But we're friends." Mala's voice grows soft. "I thought." Her expression almost breaks my heart. Damn, she's good. She's interrogating him like he's a prime suspect. I doubt he even realizes he's getting played, but she used the same doe-eyed lash flutter and pout to get me to carry the fishing poles and shove Daisy into the pond.

George sighs. "You're one of my best friends. You know that.

I didn't tell anyone about our relationship. Neither of us did. It's not that big of a deal. Landry's right. Lainey dumped me."

"When did you and Lainey get together?"

George barks out a laugh, shaking his head. "Get together? Mala, we went on a few dates over Thanksgiving break last year. That's all. I didn't have time for much more than that. After break was over, she went back to Loyola. We kept in touch for a few weeks, and then one day, she stopped returning my texts."

"Did you ever find out why?"

"No, I didn't care. It wasn't like she broke my heart or anything."

"Maybe you broke hers, prick," I say.

George frowns.

"Lainey changed into a self-destructive bitch last year. She went from caring about herself and her family to the person she became before she died. Whatever messed her up happened right after the two of you hooked up." My fists clench, and I stalk toward him. "I don't know what you did to her, George, but you—"

Mala grabs my arm. "Landry, you said Lainey never told you what happened."

"She didn't." I tip my chin in George's direction. "But I bet he knows more than he's saying. He can't be as perfect as he seems."

"Fuck you, Landry!" George snarls. He gets into his SUV and slams the door.

Mala shakes her head and winces. Her hand goes to her cheek. "Sorry. I wouldn't dump this on you if I didn't have to pick Mama up from the hospital." She holds out the cardboard box that started all the trouble. "I found Lainey's diary. It's stashed in this box of goodies, along with everything else that she left at the motel."

I snatch the box from her hands. "Seriously? *Now* you're telling—"

"*Shh*, this is why I didn't say anything in front of George. Play it cool." Mala's voice lowers. "See if she mentions her boyfriend. If not, then at least try to figure out how many months along she was in her pregnancy because the baby, uh, fetus in the vision didn't look fully developed. He could've been conceived in late November."

Worry pinches her eyes when she glances at George, and my stomach tightens into a knot. I don't want her to leave with him. It feels like I'll never see her again. *Crazy.* "Call me tonight or I'll call you." My voice grows hoarse. "Mala, I…"

Suddenly she's beside me. "Don't worry. We're due for some good juju, and I bet the diary holds the answers."

Chapter 28

Mala

Death Vision

Mama waits in a wheelchair by the hospital entrance. Her suit-case sits at her feet. "What took so long?" she yells as I park the truck in the loading zone.

"I'm sorry, boy drama."

I throw her bag in the truck bed then help Mama into the passenger seat. Her swollen nose scrunches up. "Is that cologne I smell?"

"Don't know how you can smell anything."

"Maybe 'cause it's strong enough to knock out a full-grown black bear." She waves her hand in the air. "Tell that boy you're seein' that he don't need to use half a bottle unless he's tryin' to kill the girl he's wooin.'"

She leans her head back against the seat and closes her eyes.

"How are you feeling?"

"Hush up," she says drowsily. "Let me sleep. I'm all worn out from being in that hospital. I swear, the spirits hauntin' that place are persistent. Kept bargin' into my room askin' me to give this or that message to their loved ones, like I got the U.S. Postal Service stamped on my forehead."

"I felt them when I visited. They gave me the willies."

"Wait until I die. Then you'll be able to *see* and *hear* them too." She reaches out and turns up the radio station, effectively cutting off any further attempt at conversation. She dozes fitfully for the rest of the drive, occasionally letting out a soft whimper when we drive over a rut.

I run through the list of questions I want to ask her about the man she tried to blackmail. Who was he? What did she have on him that he so desperately wanted to keep quiet? What would she think about the vision I had of Lainey's baby? But I keep quiet and let her sleep. We'll have time to talk later.

That strange prickle of premonition I've been getting since finding Lainey starts up again when we turn onto the road leading to the house. With each revolution of the tires, it grows. By the time we reach the house, I can barely keep the truck on the road. The steering wheel feels slick with sweat beneath my palms. When I see the house, I slam my foot down on the brakes.

Mama jerks forward, the seat belt keeping her from striking her head on the dash. "What?" she mumbles.

I throw open the door and run. Rolls of toilet paper drape the trees in the front yard. My flowerpots have been smashed to pieces, and the remains of my geraniums litter the front porch. The words "WHORE" and "WITCH" have been sprayed onto the side of the house in bloodred paint.

"Look what they did," I scream, spinning in a circle. "Mama, look what they did!" I kick a broken ceramic shard across the lawn. "I hate them!"

"Who, baby?" Mama asks calmly. She limps down the driveway, barely looking at the mess. "No point getting upset. What's done can't be undone. It'll just give you a tummy ache bein' so fired up. Help me into the house."

I glare at her. "Fired up...tummy ache? Are you seeing what I'm seeing? They trashed our house!"

"Yep, did a fine job of it too."

"I swear, when I figure out who did this, they will pay."

"Mala, do you see I'm about to pass out? I can't climb these stairs. Help me." She sticks out her hand. "Come on, *cher*. I know you can't hold onto a grudge for long. Let it go."

I take her arm and help her up the stairs. The front door is unlocked.

"Stay here while I check out the inside."

For once, Mama doesn't argue. She sits in the rocking chair, kicks out her legs, and closes her eyes.

I take a deep breath and slowly push open the door. I pull out the baseball bat we keep in the umbrella stand for protection and heft it, ready to knock someone senseless. I focus on slowing my ragged breathing and strain to hear a rustle, a footstep—nothing. Each room I enter has been systematically ransacked as if whoever broke in was looking for something in particular, but what—

Crap on toast—Lainey's box.

With a sigh, I go back to the porch and bring Mama inside. I help her change into a comfy nightgown and get into bed. Then I place a call to Ms. Dixie. She says she'll have George stop by once he comes on duty tonight. I dread seeing him. What if he's the guy who impregnated Lainey? I don't want to think it's him, but the timing makes sense. How do I ask my friend if he's a murderer?

As darkness falls, I lie in the hammock on the back porch. Caressed by the warm breeze, I drift between sleep and waking, surrounded by the scent of honeysuckle. I dangle a leg over the edge, and whenever the rocking slows, I give a little kick to set it back in motion. My eyes flutter open to fall on the waving mosquito netting.

I ignore the whisper, at first confusing the voice with the sound of rustling leaves. A cold patch of air settles on my skin, like a hand lain on my arm in warning. Goose bumps prick. I open my eyes to see a shadowed face inches from my own. I had left a citronella candle burning on the table, and its light falls across the guy's burned face, reflecting the full horror of the raw scars. My chest tightens, squeezing off my breath so I can't scream. He presses icy fingers to my lips.

"It's time," he whispers. "They're coming. Are you ready?"

I shake my head, unable to move my numb lips to form an answer. *Who's coming?* I think frantically, but I already know. Something terrible approaches. I can't stop it. I can only hide and pray it doesn't find me. *I'm not ready.*

His head drops as if he hears my thoughts. "Too late now. Wake up!" He punctuates the order with a hard slap on the edge of the hammock. I roll off the side, hitting the floor hard. I ignore the pain of landing flat on my back and push to my feet. My legs shake so badly that I almost lose my balance, and I clench my jaw to keep my teeth from chattering.

Voices echo in the yard, growing louder as they move closer, and I know, without a shadow of doubt, that danger surrounds my house. No one comes into the middle of the swamp. Not unless they're up to no good. Only poachers, scallywags, and murderers hiding bodies—like Lainey Prince's. *Oh crap, he's coming for us.*

I tiptoe toward the kitchen door. Each time the floor creaks, I wince, sure that I'll be heard. My hand trembles when I reach for the knob, but before I can open it, the handle's wrenched from my grasp. I fall back, sucking in air to scream, but Mama jerks me into her embrace and presses my face into her shoulder.

"Quiet," she whispers in my ear. She pulls my hand from where it clutches at her white cotton nightgown and presses a metal object into my palm. "Run, Mala. Hide in the woods. Don't let them catch you."

"W-w-why?" I shake my head, so confused I can't think clearly. The stink of her fear fills my nose. "Come with me."

"Can't. They're here for me. If they don't find me, they'll come looking and catch us both. I dreamed this, baby. I told you about my dream. The fire…darkness. Oh, sweet Jesus, I'm so scared." She pulls me tight. So tight I can't breathe. Then she pushes me back. "I love you, baby. I never showed it much, but I do. Hurry. Go before they get too close."

I step toward her, but she steps back. A crash of breaking glass comes from the living room window. Mama spins with a scream. The Molotov cocktail lands on our sofa, but the bottle doesn't break. Flames from the gasoline-soaked cloth set the couch on fire, spreading faster than I can blink.

"No! Not the house," Mama cries, running across the room.

I shove forward, but the cold spot hovering around my body grows colder. An invisible force thrusts me backward, and the door slams in my face. The doorknob twists in my hand. It's not locked. *He's* keeping me out. My hand lifts to strike the door, but I clench it at my side. I want to scream and yell. To pound until she listens and comes with me, but I don't. I can't freak out. I have to stay calm. Think rationally. If those men hear me, I won't be able to do anything to help her.

I can do this. I'm ready. I can save her.

The voices from the front of the property become more distinct. Angry male voices that don't try to hide or disguise the anger and hate that colors their words. Footsteps clomp up the front steps, and then a bang on the front door. Loud, echoing thuds send a shiver through my body each time the fist slams into the rotten wood.

I shove the switchblade Mama gave me into my front pocket, then raise my hand and press it against the back door, focusing. Magic is like breath for a LaCroix. Air enters, power exits. The door splinters, fracturing down the middle with a crack like a gunshot, then explodes inward, piercing the far wall with jagged pieces. Relief floods through me when I see the empty kitchen. If Mama had been standing in front of the door when it burst, she would've been impaled. Thick smoke rushes toward the door.

Mama screams from farther inside the house. I run inside, pulling the neck of my T-shirt up to protect my mouth and nose from the fumes. My eyes burn, watering. A sliver of wood digs into my right heel, but I ignore the pain. I peek around the doorway between the kitchen and living room. The remaining glass in the broken front window flickers with the glow of torches. I bite my lip to keep from shrieking when I see the three men, dressed in black deacon's robes with hooded masks over their faces, run up onto the porch. They hold rifles in their arms.

Mama ignores the pounding on the door, too busy using a blanket to smother the flames burning on the sofa. She gets the fire on the sofa out but still holds the burning blanket. The man in charge must get tired of waiting for Mama to open the door because I hear a loud *bang* against the wood.

"Leave it, Mama," I yell, waving for her to come to me.

She drops the blanket and stares at me with wide eyes. "Baby, no! Get out!"

I choke on the fumes. They're burning my lungs. But worse, the blanket ignites her nightgown. Mama's on fire when I run to her. I stomp on the blanket, smothering the flames, then pick up the tatters to use it to put her out. Every time I grab for her, she shoves me backward. I trip over something on the ground, I can't see what. Another *bang* from outside and the lock on the front door pops. Two masked men run inside. I scramble beneath the table, curling into a ball. They pass by, close enough I can grab their feet, but I can't move. I'm a frozen, quivering coward who watches them drag Mama across the room.

Mama wails. The sound crawls up my back and settles in the base of my brain. She keeps screaming as they drag her onto the porch. I crawl toward the door, staying low to the ground. My lungs are burning from the smoke. I try to yell for them to stop, but I can't do more than cough. She looks so small and fragile as they hold her effortlessly between them. Seeing her twist and kick in her struggle to free herself obliterates all rational thought from my mind.

A rush of steps comes from behind just as I lunge toward the door. A hand clamps down over my mouth and nose, and I'm dragged back against a sweaty chest. I struggle, pulling at the hand around my waist, but the man locks me tight in his embrace. I kick, trying to free myself, but the arm squeezes tighter. I'm dizzy. I hang in his arms while he carries me out through the kitchen door. He pauses at the side of the house, then angles his run through the side yard, heading toward the path through the woods that leads to the main road.

He's leaving Mama behind. I've got to go back.

I buck, trying to break the grip around my waist. The guy loses his balance and falls to his knees. His hand drops from my mouth. I inhale a deep breath of fresh air and erupt into a coughing fit.

It hurts to breathe, but I still try to speak, "Who—"

His hand covers my mouth again. I twist my head, trying to break free.

Mama screams again, and I freeze.

What have they done?

The front yard glows with the light from the pyre burning in my front yard. Mama struggles and twists against the ropes tying her to a wooden cross planted in my flower garden. She screams and screams. The flames engulf her nightgown. Her hair catches. I have to get to her before it's too late. They're burning Mama alive.

The hands holding me loosen. I lunge forward, breaking his grip, and run toward the pyre. If I can get to the water hose, I can put the fire out. The man grabs my foot and drags me back. Fury races through me. I dig the switchblade out of my pocket and slash at the silhouette of the guy's face. Blood drenches my hand like a sticky, wet glove. He stumbles back, crying out, and joy at causing him pain rushes through me. All this time I had a weapon. Only I'd forgotten.

I lunge forward, slamming into his chest. He falls back with a cry while I straddle him. I strike with the knife again, aiming for his heart.

Pain whips my head back. The impact of the bullet creasing my scalp spins me sideways. The guy I almost killed shoves me off of his chest with a bloody hand. He crawls away, whimpering. I start to go after him when another gunshot echoes through the trees. I scream and lurch to my feet, wheeling my arms to keep from falling. The heat of another bullet skims past my thigh, and I take off into the thick underbrush.

Voices follow, and the cries of the man who grabbed me from my house and kept me from saving Mama. I hope he dies. I hope I cut deep. Sobs well up and pour out, making it difficult to breathe. Moonlight barely penetrates the thick canopy of Spanish moss overhead. I run on instinct. I've traversed this section of the forest enough times to know it by heart, but I still trip on fallen logs. Branches scrape the skin from my arms and legs.

I veer off the main trail into the swampy area—the Black Hole. The ground turns spongy beneath my bare feet, and I slow my steps. I move carefully. Pockets of quicksand hide beneath what appears to be solid earth. I know what signs to avoid during the day, but at night…I'm not confident I can get through this area safely.

The sound of a man cursing and bushes thrashing comes from

behind me. The man who gives chase uses a flashlight that he swings in a wide arc over the ground. I hide behind a tree, just ahead of the light, and huddle against the broad base. I focus on slowing my harsh breaths so he won't hear me and peek around the trunk. He squats and touches his fingers to a leaf, then brings them to his nose and sniffs. He's tracking me like he'd hunt a wounded deer—by blood. I'm bleeding? Now I feel pain.

He rubs his fingers together and sweeps the flashlight in my direction. I duck back behind the tree and creep backward.

"I know you're there," he says with a slight lilt to his voice, as if trying not to laugh. The hunt excites him in a deep, primal way that sends shivers down my spine. "I hear you breathin'. Why not make it easy? Come on out?"

Footsteps move toward me. I try not to panic. I can't dash off into the undergrowth. Not here. Not now. It's too dangerous. I edge back, placing each step with careful deliberation, despite knowing that at this speed, I'll be visible once he rounds the wide tree trunk.

My heart hammers. The sound fills my ears. I wonder if he can hear it. I press my closed fist against my chest, imagining I'm clutching my growing panic. *Hold it together.* I force myself to place my foot down, and when it sinks into the shifting earth, I lift it and move it to the right. The ground remains firm. I take another step.

Light strikes me in the eyes.

Blind, I throw myself backward. I hit the ground and roll. A gunshot and the stench of gunpowder fill the air. Rocks pepper my body as the bullet ricochets off the earth only inches from where my head lands. I scream, throwing my hands over my face, and continue to roll, coming to rest against the rough bark of a tree.

I whimper at the clicks of the rifle being reloaded. Footsteps race toward me.

The flashlight swings upward, highlighting the masked face. The whites of his eyes glow in the light. "I found you," he sings out, taunting.

"No," I scream. "No. *No!*"

"*Yessss.*" He smiles, showing broken teeth through the mouth hole in the ski mask. "My whole life I've wondered what it'd feel like to kill someone. The Lord says, 'Thou shalt not kill.' But you ain't even a person. Not a real human being. You're a creature of evil, sent by the devil."

"No." I shake my head, pressing my back into the tree.

"Your ma drained Lainey's blood as a sacrifice to Satan. I say 'An eye for an eye.' You and your ma killed the reverend's daughter so I'm gonna kill you." He raises the rifle, cocks it, and fires.

I roll around to the other side of the tree. Bark explodes from the trunk. My ears ring, and pain blossoms in my shoulder. I cry out and press my right hand over the wound, trying to staunch the blood. My left arm dangles, numb. I try to stand but my legs won't hold my weight.

"Please, stop." I crawl, a slow inch forward. Dirt sticks to the bloody hand that still clutches the switchblade. My arm trembles. Exhausted, I roll onto my back, hiding the knife in the folds of my T-shirt. I doubt he'll get close enough for me to use it. "I didn't kill Lainey."

"I'm enjoying this," he says with another of his scary, not-quite-sane laughs. "Beg…beg me for your life. Come on. I'll kill you quick. A bullet between the eyes. No pain, if you beg for it."

"Please." I'm not sure what I beg for. *A quick death? An end to his taunting?*

He lowers the gun. A gust of frigid air blows across our path. He jerks and shines the flashlight into the shadows. A flicker of blue cloth flutters across the light. A delicate face grins at me over his shoulder.

"Lainey," I choke. "Help me."

She brushes a hand across the base of the man's neck where his bare skin shows beneath the robe. He screams, whirling around. The flashlight flies out of his hand and floats in the air.

"Demon spawn," he cries, raising his arm to shield his eyes from the light.

Lainey lunges forward and shoves him. He staggers. Flailing his arms, he tries to keep his balance, but he slips into the quicksand and sinks. Fast. And the more he struggles, the faster he sinks.

My vision has adjusted to the night. The pain and the adrenaline pumping through my veins makes the world around me appear crystal clear. The guy rips off his mask, gasping for breath.

"Mr. Acker?" I shake my head. "Why? We're blood kin."

"Help me, girl!" The quicksand has reached his armpits, but he keeps his arms lifted in the air. He stretches out the barrel of his gun toward me. "Quick. Grab the end. Pull me out."

I watch him in sluggish confusion—Dena's dad. He tried to kill me. He broke into my house and attacked Mama. Dena has four younger brothers. How will they survive if he dies? Who will provide for them? They'll starve. No. If those other men killed Mama, then the Ackers will inherit my property if I die. Other than Auntie Magnolia, they're my nearest blood relatives. Everything I own will go to Dena, unless Auntie Magnolia claims it. Hell, they can fight it out in court.

I stare at the sky through a break in the trees. The stars spin, like fireworks, shooting out sparks. My stomach rolls, and I close my eyes, dizzy. *He shot me.*

"The gun…grab the gun, please." He coughs.

I squeeze my eyes tighter, wishing I could cover my ears. *Concentrate, Mala. Think it through.* If he goes to jail, he'll still be alive. He'll pay for what he's done. If I pull him out, he'll kill me. I can't stop him.

"I'm not a witch," I mumble. "I'm not evil. I won't be like you, Mr. Acker."

I open my eyes and reach for the gun. My fingers graze the barrel sticking out of the quicksand, and I pull. The rifle comes easily into my hands. I hold it, searching the solid-seeming ground. But nothing of Mr. Acker remains visible.

Chapter 29

Mala

Owned

I let Mr. Acker die.

It doesn't matter that he was trying to kill me. I should've helped him. I tried to help him, but I'd been too late. Just like I didn't helped Mama. I had a knife the whole time, and I didn't use it. Didn't even think to use it. If I had, maybe I could've stopped those men.

How? What could I have done? There had been three of them and one of me. I shiver. When did it get so cold? The front of my T-shirt feels sticky and wet. The copper scent of my blood stings my nose. If I don't reach help soon, I'll bleed to death. Mr. Acker would win. I have to move fast. Get to the road and flag down a car.

Georgie...help me. I grab onto the stock of the rifle, use it to help me rise, and then push it into the quicksand. I can't carry it with my injured arm, anyway. A cloud hides the moon, and thick fog blankets the ground. A pulsing rhythm plays in the distance. Drums. The beat taps into my lethargy, and I limp toward the music. My head feels foggy, disconnected, like it's a helium balloon attached to a string. It floats. The drumming grows louder. Voices sing in a language I don't understand, and the sound flows through the rustling leaves. The flickering glow of a fire comes from up ahead, and I stumble into the worst place I could be. A fire burns in the center of the clearing. My gaze turns to the stone altar, and I choke back a sob. It drips red with blood.

I'm hallucinating.

Chilled fingers circle my arms. I try to jerk away, but I can't free myself. I'm dragged toward the fire. With each reluctant step, the drumming grows louder. Shadows dance. Ghostly phantoms sway around me, touching my face, my hands. I blink to bring them into focus. They look hazy, but upon making the connection, they become solid. Men dressed in homespun tunics and women in long skirts and colorful scarves. Their bare feet stomp the earth, jingling ankle bracelets crafted from beads and shells.

I've got to get out of here. This isn't right. I shouldn't be seeing them…these specters from the past. I've slipped into the between—the thin space where the spirit world and ours meet. Mama's dead, and I see ghosts.

I shove through them. It's like I'm fighting through molasses. Sticky threads bind my legs. They grab for my arms, but I twist free. The air feels thick with their collective anxiety. They want me to stay with them. They will protect me. But I can't. I'm not dead.

At least I don't think I am.

That thought breaks through whatever lingering doubts I have, and I run. By the time I reach the top of the hill, I'm panting, ready to collapse. I crouch in the bushes on the edge of the woods, hearing the sound of an engine barreling down the road leading from my house. It barely slows at the crossroad. Screams come from inside the truck, and a figure hunches over the wheel.

When the truck takes off, I remain frozen until the taillights fade in the distance, afraid to come out of hiding. This is a trick. They'll come back. They must expect Mr. Acker to return with news of my death. They'd be stupid to let me escape, not after I witnessed what they did to Mama. Stupid to think I won't find them.

My legs give out, and I fall to my knees. Pain fills every part of me, but especially my shoulder. I crawl forward. If I stay in the woods, I'll pass out and nobody will find me. Even the thought of those men finding me frightens me less than having my body decomposing in the forest for critters like Mamalama. I don't want to be eaten, especially if I'm not dead.

I inch into the middle of the crossroads before I collapse onto my back and stare at the sky, begging God to help me.

I must've passed out because, when my eyes open again, I'm not alone. "Auntie Magnolia?" I whisper.

The old woman skips down the lane, whirling her cane around her head like a baton. She wears a top hat and coat, like a man out of the Victorian age. Beneath the hat, her long silver hair hangs down her back like a waterfall touched by moonlight. *I'm hallucinating.* I blink a few times, but she doesn't disappear. When she reaches my side, she squints down at me over the rims of black sunglasses. The orange tips of two cigarettes hang from her grinning lips.

"You don't look so good," she drawls. "Looks like them evil men put a hit out on you."

Crazy doesn't even begin to explain how I feel seeing her.

"They tried to kill me." I gasp out the words. "They hurt Mama. Maybe killed her."

"Of course they killed her."

Pain shoots through me at the confirmation of what I felt deep in my soul, and I groan.

"Why you so surprised? The death vision warned this was coming." Magnolia smiles again, her open mouth a maw of darkness drinking in what little light the moon shines upon us. She touches me, running trembling hands across my neck, then strokes my shoulder with spidery fingers. She probes at the bullet wound, sticking her pinky in the hole and ignoring my scream. When she pulls it out, she places the finger to her mouth and rolls her long, snakelike tongue around it like she's licking a lollipop.

I try to roll from her, but she presses down on my chest with her knee. I convulse, pain flaring through every nerve ending.

"Stop! Please, Auntie Magnolia. Why are you doing this? Help me!"

"Not so fast, little one," she hisses, and the sound sends a chill down my spine. "You cried out for help at the crossroads. You lucky I'm full up with juice from your mama's passing so I could come for you. Other things out in the world could've come. Worse things. Demons haunt the crossroads." She arches her back, like a cat stretching on a scratch post, then presses her face into my neck, drinking in my scent. "So much power, ah, *cher*. Been waiting for this moment since the day you were born."

"P-p-please, stop." *Oh Holy Mary, please make her stop.* "You're not real. This isn't real."

She leans forward, snaking her tongue into my wound. She laps up the blood, shivering with ecstasy. A pulse of revulsion shoots through my body. She revels in my pain—sucking it up in mouthfuls that overflow to drip down her chin in a crimson waterfall.

Oh God, the pain. I choke on it. I can't catch my breath, and my vision blacks out for a minute. When it comes back, everything goes fuzzy and kind of glows.

"You've given me blood, so I own you."

"W-what are you?" I ask, even though I already know the answer. She isn't human. Far from it. Maybe she started off human, but over the years, she delved too deep into the dark arts. This was the reason she fell out with her sister. Grandmère Dahlia foresaw her corruption and tried to keep our family free. *This can't be happening.* "Am I dying?"

Auntie Magnolia straddles my hips. "You this close to crossing over to the spirit world," she says, pinching her fingers together. "But you my child now, and you'll do me no good if you dead. So is being mine a worthy exchange for your life, *cher*?" She seems impatient and, worse, hungry. Her tongue licks the blood from my cheek and she moans, eyes rolling back in her head. "Mighty tasty, so much power in your blood. Better decide quick, before I decide to make you a meal." She cackles. "Swear allegiance to me, *cher*. Here at the crossroads where bonds are forged. I'll save your life. And more. I'll give you vengeance."

She presses a sharp fingernail to the middle of my forehead. Her touch burns, and I cry out. My eyes roll back. The memory of Mama being burned by those men races through my head. The pain grows and grows until it feels like my liquefied brain will shoot out of my nose in a mucus-filled jet.

"Ah, I see," she whispers. "I'll take your sacrifices."

I scream.

She laughs.

* * *

I wake cradled in a man's arms. Wind cools my face, and I cling to his shoulders as he runs. With each step, pain rushes through my body. I fight to keep breathing. Tears roll down my cheeks, and I hear myself whimpering. We reach a police car, and I tense as he jostles me to open the door then lays me gently in the backseat. He vanishes. I'm not sure for how long, but then he reappears. He messes with my shoulder, and I do cry out this time. He presses something against it, then wraps gauze around my arm. Afterward, he fusses with my head. I want to tell him to stop, or punch him. But my lips and arms won't work.

In the distance, a siren wails. The sound becomes piercing the closer it gets to our location. The guy stares at me with tears standing out in his green eyes. The overhead lights reflect off his red-gold hair.

"Hold on," he says, pressing harder on my shoulder.

I look down and see blood. It covers his hands and the dressing he holds. "I'm bleeding," I whisper.

"Not bad, you'll be fine. The ambulance is coming."

My eyes dart around the car. Is he talking to me? We're alone in the car. Just me and the girl in the blue dress huddled in the corner. Nobody else is here. But she doesn't answer, and he never glances in her direction.

"Who did this? Tell me who hurt you."

"I don't know..." His face gets fuzzy. My vision fades, but the blare of the siren echoes in my head.

Chapter 30

Landry

An Eye for an Eye

White-hot pain jerks me awake.

I scream and hot, sticky liquid runs into my mouth.

My blood. I'm drinking my own blood.

My stomach lurches, and I roll onto my side, gagging. The coppery taste lingers on my tongue and mingles with a charcoal, burnt-beef stench that claws at the back of my throat and makes my stomach heave over again and again. Pressure in my head keeps me from curling up into a ball to ease the ache in my gut. The fire burning in my left eye won't stop. My eye socket feels bloated with fluid that leaks down my cheek. It throbs.

I can't see.

Darkness presses down, a heavy weight on my chest. Each breath wheezes. A cough tickles my throat, and I hold my breath, fighting it back. Maybe if I don't move, I won't hurt. What total bullshit. I won't hurt as much. *Why is it so dark?*

The distorted shouts of male voices echo in the distance, broken by the crack of gunshots even farther away, but loud enough to jerk me upright. My head explodes in agony like I sucked on a live grenade. A scream rips its way upward, scratching and clawing at the lining of my throat. It doesn't stop until I'm gasping for smoke-tainted air. Wheezing. Choking. Suffocating.

The darkness eats me…

Rough hands roll me onto my back. I can't see who kneels at my side. It's too dark, and I can't focus my eyes. Whoever it is presses a smoke-tainted cloth against my injured eye, and I shove at a thick chest. The man shoves my hand away and continues to wrap the bandage around my head. He's not gentle.

"It hurts. *Don't touch me.*" I scream the words.

Hands slide beneath my armpits and circle around my chest. Another pair of hands grips my legs. I'm lifted. My head thumps against a chest. *Stop running? It hurts.* Each step stabs a shard of agony into my eye. My throat burns, raw and scratchy. Whimpers come from deep in my chest with each ragged breath. Voices yell over my head, but I don't recognize them. It takes too much effort to focus. I let their words wash over me.

An approaching engine jerks me awake. I'm lying on gravel. Rocks dig into my back. A bandage is tied around my head. I want to look around, but I can't move. I'm scared of the pain. Thick smoke mixed with that acrid, burnt-meat stench fills the air. Orange flames flicker. The fire dances, twisting and weaving. I try to focus on the source of the blaze, but my narrow field of vision contracts, cutting off.

Darkness swallows me whole.

My heart races. It pounds in my ears, throbbing.

The pop of rocks beneath tires grows louder, then stops. A car door opens. Feet run in my direction. I tense.

"Landry!"

Relief surges through me, momentarily dulling the pain. When it flares up again, I want to die. *Help, Dad…please.*

He skids to a halt right beside me, kicking dirt and pebbles across my chest. *It's so dark. I can't see.* I reach for my father, but he pushes me back down before I do more than twitch.

I'm lifted into the passenger seat of Dad's truck. That small bit of movement sends a wave of fire rolling through my eye. My head lolls against the headrest. I smell the pine from his air freshener and the cinnamon spice of his cologne. I'm safe. He'll know what to do. I want to pass out. Why aren't I passing out?

My shirt's soaked with blood and sweat. The smell of smoke and offal begins to overpower the other smells filling the cab of the truck. The seat shakes when Dad gets in, and I groan. He buckles the seat belt. When the strap touches my shoulder, I cringe. It's like every nerve is on fire.

"It'll be okay, son." Tears thicken his voice.

He hits the gas. I rock sideways when he makes a quick U-turn. I black out.

When I come to, I can see. The interior dashboard lights look blurry. Even the high beams can't pierce the seeping fog licking the outer edges of the light. Trying to focus brings on a wave of nausea, and I clench my teeth, swallowing acidic vomit.

Why does my head hurt so bad?

I should know the answer.

Dad pulls my hand down when I touch a wet bandage around my eye. In order to see him, I roll my head to the side, panting against the pain. "What happened to me?"

"An accident…" Dad says, not looking from the road. "Don't talk. Rest. We'll be at the hospital soon. They'll fix your eye."

They'll fix…No, I don't think so. I don't know why. It feels permanent. It feels right, like I deserve to suffer. But why? What did I do?

I stumble through the confusion, searching for answers in the fog filling my mind. *No. Smoke.* "The house was burning. I ran into a fire." Flames licked at a couch. The woman screamed as her hair burned.

Oh God, Mala…

I ran inside to get Mala. She fought, but I dragged her out. Her mom burned, but I got her out. I gasp. "She stabbed me in the eye."

"Landry—"

"Men in masks. They set fire to her house, Dad." Mala sat on my chest with the knife held over my heart. She thought I was one of the bad guys. I wouldn't let her go back to save her mom. They would've killed her too.

The gunshots. Mala got shot before she could stab me. She ran into the woods, but one of the men followed her. He had a gun. He'll kill her. "Turn around."

Dad's jaw flexes. "No."

"We've got to go back. He's after Mala. He'll kill her!"

"She's dead. Acker went after her. There's no way she escaped him."

A shiver goes through me. "Oh my God. You helped murder Mala's mom and you…"

"No, Landry—"

I lunge sideways, grabbing the wheel. I yank it hard.

"Landry, stop!" Dad yells, fighting me for control as the truck weaves from side to side. The right front tire skids in the mud. For a second, I think we'll slide down the embankment, but Dad jerks the wheel and all four tires return to the road.

"You almost killed us!"

My heart tries to leap up my throat. I can't believe I could be so stupid. We could've died. I've got to figure out a way to make him stop that doesn't involve crashing.

I glance up to see him staring, then my attention shifts.

A shadowed figure stands in the road. Misty tendrils lick her bare feet and curl up her legs, like it's a living coat. White hair floats around her head. I squeeze my eye shut. Clearly, I'm hallucinating, but when I look again, she's even closer.

"Dad, watch out!"

He jerks, eyes widening. "Do you see…"

I swear it's a wraith in a *Stargate Atlantis*-inspired costume, only instead of leather, she's wearing a black top hat and coat. She even holds a cane, which she swirls around her head. The spinning gold head reflects the headlights back into our eyes. I'm not sure how, but I can't see worth a damn. Dad slams on the brakes, but we're moving too fast to stop. The spinning cane leaves her hands as she flings it. It crashes against the windshield. Cracks spiral through the glass.

Dad shouts, twisting the wheel. He slams on the breaks, but the truck skids into the turn, weaves, then runs off the road.

We're airborne. Then we hit the raised embankment. My arms rise instinctively to protect my face as my head whips forward then back.

I'm surprised I don't black out.

The truck lands in a ditch filled with runoff from the bayou. Muddy water flows into the cab and soaks into my shoes. The carpet squishes when I unbuckle my seat belt to check on Dad. Blood flows from a gash in his hairline. I find a heartbeat, but he doesn't wake up when I shake him. The fucking airbags didn't deploy on either side.

Dad's cell phone is in his pocket, but it doesn't have service.

A shadow moves at my window. The woman who had been standing in the road presses her face against the glass. She studies my face then smiles, motioning with a hand for me to roll down the window. Like I'm crazy. Shit! The bitch ran us off the road on purpose. Why?

Her eyes narrow.

Her shoulder moves. I can't see what she's doing with her hand. I hold my breath. Too terrified to move.

The click of the latch startles me. The door's unlocked.

I grab for the handle. I yank hard, but it's a fight. The woman's old, but she's strong enough that, for a second, I think I'm going to lose. Then I hear Dad groan. I can't let her get in. She's dangerous. We won't survive if she gets in. I grab the handle with both hands and slam it shut, then hit the lock.

The woman stares at me with yellow eyes, then shrugs. She walks off, vanishing behind the truck. I sit there for I don't know how long. Maybe I even fade in and out of consciousness. Blaring sirens bring me fully alert. I glance at Dad. He hasn't woken up.

His head wound isn't bleeding anymore. The pain in my eye still makes me sick to my stomach, but I must be able to tolerate it better. I can think clearly…not rationally, but I know what to do.

I get out of the truck. My feet slip in muck. I thrash until I get balanced, then wade through chest-high water to the raised bank. It's slick. My feet and hands sink into the mud as I climb up the steep hill. I lose a shoe but don't stop to dig it out. Each minute that passes scares the piss out of me. Dad's hurt. He's waiting for me to get help.

Chapter 31

Mala

Poker Face

I wake in a white room. Sunlight filters through the drawn shades to fall on the sleeping man's face. He looks uncomfortable scrunched up in a tiny chair beside the bed. But his faint snore proves he rests. My mouth feels dry as sand, and my tongue doesn't seem to be working, much like the rest of my body. A dull throb echoes through my head and settles in my shoulder. When I reach for a cup of water next to the bed, the throb turns into a sharp pain, and I gasp.

The guy in the chair twitches then sits upright. He blinks at me with swollen eyes.

I point a finger at the pink plastic pitcher on the nightstand and grimace when even that small movement causes me pain. "Water, please," I croak.

"Mala, thank God." He grabs my hand, and I hiss. "Sorry, are you okay? Did I hurt you?"

"I'm thirsty."

"Sure thing." He moves slower than I'd like. I'm a step away from drying out like a salamander on a stoop. He turns with the glass. Condensation fogs up the sides and little, happy chips of ice dance in the water. I can almost taste the cool silkiness sliding down my parched throat.

"Hurry," I beg, unable to take my eyes from the glass.

He holds the glass out to me, but pulls back before I can take it. "Oh, I don't know. Maybe I should get an okay from the doctor first."

"No, I'm thirsty." Tears fill my eyes and the guy melts. Literally. His shoulders slump, his head lowers, and he takes that extra step to reach the bed. He wraps his arm around my shoulders as he helps me upright. His hands are gentle, and he smells nice.

"Thanks." I take a sip. My eyes close as the cool liquid slides down my parched throat, and I shiver in ecstasy. *Heaven.*

"I remember you," I say, lying back.

He frowns, scrubbing a hand through his copper curls. "Remember what?"

"When you carried me to your car and stayed with me the whole ride to the hospital in the ambulance. Then they tried to kick you out—" I smile at the memory. "You put up such a stink that they let you stay in my room."

He sits in the chair with a grin. "You remember all that, huh?"

"My hero. You kept your promise. Thanks."

Darkness settles over his features. "I don't know why you're acting all surprised. Of course I stayed. You were dying. Hell, you almost bled to death, and it's my fault."

"Why? Did you shoot me?"

"No! Don't be stupid. I—" His eyes narrow. "That wasn't sarcasm, was it? Are you seriously asking?"

"Someone shot me. If you didn't do it then it can't be your fault. You saved me."

He collapses back into his chair. "How much of that night do you remember?"

"Everything. You found me in the road and carried me to the car. You kept me from blacking out."

"What else?"

"What do you mean? That's everything."

"Think back before I found you. What do you remember?"

I close my eyes and concentrate on the gray shadow in my head.

"Mala, do you remember?"

"Nothing's there. It's all gray and cold. Nothing's there before you." I try to turn onto my side, but pain flares in my shoulder. Something bad happened to me and continues to affect me. Why am I so calm about not having any memories of before he found me? I should be upset, but truthfully, I don't care.

He rises quickly. "I'm getting the doctor."

"No!" Panic fills me to the brim, hearing those words. "Don't leave me alone."

"I have to. This isn't right." He backs toward the door, his face filling with fear. "You know me, Mala. You know who I am."

"You keep calling me Mala. Is that my name? Wait. Come back."

He practically runs out the door, leaving me alone and terrified. I don't know who or what I'm afraid of, other than myself.
I focus on slowing my breathing, not wanting to lose control.
The wait stretches. The man doesn't return, and with each minute
that passes, terror builds along the edges of my thoughts.

After about ten minutes, a nurse wearing fuchsia scrubs decorated with white daisies, with a nametag reading Delores
Lindquist, enters the room. She proceeds to check my temperature and the fluid level in the IV bag attached to my arm by a long
tube.

The man enters the room as she asks me to hold out my arm so
she can check my blood pressure. He runs his fingers through his
mussed hair. "I can't find the doctor. Did she come while I was
gone?"

"Not yet, but at least the nurses haven't abandoned me." I give
Delores a little smile as she fiddles with my IV.

The man focuses on me. "Did the nurse say what time to expect the doctor?"

Why don't you ask her yourself? "No, I expect the doc will be
here when you see the whites of her eyes."

"Cute, Mala."

I shrug. "Why are you asking me? Ask the nurse yourself."

Delores's expression grows severe. "George has been told the
last four times he's asked that Dr. Morris will be in later this
morning. She'd been on duty fifteen hours by the time she went
home last night. She needs the rest." She pats my foot and gives
me a little smile. "He's kind of stubborn. In a cute way, I guess."

My eyes widen, and I glance at this guy named George, but he's
too busy stretching the kinks out of his back to pay attention to

Delores's remarks. That or he doesn't hear her. Which makes no sense. *Right?*

"You're healing just fine, Mala," Delores says. "Breakfast should be coming soon. Make sure you eat a lot before they start running tests." She writes a note on her clipboard, then vanishes.

I blink, waiting for my vision to stop acting wonky. Surely she didn't disappear, like for real? I glance at George, mouth opening, and then shut it quick. Just because I'm an amnesiac doesn't mean I'm crazy. I hope.

Dr. Morris arrives an hour later and asks me a bunch of questions about how much I remember. She orders a slew of tests: an MRI, EEG, blood work…*yuck*.

Once they finish treating me like a human pin cushion, they move on to psychological testing to see if I've lost my mind. Judging by the expression on the face of Dr. Rhys, the hospital psychiatrist, I failed. Probably because I'm talking to people he says aren't actually in the room.

Which is total bullshit!

George goes missing about three hours into the testing. He leaves a message with a nurse named Isabel, who I hate on sight, about being called in to work. His absence brings on a panic attack that traps me in a waking nightmare for a day and a half. With my emotional control so fragile, my hallucinations become stronger.

Ghostly specters float in and out of my room. Some, like Nurse Lindquist, look and sound so alive that I confuse them for real people. Others terrify me by the violence of their appearances. Those are the worst: blood-covered torsos, missing limbs, burns. Nurse Isabel keeps a syringe of a powerful sedative tucked in her pocket. One quick jab of the needle into my IV line, and I'm out like a beagle curled up in front of a fireplace.

The drugs trap me within nightmares. I can't escape. No matter how fast I run or how hard I fight, I can't wake up. I run through fire, sink in quicksand—suffer one terrible, life-threatening event after another. Over and over. I find myself wanting to die and go to hell, rather than be stuck in the endless, revolving loop of my dreams.

I wake with a cry. A hunched shadow fills the chair beside the bed. When I scream, it moves forward.

"George." I hold out my hand. "I had a nightmare…of fire…and a girl with blue eyes."

His warm hand takes mine. "Shh, you're safe now."

With a startled yelp, I snatch my hand back and turn on the lamp beside the bed. I pull the blanket up to my neck, making sure to cover all essential private areas. "Who the hell are you?"

"Don't you remember me?" he asks.

Am I supposed to? Will his feelings be hurt when I say I don't remember him? More important, will I be the only one able to see him? I think he's real. Unlike my previous visitors, he doesn't set the hairs on my body on end. He also doesn't seem to have the ability to walk through solid walls or vanish on a whim. But I've been mistaken by how real my delusions appear and embarrassed myself enough that Dr. Rhys wants to start me on antipsychotic medication.

I reach out real quick and pinch his arm.

He yelps, jerking his arm free. "Hey, no groping."

"Uh, sorry." I tap a finger to my bandaged head. "I have a head injury. A few quirks come with the territory. Like the whole remembering-who-you-are thing. My doctor says the amnesia is my mind's way of protecting me from a traumatic experience. I figure it must be pretty horrible since nobody will tell me what happened. They think that if they say something, it'll trigger a memory before my mind's ready to deal with it, and I'll go crazy."

I brush a shaky hand through my hair. Why am I telling a stranger so much? He probably doesn't even care.

"What do you think?" he asks.

"That I'm already insane." I cringe at the confession. Wanting to change the subject, I ask, "So, what are you doing in my room? It's the middle of the night." I squint up at him, then it hits me. "Oh my God! You were watching me sleep, weren't you?"

"Yeah, you got a little drool." He circles his chin with a finger and laughs when I hastily wipe my mouth. "You also snore, but don't worry. It's pretty cute. Like a little flute whistle."

"I don't snore. I know that for a fact."

His head dips, and a shock of midnight hair flops over his forehead. "Can I sit? I'm not feeling too good myself."

I wave toward the chair.

He collapses into it with a groan and lays his head back.

Curious, but not wanting to offend, I fiddle with the edge of the blanket until I work up the courage to ask "What happened to your eye?"

His single gray eye closes. The bandage swathing the other stands starkly against his olive skin. "My dad and I were in a car accident. He's still in intensive care. He hasn't woken up yet. It's been three days."

"I'm so sorry. I hope he'll be okay."

"Thanks." He sits up to lean forward. "So you really don't remember me?"

"No. I really don't," I say, trying not to sound annoyed since he looks so sad. I don't want to run him off. "I know. Let's pretend like we've never met and introduce ourselves. Like this. They tell me my name's Malaise. Not a name I'd choose, but I'll work with what I've got. Now it's your turn."

He thrusts forward, rising quickly to his feet. He wavers, catching his balance on the end of the bed. Sweat pops up on his forehead. "Sorry," he mumbles. "I shouldn't have come. I just couldn't believe…The nurse told me about your condition, but I had to see…to know if losing my eye—if it was worth it."

His words make no sense, but when he turns to walk to the door, something in me rebels. "Wait, don't go." I throw back the covers. All the wires attached to the various machines tangle me up, preventing me from leaving the bed.

Pain shoots through my bandaged shoulder. I grit my teeth, breathing hard until the searing agony subsides to a dull throb. "Nobody's been in to visit all afternoon. Even when people do stop by, I don't know them. Please stay. I'm sick of being alone."

The boy paused at the door when I cried out, and he slowly turns to face in my direction. "So am I," he says. "And I miss…talking to you."

"Why? You act like you know me. But you're saying things I don't understand. Will you at least tell me your name?"

"I'm Landry, and yes, I do know you. We're friends."

"Oh? Well, why didn't you say so in the first place?" I grin and pat the bed. "Nobody else seems to know me at all, except the police. Tell me what I'm like. How long have we been friends? Do I have a favorite food?"

Landry laughs. "I could totally make up all the answers, and you wouldn't know the difference."

"Yeah, but why would you do that?"

"Just to see you eat broccoli because you think you like it." He sits on the edge of the bed. "I could say that we've been madly in love since the eighth grade."

I snort at that one. "Somehow I don't think you're my type."

"Oh, how would you know?"

"A feeling I don't have when I look at you."

"How could you've forgotten our long-standing love affair?" He lifts my hand and brings the back of it to his lips. Warmth floods through my body at the tender kiss, and I scowl.

He meets my gaze with an intensity that makes my heart race, and the stupid machine tracking my heart rate beeps like crazy. All I need to complete my humiliation is for a barrage of nurses to race into the room to administer CPR.

He gives me a smug grin. "Ah-ha, confess. You felt that, didn't you?"

"I did not." I disentangle my hand from his grasp as I study his face. Damn, the boy has good genes. Handsome barely cuts the mustard in describing him. Yet for all his beauty, I still feel disconnected from him, like I'm looking at a painting that is visually pleasing to the eye but would be dowdy in comparison to the original.

"Hey, enough about me," I say, after I remember how to breathe. "I'm a partially open book. What I know, I'll be up front and honest about. Everything else is locked in the vault of my damaged mind."

"Guess that means it's my turn."

"Well, your memory's intact. Tell me about yourself. Start with the basics: name, age, hobbies."

He bends forward at the waist in a mini-bow. "Landry Prince, at your service. Age twenty-one. My hobby is chatting up cute girls with memory loss while they're stuck in a hospital bed and can't run screaming in horror."

"Oh, please, I bet a girl never ran from you in your life," I say laughing.

His raven-wing eyebrow rises. "Oh, you'd be surprised."

I giggle.

Landry reaches into the pocket of his robe and pulls out a leather-bound book. "Well, since we're both bored to tears, I've thought of something to help pass the time. Maybe help you get your memory back."

I lean forward. "What is it?"

"I found this in a box you gave me before you were hurt." He turns the book over in his hands. "I thought it was *The Color Purple*, but when I opened it, I found the dust jacket concealed the real mystery."

"Uh-huh, and why would I be interested?"

"Because you like mysteries, and I know you took at least two years of French in school."

"'Cause we're secret lovers and you know everything about me."

"That's right."

I search my feelings for Landry—strong and tightly bound.

My mind may not remember the connection between us but my body does. "Okay, I trust you."

"Good. I need you to read this diary. It belonged to my sister, Lainey."

I roll my eyes. "What's up with trying to take advantage of the brain damaged, Landry? Ask her about what's in it if it's so important."

"She's dead, Mala. She wrote these last entries the month before she was killed. It's my last connection to her, and I can't read it because it's in French." He clenches the book so hard I'm afraid he'll snap the spine.

"And I can decipher it for you?" I rescue the book from his grasp. The leather warms beneath my palms. "How am I supposed to remember how to read French when I can't even remember my name?"

"Open it and try."

"This is stupid. I shouldn't have this. It's private. Her personal thoughts. It's an invasion—" I sigh. The book opens beneath my hand, and I force my gaze away from the girl with the blue dress who hovers over Landry's shoulder. She wasn't in the room before he showed me the book, but now her presence blazes with a chill so deep it burns.

Landry shivers but doesn't comment on the sudden drop in temperature. "What does she say?"

"That her little brother is a nosy pain in the butt."

"Seriously?"

I glance at the scowling girl. "Yes, seriously. Geesh."

It takes a lot of effort to read the first page. The whole time, I feel like a voyeur. "She's talking about how her day went. She and Mommy Dearest argued about her wearing baggy clothing. She goes on for a couple of paragraphs about how angry she feels about being treated like a teenager."

"Mommy Dearest," Landry says with a small laugh. "My mom hated when Lainey called her that. What else?"

My head starts pounding again. Part of me wants to call in the nurse and request painkillers. The other part doesn't want to pass out on the first interesting conversation I've had since waking up in the hospital. I lay the book on my lap with a pained sigh.

"Look, is there anything specific you want me to search for?" I ask.

Landry stares hungrily at the book. "Yeah, she had a new boyfriend right before she died. I tried to find a name, but she used some sort of code or something. But maybe there're clues. I need to find out who he is. How they met, and what happened the day she died. That would probably be the last entry. I think she wrote in this every night before bed."

"Okay, I'll work on it tomorrow."

"Why not now?"

"I'm tired, Landry. My head hurts, and I want to sleep without having nightmares. I'll work on reading when the words don't make my brain bleed. I promise."

"This is real important, Mala. Not just to figure out what happened to my sister, but also to help you get your memory back." He squats beside the bed and lays his head on the blanket. Without thinking about it, I thread my fingers through his hair and brush the tangled strands away from his face in long, soothing strokes. His shoulders shake, and when he finally lifts his head, tears stain his flushed cheeks. He takes my hand.

"You don't remember this, but we went to a psychic named Madame Ruby. Now, don't scrunch up your nose and start arguing with me about there being no such thing as being able to talk to the dead, because there are such things as spirits."

"Why would I argue?" I whisper, my eyes firmly on his face and not on the shadows that rustle on the edges of the room. Night brings the spirits out in groups, wandering, confused forms that barely hold human shape. Their whispers echo through the room like static on the radio.

"'Cause that's what you did that day. You told me in detail all the reasons why Ruby was a fraud. Looking back on it, I think she knew what she was talking about. She said we'd have to fight to be together, that we'd have to choose between our love for one another and our love for our families. I never thought I'd ever go against my father, but when it mattered, I chose you."

"I don't understand." He chose me over his love for his father? Does Landry love me? Is he right that I'm in love with him, but don't remember?

He studies my face then frowns at whatever reflects back. "Don't worry about it now. When it's important, you'll remember."

"Fine. Whatever." I blow out a deep breath, sick of the evasions. My brain's too fuzzy to figure out this love business. The energy emanating from what Dr. Rhys had almost convinced me are hallucinations makes my nerves tingle, like I hit my funny bone, but throughout my entire body. If these people are ghosts, then I'm not going crazy. "Tell me about the spirits, Landry. Do you believe they're real?"

"My sister possessed Ruby, and it killed her. I didn't believe that Lainey was powerful enough to do that to a person, but I spoke to the doctor who did the autopsy. Ruby died of a brain hemorrhage."

"What does this have to do with me?"

"You told me that, if Lainey possessed you, it would blow out your mind. Now you don't remember who you are or what happened to you. I think my sister attacked you."

"Well, I don't know about that."

"Did you feel how cold it got when we read the diary? That was Lainey's ghost." He squeezes my hand. "You've got to believe me."

I do, and he'll understand when I tell him about the spirits haunting me. Finally, someone who won't think I've lost my ever-lovin' mind. The boy's a blessing and a relief. "Landry, there's something I need to confess—"

The door slams open, and I jump as a man in a uniform bursts into the room. "He's in here!"

George and two other deputies follow him into the room in a determined rush. "Get away from Mala, Prince," George yells. "Move!"

Landry pushes up from the bed with his hands raised. "What's going on?"

George grabs his upraised arm, spins Landry around, and throws him forward across the bed. I curl my legs up seconds before he lands. "Landry Prince, you're under arrest for attempted murder."

"Wait! I didn't do anything," Landry cries, rolling onto his back.

George flips him back over and pulls his arms together so he can clip on handcuffs. "Stop resisting…damn it."

"You're making a mistake," Landry says.

"You have the right to remain silent. Anything you say can and will be used against you in a court of law—"

"Go to hell!" Landry's voice breaks.

"That's where you're heading, Prince." George moves until he stands over the bed. A hard smile flits across his lips. "I had enough evidence against you for the judge to sign the arrest warrant. Mala was still holding the bloody knife she used to carve out your eye when I found her bleeding to death. The blood type matches yours, and I bet the DNA will too."

My mind reels. Betrayal hits hard. My knife...Landry told me he injured his eye in an accident. He lied. Did he shoot me and leave me for dead?

I slide off the bed. "Tell me this isn't true, Landry."

"I've never lied to you." He lifts his head and meets my gaze. The tape holding the bandage to his face dangles on his cheek. My stomach clenches at what remains of his eye. Swollen and pus filled, it looks like rotten meat. "I won't start now."

The deputies drag Landry's unresisting body from the bed. I feel frozen, then realize the chill settling across my skin comes from more than shock. Lainey returns to rescue her brother in vengeance-packed fury. Her rage consumes me and spits me out of my own body.

With a bloodcurdling scream, my body launches through the air at George. My good arm wraps around his waist, and we slam to the ground. I think the reason he lets me bang his head repeatedly on the floor is because he doesn't want to hurt me.

He should've fought back sooner.

Chapter 32

Mala

Possessed

*P*_{oor} *Georgie*, he doesn't look good at all. Blood pours from his broken nose, and his left eye starts to swell shut. That psychotic ghost Lainey possessed me—fucking shoved my soul out of my own body and now uses *me* to wreak havoc on everyone who stands between her and her brother. And I can't stop her!

How can I be suffocating when I don't have a body? Wheezing, I double over. I reach for George, but my fingers pass right through his bloody face.

"Help me." I gasp. "Please. Somebody."

"Mala?" Landry yells, and I jerk upright.

His chest heaves as he jerks his arms, trying to break free of the deputies holding him. He stares, horrified by his sister inhabiting my shell. I look crazed. The whites of my eyes roll, furious. Blood and scratches cover my face, but Lainey doesn't seem to feel pain.

She punches and kicks at two gigantic orderlies who try to pin her. Teeth flash as she bites down on one's hand, and blood spurts from the wound when he rips his hand free.

The deputies finally realize where Lainey's headed and drag Landry from the room. He stumbles out but keeps looking over his shoulder at me/Lainey in horror.

"Landry, I'm here!" I push off the ground and run after him. The door closes. I try to stop, but I'm moving too fast. My hands rise to stop myself from running headfirst into the door, and I stumble forward, losing my balance when my hands pass through the frame and wall. I sprawl in the hallway, panting for air that I shouldn't need and trying to figure out if I have any injuries, but I feel no pain.

Once he reaches the hallway, Landry starts fighting. He throws his body sideways, slamming one of the deputies against the wall, then twists to fling the other off. His shoulder slams into the second deputy's jaw. Both of them release their hold, stunned. He breaks free and lurches toward my room. Blood drips from his fingertips where the handcuffs cut into his wrist. His good eye looks puffy, starting to swell. I'm not sure how well he can see, but he remains focused on reaching the door. Reaching me…

I block his path, waving my hand before his face. "I'm here, Landry." He stumbles to a halt, swaying on unsteady legs. His head dips forward, and his hair falls across his eyes. Blood stains the ebony tips crimson. Only an inch separates us, but I'm not sure it's a distance we can cross.

Vapor condenses in the air between us, and his eye widens. Can he sense me?

A flash of movement comes from behind him. "Watch out."

The deputies rush Landry from both sides. They use their weight and his distraction to throw him to the ground. He hits hard. One presses his knee into Landry's back, and the other sits on his legs.

I crawl next to him and lay a hand on his back. Landry shivers at my touch, and his good eye closes. The other eye leaks mucus and bloody fluid down his cheek. He begins to shake, and the hairs on his arms stand on end. He feels me!

"Landry, it's me. I'm here." I run my finger across his back, spelling out my name on his skin.

"Mala?" he whispers.

"Y-E-S, H-E-L-P," I spell out, then lean back to wrap my arms around myself. The energy that I expended leaves me shaking and dizzy.

"Oh, God," he whimpers.

"The boy can't help you," a familiar voice says.

With a yelp, I look up to find the burned soldier standing over me. "Uncle Gaston?"

His scarred lips lift in a half smile. "Ah, you remember me now."

I take the hand he stretches out to me, and when his fingers close over mine, I cry out, throwing myself into his arms. "You're really here. You can see me. Am I dead?"

"That's the least of your worries."

I hiccup but force a watery scowl. "Tell me something I don't know."

Mama steps out of the shadows and whacks me upside the head. Even in spirit form, it stings. "Stupid girl, I thought I warned you not to let Lainey possess you."

I rub my head ruefully. "Sorry, Mama. I forgot."

They're back now…my memories. And the reason why I can see Mama and Gaston and why they can communicate with me suddenly hits. I inherited Mama's power when she died. I see and hear the dead. Just like Mama said I would. *Crap!*

Mama puts her arms around my waist and pulls me into a hug. "Forgettin's no excuse for lettin' your guard down. Lainey's done stole your body. How are you gonna get her out?"

I sigh. "Hell if I know."

The door opens to my room, and the bloodied orderlies stagger into the hallway carrying my body. One has Lainey in a bear hug, pinning her arms, and the other holds her thrashing legs.

Uncle Gaston eyes Lainey. "She's a good fighter."

How dare he be impressed by her? A surge of anger pushes aside the fear. "Not good enough. The orderlies have her now."

"Not yet," Gaston says with another of his ghastly smiles.

Lainey twists her torso and frees a foot, which she jams in the stomach of the guy holding her other leg. Air whooshes out of him, and he falls to a knee. The other orderly loses his grip on her upper body, and she drops to the floor.

"Damn it! Uncle Gaston, do something," I cry, running forward to grab for Lainey, but I can't touch her. Her eyes meet mine, and she grins savagely and rolls. The orderlies scramble after her. "Make her stop! She's screwing me over. They're gonna lock me in a padded room and throw away the key. Even if I get my body back, I'll be trapped in a psycho ward for the rest of my life."

"You're not who's important right now, Mala," Gaston says, reaching his hand out to me. "Are you ready?"

Mama gives me a smile. She takes Gaston's hand then mine, linking us together in a chain. My spirit crackles with the energy flowing between us.

"Why do you keep asking me that?"

Gaston tips his chin in Lainey's direction. "A vengeful spirit can manifest only by tapping into its rage. It's a being lacking in sanity…empathy. Hate consumes Lainey. The more hate she draws on to speak to the living, the less she has to keep her sane. Lainey seeks justice so she can rest. Your job as a spirit guide is to lend her your strength. Are you prepared to send her home?"

Like I have a choice if I want my body back. "Yes, yes. Whatever I've got to do, I'm ready."

A commotion draws my attention from Lainey. Dr. Rhys and Dr. Morris run down the hall. Andy, the K-9 deputy, exits the room. Luckily, he hasn't brought Rex, or I'd be getting chunks bitten out of me. He blocks the doctors from passing, and they begin to argue. The two deputies holding Landry pull him to his feet. He sways between them with a dead look on his face, like he's gone catatonic.

George staggers out of my room. He focuses on Lainey and raises his bloody hands toward her in supplication. "Mala, please. We're trying to help—"

Gaston touches Lainey's head. Energy travels into my body. Lainey lurches forward, and her eyes roll up in her eye sockets, like she's touched a live wire. When her eyes pop open again, I stagger. Only Mama's hand keeps me upright. Lainey's blue eyes stare from my face, and I shiver at the fury blazing from the cobalt depths.

"She killed him," Lainey screeches.

Everyone freezes.

Lainey crouches on the balls of her feet, rocking back and forth like a wild animal. She points a bloody finger toward the middle-age woman who came up behind the doctors. Mrs. Prince, the woman who slapped me silly.

Lainey hisses, but her eyes don't turn from her mother.

"W-what?" Mrs. Prince stammers, backing up. She glances toward the officers holding Landry, and her expression changes. Rage fills her blue eyes, and her back straightens. "What's going on? Why are you arresting my son?"

"We'll explain later, Mrs. Prince." George tilts his chin at Andy, who blocks Mrs. Prince when she tries to go to Landry, but his eyes never leave my body. "Mala…"

"Mala's gone," Lainey snaps, then smiles. Blood stains her teeth. "Just me. Only me," she singsongs in a voice that sends chills across my skin. "Mommy Dearest killed my baby. She buried my son in the roses."

Mrs. Prince pales beneath her heavy makeup. "What did she say?"

"Mala, you're not making any sense," George says, keeping his voice calm.

Landry's head lifts, but he holds his body unnaturally still. He glances at Lainey then stares right at me. My hand lifts, and he flinches. "She's Lainey, George. Not Mala but my sister." He looks back at his mother's bloodless face. "Mom, is Lainey's baby…" He pauses, swallowing hard. "Did you bury the baby in the garden?"

"Shut up, Landry. You're not helping," George yells.

"She killed my baby," Lainey sings.

"Don't…" Mrs. Prince stumbles backward. Andy reaches out to take her arm, but she twists free. "How…"

"Why, Mom?" Tears run down his cheek as Landry whispers, "Tell the truth."

"Tell the truth," I echo, infusing power from Gaston and Mama into the order.

Mrs. Prince twitches, like she hears me. Her eyes glaze, and her head jerks toward Landry. "Family first, Landry. Lainey's behavior brought shame upon us. I couldn't let her damage your father's reputation by giving birth to a bastard."

Tears fill Lainey's blue eyes. "She refused to take me to the hospital. She let me bleed to death."

Uncle Gaston removes his hand from Lainey's head and places it on her shoulder. She shudders, leaning against his knees. "It's done. The truth's out," Gaston tells her, then looks at me. "Mala, are you ready?"

My hands tingle, and my vision blurs. I'm sucked forward, spinning, then, with a lurch, my position changes. My knees ache. The skin on my face burns. I raise my hands…my hands…my body.

"I'm back!" I yell, so happy I want to jump up and dance. The orderlies get their second wind and start toward me again. I give a Lainey-inspired growl, and they freeze.

Landry's knees buckle, but he's held upright by the two deputies. He looks broken. I want to throw my arms around his neck and squeeze all the sadness out of him. His eye lifts to my face.

"Mala?" he mouths.

I nod, putting a finger to my lips, shushing him.

Lainey appears beside Mrs. Prince, an invisible wraith only I can see. *Lucky me.* She touches her mother's cheek. "Mala, she can't hear me anymore. I begged her to help us, but instead of calling an ambulance, she called James."

"Who's James?" Lainey grimaces at me like I'd been dropped on my head too many times as a child, and the puzzle pieces finally come together in horrifying detail. "Saints, I'm stupid. James Rathbone. The only doctor your mama would feel comfortable telling her secret to. That's why he faked the autopsy results. To hide the fact that you delivered the baby."

Mrs. Prince thinks I'm speaking to her. She covers her face with her hands. "I thought James would help her. He promised to keep the birth a secret and help find a home for the baby. But he couldn't stop the bleeding."

"More likely, he didn't *want* to stop the bleeding," I say. "It was better for him if his secret got buried. But you could've called an ambulance. You could've saved her."

"I begged Lainey to stay with me, but she died in my arms. Imagine my pain upon hearing that James tossed my baby girl into the swamp like trash. But I'm glad I decided to keep that tiny piece of her close to me. Every day I see their spirits in the vibrancy of my roses." Mrs. Prince squeezes her eyes shut, but when they reopen they remain dry. She smiles slightly. "This year my roses will finally beat March Dubois's in the annual garden competition."

Talk about sane on the outside, but ewwy gooey on the inside. I guess it is true what they say about crazy people not knowing that they're stark raving nuts.

Then the implications of what Mrs. Prince is saying sinks in.

"Oh my God! That bastard—" I swallow around the lump in my throat and spit the words out. "Rathbone knew it was only a matter of time before Mama exposed him to the police. His first attempt to get rid of her failed, so he came up with a better plan." I shake my head. "What I don't get is how. How did he convince two other men to help him murder someone in cold blood?"

Mrs. Prince answers my question with hardly any inflection in her voice, like she stands outside of herself. "James twisted my husband's grief." She squeezes her own hands together as if in prayer. "I helped too. I begged my husband to avenge our daughter. And he did. I just never thought Landry would help, but he's such an obedient son."

"Mom, no!" Landry yells. "I didn't help Dad. I saved Mala!"

Mrs. Prince ignores her son the same way she ignored her daughter when Lainey begged her to take her to the hospital. She glances at Andy who started down the hallway at her words. "You're too late. My husband's gone." Madness tinges her rising voice. "I protected him at the expense of my own child, yet he abandoned me."

Lainey lets out a little cry, turning toward her brother. The energy powering her dims like a draining light bulb, making her appear less substantial—a ghostly copy of her former self, slowly fading away.

"It's time for us to take Lainey home, Mala," Gaston says.

He and Mama leave my side and go to Lainey. She takes their outstretched hands and smiles. "Good-bye, Mala. Thank you."

Mama gives me a little wave and disappears.

The reality of their absence hits hard. *I'm alone.* "Oh God," I wail, falling onto my backside. "Mama's really dead."

Images, hard and heavy, rush into my mind. Fire. Death. Mama screaming as I try to break free from the man holding me so I can help her. Stabbing the man—stabbing Landry. The knife sliding through his eye like jelly. Landry in the hospital, telling me he'd been injured in an accident. Oh God, how could I have forgotten?

"Mala, I swear. I tried to keep you safe. You've got to remember, please," Landry pleads.

"No! You're a liar. It's your fault!" I scream at Landry. "You wouldn't let me help her. Mama died because of you!"

I double over at the waist. My stomach clenches. I choke, pushing the words from deadened lips: "I hate you, Landry!"

Chapter 33

Mala

Closure

To day I look fairly normal. If normal wore hot pink Hello Kitty flannel pajamas. I don't know what my boss, Ms. March, had been thinking when she picked out my clothing. She ought to have known better. Maybe she thought I'd gone completely around the bend and would actually like being dressed up like a toddler.

As embarrassed as I feel in this ensemble of bad taste, I perch on the edge of the windowsill, staring across the heat-shimmering asphalt of the hospital parking lot. I search for one vehicle in particular, a forest green Land Rover. There's one in the parking lot. It's him. Finally.

I hate crowds. Now, not only do I have to deal with the living, I also have to contend with the demands of the dead. Their constant chatter leaves me restless and jittery. I can't block them out.

My mama once told me that, after she died, I would sit on her grave and beg her spirit to teach me to control the horrors I saw. When Mama burned, her ashes were scattered to the four winds. And like Uncle Gaston, who'd been crisped by the Viet Cong, she roams like the free spirit she'd been in life.

I'm more likely to find her sitting on the edge of Dr. Rhys's desk than a grave. She keeps baiting me into responding to her in front of him. Talking to invisible people convinced Dr. Rhys to shove medication down my throat and lock me up in the hospital's psychiatric unit on a thirty-day hold for observation. For the first week, I resembled a zombie with spit drooling down my chin. Thank heavens I wasn't allowed to receive visitors until my body adjusted to the meds.

I draw in a deep breath of air-conditioned air. The smell of burnt chili, hot dogs, urine, unwashed bodies, and a score of other scents I don't want to break down too closely fill my nose. Ms. Anne, one of the older patients, plucks a few keys on the piano, not putting much physical effort into reproducing the music she hears playing in her mind. Her daughter sits silently beside her. Out of the fifteen people committed to the psychiatric unit, Ms. Anne and I are the only patients who have visitors.

When the door opens and George walks into the room, my heart lurches. I try to play it cool, but my feet, clad in fuzzy, zebra-striped socks, wiggle with excitement. He's so beautiful, like a rainbow after a thunderstorm. He glows. He walks toward me with a slight bounce to his step, wearing a short-sleeved, white T-shirt with purple and gold LSU lettering and worn jeans. The smile lighting his green eyes brings heat to my cheeks. I jump off the sill but wait for him to come to me. I've learned my lesson the hard way—no sudden moves in the psych unit or the orderlies take you down.

"Hey, Mala," he says, opening his arms.

I glance over my shoulder at Kevin, my favorite guard, who nods. Permission granted.

"Georgie," I cry, throwing myself into his arms. He lifts me in the air and swings me around. "About time you came for a visit."

"I've been trying to get in for three weeks. This is the first time they've said yes."

I give him a peck on the cheek. "You'd better put me down now. Kevin's getting the wrong idea about our relationship." I nod toward the orderly. "It's okay, we're just friends."

George gives me one last squeeze. "The best of friends."

"Always," I say, waving to the orange plastic sofa. "We can sit. How long can you stay?"

George doesn't release my hand as we walk over to the sofa. I curl up in the corner so I can stare at him. Gosh, he looks good enough to eat. I spent a lot of time fantasizing about seeing him again. About what I'd say to explain what happened with Lainey taking over my body. She beat him up pretty good, but he thinks I did the damage. How do I apologize for something I didn't, but also did, do?

I bite my lip, feeling guilty and confused. Silence stretches between us, and I don't know how to break it. Finally I jump in with both feet. "Georgie, I'm sorry."

He jerks, like he'd been lost in thought, then frowns. "About the hug?"

"No. Kicking your butt."

"You did not kick my butt," he protests, scowling. "You

cheated. I would've taken you down if you hadn't caught me by surprise."

"Dream on, buddy," I say with a laugh, then sober. "Seriously, I *am* sorry. I lost control of myself for a while. It doesn't excuse what I did, but I'd never deliberately hurt you." *All true. Every word.* "You must know how much I care about you, right?"

"Yeah, don't worry about it." He fidgets with the frayed cuff of his jeans. "When do you get out of here?"

I hold onto my sigh. Not the enthusiastic response I hoped to get. "I have another week. Dr. Rhys says he's pleased with my progress. I've done everything they've asked: group, grief counseling, meds." My face puckers at the thought of those horse pills. *Bleck.* "You know, I didn't think I'd accept what happened to Mama for a long time, but it helps to talk about it."

George leans forward, placing his hand on top of mine. "Have you remembered yet?"

"The actual attack?"

"Yeah, do you remember how much Landry participated in your mom's murder?"

I jerk my hand free and scoot up onto the arm of the sofa so I look down into George's wide eyes. Fear flickers in the green depths, bringing out a hint of gold. I wrap my arms around my upraised knees. "So…we get to the real reason why you're here. To see what dirt I can give you on Landry."

"That's not the only—"

I wave him silent.

Kevin leaves his position by the door and moves ponderously in our direction. "Everything okay, Mala?"

"Yes, sweetheart," I drawl, batting my eyelashes.

"Let me know if you need me."

"Will do, Kev," I say, not taking my eyes off George. "My, you've only been here five minutes and I already want to pound your head again."

"That's not funny, Mala," George says with a scowl. No trace of fear remains in his eyes. Now he looks annoyed. "Answer my question."

"Why?"

"Landry's preliminary hearing is in two months. The district attorney needs you to testify against him, or he'll have to drop the case."

"Well, I won't! I'm not testifying to him helping to murder Mama. How many times do I have to say that Landry saved me from his father that night? I'm not crazy or suffering from amnesia anymore. I know what I remember."

"Why did you fight him if he saved you?" George yells, rising. "You stabbed him in the eye. That's not something you'd do without provocation."

Kevin starts over. "Yo, man, calm down or you'll need to bounce."

"I'm sorry," George says quickly, raising his hands. "Look, this is ridiculous. I didn't come to fight." He turns pleading eyes on me. Hellfire, whenever he looks at me with those puppy-dog eyes, I forget my reasons for being angry with him.

The air cools, and tingles spread across my arms. I grit my teeth. The air shimmers beside George, and Mama appears. I keep my gaze firmly on George. "I'm sorry too, Georgie."

Mama crosses her arms and paces around him. "What are you apologizin' to him for? He's the one stirrin' up trouble."

I catch myself rolling my eyes.

I've gotten used to answering her questions by directing them at another person. "Georgie, I may hate that Landry kept me from trying to save Mama, but I won't condemn him to the death penalty for murder. It's bad enough he's been in jail for three weeks on assault charges, with no proof he hurt me, I might add. Being locked up can mess with a person's mind." I wave my hand to encompass the room. "I know from firsthand experience how degrading it feels to be blamed for something I didn't…didn't mean to do." I shake my head. "I'll do whatever I can to help him."

George's lips tighten. "He did it, Mala."

"I'll prove he didn't." *If I ever get out of here.*

George stalks over to the window, breathing hard. I stay back, waiting for him to calm down before he loses it. I don't want him getting kicked out. He thinks I'm being naive. But I heard the evidence against Landry from his own mouth during his police interview. The problem with having my soul ripped out of my body by Lainey is that now my spirit doesn't want to stay cooped up. Every night, I find myself floating out of my body and wandering the town. I can go anywhere in spirit form, spy on anyone, including that District Attorney Cready who's trying to dig up enough evidence to fry Landry. No walls can keep me out.

Landry couldn't deny being at my house. The DNA found on the knife I used on him proved it. He said he came over to have me translate his sister's diary. He arrived too late to save Mama, but he ran into a burning house to rescue me. I don't know how to forgive him for not trying to help Mama and for hiding his dad's involvement in the attack from the cops. I've tried.

Still, even with all the hate bottled up inside me, I'm drawn like a moth to a flame to Landry's jail cell every night. The boy looks seriously scary. Since he's been locked up, he spends his free time in the yard lifting weights. The intense workout has put muscles on top of muscles. With the eye patch and his long black hair, he looks like a pirate. He gives me the chills, both the good and the bad kind.

I finally can't take the silence. "Look, George, let's agree to disagree. I'm gonna do what I need to do to prove I'm not insane so I can get out of here. Then I'm gonna get Landry released from jail before his perv of a roomie shanks him in his sleep."

George leans against the windowsill. "Fine, I'll let it go. For now." He thrusts his hand into his pockets. "I guess I wouldn't worry so much if we could get a lead on Rathbone's and Reverend Prince's whereabouts. Although, if I were the rev and found out my best friend impregnated my daughter then murdered her, I'd make sure his body got fed to the gators."

"The rev has proved he's quite capable of taking it old school with the vengeance. Rathbone had better run long and far…" I stare at my socks, wiggling my toes. "I'm getting out soon. The rev will come after me again, won't he?"

"I won't let anything happen to you."

He didn't answer my question.

Mrs. Prince turned catatonic after her confession. She's locked up in an extra-secure wing of the psych unit. I've peeked in on her a few times. She drools. Landry and I are the only ones who can testify against Reverend Prince and Doc Rathbone. If they get rid of us…not that I think the rev would murder his own son, but Rathbone wouldn't have a problem with it. He proved that by letting Lainey die. But me? There's no reason why I wouldn't be a target.

George clears his throat, and I look up. His smile sends a burst of warmth to banish the chill of worry. "Time for a happy topic—what do you plan to do after your release next week?"

Mama had flitted over to hover next to Ms. Anne. Every so often, she flicks the woman's ear and laughs when Ms. Anne tries to hit her. Kevin thinks Ms. Anne is attacking her daughter, and he calls another guard to help shuffle her out of the room, giving me a meaningful, don't-do-anything-wrong-while-I'm-gone look.

I roll my eyes and fold my hands primly on my lap. "Well, Georgie, I've been thinking of getting out of town for a while," I say slowly, rubbing my arms. As usual, thoughts of Magnolia make me break out in a cold sweat. I'm not sure why. The only thing I know is I *have* to go to her. No ifs, ands, or buts about it. If I don't, something awful will happen. "I'll head out to New Orleans. Before all this happened, I promised to work for my aunt over the summer, and I think being with her will help to clear my head."

A gust of air bursts from George's mouth forming a strangled "No!"

He moves so fast I barely have time to squawk. His hands fall onto my shoulders, and he yanks me against him. My hands rise between us, pressing against his chest. His heart hammers beneath my palms.

"Georgie?" I stare up at his face. "What's wrong?"

A broad range of emotions flicker across his features, but the last one takes me by surprise. The turmoil seeps from his eyes, and they soften. "I've been an idiot, haven't I?"

My tongue runs across dry lips. "I'd say yes, but I'm not sure which time you're referring to."

He cups my face between his palms and tilts my head up. "I'm thinking of all the times I saw you but didn't really see you. You've been right in front of me, and I kept telling myself you were a kid. I never noticed how important you'd become to me."

Oh God, what's happening here? My heart speeds up. I stare at his mouth, reading his lips shaping the words because I don't think my ears are working right.

"You've got to stop scaring me, Mala LaCroix. I almost lost you once, and I just got you back." He leans down until his warm breath blows in my ear as he whispers, "Don't even think about trying to ditch me again."

My mouth drops open. I can't believe the words I'm hearing or what they stir up inside of me. Confusion, anticipation…*Crap!* "Are you real or a hallucination from the meds?"

"I'm gonna kiss you now. Okay?"

"Kiss me?" I say with a shaky laugh, then his words sink in. "Oh, wait. What?"

His lips meet mine in midprotest, and I gasp. He thrusts his tongue inside my open mouth with a groan of desperation. He trembles as his hands slide down my shoulders to wrap around my waist. The hunger in the initial kiss softens into gentle exploration. I trail my fingers up his neck and thread them into his silky hair.

The deep rumble of a clearing throat jerks us apart. Kevin's six-foot-plus frame hovers over us. "Keep it PG, folks."

"Jealous?" I ask with a giddy grin.

Kevin harrumphs.

I fan my heated face. Kind of glad at the interruption. The wheel in my head spins threads of confusion, not gold. Oh boy. I kissed George.

I'm going to hell for this.

George's kiss was nice. *Very nice.*

Landry's kisses could wake the dead. But I hate him now, right? So he shouldn't matter. Except he does. And always will. He gave me my first kiss. All others will forever be compared to his. *Damn.*

George squeezes my hand. He sinks into the sofa and pulls me across his lap. "Stay with me this summer. I mean, with Bessie and Maggie, but I'll visit. We'll take it slow and get to know each other."

I bite my lip and meet George's worried gaze. How would he react if I told him I see spirits? Would he believe me, like Landry did? Or run so fast that I get rug burn trying to hold onto him?

"I have to go to New Orleans, Georgie," I say with a sigh. "I don't have a choice. I made a promise. But mainly, I need time to figure this out, 'cause, yeah. This is totally unexpected. I mean, we're friends. I'm scared you're just feeling protective because I almost died."

"I know my own feelings." He's wearing his gunslinger look again.

"Yeah? Well, I don't." I slide off his lap onto the sofa. "This probably isn't what you want to hear, but I still care about Landry. I don't know how we can be together. Not after what happened with Mama, but I owe it to him, and to myself, to figure it out. I'm sorry. I don't have a better answer."

Mama leans across the back of the sofa and taps my nose with a finger. "Yep, best bet all round if you want to control me is to learn from Magnolia. Otherwise, I'll haunt you till the second coming."

"I guess I can agree to take it slow," George says. "'Do you think Kevin would complain if we did a little more smooching? You know, like a test drive." He smiles, and his lips meet mine.

I shove aside my guilt and allow myself to get swept up in the moment. My first crush is kissing me. The guy I gave up as someone who would never in a million years want to be with me. For this shining moment, he captures me utterly and completely. 'Cause I deserve a bit of happiness, and who knows what kind of shit's gonna go down tomorrow.

Mama cackles and does a jig around the sofa. "My daughter's gonna be a hoodoo queen's apprentice."

Acknowledgments

I am grateful to the many people who have helped me along the way. Without your support, I would not be seeing a lifelong dream come true. My love and gratitude goes to my family, whose unwavering support inspired me. Nate, my soul mate, thank you for talking me off of the ledge whenever I wanted to quit and for keeping me supplied with chocolate and peach tea. Kierstan and Maxwell, Mama could not have done this without your patience and love. You inspire me every day. Dreams are attainable when your loved ones believe in you. Never give up. To my parents and, later, my in-laws, you cultivated a love of reading and writing in your children and grandchildren. Thank you for that gift. To my supportive siblings, I love you.

To my amazing agent, Kathleen Rushall, you are my champion, a friend, and the Ned Stark of my heart. You never gave up hope and found us the perfect home in Grand Central Publishing. To my amazing editors, Alex Logan and Erica Warren, I appreciate the opportunity that you have given me. You amaze me with your questions, your insight, and your willingness to push me to be the best that I can be. My gratitude to Madeleine Colavita and the extraordinary Grand Central team, who work so hard behind the scenes to make their authors feel special and wonderful.

A special shout-out goes to the amazing folks at AQC, especially the Speculative Fiction group. I found you when I needed you the most. Thank you to my amazing critique partners. Kate Evangelista, you were the first person other than family to read my work. Thank you for letting me know that I didn't completely suck at writing and for being a mentor, a friend, and a psychic twin. You taught me how to grow in my craft, supported me when I thought all was lost, and cheered me on when things went well. Carla Rehse and Sarah Gagnon, my writing sisters, the two of you mean the world to me. We've been through the thick of it, and we've come out stronger. Thanks for reading my rough first chapters and making them shine. Donald McFatridge, King of Echoes, thanks for getting my twisted sense of humor by being even more twisted. You're the funniest man I know. Michelle Hauck, Queen of Plotholes, thank you for catching my dangling threads. Without you nothing in this story would make a lick of sense.

Thank you to my awesome betas, Joyce Alton, Jennifer Troemner, Diana Robicheaux, Debra Kopfer, Jordan Adams, Jason Peridon, Kierstan Sandro, Bessie Slaton, Jonathan Allen, Christine Berman, and Margaret Fortune. You all rock! I couldn't have done this without you and so many others from AQC.

To my wonderful friends and coworkers at BCP, thank you for listening to my crazy ideas. You supported me when I only thought of this as an unattainable dream. I appreciate each and every one of you.

And most of all, to the readers of this book, thank you. If this novel allowed you to escape for a single second from the troubles of your daily life, then I truly have attained my dream. This novel was a labor of love, and I appreciate you allowing me to share it with you.

Please see the next page for a preview of

Dark Sacrifice.

Landry

Jailhouse Blues

Jail sucks.

Prison's got to be worse. I don't even want to imagine how much, and since I haven't been hauled before the judge and sentenced yet, I don't have to. So while it's not all sunshine and daisies in my ten-by-five-foot steel-barred world, I count my blessings and pray for an out that doesn't involve me getting shanked.

I walk in front of the guard, making sure I don't stray too close to the bars of the other cells, and keep my gaze trained on the far door, ignoring the shouts of the prisoners. My shoulder blades twitch. Tingles run up my spine. The crinkling of the orange jumpsuit, the clank of the shackles attached to my wrists and ankles, and the *shush* of my shuffling feet on concrete add to the humiliation of being accused of attempted murder.

I'm innocent of that allegation, but I kinda think I deserve to fry for all the shitty things I did that led me here.

I feel like the lowest piece of shit.

The temptation to ask the guard who my visitor is builds with each step, but I keep my question behind clenched teeth. I've been locked-down in Cell Block A for eleven days now, classified as a high-risk violent offender and housed with all of the other rapists and murders. If I want to survive, I've got to follow the rules—the spoken and unspoken.

Rule One: *Keep your mouth shut.*

Rule Two: *Watch your back.*

Since my case is a high-profile crime, I take it a step further and also watch who's in front, side...*fuck*...I need another eye. Although exhausted 'cause I'm so on guard, I can't get a good night's sleep, which doesn't help keep me alert when I need to be. It's a catch-22 situation.

"Who's here for me?" I blurt out. *Damn.*

"No talking, Prisoner 245." The guard sounds bored. He probably says the same line every time he takes someone out of their cell. Only the prisoner I.D. number changes.

I must look pathetic. I broke Rule One within minutes of hearing about my visitor. It's just driving me crazy not knowing who's here. I'll know soon enough, but the anticipation gnaws at my insides. 'Cause I hope it's her. Pray it's her. That she's finally forgiven me.

Hell, who else could it be? My so-called friends on the *outs* think I'm dirt. Nobody visited me in the hospital while I recovered from my injury. After I got arrested, not even the nurses spoke to me unless it was about my missing eye. *Keep the socket clean. Take your antibiotics. Let us know if you're feverish. Are you in pain? Here are some meds. Oh, it's not about your eye. Your chest hurts. Why?*

'Cause Mala LaCroix hates me.

How do you know?

'Cause she said so. Rather, screamed it. "I hate you, Landry. It's your fault Mama's dead." Not a lot of room for doubt…or hope to hold onto when the girl you're in love with accuses you of murdering her mother.

The guard unlocks the door from my cell block. The shouts of the prisoners fade as the heavy metal door clinks shut. The narrow, gray hallway stretches before me. At the end will be the visiting room.

God, please let it be her.

This is the longest walk of my life.

The chain catches my ankle, and the stumble takes me to a knee. The guard yanks on my arm, and I stand fast. "Keep moving."

With a grunt, I shuffle forward.

The spirit of my dead sister, Lainey, possessed Mala and used her body to rain mass destruction over the cops and orderlies. Lainey also exposed her murderers. A win for my big sis. Not so much for the girl whose body she inhabited. Mala's pretty nonviolent, but her eyes burned with hatred after she remembered my part in her mom's death. If the doctor hadn't sedated her before she could reach me, she gladly would've plucked out my other eye.

My hand lifts, but the handcuffs are connected to a chain looped around my waist, and they keep me from rubbing the ache in my chest.

The hallway ends at a door. The guard pulls out a key and opens it to reveal a small room divided in half by a glass window. A telephone hangs on the wall. I duck my head and shuffle forward, afraid to meet the eyes of the girl on the other side of the glass.

"Sit down. You have five minutes," the guard says.

I slide onto the metal stool bolted to the floor. "Thanks," I say, staring at the roach crawling across the cement. I lift a foot and squish it. The guard grunts and leaves the room, locking the door behind him. A banging on the glass brings my head up.

Dena Acker scowls and waves the phone at me. I read as her lips move. "Pick it up, idiot."

My mouth twitches.

The phone's dirty, but the short cord won't reach my jumper so I can't wipe it off. I put it to my ear with a grimace. "Hey."

"Hey? Is that all you've got to say?" Dena scrunches up her nose, reminding me of her cousin, and the pain in my chest flares again. It's amazing how much alike she and Mala are. It's hard to look at her.

"Dude, you're totally blowing the best five minutes of your short life."

My gaze flicks up to meet hers. Worry flickers in the green. "Are you serious?"

"Have you gotten a better offer lately?" Springy red curls, only a little darker than the color filling her cheeks, fall across Dena's face as she shakes her head. She brushes them back with a huff. "Gosh, that sounded dirty. Didn't mean it to be, you know?"

"I know." I lean forward. "Thanks for coming."

"Sure."

"No. I mean it. You're my first visitor."

"Well, technically, I'm here for someone else so it doesn't really count. Not that I wouldn't visit you on my own, but I'm not."

"You're not making any sense."

"I know. Sorry. I'm here because I'm worried about Mala."

I suck in a breath, gripping the phone. "What do you mean?"

"Did you know she's still stuck in the psych unit?" She leans forward, gripping the phone so hard her knuckles whiten. "I tried to visit, but they said she can't have visitors unless it's immediate family. I guess distant cousin doesn't count. But she's being re-leased in a few days. I thought maybe you'd like for me to give her a message."

I stare at the fingerprints smearing the glass. *What do I say?* "She thinks I killed her mother. She won't want to hear anything I've got to say, Dee."

"But you didn't…"

I did. "Doesn't matter. Let it go."

"Landry, we both know it's not true." Her voice chokes. "I was there too. I saw what happened."

Panic rushes through me.

"Shut up!" Sweat runs down to sting my good eye and soaks the patch over my dead one. Dena wraps her arms around herself, shivering. I'm hot; she's cold. We're both terrified because we're so fucked.

All of us. Mala too. Only she doesn't know it yet.

Air fills my lungs. It smells—a putrid body funk oozing from the walls. I take another deep breath anyway, trying to slow my racing heart. I glance at the sealed door, then the phone. If this conversation's being taped, then Dena just buried herself. "God, are you crazy, Dee? Keep your mouth shut," I whisper. "It's not safe. You're on the outs. At least with Mala and me locked up, we're safe. Rathbone, my dad, your dad…they're still out there."

Her voice wobbles. "I'm not scared of them."

"You should be." We both witnessed what they're capable of.

I scratch around the healing scar partially covered by the eye patch. The stitches itch.

Dena stares at me for a long moment. Her eyes flicker with whatever she's considering, then her jaw firms. "Doesn't matter what they try. I can get you out of here. If I tell the DA what I saw, he'll let you go. This isn't fair. It's not fair for Mala to think you had anything to do with Ms. Jasmine's murder. And it's not fair that I'm not doing a damn thing to help." Her lips pinch, and her gaze moves over my shoulder. The sound of the opening door makes her sit back. "I can't let it go, Landry. I *won't*."

The pain in my chest intensifies as my lungs constrict. My breathing grows harsh. I know the signs of a panic attack. I've had a few in the last couple of weeks. It takes a few seconds to slow my racing thoughts.

"Give me a few more weeks, Dee. The DA doesn't have the evidence to take my case to trial. He'll have to drop the charges, and you won't have to get involved. I'm fine. This place sucks, but I get three meals a day. I'm learning to make license plates…"

Dena's harsh laugh trails off into a sob. "I don't have a few more weeks. Dad disappeared. H-he hasn't even tried to contact us. The money's running out. I can't support the kids on my paycheck from Munchies. I don't know what to do, Landry. I want my best friends back."

"Mala doesn't know about *us*, does she?"

"No, I never told her. I promised you I wouldn't, but this secret makes me feel like I'm the worst cousin in the world!" Her wail cuts off with a choked hiccup, and she runs the back of her hand beneath her nose, then looks at her hand in disgust. "Eww..."

"Yeah, not the brightest move."

She gives a soggy laugh. "Shut up."

A shadow falls over the table, and I whip around. The guard walked up on my blind side. I'm still not used to people being able to sneak up on me so easily. It makes me jittery.

The guard takes a quick step back, balanced on the balls of his feet in case I've lost my mind enough to attack him. It must happen more often than I think—crazed prisoners flipping out in the visiting area.

When he sees I'm okay, his raised hands drop. "Two minutes."

I nod and turn back to Dena.

Her wide eyes flicker. Rather than showing her that I can handle myself in here, she just witnessed how much of a disadvantage I have because of my injury. Not good. Dena's impulsive, and she doesn't have a clear sense of self-preservation when it comes to helping her friends. I'm scared for her.

"I've got to go. Don't come back here...and be careful, okay?" I lay my palm against the sticky glass.

Dena presses her hand adjacent to mine, and for a brief second, I imagine her warmth through the thick glass, then she hangs up the phone. Her shoulders slump as she walks to the locked door and waits to be buzzed out.

* * *

I stare up through the wire springs at the saggy, stained mattress above my head. Thank God my cellmate isn't a bed wetter. A murderer, yes. I think waking up with a mouthful of piss every morning is ten times worse than worrying about whether I'll wake up at all. So far, Caleb has kept his psychotic impulses under control. If I'd been thirty pounds lighter and three inches shorter, I'd have "CALEB'S BITCH" tattooed on my ass.

A quick elbow to the face kept him from going hands-on in the shower. We've kept an uneasy truce for the last five days. I sleep with my only eye open. Okay, that's a slight exaggeration. But I'm definitely on edge, all the time. Going out into the rec yard is like rolling the dice. Who's gonna try to increase their rep by stepping up to me today? Will I make it back to my cell? So far, double sevens say it's my lucky day.

A snore comes from above, and I squint, wishing I had X-ray vision to see if Caleb's faking it. The tension between us has been building over the last day. A snitch, wanting to get on my good side, told me someone offered a lot of cash—more than most convicts see in their lifetime—to take me out. Money like that is hard to say no to. It's maybe even worth the risk of frying in the electric chair if it lets you take care of your family. Especially if you're already looking at a life sentence.

Caleb's looking at twenty years, less if he gets parole. Only an idiot would try to take me out while we're stuck sharing a cell with no one else around to shift the blame onto. Paranoia has me searching for threats where there may be none. It's more likely I'll get hit when the guards aren't around so I make sure to stay in groups. I need to find a protector, but so far I haven't been willing to do what it takes to earn a spot. I'm screwed. I'm just not desperate enough to *be* screwed.

Yet.

God, I've got to get out of here.

Dena said that Mala's being released. What's gonna happen to her? Where is she gonna go? What if I'm not the only one with a death threat on me? I can't protect her from in here.

Hell. I couldn't protect her before.

My brain itches—a tickling at the base of my brain. A rush of anticipation floods through my body. I squeeze my eye shut as warmth spreads from my toes upward until I'm blanketed in it. The scent of orchids overpowers the stench of Caleb, and I draw in a deep breath. My muscles relax and the ache behind my eye drains like water trickling down a drain.

She's here.

A whisper of a caress traces across my cheek. I want to press my face against the hand, but I don't move. Too afraid I'll scare her away. Her emotions ripple across my bare skin…that's the only way I can think to describe the sensation. Only, I can't tell what she's feeling: anger, fear, disgust…hate? No. That's what I'd feel toward me in her situation. I don't know for sure how she regards me. A tiny piece of me hopes the reason Mala comes to me every night isn't to plot her revenge but 'cause she still cares.

About the Author

ANGIE SANDRO was born at Whiteman Air Force Base in Missouri. Within six weeks, she began the first of eleven relocations throughout the United States, Spain, and Guam before the age of eighteen.

Friends were left behind. The only constants in her life were her family and the books she shipped wherever she went. Traveling the world inspired her imagination and allowed her to create her own imaginary friends. Visits to her father's family in Louisiana inspired this story.

Angie now lives in Northern California with her husband, two children, and an overweight Labrador.

9 781455 554829